BULLSHIT

PETER GEORGIADIS

CIRCLE OF PENS

Copyright ©2024 Peter Georgiadis
All rights reserved.

Peter Georgiadis has asserted his right to be identified as the author of this work in accordance with the Copyright Designs and Patents Act 1988

This is a work of fiction. Names, characters, places and incidents either are products of the author's imagination or are used fictitiously. Any resemblance to actual events or locales or persons, living or dead, is entirely coincidental.

No part of this publication may be reproduced, stored in or introduced into a retrieval system, or transmitted, in any form, or by any means (electronic, mechanical, photocopying, recording or otherwise) without the written permission of the publisher except that brief selections may be quoted or copied without permission, provided that full credit is given.

Chapter 1

All five feet ten and a half inches of David Cartier was feeling nervous, he didn't actually shake, but his stomach was playing up by rumbling really seriously, the muscles around his upper legs and also his reasonable well-proportioned biceps, were twitching annoyingly, all this was going on while he waited to be called in.

He wondered if he should maybe take a walk to the men's toilets and relieve himself. He had managed to go that very morning he started to wonder if he should try yet again. No, he thought better of it. It would be his luck if they called him in when he was sitting waiting for the world to fall out of his bottom, that would have meant the bottom would have most definitely fallen out of his world.

He sat there, rubbed his hands together gently warming them up, not that he was cold. Straightening his tie for the third time, he then slicked down his mousy blond hair, not that a single follicle was out of place. He wished, and not for the first time that he had thicker hair, his was always blowing about in the wind because it was almost silk like in texture. Also, it was so straight, he always envied fellows with thick wavy hair.

There was a mirror opposite where he was seated and if he strained slightly to one side, he could see himself in it; 'Just check your jacket looks smart, is that a piece of fluff on my collar? No, just me getting edgy. Oh, do stop tapping your fingers on your knees. I wish they would hurry up. Let me get this over with. A cup of coffee wouldn't go amiss right now.' Trying once again to relax, he inadvertently thought of his father, then immediately wished he hadn't. Those tender words of encouragement that he had given him still stuck in his throat. "You are a bloody failure; you will never amount to anything. Your mother was offered the opportunity to abort you when she was evacuated to Darlington. I always said she should have done it."

The memory of the venom that spouted from his mouth was pure nastiness, a sneer from a large flabby turned up lip appeared.

"And now you think you are a musician; no bloody orchestra is going to use you. Stop wasting their time and your own."

Now the aging mater shook with rage, a fit of temper that usually led to some sort of violence, either against David or his mother. "Get a proper job, the building industry is crying out for labourers with all the bomb buildings still hanging precariously awaiting to fall down."

He snuffled a grunt, then continued in the same vein,

"Yes, that's it, the building trade would be a more apt career for the likes of you, you a nasty young thug."

He gave yet another sneering grunt and then concluded his tirade of unadulterated venom with,

"The very idea of you thinking you could compete, joining an orchestra, ha!"

His father wasn't a cheerful chap, which many people noticed, and his aggressive nasty way of talking to David was one of the many things that knowing people really didn't like about him.

He came in all flavours of aggressiveness, this included arrogant, bullish and thoroughly mean and unpleasant, especially to this his young son David who for some unfathomed reason he despised, almost to a degree of loathing.

Of course he wasn't entirely wrong about young David, something that the young fellow was aware of. He had hardly shone as the brightest star in his schooling. Having only just managed to attend a secondary modern school in his hometown of Tenterden, Kent and there he managed to successfully fail most subjects, but failing was done with always a certain flair and panache.

David thrived in only two topics, first music, a subject that he knew, he knew more than the teacher that was desperately trying to impart knowledge into the bored and irritating students that reluctantly attended his classes.

Mr. Woods was the music teacher and David was his nemesis, always there to disrupt and argue points about various aspects of that abstract art form, while his classmates just watched and listened in moods of mild amusement.

The teacher was named Martin Woods, an unscholarly man in his early forties. Having survived the war he had taken to teaching as an easy alternative to soldiering, it was a reasonably well-paid job with short hours and long holidays and to Woods, after fighting Rommel in the desert, and winning a gallantry medal to boot, long holidays was what he wanted.

Sadly, he knew that this pupil Cartier knew his inadequacies and that knowledge had turned him prematurely grey, something that had made his spouse become more interested in the older students than her quickly aging husband. To David though, music lessons gave him his chance to dominate the room and show his pals that he was the main man, not that fool Woods.

The only other theme of schooling that Cartier enjoyed and showed a certain aptitude for, was mathematics. Somehow and all through his life he never understood how, maths had sort of come easy to him. He was not a budding genius, no Einstein more an Epstein, but he got a buzz out of being able to solve mathematical problems. It totally astonished his form teacher; one grey cropped headed Brian Cluff.

Cluffy as he was known as by the students was always amazed at how David performed with oral maths. He solved very complex sums and equations all in his head, never using pencil or paper.

Brian was a much older man, in fact the oldest teacher in the school. He was well past retirement and pension age, it suited his character to work on into old age, he never wanted to leave, teaching was his life.

He had fought with distinction during the Somme offensive in 1916. He had personally saved the life of a young piper who had been shot in the stomach, as the piper lay screaming for his mother in no-mans-land with the Germans raining a continuous fire of hot lead down to where the boy lay. But he had been lucky, he was still alive and had taken just the one bullet. Sergeant Cluff ran from his cover down to the lad picked him up and single-handedly turned and ran in the direction of the aid post. His fellow soldiers cheered as he covered the hundred yards in an Olympic turn of time and more amazingly as he was carrying the young soldier as well, and all the time he ran tracer bullets flew all around him but none never hitting him. For this action he received the Military Medal. Because of his heroic action the young piper went on to fight in the second round in 1939.

Brian Cluff was the science teacher of the school, a very clever and understanding man. He could be a strict and severe teacher who would take no truculence from any young soul, so if pushed he would come down hard on any offending lad and when he used the cane, it was always with a will, but most pupils accepted the punishment as a small price to pay, as punishments were only metered our against a need for discipline.

So, to sum up, Mr. Cluff was appreciated and respected for that honest side to his character. Yes, that was what he was most liked for, his fairness. But he always found personal enjoyment and pleasure in having his young charges around him, he sparkled with their vitality and, his enthusiasm rubbed off onto those young folk. For some strange reason he specially liked David Cartier, he knew the hard rather sadistic background that he came from, and he admired the boy's stubborn determination, even though it was usually in failing most academic lessons within the school. Cluff thought that Cartier failed for two reasons, first because that what was expected to happen by his own father and second, because he somehow preferred to fail, strangely to Mr. Cluff it seemed to give young Cartier boy some sort of inert pleasure.

But when Cartier did do something very well, either on the piano or viola as music was most definitely his thing and the viola being his main instrument, Cluff would always be there to watch, then to praise him, knowing that it was extremely unlikely that any other members of his family were likely to be there to encourage him.

David Cartier was to most of the teachers a complete waste of space and he really didn't deserve to be breathing the same oxygen as the rest of humanity.

But Cluff knew better.

When David finally left the school, Brian Cluff with more than a small tear in his eyes, said,

"David, I don't know why you have wasted most of your school life, though I think I can guess. Who have you been fooling? Not me old son! I think in the end you are going to be a great achiever. When you feel ready, go to night school and start again. Good luck boy, now bugger off before I give you one last thrashing for the sheer fun of it!"

David walked through the portals of Tenterden High Road School for the last time, he didn't once look back.

Years after though, he wished he had.

Once again David fidgeted as he waited to be called in for the audition, he hadn't enjoyed those last memories, they made him think and, thinking wasn't something he wanted to do at that particular time. But memories are something that always come back to haunt one and David's were no exception. While feeling more than a little sorry for himself he went back into the land of dreams.

David Cecile Cartier was born July 1944, his mother Janet Broughton, married his father John Norman Cartier in early 1933, why they married neither could really answer honestly, they had absolutely nothing in common. Janet was a political soul, favouring the far left in her beliefs, whereas John was not interested in any political movement preferring to make money instead.

He had come from a Welsh and Northern background, whose own father had been a teacher, librarian and then a furrier, an eclectic mix of professions if ever there was.

Janet was predominantly East End of London. The Broughton family had been shipbuilders of the river Lee. Probably their only joint interest was music, and it was classical music that was their love and delight, not one another.

A daughter had been born in early 1938, in fact the day war broke out. The daughter was called Nevillia, after Neville Chamberlin. Had she been born a year later; her name might have been Winstonia. Immediately Nevillia was born John was called to do his duty in the tank corp. He hated being in the army, and though not a complete coward, seemed to have a weird aversion to the possibility of being killed.

He made sure that the training lasted as long as possible, being posted to Bovington in Dorset. His job was to drive a newly built Churchill tank, this he enjoyed and showed a real flair for knocking down walls and trees. But sadly, for John a very serious event occurred. Whilst out on manoeuvres on Salisbury plain, the tank had been parked up for the night on shingle. The crew had made a brew over a fire and were enjoying a smoke and a drink from an illicit flask which filled to the brim with whisky. Unfortunately, it started to rain and then the rain turned into a deluge in which one couldn't see beyond one's nose, but not only extremely heavy, it was persistent in its ferocity.

The commander ordered John to stand guard under a tree while the other three crept under the vehicle to be out of the rain and hopefully to snatch some very drunken sleep. It rained and rained even more heavily than before, but John who was supposed to warn the others in case of a surprise attack from other sections of their corp. But not that any of them was compos mentis enough to have withstood a raid. This was all part of the manoeuvres, grubbing around trying to catch this or that tank in an unguarded moment. But for poor John, who was completely out of his depth in the army, it was most definitely not his brightest hour, for he too accidentally fell asleep.

The trouble was that his oilskin was draped over his head and body, though that wouldn't have made any difference because anyway it was completely impossible to hear or see anything above the storming weather and it was getting ever worse as the time passed by and the alcoholic drink had long since taken its toll. This was seriously bad news, as the rain worsened the tank started to sink into the shingle eventually crushing the other three luckless men.

All three died without a word being said. John woke up the next morning with a stiff neck and a very slight hangover, but he had been tucked nicely into his waterproof clothing for the duration of the storm and though he was damp from perspiration, he had passed a somewhat peaceful night. Very gradually his condition improved as the morning sun beat down on his now warming body. Calling the others to rise and shine, he noticed that this might indeed be a problem as the tank had sunk down completely to the top of its tracks.

John broke down in a heap, he felt that this whole tragedy had been of his making. He climbed into the tank and called on the vehicles radio for help. Help of course was too late for the three crewmen and sadly to late for John too. He promptly had a nervous breakdown and was discharged from any future conflict at least as far as army and wars go.

Nevillia was the apple of John's eye, she was instantly bright, talked by the time she was eighteen months, knew here numbers and alphabet at three and a half.

At her tender age of five a further extension to the family appeared, a son which was immediately named David after David Lloyd George. But young David didn't do it for John, who only loved Nevillia, and he doted even more on her once David appeared on the scene.

Very soon after David was born John bought Nevillia her first small violin and sent her for lessons. She flourished and blossomed with music, so much so that John quickly had to upgrade her instrument. Nevillia was born for the violin, it had very quickly become an extension of her being, this was what she wanted even at that extremely early age, she knew it and so did John and Janet, her doting parents.

As the years went by Nevillia got more and more proficient. By the time she was eight years of age and her small annoying brother David, who at three years of age was only just talking, she went to study the violin with Professor Glencross the very eminent exponent of that stringed instrument. At the tender age of ten she was invited to become a junior member of the Royal Academy of Music, and it was obvious to all that her future career was assured.

On the other hand, David was not the apple of anyone's eye. John despised his son for not being as quick on the uptake as Nevillia and anyway, David had been somewhat of a mistake being conceived on the very last air-raid on London before Hitler turned his attentions elsewhere. Then to John's sanguine, Janet heavily pregnant with David was encouraged to evacuate to Darlington as the doodlebugs and V-2's were dropping around the capital with an ever-increasing gusto of German enthusiasm.

The pregnancy had been a harrowing affair for Janet and almost up until the day of birth, doctors had advised on termination as the actual birth might kill mother as well as the baby. Mother refused and went ahead and gave birth, it was long hard and painful but eventually David was born and survived, as did Janet.

But it was perfectly obvious that John was extremely upset by the simple expedient that he had been left to his own devises along with his beloved Nevillia and if they had to run the gauntlet of Hitler's weapons of mass destruction why couldn't Janet and the new sprog have done the same. After all it was his earning that was giving them the support and comfort that all humans, including the Cartier craved.

Anyway, he was after all the head of this family, or so he told himself. From that moment on when Janet and young David reached their home war was once more declared, but this time the enemies behind each trench line were John and Nevillia against Janet and her son, anyway Janet showed no emotions towards anyone on any side, she was completely indifferently ambivalent to any family member doing battle.

But if father and daughter wanted to be more venomous towards David, that at least took the pressure off her, after all David might be her offspring but Janet wasn't a serious mother and would have preferred being barren as to motherhood.

But David always fought back and often in a way that just showed contempt for his sister and father, then later on, to his mother as well and that was for Janet a moment of momentous monstrous indifference, now she could bleep about anything, so finally she had now gotten what she craved, just wanting the quiet life and of course the chance to moan about this government or anything that took her fancy.

Why Stalin had let her down so badly was totally unforgivable, she had predicted England becoming a Communist country by as early as 1947. She never forgave Stalin for that gaff, and she never forgave John or Nevillia for holding her back in the fight for the masses, whom-ever-they-were, not that Janet could even stand or seriously give a monkey's kiss for the so-called masses.

She was, or better still had become, a middle-class lefty and consequently that never stopped her spending more and more money on the trivia and luxuries of the bourgeoisie.

When David was nine years of age the family moved to Tenterden in Kent, the reason was that John's business, which was dealing in leather bags and belts and various other items all made from cow hides, was flourishing and needed more space.

A house close to the railway had become vacant, along with the house was five acres of land and many outhouses that were going to be converted to industrial premises for Leather Now and Forever. Tenterden had also been chosen because the famous Russian violinist Faberge Volstead lived there and had agreed to give Nevillia lessons.

At the age of eleven David entered the tired dreary looking grey bricked Victorian place of learning, Tenterden High Road School, a faceless secondary modern establishment, with prospects for the children as grey as the school itself. As his eleven plus had been a total failure and he had achieved the record of getting the lowest marks in the examination since before the war he was placed in grade D and that was assumed to be D for dunce. And there he stayed until he left at the age of fifteen.

While he had been a student apart from the two subjects of music and maths David rarely showed any interest in any other academic theme. He had managed to perform well in athletics and especially high jump and much to his own personal pleasure had managed to break the women's world record by jumping five feet eleven inches.

He was also a comparatively good runner that is as long as it didn't go on for too long. He had achieved a somewhat personal best by managing to win the half mile race on a sports day at least once, which had been towards the end of his less than scholarly time there.

He had developed into a healthy extremely strong young man when he left school, and this was down to having to work for his fathers business and this entailed having to hang the heavy still wet hides of the cattle onto things that resembled extremely strong clothes lines. This of course, was after the said skins had been bought and brought back after being dipped and treated by the leather tanners. These were then strung up high in some of the converted barns where they would stay and dry before being turned into leather.

Sometimes he was made to do this chore very late into the night, it was his job to get them hung and if one of the vans brought them back late, then tough on him, he always had to carry the burden until they were all up there hanging and smelling and that reeking smell got everywhere, which much to David's personal shame often drifted over the town making the locals resent the filthy business that was the Cartier's trade.

He hated this work and resented the fact that he was made to do it. But John was canny and far to mean to pay anyone else for doing that job, anyway very few people would want to do it which would have meant having to pay even more. But David found one reward for this labouring toll, the strength he got from all that lifting gave him muscles far beyond his age and strength that made him very quickly street wise when coming across his peer group.

And finally, because of all this strength got used for the purpose of school sports whilst attending the school, it gave him the chance to show-off his excellent physique to any girls that may be glancing in his direction. It was that strength that helped him to become the shot-put champion, he actually broke the school record for throwing that sixteen-pounder ball of iron further than anyone else had ever done and that also included the teaching staff.

What he didn't know and the teachers had completely forgotten, was that the very same shot had actually been a ball of iron used for trying to sink a French ship of the line during the battle of Trafalgar, many had been salvaged after the battle with the sole purpose of re-using them, but instead had been brought back to Britain and eventually been distributed to small towns where men had died in the battle as mementoes of the great victory, in the case of Tenterden, to become an iron ball for the local schools shot put seemed somewhat disrespectful to the memory of the fallen, though I doubt if the dead heroes gave a tinkers cuss about its use.

When David became fifteen and soon to be leaving that school forever, he met his first serious love. It was a young dark-haired beauty named Carol Allenby. She was petite and charming but had very little conversation other than Elvis Pressley or Cliff Richard, so that when David took her home to meet mum and dad, they were both rude and patronising to her thinking her to be stupid and Nevillia was positively beside herself with aggression towards Carol. Carol was not dumb or unintelligent, she was just shy, and she certainly didn't deserve the treatment that she had received from the Cartier family. Just because she knew nothing about classical music or the communist party and that she tended to keep her mouth tightly shut while close to the offending family, they despised and belittled her even in front of David. She was never going to talk much knowing that he in fact knew a great deal, at least about music and the classics and because of his families influence he too started to look down on her, so in many ways their love was doomed long before it ever really got started.

But to David she in some ways had everything he wanted within a woman, he became confused and disappointed, firstly in Carol's lack of intellect and secondly in his own inability to understand her or her lack of interests in what the Cartier family thought to be the most important aspects of creation itself.

David went through his adult life having many love affairs and falling in and out of love with many women, but strangely never being able to forget his first love Carol Allenby, so even as he sat there awaiting his future fate, his mind once again drifted back to this petite young Carol Allenby.

Chapter 2

Maybe, the reason that they didn't stand a chance was three-fold. Firstly, his own families unsettled feelings towards her, secondly her parents having realised that the Cartier's were an arrogant bunch of near-do-wells who thought themselves superior and far too good for their daughter and thirdly maybe it was something to do with the simple fact that their love for one another had been completely unrequited, leaving them both very sexually frustrated.

So David left school with no real acceptable examination results and no real ambition for anything other than to leave the family hearth as quickly as possible.

Where to go? How to earn a living? His piano playing had slid, as he had no real interest in that and his viola playing was lacking real technique which had allowed him to reach one level but there it had seemed to slow and then stop in its progression.

Like the rest of his disjointed family he loved music, in fact you could say he really loved music, but he really didn't think that he had a future in that industry, unlike Nevillia who was now twenty years of age and studying full time at the Royal Academy of Music.

David somewhat despised his older sister though he always wanted to at least be accepted by her, she seemed to be a snob and a progressively active bully, not that she could physically hurt him, no her torture was always a form of mental torment and it never ever ceased, though David had long realised that this torture was just part of her family motivation from her and his father John.

But though he disliked her bullying tendencies and sneered at her short-sighted ways towards him, on the other hand he admired and understood her talent. She was a border case for genius and the sounds she made were a delight to one and all. She was going to be a star and that, was at least admirable. Now that she was doing so well, much to Janet's surprise John went out and spent several thousand pounds on a fine Old Italian violin, made by the master Luigi Ponsiochelli of Milan 1739.

Strangely enough, knowing that all that money had been spent on Nevillia never fazed David, he felt no sense of jealousy, really only pride that the talent of a sister was brilliant enough to warrant such a great piece of instrumental artwork.

So, what to do? Firstly, being strong he got a job labouring on a building site in south London and then managed to find digs in Forest Hill. The work was hard with long hours and his colleagues were not the most intelligent interesting stimulating people on this planet. Most were, to be kind, thick and rather naively stupid.

But they were also strong and sometimes very dangerous. Cards always became the pastime should it be raining, and work was stopped. Wages could and did change hands, which in turn created appalling violent fights, sometimes so bad that a person might be seriously hurt and end up in hospital, then the police would be called in much to the chagrin of those involved and to the management. David hated this life and only managed to stay sane for six months and then he knew that enough was indeed enough. He left work one Friday night, money in his back pocket, tired from extreme labouring, cold wet and muddy. It was at this low point that the penny dropped, and he heard his old mentor saying those last prophetic words before he had walked out of the school building for the last time.

"Get your learning done at night school, don't waste all your life. You have the ability and I for one believe in you. Stop pissing about boy, grow a pair! There is a world out there waiting for young men to explore and conquer it, you could be one of those lucky people if you want it enough?"

Well, he remembered it somewhat differently to what might have been spoken. But whatever the words had been, he now heard these words and yes, it was indeed time to learn, and this time do it properly.

Instead of returning to his digs in Forest Hill, he went straight to the local school and asked for the prospectus for evening classes. David was not totally surprised to be looked at in a very strange way by the admissions adviser of the school. She looked at him, noting his dirty face and clothes, wondering to herself why this obvious scruffy individual should want to take lessons again?

But she was pleasantly surprised how succinct his speech was and the way that his diction and use of words made her realise that Mr. Cartier was not a scruff, at least not entirely When he finished explaining that he now felt the time was right to proceed with his education and in fact he wanted to get enough certificates to be in a position to either go to University or at the very least a place at a college of some sort. But now deep down he knew where it had to be and what he wanted to do for a living, he just didn't want to say it out loud in case the bubble burst.

"Well, what was that Mr. err, Cartier, what did you say? Well of course we can help with your further education but what really do you need the certification for? And what sort of college or university do you really have in mind to go to? Let us, meaning you and

I ascertain your needs from the information you give me."

She was still of two minds about this young man standing there in front of her, but the idea of taking someone off the street and giving them a real chance in life was why she was there, and that prospect made her smile inwardly.

Her life was about wanting to help young forgotten people, the no hopers of this world and this young man, this young Mr. David Cartier was just that, he seemed to be a complete lost cause, but now with her help he might just have a chance.

"Before you answer me, I should tell you that to study is hard! To obtain A-levels means work and yet more work. You will find it extremely difficult if you are working on building sites which anyone can see is exhausting, how can you study after a day labouring? You really need a job where you can get the time you will need to study, if necessary, take time off."

She looked at him, a smile crossed her countenance and without saying much at all he had somehow won her over to his way of thinking. He smiled back and then told her what he thought he might need.

"I need at least two A-levels, possibly in music and mathematics, but I would also like the chance for some other subjects, maybe Geography, History and something that just might suit. As to where I want to go, you will be surprised. I wish to get a place in the Royal College of Music in Kensington."

He blushed a full bright crimson colour which would have shone brightly even at night had it been so.

He then continued,

"I play the viola as a first study, but I have studied the piano for many years and that would give me a second study. But I really don't think I can get in without these qualifications, my playing just isn't enough."

Yes, she was won over. Miss. Megan Vaughn-Thomas had come to Forest Hill, South London on a personal mission, a crusade to get the youth educated. Her hometown had been Neath in South Wales, and her background was very chapel and very strict chapel at that. She never missed a Sunday service always believing that God had given her this chance to help others, and she knew she must never fail God. She was slight in build, thirty-two years of age, but though she had actually interesting, nice looks she did nothing for herself. Never ever wore makeup, never wore bright feminine clothes, always dressing somewhat tweedy and frumpy. But there in her eyes was a sparkle, those two blue deep pools shone like headlights on a car pleading for some sort of recognition for her hidden beauty.

For the first time in her life, she looked at a boy with more than just academic interest, she saw a sixteen-year-old boy with a body of a twenty-five-year-old. He was a very fit young man with obvious great sexual appeal that had now awakened something within Megan, something she didn't quite understand as yet. What she was looking at and listening too excited her with feelings that she was totally unaware of within herself until this actual moment in time, feelings she just hadn't known where there.

"David, I hope you don't mind if I call you by your Christian name? I suggest that we sit down together and seriously discuss what you need, then how we can best give you that knowledge you require to pass the exams."

Unknowingly Megan too was blushing profusely.

"I have so much work to do at this time, may I suggest that you come back here tomorrow if you are not working. Come at lunch time and I will meet you outside. Maybe we can find a coffee house where we can sit down and get to grips with the whole work concept."

A smiled that warmed the entire room came to her lips, but she ignored those feeling that were stirring within her very soul and continued with her challenging talk,

"But I think we can help and what you have told me sounds very exciting and a real challenge for both of us. Can you make tomorrow?"

"Yes, Mrs. Vaughn-Thomas. And to show you that I am grateful I will buy the coffees. Plus, I will come washed and dressed somewhat better than I am now."

A huge smile came over David's face, almost lighting up the room with its obvious pleasure.

"Twelve o'clock you say?"

She had once again reddened with tinges of pink in her face ever since he had mentioned the word Mrs.

"David, for the record I am still Miss. Thomas, but I would prefer that you just call me Megan; formality is not necessary for night classes."

She held out her hand to be shaken, and then concluded with,

"Twelve o'clock right outside here."

And then one more vast sparkling embarrassed grin which once again lit up the reception area. Between them both, they had generated enough lighting to keep the school bright for the entire day, plus even maybe the night.

"Until then."

Young Cartier was up early on the Saturday, he dressed and had a very quick breakfast. He wanted to go for his normal run, and then he would come back have that all important bath and get ready for the meeting with Megan Vaughn-Thomas.

His run lasted an hour; he ran all the way up Kirkdale Hill past the large house that Franz Liszt had acquainted himself with along with an entourage of belles that always followed in his footsteps while living in London. While passing by this dwelling he subconsciously hummed the main theme from one of Liszt's Hungarian Rhapsodies. He then ran down past the burial mounds of plague victims from centuries past.

Here David always paused though still jogging on the spot. He was always fascinated by these simple mounds and, he always felt pity for the poor souls that were in them, almost certainly up to five hundred bodies in each mound yet only taking up approximately twenty square feet of land each. Every time he stopped here, he seemed to feel their pain and suffering. He knew they were all wretched bedraggled misfits, the poorest of the poor whose very existence without disease was hard and tortured at best.

A large heartfelt sigh gave way to his normal feelings of sadness for all the poor and misguided peoples of the world, though mainly centralising his pity upon himself, then he ran across the busy road and around Horniman's Museum into the flower gardens then down into the playing field, after which he back tracked till, he was in his digs again.

He always felt better for having achieved the run, it probably was no more than two and a half miles but going up and down the hill was what made all the difference. The bath was delicious and soothing, soaking in really hot water seemed to give him new impetus in life. It allowed the weeks grime to percolate from his skin and from that moment on he could feel like a new man once again.

He was fresh bright and clean and smelling like a new rose. Always a layer of scum coated the surface of the bath reminding him of a hot Rice Pudding gradually setting.

David knew that one day he would have his own home and then he would bath at least twice a week whether he needed to or not. He dressed in his silken mohair three-piece suit, put on his winkle picker patent leather shoes, looked in the mirror to adjust the thin leather tie and then placed a tie pin through his rounded collar. He stood there admiring himself, he knew he looked like a million dollars.

He reached the appointed meeting place with ten minutes to spare, yet there was Megan already waiting eagerly for her new charge.

"Good morning, David. My, you look dressed to kill, going anywhere special?"

"Well, I hope so, I am taking you out."

Megan flushed as she was prone to do. 'Of course he is taking me out, why did I say such a stupid thing?'

"So, where are we going? Somewhere nice I hope?"

"I thought we could talk at the Italian Coffee Bar at Clockhouse Station. How does that sound?"

"Well, I have never been to a coffee bar before, this should be fun."

Fortunately for the both of them, they didn't have to wait long for the 12A bus that would run them all the way to the station. David sat next to Megan on the public vehicle, he could smell her scent, and he liked the fact that she also smelt clean and nice. Her clothes were a little softer than she normally wore and she for once sported a very pretty blouse that had a flower print in various colours but showing off the predominantly obvious blend of yellows and light blues. Her dark hair was brushed neatly, but also pushed up into a slightly different more feminine style and David liked what he saw and smelt.

As they sat there, they both struggled to find something to say, Megan made a comment on how dirty the houses looked, but she was looking straight ahead not out of the window. At last, just before they arrived David found the courage to say,

"Megan, you look different, really nice."

He turned his head slightly eschew and finish his sentence with,

"And you smell, err, lovely too!"

Then they both went bright red, refusing to look anywhere but straight ahead.

Now he became aware that now they would have to stand to get off and he was sporting an excessively large protrusion within his rather tight trousers. As he stood up within the bus, he rapidly thrust his left hand into his pocket to pull the offending member to somewhere that was not quite so obvious.

There was no question that a young Cartier knew how to be polite especially in the attendance of a woman, in fact he had somehow instinctively always known how to behave, it was just that in his parent's presence he normally refused to do so. But now he was quick to alight the vehicle so that he could help Megan off the bus just like the gentleman he wanted to show her he was.

Miss Vaughn-Thomas was so far delighted to be with this young man who, though she didn't want to think about it she knew that he was almost half her age. He was something very masculine to look at sporting extremely bulbous muscles for his age. He was also smart well mannered and polite, to her a complete Adonis.

Megan was already melting away from that rather frumpy person that she personified in her normal day to day environment. For the first time in her life she felt like a young woman and was enjoying that new exciting experience.

The bar was squat in size being not more than twenty feet by twenty. There were garish paintings of Italian scenes on all the walls, at least scenes that the artist assumed would fool the local punter to believe that they were viewing panoramas of beautiful Italian views. Plus supporting the idea that one was in some sort of tropical paradise, there were five tables made from bamboo all filled with young rather Bohemian types, the men mainly sporting beards and the women generally fitted out with bright coloured loose fitting clothing with many, many petticoats all pushing out the most flamboyant skirts, all were stereotypes of what one would expect to see in Bohemian so called beatniks.

All were in deep obviously profound conversations and listening to the Lonnie Donnigon record that was exploding from rather cheap noisy scratchy speakers.

And as the excruciatingly rough sound of -

"Does your chewing gum lose its flavour on the bedpost overnight…?"

Up stepped the owner.

"'Ello Dave, where 'ave you bin hiding? We 'oped to see you last Sunday, we 'ad a right ol' jamboree 'ere an' we certainly could 'ave used you and your old banjo viola, fing."

David smiled deeply and warmly at his friend. Then looked around to see if there were indeed any tables left on the ground floor, or would they have to sit downstairs? There were none, and yes downstairs was the only other option.

"Yes, sorry about that Ted, but I went home to visit mum and dad, though to be honest I wish I hadn't bothered. Any tables left downstairs?"

Ted was a middle aged seriously cockney hippy, carrying a rather large very distinct protruding bear gut. Like all the other men there he sported a small greying goatee beard. But the one thing that was genuine was his winning smile which was indeed warm and real, he was liked by one and all and he liked being popular.

"If there aren't any, I'll make some room for you, no problem my boy."

Down the narrow spiral staircase to the room that was exactly the same size as above except there were no windows to see the lower unmade road that was at the back of these buildings and shops. There was an emergency exit, but no one would have been able to use it as it was padlocked inside and chub-locked outside, ideal for any emergency.

David stumbled over the closest chair as his eyes adjusted to the dimmer light. He helped Megan with a seat at the table furthest away from the appalling scratchy sounding speaker that hung loosely on a wall. David knew that just one Little Richard record blasting away would have shaken the speaker off the wall.

"Megan, would you like some real Italian coffee?"

She smiled at him, but it was entirely wasted as there was no way he could see anything better than an outline of the lady that sat opposite to him.

"Yes, that would be nice. David, I have never been to such a place before in my life, what was he talking about when he said you should have been there for the jamboree? I thought that was a scouting thing?"

Her words had a seriously puzzled ring to them, it was true she was completely in alien territory.

Megan carried on with,

"No, I am sure that wasn't what he meant?"

Cartier smiled again, and then laughed with a chuckle.

"No, a jamboree here is a bunch of amateur musicians that come together to play and sing skiffle music. It is all very silly but really good fun. I am the odd ball though as my so-called banjo is my viola, but it does go to make a different interesting sound something that many of the listens have enjoyed and told me so."

For a very brief moment, he felt his chest heave slightly with a certain pride.

The coffees came, two very frothy cups of quite strong Arabian beans, made fluffy by blowing very hot air and milk into the cups. David was used to it but preferred the Turkish coffee that his father loved and made. He always felt he ought to appreciate something that was destined to have come from his dad.

"Oo, I like the taste of this Italian coffee. Though I am sure I shall be covered in froth after this."

Her attempts at joking sadly fell on deaf ears. But David was enjoying being there with this Welsh lady. After the drinking had finished, Megan looked in his direction and asked in a soft low but typical singing South Welsh accented voice,

"So, now to some work. I have thought about what you need for your college examination qualifications, and I want to help you get them."

She paused briefly for some response that didn't occur, so then continued,

"I think by what you have already told me, that you might be capable of sitting music A-level and possibly a maths A-level; though I warn you now, they are both going to be very hard. But I have a degree in maths, so I am prepared to help you get past that first hurdle."

Again, another pause for breath.

"Then for your own personal quest for knowledge, what about a couple of O-levels, in fact you will have to get O-level music and maths before you can take the A-level, but why not combine the two O-levels with, say Geography and History? That would give you a complete rounding of subjects and would look good at any interview."

"That is exactly what I had in mind. Why are you being so very good to me, I am not sure I deserve all this personal attention. Do you give so much time to all your students?"

No answer came back, just a knowingly embarrassed silence. Had he been able to see her face he would have been perfectly aware that he was getting very, very special treatment.

David stretched his hands across the table took her hands and squeezed them gently, this was done as a sign of thanks, but when he tried to remove them, Megan kept her grip. This moment of tenderness she liked, and she was not going to lose this feeling. Once again red flushed faces presented themselves, but neither could see so were to a degree wasted. After another cup of froth, David took the bull by the horn.

"I, err, I thought that maybe we could go up to London together? There is a film on which sounds like good fun, it is called: How the West Was Won, everybody who is anybody is in it and it is something called Cinerama Panorama Vision or something like that. Evidently, the screen is all around the audience. What do you say, fancy that?"

He didn't have to ask twice.

"Oh, yes David, I would love to come with you, but you must let me pay for myself."

And as he had so very little money David was never going to argue with that! It was a bright sunny day, and the warmth was not just in the weather, they both felt that heat towards one another. They enjoyed the movie, and they excelled in each others company.

Megan was as good as her word, she worked out a tough but doable schedule for his learning, then just to make life easier for him he was given a job as librarian in the school. Not only was the pay better than a building site but it gave him long hours to study in.

But for Megan it was the chance to keep him near to her, she was growing more and more fond of him as each day passed.

As the weeks went by David worked with a will, enjoying knowing that in fact he was bettering himself. After classes in the evenings Megan would always be there waiting outside the classroom, then they would immediately go through that day's work and she would explain how he could solve this or that problem in the mathematics and how to absorb these facts in the brain in any subject.

She was loving every moment of this project and though she tried not to think about it to much she was aware that her feelings were indeed becoming very deep and caring towards him. She realised that she was in love with that scruffy reprobate that first introduced himself to her those long three months back.

She longed each day just to catch a sight of him, either dealing with the books for students or just sitting there making notes or reading his own studies. After work and studies Megan would always ask him to go either to the coffee bar again, or the new Chinese restaurant that had opened just around the corner from the school. Megan knew that David was short of money, so she always offered to pay and David Cartier being a well trodden Cartier never refused a ladies offer.

David liked Megan and what she was doing for him and come to that what she had already done. But he was male and sometimes his thoughts turned to the possibility of a more sexual approach to there so far chaste friendship.

They often held hands when walking out and, on several occasions, David had dared to kiss Megan, but sadly this failed badly as she had no idea what to do when kissing so that had been quickly abandoned. Now his thoughts once again turned to a more carnal knowledge, or in Cartier's case lack of carnal knowledge.

He dreamt every night of having sex with women and often had to wash the sheets or his pyjama trousers when accidents occurred. Lately he been dreaming of Megan, wondering what it would be like to throw his legs over this thirty odd year-old Welsh lady. He was determined to once and for all achieve his goal in the academic pursuits, but at the same time lose his virginity. These two desires in his mind were worthy goals to achieve. They were having a meal of the Blue Dragon when once again the thought came to him.

"Megan, you know I am so very grateful for your friendship and what you are doing for me. I want you to know that I feel very strongly that there is a bond of err, deep friendship between us."

He looked her directly in the eyes and took the plunge.

"Maybe more than friendship?"

Here he paused to take stock of what nonsense he was in fact spouting. But one look on Megan's face told him that maybe it wasn't nonsense after all. She put her chopsticks down and reached across for his hands. There was a warm smile on her face, and he noticed that her eyes had misted over she was close to tears.

"Carry on David, say what we are both thinking."

He stuttered slightly but, in the end, managed finally to say what it was that had been on his mind for weeks.

"I err, want you, Megan."

He almost gasped with excitement.

"I want to feel every part of your body. I want to kiss and caress every nook and cranny; I want to make mad passionate love with you. I want to enter your body with my, err, you know what. And I want to do it now, I have been trying to ask you for weeks and now I just have to have you."

He was almost breathing like he had just finished a marathon race.

"Can I come back to your flat and stay the night with you?"

Megan had flushed even deeper than normal; this wasn't quite what she had been expecting. She was hoping for a declaration of love. She withdrew her hands, looked closely at her meal and then sat there very quietly contemplating. Cartier thought he had blown his chances, was now cursing for what he had just said. Maybe she would throw him out of the school and after all that work, they had both put in.

Then in a whisper came her answer.

"Yes, you can stay. But I must tell you, I am a virgin."

David barely heard her faint sounds, but he got the gist, then he took her hands again and said in return with a warm smile on his face,

"So am I!"

He had never been back to her flat, in fact he hadn't even known where she lived. It turned out to be just five minutes from the school in a quiet back road with no real traffic problems. She had a basement apartment which consisted of a bedroom and a lounge living room with a kitchen section in one corner. The toilet and bathroom were off the hallway. Fortunately, it was not used by anyone else, but other tenants could and did walk by to get into the garden, this simple act did sometimes cause some dire embarrassment.

The two rooms were as David imagined them to be, neat, tidy and clean. There were two prints on the walls both scenes of Welsh countryside, but in themselves pleasant enough in an innocuous way, the wallpaper was old and dirty but that was hardly Megan's fault. The ceiling was quite low and anyone taller than David would have had to stoop when standing and, there was no way from keeping the noise from the people that lived in the flat above quiet.

When the tenants upstairs moved around their footsteps rattled the floorboards and echoed down to the basement like a rain forests tropical thunder. David had already decided that this would not suit him to live here, how could he practice the viola with that din going on and how would he study there? And more to the point, how would he sleep. No this was not for him.

Megan offered him a cup of tea which he gladly accepted. His mouth was dry from anticipation and a slight tic appeared within his right eye, but worse of all he was seriously nervous about how to approach the actual act of sex. Like all men throughout the world, he knew what sex was and how it should in theory be done, but the practice needed just that, practice. He was a virgin, she was a virgin, so after a while his thought was, 'Oh well, I guess we both will learn on the job!'

They had their tea and David started to get an erection that this time he didn't try to hide. Megan saw this protrusion and that excited her as well, her heart was starting to heave and she felt all a flutter, just like a young teenage girl again.

Finally desperation got the better of David Cartier and he got up from the chair that he was sitting while having his tea, walked over to her pulled Megan gently to her feet and then kissed her full on the mouth making sure that his tongue gently explored into her mouth, this he noted got her complete attention and then in a tremble, David felt Megan's body shudder. When he pulled back Megan nearly fell to the threadbare carpet which was in her lounge. She gasped slightly steadied herself and, then to both their surprise pulled him back and this time she kissed him. Her tongue went into his mouth, and she explored his inner lips and then his tongue. As they separated, he noted with a certain smug feel, that she was now shaking quite openly, and her smile was the broadest he had ever seen it before this particular day.

David gripped both her arms; his smile had become almost a grimace.

"Megan, can you please show me your bedroom? I am not sure I can hold out much longer."

She took his hand and led him the five paces into the next room. Her bedroom was just as neat and tidy as the lounge was. Again, a wall was filled with pictures, but this time they were very old photographs. He didn't ask the obvious question as his mind was already elsewhere, but he guessed they were portraits of past relations. She held his hand very tightly not quite knowing what to do next. He had to prise his fingers from hers just so he could sit on the edge of the bed and try it out for softness. There was a sinking feeling as he sank into the old-fashioned bed with its worn iron springs. But he didn't care about any of that he just wanted her to take off all her clothes and show her delights to him, then to get on with the act of sex. He was sick of masturbation and wet dreams, this was finally after seventeen long lonely years going to be the real thing, so let's not waste precious humping time, were his thoughts.

"Megan, please let us take off our clothes and get into bed."

She looked shy and vulnerable, but at his command jumped as to get into bed fully clothed. David stopped her doing that he wanted to see and experience everything, this moment he had to savour, they both had to savour, this was going to be a joint experience that they would both never forget.

"Megan, no please. Let us both get undressed together. I want to see you completely naked. I wish to explore all your private parts, as surely you do to mine."

As she looked almost terrified, he asked again,

"Anyway, don't you want to see me also?"

"Well, I do and I don't."

She reddened making David wonder if her blood pressure was about to pop.

"David this is my first time, I feel shy, embarrassed and more than a little foolish."

"I will take off a piece of clothing and then you can do the same, that way we will get there together. I shall remove my shirt first, now you."

"Please David, at least turn off the light."

"No way, that's the whole point, I want to watch and enjoy this moment. Trust me and don't be shy."

At that last command, she sighed looked embarrassed but decided there and then to be resolute and do as David asked. She took off her blouse exposing a vest and bra underneath. David kept a straight face as he knew he could have spoilt the whole ambience of this moment had he laughed, chuckled or even smiled, it was the vest that did it for him. But inwardly he laughed out loud. 'Those woolly vests, oh those woolly vests.'

Too far now to turn back! He needed her body and whatever it took, he was going to get it. The next item was his trousers exposing a pair of boxer shorts underneath, he hoped that they were not soiled in any way. She then removed her skirt, showing her stockings and her panties, which were grey in colour and looked as if they too were made from wool. 'Oh, Megan dear, you are so old fashioned in what you wear and what you do and what is more, generally you are old fashioned even in life. This is 1961, come on girl, get with it.' David then put on a spurt by removing his socks and vest, just leaving his underpants; his erection was almost forcing an exit of its own through the material and a small wet patch appeared on the outside of his pants where his penis was, she noticed that stain, but he didn't care any longer.

Megan had watched this with growing fascination and was fully aware that she too was starting to get very wet in her nether regions. She closed her eyes and decided to go one further, she took off her vest and then removed her bra revealing two lovely plump firm breasts. Her nipples stuck out like two cherries. This excited David almost to exploding so he quickly took of his boxer shorts. She had never seen an erect penis before, it seemed so big that she thought she could hang on and swing to and fro from it. At this point she too, first removed her stocking and suspenders and then her knickers. There for Cartier to see was her pubic hair, masses of black thick pubic hair. He had wanted to see her crack, he wanted to touch it, kiss it, eat it, stick his fingers in, stir it around then enter with his penis. But where was that crack, he would have to explore clearing away through the jungle of pubic hair. 'This is going to be fun! I hope there is an opening for me to find in there somewhere?'

He gently pulled Megan down onto the top of the bed, they at once both sank into the middle but that was cosy even though between them, they almost touch the floor. He leant over and kissed her hard on the lips, she responded in kind. Her breast beckoned to him, he cupped them in his hands, and they were warm and soft and lovely, they both welcomed him. He went down and kissed each nipple then started to suck quite hard on them both. She gave a sigh then a small moan, she was in ecstasy. She had never ever done anything like this before, she never masturbated, never even had impure dreams.

Now though she didn't care anymore, she just wanted more and more of the delightfully pleasurable feelings that tingled through her being. While he was kissing those two cherry red nipples his right hand drifted down her body tickling her as it went, he came to that incredible mop of pubic wiry hair and explored around for some sort of entry point. He had seen naked women before, mainly in smutty magazines but none with such an amount of hair down there. At first it bothered him but now it was exciting and different, and both were enjoying every second as he explored around her body. It was now time for Megan to feel some of his various erogenic areas. First, she probed his face and his ears, feeling and tickling as she went, her fingers brushed around his lips, she pushed slightly into his mouth even touching his tongue with her finger. Then she felt his breast and, noted with some satisfaction just how hard his nipples had become through the caresses that she was doing to him. Then she went down to his penis, she had never seen one before on a man let alone touched one. The touch made things critical for Cartier and he shuddered a couple of times then deposited a large amount of semen on her hand then on the eiderdown. Neither of them cared about the mess at this stage of exploration, everything could be cleaned up later, much, much later.

David found the entry point and found that Megan was still completely intact, he pushed very slightly, she jerked and gave a small squeal, her hymen had parted. It startled her because again she had no idea of what to expect. He then withdrew his finger and noticed a small deposit of blood at the nail. He crawled his way down her body made her open her legs wide, wide enough so that he could see what he wanted to do next.

His nose was three inches away from her vagina and the smell was somehow sweet and pleasant to his nostrils. His tongue extended and just for his troubles got a mouthful of hair, so he parted her further with his two hands, wide enough so that he could lick and suck her. She moaned and started to writhe from side to side, at first this disturbed David as he knew nothing of women's orgasms but when he realised the sounds were of pleasure and not pain so without further ado he continued. His tongue had now found her clitoris, which was large and as stiff as his member. This his tongue caressed from side to side, gently at first then increasing the pressure and licking and sucking with more and more speed. Megan tossed so hard then slumped exhausted, which was just as well, as David had obtained a small but very sore blister on his tongue.

Now was the time, he opened her legs again, then climbed over putting his arm around her neck, with his other hand manpowered his penis into her waiting cavern of delight. It was at this point that he became aware of the noise that the bed was making. Bong, bong, bong it went with the rhythm getting faster and faster. It only took roughly two minutes when he couldn't hold back any longer. Both of them gave shouts of approval as they both erupted at the same moment, David filling her vagina with life giving semen. David was panting hard and could feel his own heart pumping blood at a rate of gallons not pints. Megan just laid there with her eyes filling. Then she burst out crying. He withdrew his member quickly and, then feeling concerned and more than a little guilty he asked,

"Megan my sweet. What is the matter, did I hurt you?"

"No you lovely man, you didn't hurt me. I just feel marvellous and sad at the same time. Great because the whole experience was wonderful and sad that it has taken thirty-two years to reach this point. I feel now as if I have wasted all my life."

She turned away from him tears streaming down her now tired looking face. Then she very quietly added,

"Thank you, David."

It was a hard night for David as Megan demanded repeat performances every hour on the hour. There was no way that he was going to work the next day, bugger that!

David told Megan straight that he would not move in with her, he was crazy about her this he admitted openly, but he didn't want to stay too long in her flat. Anyway, his excuse was that he needed to work and sometimes to sleep. They spent Christmas together and it was a wonderful time for them both. Megan bought him a beautiful watch, a Swiss twenty jewelled movement with a gold frame and wrist band. David bought her frilly silk knickers. She cooked a chicken with all the trimmings; she had received a letter from her mother demanding to know why she was not coming home for the festive season. Megan didn't even bother to answer instead just sent a card.

Megan Vaughn-Thomas, a brilliant scholar and teacher, sadly had now more or less abandoned the chapel that she had grown up with and so quickly did God go out the window as to make even an atheist shudder with doubt. She pondered about those puritanical years that she had spent and for what! Why had the church wanted women to stay virgins for life? Wait until you marry, but then nobody unless they too were chapel is ever going to be good enough.

Well marry, David, probably not, anyway he was as she always knew far too young for her, she was going to live and to enjoy each day as it came and damn the rest. It wasn't that she now no longer believed in a God, it is just that she now knew that God was a creature she hoped, of love and tenderness, not fire and brimstone as foretold within those red bricked walls of the Welsh church. Megan Vaughn-Thomas now saw Christianity for what it really was, a religion that relied heavily on fear, in fact the fiery damnation of hell itself. If God had created man and wanted celibacy, then why had he made sex so wonderfully fantastic something to be enjoyed all one's life, not just for the procreation of future children.

Megan always knew that her parents or the church would never understand the way she had become thanks to David Cartier. Now she loved him from the top of his head to the bottom of his bottom, which she particularly like touching and stroking. How she praised the day that she had decided to give aid and sucker to this gentle and loving being.

June of 1962 came, and it was time for David to take his O-level exams. He knew that he was ready for them, thanks that is to his sexy Megan. The only test that he found hard was the mathematics. But he lived in hope that anyway he would pass, maybe not a high pass but a B or C, would be okay. The music had been easy, he played his grade eight viola and passed with flying colours, he had successfully managed his grade five theory, not that theory was really his forte. But he knew that he would get a good pass mark on the whole exam, so he felt relieved and satisfied at the same time. As for the two other O-level exams they were a doddle and, he knew that these were just a formality something for him to be pleased about, as apposed to being of great importance to any future job or entrance to University or College.

Now that studies were over for the O-levels, he knew it was time to party. Though he went to work every day, he would now often take his viola in with him. Megan didn't mind as there was very little for either of them to do at this time. Listening to David playing and practicing was a pleasure for that Welsh lass, who anyway had been brought up with singing and brass bands playing which she also enjoyed and loved. But here and now with David, here was something different, a string instrument that had these beautiful mellow tones.

David had managed to buy himself a 19th century German trade viola two years ago when his father in a mad moment had given him some money for all the work that he had done within the company, that reward was for his past graft and what was expected of him to do in the future.

He was told about the auction house called Phillips, which is situated in central West End London. He went to a viewing of just string instruments and was amazed to discover that there were literally hundreds for sale at any one auction.

He had spent hours trying various instruments until he found a rather nice copy of the Cremona school founding son Amati, but his one was made by a German maker called Kesslering and made in Mittenwald probably 1880. He measured it and to his delight the back was sixteen and a quarter inches, perfect. This was going to be his baby no matter what he would have to pay. When the bidding started, it looked as if he would never be able to afford it, but it stopped at just fifty pounds and then was withdrawn for not reaching the reserve. Cartier was heartbroken, but decided anyway to ask after the auction had finished if he could in fact have it for just fifty pounds. Much to his amazement he was told after a telephone conversation with the owner, the answer came back as yes, he could have it for that price. It came with a case plus a usable bow. David was indeed in musical heaven.

Since being with Megan, he had never stopped practicing, but he knew that he was in serious need of help, his technique was not allowing him to progress.

He needed that help and quickly and by jingo he knew it, so important that David was aware of his own short comings, he didn't fool himself into believing that all was fine with his style of playing, he knew it wasn't. It was Megan that found an old viola player living in Deptford not more than a few miles away.

His name was Charles MacFlatten, though having a Scottish name he was in fact originally from Dublin and was famed for being the first viola in the London Philharmonic Orchestra until his retirement in 1958. He was a very gentle man who was glad for the chance to help young David, especially as he wanted so badly to work hard and attain a highly proficient standard. David went regularly to have lessons; it gave them both an incentive to work hard. There was a goal to reach, David needed it to better his life and fulfil himself, Charles needed it to give the last years some sort of meaning. Charles had many facets of his life that he wanted to expel from his thoughts by doing good deeds to others, he needed some sort of fulfilment not because he had been a bad or villainous person, oh no! But purely because he had fought in two world wars for the accursed English, after all he was a true four-leaf clover green Irishman.

In the Great War he had fought alongside men from Northern Ireland, he had fought at Ypres, Loos, Somme and Passchendaele, he knew he had personally killed several Germans, on one occasion he had thrust his bayonet into a wounded Germans stomach.

Though he wouldn't recommend fighting in any army, battling for the English was extreme bad news; to do it twice bordered on insanity and treachery to the Irish cause, those thoughts didn't bring him joy but he didn't flinch from them either. It wasn't the fighting that had bothered him, it was those bloody awful Protestant bastards from Belfast. He knew and perfectly understood that he would have been better suited to have fought for the Hun.

Then in the return match of 1939, he once again fought for the British. He could have gone back to Dublin and almost certainly have had a good life, after

all the Irish had stayed neutral in this scrap. Perhaps he would have been more suited to playing for the orchestra there, but no, somehow, he managed to get himself tangled up with a recruiting sergeant in a Catford pub and before he could say,
"God bless King George the sixth!"
There he was signing on the dotted line once more. This time he managed to become a sergeant himself with his specialist expertise in killing, plus the fact that he was a musician he became a drummer in the Scots Guards.

His saintly mother was now and forever more turning somersaults in her grave. He survived both wars without a scratch, though he did get a bloody nose on V - J Day, when he bumped into a bloody protestant bastard from Belfast, after drinking too much he told this particular Paddy what he thought of the Royalists, the offended chap had no sense of humour what-so-ever and promptly thumped him on his snout.

After the war he practiced hard once again and immediately got the position of first viola of that fine London Orchestra. He was almost happy now, after all it was a good orchestra, but to work with those bloody Anglo-Saxon children of swine, was bordering on almost too much for man or beast to bare.

Now long retired Charles was now finally trying to reconcile his purpose in life, plus coming to terms with living and working with bloody English people, he could at any time have returned to Ireland but never did and now he knew he never would.

So David had come at a perfect time, it was time for Charles to give something back to the country that actually had kept him in housing, clothing and Irish whisky.

David enjoyed going to Charles MacFlatten and managed to try and get a lesson in at least once a week.

His practicing time was now extended to at least four hours a day and was expecting to have even more hours to work soon. David's technique improved quickly, he held the bow in a more positive way giving him more flexibility, thus able to control any action that might be called upon to do. He was given huge amounts of sight-reading tests and, his knowledge of the difficult moments for solo viola soon became very familiar lines to practice. But David knew within himself that things were most definitely going in the right direction.

It was late August when David now eighteen, received his exam results. He was shocked, and shocked to the core. O-level mathematics, grade A, music O-level grade A-star, then looking at the O-level results, all excellent passes.

Looking towards Megan he asked,

"How can this be? I know I didn't do that well in any of the subjects." David looked towards the floor and then screwed up his eyes,

"Megan, sweetheart, what have you done?"

He was looking at Megan in a sideways glance, though he had a smile on his face his teeth were gritted, inside he felt sad about the results.

It was perfectly obvious to him that Megan had done something to those papers. After all the work that he had put into taking these exams was it all for nothing? He hadn't wanted any special help, this was something he wanted to achieve through his own common sense and his own ability to learn and through long hours of hard work. Now he felt like a failure, who had passed these tests? Him or Megan?

Megan was a little puzzled by David's attitude, surely all he wanted was a chance to get into a music college did it matter how he did it? Tears welled up into her eyes she was not sure if she was going to burst out crying for somehow letting David down, or was it because she felt indignation for being made to look like a fool after trying to help the person she loved? 'How could he get so agitated by receiving passes?'

Those tears were starting to be replaced with a feeling of annoyance. Her indignation was quickly turning to anger.

"I did what I did for you, because I thought you loved me and because I stupidly love you? Maybe I was badly mistaken, maybe you don't love me? If I hadn't cheated on your behalf, you would not have passed your maths exam you would have failed it, is that what you wanted?"

Then her voice softened slightly as she continued,

"I did it for you David, this way with your abilities to play your viola you will have no trouble getting an entry into college."

His slight sneering smile had now turned into a smile of scorn. Inside he was shaking with rage.

"So Megan, I didn't really need to do any of the work, you were quite prepared to take the exam on my behalf. I didn't have to work in the school, I didn't have to suffer your bloody mood swings during your accursed periods, then the continuous lecturing that you gave, was all that just for your own fun or did you just enjoy being a bully?"

David was almost in tears himself; he had never ever felt so put out.

"On exam day, I could have just given you the empty paper with my name scribbled on the top."

Almost spitting out the next sentence,

"Is that how it should have been?"

David was now spitting the proverbial feathers, he felt hurt and disappointed all in one fowl swoop. Megan realised immediately that unless she pacified the situation real quick, she was destined to be alone once more and as the last months with David had been so wonderful, with the feelings of great satisfaction on discovering her own sexuality and the experiencing this young man's body, what a complete shame that would become.

Then there had been the pleasure of helping him to learn from reading and testing, giving him her own educated knowledge, these had all been very special days.

To her way of thinking just making sure was the right thing to do, after all had he failed for sure he would be cycling away from her and Forest Hill forever anyway!

"Look darling, I realise that maybe I was a little zealous in my interference, but I promise you David I only changed a couple of the answers on your maths paper and it was more to show how you reached the answers than changing the answer itself."

She was now lying through her teeth, but this at least gave him back some self respect.

"Honestly, I never touched any of the other papers. Your history and geography answers are all your own. You just did better than you imagined you could."

Better to win him back at any cost, she knew loneliness was a costly unpleasant experience that she no longer wanted or needed in her now contented fuller life. So, Megan carried on in the same vain.

"Now look darling, I want to take you out to the Blue Dragon and let us celebrate, we shouldn't be arguing. Then I want you to take me home and have your evil way with me. You deserve it all!"

David knew that the entire rhetoric that had preceded was complete bull shit, but after all what is done cannot be undone, at least not without causing huge amounts of trouble for himself and Megan, better to leave well alone. But inside he knew that his days with Megan were fast climaxing and once you reach the top, there is only one more way to go, down!

"Look, in a few more months you can take your a-level maths and music, though I will help you cram I promise you now, it will be all your own work. Now, not another word, food then loving please!"

They ate well, at least he would make sure that this meal was going to cost a pretty penny, after all good old Megan does everything, arranges everything and these days she gets the most pleasure out of the sex, so it's only right that she pays for everything too.

When they got back to her flat Megan excused herself and disappeared into the bathroom. David turned on the radio and listened to a moderately funny programme called the Navy Lark. He had heard it many times before but never really liked it. He didn't enjoy the somewhat effeminate ways that many of the characters presented themselves. But there were several occasions when without realising it he chuckled at one or two jokes.

As the programme ended in strolled Megan. David casually glanced in her direction and then quickly did a double take. There she stood, and all she had on was a very flimsy nightdress showing off her proud breasts and voluptuous figure and as he looked down he noticed that there was absolutely no thick black pubic hair, she had shaved it all off and for the first time he noticed just how proud her Venus mound stood. She might not be the world's beauty Queen, but for age she looked quite desirable in fact more than quite, very desirable.

David's jaw almost touched the floor. Nothing was said, she just beckoned to him with her index finger to follow to the bedroom. Once in there she bent over to light several candles and then turned off the light. As she bent over the bed to pull back the sheets David could see her bottom quite clearly, he had never noticed before just how beautifully shaped it was before this night. For a moment he wanted to get on his knees and lick every part of it, then quickly thought better of that one.

Megan turned towards him and then said in a low voluptuous voice,

"This is for you, just for you, nobody else but you. I love you and this is the best way I know to show my feeling."

She pulled up her nightdress and slowly removed it, then calmly and deliberately lay on the bed with her legs wide apart. To David's utter delight he could see that she had very, very cleanly shaved off all that mop of wiry black pubic hair, so not just shaved but completely bald, not so much as a sign of any stubble. She was bald and pink. He looked and melted, her vagina was beautifully round and plump, the Venus mound extending down ready to be cupped in his hand. And there before his bulging eyes he could see that her clitoris stood erect in the air with anticipation.

'Wow!' he thought, 'Megan has her own small but distinct penis'. David once again lost control of his ejaculation powers and managed not for the last time to leave a huge deposit in his underpants that soaked through to his trousers. 'Who cares anyway?' Certainly not David Cartier, plus he knew that Megan would clean everything afterwards. Quickly he scrambled out of his clothing. To Megan's delight she saw that he was already gaining another erection and once again she wanted to swing on it.

He lay on the bed beside her, but before he could manipulate the situation to what he wanted, Megan had taken his member in her hands and was slowly caressed it. When she knew he was close to climax she got down and did what he always wanted her to do, she was going to put it in her mouth.

She pulled his foreskin back to reveal his crown in all its flushed red glory, she licked around the edges making sure that it was well lubricated, then she gently pushed it into her open mouth. She placed her head in such a position that his member could be harried gentle but firmly into one cheek then the other cheek, this was done with the clever use of her tongue, while doing this in a steady rhythm she passionately sucked, at the same time her left hand was tickling his testicles and the right hand was playing around his anal regions, sometimes lightly sticking her finger inside then tickling around the orifice area. It took less than one minute before David was fit to explode. 'Please take it in the mouth, I have tried and tried to get you to do this before, so now you are going to get the load. Don't let me down.'

At the end of that thought Cartier jerked and moaned, he had expelled a massive amount of sperm and it all went into her mouth. He looked to see what she was going to do next, and it was his delight to see that she swallowed the lot. When he had finished, she crept up the bed towards him and then put her mouth to his own and kissed him pushing her tongue all around his lips and the inside of his mouth. He could still taste the slightly salty flavour of his own life juices.

This act was singularly the best sexual experience that Cartier had ever felt. He was truly elated, he felt complete and now it was his turn and this time he truly wished to please her. He climbed out of the bed taking his pillows with him. He placed them on the floor and got Megan to slide around and across the bed, placing her in such a position that he could explore those shaven vaginal regions not just with his tongue, but also with his fingers and then his penis.

He got down with his knees resting on the pillows and then he gently pulled her over towards him making sure that each leg could go over each side of his shoulders. The sight that was before him was one of simply delicious pinkish wet flesh. Once again, he had already started yet another erection and he wasn't about to waste it. He touched the area gently with both hands, he cupped her mound and then licked all around it. Megan was already breathing heavily, and her hands were gripping quite tightly on his head her fingers being intertwined with his hair. At one point he wondered if she was going to make him bleed as her nails seemed to be digging deeply into his scalp. He opened her up, looking directly into the pink flesh. In his mind it was now time to take that long-awaited drink.

Tasting her life juices and returning the compliment of that wonderful adventure that had just been bestowed on him first. His tongue shot in as far as he could make it and he was pleased to experience a pleasant taste of womanhood. Her own liquid lubricant was flowing quite openly and to David this indeed was manna from heaven. He then put his right index finger into the gaping chasm much to her delight and his. She was so wet but also so active. She was now writhing from side to side making it extremely hard for him to do his duty. Then he pushed two fingers in and this made even more excitement for her, soon he had forcing entry for all five and, Megan was actually screaming with the delight of her passion. David thought that it was now time to try something else, something that had played on his mind ever since he got familiar with Megan. But when mentioning what his fantasy was to Megan, he had been sharply rebuffed.

It was time to try again.

"Please Megan, turn over and get on your knees."

"Yes darling, anything darling. Shall I put my head up or down?"

"Down, stick your bum into the air, I intend to penetrate it."

At this Megan stiffened slightly, but after thinking for a moment relaxed and did as she was bid.

Cartier stood up and noticed that his member was now as stiff as a iron rod, he just couldn't remember when he had been so stiff and large. He was amazed that he had managed two ejaculations and now was ready for a third and all in under an hour. He opened up the cheeks of her bottom and was pleased to note that not only was it clean, but there were no hairs there either. Pushing her cheeks apart quite firmly he managed to open her waste exit region up enough so that he was looking into at least an inch of pink flesh. Now with a fully erect penis, he placed it at the entry point and tried to enter. But Megan's automatic reflexes had cut in and he could not make it in without her relaxing.

"Megan, please relax. Let yourself go, who knows you might just enjoy the experience and if you don't then I shall be quick and that can be that. At least I will have the satisfaction of knowing that there is indeed no orifice on you that I have not explored, err, in depth."

They both giggled like a couple of naughty kids.

Somehow Megan managed to relax her muscles and David managed entry. At first, he pushed in gently, half an inch, then an inch, and then two, three, then all the way. He pushed hard and fast, but being honest to himself, he was not entirely sure that he liked what he was doing and one thing that somehow made his feelings turn aside was the fact that Megan was once again squealing with ecstasy. In David's mind women shouldn't like or appreciate the act of buggery, it was rude, unclean and could lead to all sorts of medical problems. He had heard a story of a man getting warts on the end of his penis after having anal sex to much, or was that a woman having the warts, he wasn't entirely sure, but it did all seem very seedy and smelly and shouldn't really be done? This in some way upset him so much that he knew he wasn't going to ejaculate, so he withdrew, much to Megan's disappointment. He then thought about the proper entry point and as she was still holding the position he pushed it into her vagina. Somehow this seemed maybe the right thing to do. Maybe acting like a homosexual was not right, at least not for him, David Cartier. 'Arse holes should be left for the faggots of this world', were his distasteful thoughts.

David could be quite homophobic when he put his mind to it.

Once started in her vagina there was now no stopping, this felt right and he made sure that he was pushing in as far as it would go. This was extreme pleasure for them both, he could feel the walls of her inside pounding against his penis, she was in heaven, and he once again was close to exploding. Just one last deep penetration and the job was done. Megan was quivering and David was moaning, in his case partly because he was now extremely sore. He was standing with his knees shaking with fatigue, he knew that if he didn't sit soon, he would fall over, so he sat down on the side of the bed and panted with exhaustion. Megan had had three orgasms but was still in the mood for at least three more.

David in return just wanted to die. He had enjoyed it all, but like most of the male species he was never happier than when he had had enough. Megan came up beside him, she stroked his wet face and hair and then seeing that he was in fact holding his penis as if it hurt, she took it on herself to do the job for him.

He had filled all her exit points and now felt wet, grubby, smelly and very dirty. To Megan none of those things mattered. She once again took his member and licked it all over then placed it once again in her mouth. David squirmed deeply. This was now most definitely not the thing to do, instead of exciting David, it made him feel nauseas.

'What is she thinking, I have just been up her arse and in her fanny and I must be covered in everything. Now the silly cow has put it in her bloody mouth. If she gets ill, I'll have nothing but contempt for her.'

He made her stop much to her sanguine. He looked at her now as if she was something that he had just stepped into.

"I am going to wash and clean up. I suggest you do the same. I am very tired and well, actually I am completely exhausted. Sorry Megan, but I need to sleep and for that I shall go back to my own digs."

When he came back into the room after washing and making himself feel decent!

'Yes, that's the word, decent!' Even David understood the hypocrisy of those incredibly naïve selfish homophobic thoughts, but it didn't stop him thinking them anyway.

He still felt a certain amount of rage welling up inside of him, first about the exam results, second for the obvious contemptible attempts of seduction from Megan, though nice at the moment of doing, now leaving him feeling low and repugnant and the venom from that lack of self esteem was aimed firmly in her direction.

He knew he needed space, time to think alone. Maybe just a day or two, but he wanted his own company, or maybe the company of some other males. Megan was still lying in the bed, he could see that she had been crying and though he felt pity, there was another sensation creeping over him, it was an awful feeling of being trapped, he had fallen into the age old trap, seduce the woman and spend eternity being held to ransom. Yes, that he thought was what had in fact occurred and now he understood, he knew that feeling had sprung up like a coil of wire to imprison him. Yes he knew he now had to get away and be free once more.

"Why are you going David? What did I do, have I done something wrong? I only wanted to please you, and I did do everything that you asked. When will I see you again?"

Her voice was shallow and tired, tears were streaming down her flushed cheeks. He couldn't tell her his inner most feelings, no that would have been extremely cruel, anyway he wasn't entirely sure what they were himself. He knew that she had indeed within the boundaries of this sex session, somehow had sold herself short and that made him feel somewhat disgusted with her, or was that himself? Maybe a form of guilt was creeping into his brain, and possibly not before time.

"I am sorry Megan, its, err, those bloody exam results!"

He lied, but kept going anyway,

"Its not you it's me."

He couldn't quite bring himself to look her directly in her eyes, he just stood there like a naughty boy waiting for the headmaster to come and chastise him.

"I am fond of you, and I am extremely grateful to you. Oh, just give me a few days. I will be back, and we will bonk and screw and even make mad passionate love again!"

He knew that he had not been convincing, he also knew that she knew that simple expedient too.

"See you in a day or two. Bye Megan!"

But all he heard were the sobs of a broken heart, in his minds eye he saw those tears streaming down her countenance, but then from a sob came a wailing sound gurgling from her throat.

'Oh Christ, let me out of here! This day has turned into a complete nightmare.' As he went out into the nights cold but clear clean air, those were his parting thoughts.

Chapter 3

David Cartier went home to his digs, changed his clothes which were dirty from passion thus also very smelly. Though he had washed thoroughly at Megan's he still felt unclean and knew he probably would for a long time to come. But to combat those feelings he went and had another wash. He could wash away the dirt, but he couldn't wash away that dirty feeling that clung to him like a limpet. He wasn't going to try and wash her out of his mind, at least for the time being. He already understood that a time would come when he would long for intercourse again, and Megan Vaughn-Thomas had the sort of body that he would always lust after. 'To hell with it, to hell with women and especially that bloody Megan.' He looked into the mirror but only half admired the person looking back at him, some valuable self respect had left his being to be replace with an iota of self repugnancy.

His hair was clean and well brushed, though it would be thought by others to be slightly too long, he personally liked it that way. He was mousy blond in colour and the texture was silky fine, which made styling very difficult as he didn't like gels or lacquers. When David went to the trouble of trying a new hair style, the first hint of wind and that style was blown into nothing that could possibly be recognisable to anyone, but if nothing else persistence was an on going event in hair displays as far as young Cartier was concerned, nothing ventured nothing gained, but the truth be known everything was ventured with his hair, but nothing was ever gained.

He had put on a simple two-piece suit, dark brown in colour with slight pin stripes running through the cloth. His trousers were tight but well fitting with creases that could cut paper. His brown Italian style patent leather shoes were so clean, he could use them for looking up girls' skirts, though to be entirely fair to young David Cartier that thought hadn't as yet crossed his mind.

As he looked himself over, he felt a certain pride and confidence reappearing, he was once more a Jack-the-lad! He grabbed his viola case, after all it was Friday night, and it had been months since he last had a jam session with the boys at the coffee bar at Clockhouse.

"Ted, you old fart, how the heck are you? Keeping well, screwing women, making money or generally making a nuisance of yourself, I hope?"

David marched up to his aging friend and slapped him hard on the back. Fortunately, Ted was actually happy to see him again.

"Ah, David, what a pleasure; I was hoping to see you some time, there has been an American Yankee Doodle Dandy in town, and he has been a few times to listen to the various groups that have been here playing. I'll give the old blighter a call on the blower and see whether he will appear tonight? I've got 'is number somewhere. Err; I am assuming you were coming to gig?"

"No, it's the coffee that I come for, you know how much I like drinking dirty muddy water!"

And then the smile departed and for a moment he became serious.

"Who's playing tonight anyway?"

"Don't know, just hang on for about an hour, it'll all start up about nine."

He then added as an afterthought.

"You'll still 'ave to pay for the coffee."

David smiled, touched his viola case and said,

"See Ted, I brought my banjo especially for you, surely that's worth the price of a cup of muddy brown watery coffee."

It was nearly ten-thirty when the American turned up to listen. The high-flying wiz-bang group consisted of one drummer, with just a snare drum and a cracked cymbal, one bass player with a very fine Cremonese tea chest, with the various attachments needed, i.e. good solid obvious vintage broom handle with a length of sisal string attached. Strangely enough he was making a very good sound and kept rhythm and some sort of tuning all the way through every piece they played. Then there was a very fine flautist who was studying at the Guildhall School of Music and Drama and like David, he had come to these silly sessions just for the fun of doing something completely different from normal musical studies, he was there just for the fun of jamming it up, his sound was so beautiful and somewhat out of place but somehow it added to the ambience of the entire evening so it really didn't matter a fig that real rubbishy amateurs were performing with top class music students.
The piece de-resistance was the singer come real banjo player. His name was Stanley Everett and young Stanley played that banjo very well, with panache and gusto all in one, he could also sing and knew all the latest skiffle and pop songs. Lastly David Cartier followed up the rear, David now was playing the viola really well, he was extremely thankful in having had the chance to study under Charles MacFlatten, he had spent his time well and it now showed, he was playing the best he had ever done before, but like the flautist he enjoyed these silly inane sessions, it provided him with the chance to improvise, this made him listen and keep the tempo,

plus watch his intonation against his fellow musicians, not that intonation meant much to the bass player or the drummer, the word musicians in this context was said in a loose dandified frivolous fashion.

None of them knew who this American was or if they saw him, what was he even there for? They just played and generally at a decibel level that was close to turning purists deaf. But all the punters there joined in with various choruses and a good time was in theory, being had by one and all. Especially Ted who sold more soft drinks on Friday nights than all the rest of the week put together. After finishing the last verse of Cumberland Gap, the five weary but elated players took a well-earned rest. Ted supplied them with they salary for their nights work, one cup of frothy coffee each, anything else they paid for! As finally silence descended within that small but homely innocent coffee bar, a figure came across that speak to the group of five.

"Hi-ya! My name is Stuart Holstein. I arrange bands for touring around entertaining the U.S. army, all over the world. I am here with a group now, but one of my members has gone and died on me."

He didn't look remotely concerned, just somewhat annoyed that he was out by one musician, which implied taking time out to train another one to take the blighter's place.

"I need!"

And he looked directly and squarely at Cartier's face and eyes,

"Someone who can busk, play the string instrument for quartets and light classical concerts, but also have the ability to work in a dance band, preferably playing the piano or the drums as well." Still looking directly into David's eyes, he continued,

"Does any of that ring bells with any of you? Perhaps you, Mr.?"

"Who me, oh, my name is David Cartier. Yes, I play the piano and I am expecting to go to the Royal College of Music next year. How long do you need someone for?"

"Well David, it would be approximately six months. But the pay is good, you would earn at least five hundred bucks a week."

"What! Err, let me work that out."

He paused, looked at his fingers and counted, then said,

"Why that's one hundred pounds and, for a week's work?"

He sank down in the chair next to him wide eyed and wondering. "And you want me, from when?"

"Well, we have some gigs at various aerodromes around your East Anglia. These are for American bomber pilots and crews. There will be a couple of dinners, there you will have to play some chamber music which you practice with who ever else will be playing and in your own free time. Then there are a couple of dances, local girls come and strut their stuff with our boys and in return get taken outside and shagged rotten."

He smiled at all that were listening, then said in a flat tone,

"Err, shagged, that is an English expression, isn't it?"

He then took time out to see if anyone was laughing at his joke, no one was.

"Then before we go off to Germany and then the Far East, there is one cabaret for an office's night. Believe it or not that should be fun, strippers and such like, those buggers are a dirty bunch, the officers I mean. So, what do you say, interested?"

Then at the last breath as if he nearly forgot,

"Ah, yes. We will need you to start on the first of December, that gives you twelve weeks. Can you get your life in order for then?"

"Bloody hell, I'll say I can. Many thanks, this is just what I need. A chance to earn some real money and the excuse to travel the world, wow, maybe even meet some lovely oriental ladies. And the timing is perfect, I shall contact the college on Monday and see whether I can have a chance to play to them now?"

David turned to his friend the flautist,

"Steve, you old bastard, what do you think of that then?"

"David, one thing, or maybe even two. Keep up your practicing, never stop, you will need to practice even when you are in your sixties."

Sharp as an eagle, Steve Preston added,

"You must remember what Sir Thomas Beecham once said?"

He then took on the voice of a aging conductor,

"You forget to practice for one day, you are aware of it, if you leave it for two days, everyone is aware of it."

He placed his hand firmly on David's shoulder and concluded with,

"Also remember, you want to be a classically trained player, and a good orchestra is your goal, don't get sidetracked by money, keep your dream alive always."

David shook his friend warmly by the hand, smiled and said, "Screw you! I shall always want to be a player in a symphony orchestra, that's my aim and ambition nothing will side track that part of my life. But, money, money, money; girls, girls, girls. Do I have to say anything else?"

On the Monday David didn't go into the school library, instead he contacted the secretary of the Royal College of Music and asked politely if there was a chance of coming to play to someone, this was concerning an entry into the college. He explained that he was in fact going abroad for anything up to six months, so if he was to know that there was a position there for him when returning to England it would have saved time and given him an incentive to work and to save that money.

The secretary, one Janet Church, a budding composer herself, liked this young man's tone of voice. She explained that though there were special times in the year to take an entrance examination, it would appear that David Cartier might be in with a chance as he played a string instrument, the country was extremely short of string players and there was always a special need of viola players, she would ask the principal Sir Archibald Sanders if it was possible for him to come and play to the examiners more or less right away.

"Could you give me an hour then telephone me back Mr. Cartier, I should have an answer for you by then. Oh, by the way, are you any relation to Nevillia Cartier?"

David thanked her profusely, even though the answer hadn't yet been in the affirmative. He virtually jumped for joy even though the association with his sister was now confirmed. Things were finally starting to seem very positive for him.

Miss Church having replaced the receiver went directly to the principal's office. There leaning back in his captain's chair with the morning sun cascading down upon his person, this was giving him the appearance of a saint surrounded by one huge halo. Sir Archibald Sanders was an aging, rather plump, balding man, who when smiling showed a row of rotting teeth. So bad were these brown moulding stumps, which when he came up close to anyone else, it became an extremely unpleasant matter for the visiting person as he suffered from the most appalling halitosis. Janet was always careful to have at first before entering sprayed a little rose water on her face, that at least took the worst of the reeking smell away.

"Sir Archibald, something interesting has just occurred. I have just received a telephone message from a young man who plays the viola and piano. He has just been offered and accepted a position with an American military entertainment orchestra, but he wants after finishing the tour, to come back and start music studies proper here afterwards and you will never guess who he is, only the brother of Nevillia Cartier."

She paused giving the principal a chance to break into the conversation.

"Why should that affect us? What is so special about this young man?"

Sanders was a man now almost completely out of touch with who is who in the musical world, his days were now spent reminiscing about his friendship with Ralph Vaughn-Williams, Edward Elgar, Gustav Holst, Delius and Parry, composers whom he had grown up with.

This was Janet Church's chance to show some real initiative, and she took it with both hands spread wide.

"Well sir, it's a two-fold reason really. First, because of the real shortage of men due to the war, this country like many others, finds itself short of good string players and what is more he plays the viola, hardly a seriously popular instrument at any time. Second, his name is,"

She added with a certain zeal,
"David Cartier."

"Well, who the heck is David Cartier when he is at home?"

"David Cartier sir is the brother of Nevillia Cartier, like I said before. She is that brilliant violinist who is now leading the Birmingham Symphony Orchestra and she is a truly wonderful musician. If David is half the man that Nevillia is woman, he might well turn out to be a very important catch for this establishment?"

"Ah yes, I get your drift. Well, what do you suggest then?"

There, that was the rub, she had him! If this David Cartier was any good at all she would make sure that she Janet Church would get the plaudits. This might be her chance to get a position where she can indulge her composing talents, being a secretary was just not going to cut the mustard in the long run.

Rubbing her hands together with more than a certain amount of satisfaction glowing from within each side of her being, she returned to her own office, anyway once back there she could start breathing in again.

Janet Church was the only daughter of that fine English composer Alexander Church, who after completing his eighth symphony called his wife Agnes in to listen to the completed rushes from the piano. Agnes got so excited listening to the work that there and then they celebrated the completion in the traditional way, on the living room carpet. Nine months later Janet was born. Alexander loved his only daughter, so much so that he composed the next and last symphony especially for her. As is commonly known by one and all, the ninth symphony has the subtitle of Little Janet. After completing this work

Alexander realised that this was the climax of his life's work and promptly died.

Janet was just old enough to miss her father terribly, so as a gesture of love to the memory of her father she also took up composition. Though she had studied music at the Royal College of Music, little to nothing in the way of chances for performances had ever opened to her. Her output was tremendous but sadly Janet was the only one who ever got to hear her own music. To help her non existent career move forward and stay within the environment of a musical establishment, she managed to get the job as secretary in the very college that had given her theory and composition lessons. To Janet, this was indeed at least a step in the right direction, to everybody else, it was just Janet Church, college secretary!

She was now in her fortieth year and had worked at the college for the past fourteen years, but nobody was going to say that she was not a go getter; she had plans for this that and anything else, always with the grand design of getting her compositions heard and appreciated, but alas always generally to no avail.

She had never got married, never even had a boyfriend. Always in the back of her mind the thought, 'Plenty of time for all that nonsense after the world hears my music and I am famous.'

But time was passing quickly and what had once been a very attractive lady was fast becoming a weird strange frumpy spinster with only the occasional look of lust to accompany some young man who might be special either in his ability to play an instrument or to write music that somehow gets performed.

David telephoned as requested just one hour after he had first done the deed. It was Janet who answered.

"Hello, this is David Cartier speaking, I spoke to you…"

"Ah yes; Mr. Cartier. I have spoken to the principal and, he has agreed with me that you should come and give an audition. Can you make tomorrow afternoon?"

Young Cartier was completely thrown by the suddenness of her response. But gathering his thoughts quickly and managed to get the right answer.

"Absolutely, what time do you want me to be there?"

"Let's say, err, two o'clock, would that be acceptable? Oh, and please have a concerto ready for performance, then you will be given some sight reading test on the viola, I do hope your reading is good? If that goes well there will be a short theory and harmony examination. You should be finished by five to five thirty."

"How can I ever thank you. I shall be there never fear and I have the opening movement of the Bartok viola concerto under my belt, surely that would do?"

"That would be splendid. One last thing David, I hope you don't mind me calling you by your Christian name, please wear the right sort of clothing. Too many young people turn up here dressed in Beatnik or Teddy boy attire, please come sensibly dressed. You might also be judged by your demeanour."

David thanked her once again and then immediately returned to his digs. He would make sure that he was totally prepared for the next day's adventure.

Janet went back to her office work, but there was a nagging thought that had somehow crept into her head.

She liked the way he spoke; he was polite yet somehow a quite subdued tone of authority came from his manner. Why had she called him David? This had puzzled her. She was never informal with the students and especially not with potential new students. But somewhere deep inside her there was a volcano awaiting eruption time and maybe the magna was just starting to rise.

This she was not aware of only within her sub-consciousness, but there it was, a tingled in her loins, something that had never manifest itself before, at least not that she had ever been conscious of, and now she felt trepidation as what this young fellow was going to be like. Why should she care it all seemed so crazy. She shivered ever so slightly and then got down to her registers.

Cartier was excited, he had got a proper job playing, albeit a cabaret come entertainments band, but how well paid it was. And tomorrow he has finally managed to land an audition for a place at college. Surely life didn't get any better than this! He practiced hard that day, he had been working on the concerto for several months with Charles and thought that he was quite proficient in playing it, at least the first movement. His landlady had a fall size mirror in her hall so he stood in front of it and practiced, at the same time watching his own technique in the reflection.

Charles had improved many things about his playing, but the biggest problem was his sloppy bowing arm. He had been working for nearly three hours and was starting to tire. Then in came another tenant, a normally friendly lad of early twenties. His name was Chester Gibbs and Chester worked as a baker in a huge bakery in Beckenham, one called Ackerman's. He had just finish work for the day having started his shift at four that morning. It had been a terrible day, and he was absolutely finished, all he wanted to do was sleep. His head ached and he felt as if he was coming down with some sort of flu virus. Then to come home expecting peace and quiet but getting this caterwauling sound echoing around the building and to top it all having the idiot who was making the din standing in the hallway taking up space. 'Oh, give me strength,' were Chester's thoughts.

Then almost in despair, he looked at David, went up to him and quietly enquired at the top of voice,

"Stop that awful noise. I'll take that bloody piece of wood from under your chin and then stick it where the sun never shines. Shut the buggery up..."

Then shaking from the physical exhaustion that raising his voice brought on, he added in a more peaceful calm subdued tone,

"Please!"

David thought that he owed it to Megan to inform her of his plans. Let her off the hook gently, then he would write a resignation letter to the school and thanking them for giving him the job in the first place. When he reached the school, it was almost leaving time, Megan was nowhere to be found. He asked the secretary if she was about and was told that she had not appeared that day at all, nor had they heard anything from her. They thought that she had been with him and were just having a day of fun, going out somewhere together.

David started to feel some guilt once again thrusting up like cruor in his throat. He explained to the secretary what had occurred today and that though he would of course give a weeks notice as from the next Monday he would in point of fact be leaving. He gave the secretary his letter of resignation, but before leaving explained that there had in fact been a little misunderstanding with Megan.

"We had a right fracas last night; it didn't end well. I then went out jamming with some musician friends and out of the blue yonder I have been offered a job playing the viola and piano. In fact, it is a world tour. You can see I cannot possibly turn it down, can I! The trouble is I haven't told Megan yet, so I think I had better go around to her flat and explain."

He then turned on his heels and speaking only loud enough that he was the only one that could hear, added,

"Oh shit, I hope she's alright?"

David knew that Megan was a very clearly defined person, though since knowing him she had become emotionally besotted, but somehow underneath he always expected calm thought out responses to any eventuality. Not in all the time since becoming her lover had he known her to miss a day's work. She loved her job, work in many ways was her life, you could say she lived to work and not worked to live.

He ran all the way to her flat, he was very glad to see at least there were lights on when he got there, and some classical music was playing on her gramophone. His heart rate slowed, and he gave it several minutes before he knocked on her door.

David knew that it was not going to be easy telling her that he was leaving the country even though he would be back. He made sure that his hair was tidy and then he brushed down his coat which was getting very slightly wet from the misty rain that had come with the dusk. Finally, with a certain resolve he knocked on the door. He waited, one minute, then two minutes then knocked again, but this time harder. Still, no one came, so he tried the door, and it came open to his touch. Once again, his heart was pounding; something was dramatically wrong here. He went to the flat door and didn't need to knock as he could see that it was already slightly ajar. He felt like the criminal returning to the scene of the crime. But was he a thief or worse, maybe a murderer?

He pushed the flat door very gently open, first putting his head around to see anything that might be seen. The room was as always neat and tidy, so he entered. As she wasn't there, it made sense that she would be in the bedroom. In fact, he could once again see that the light was burning through the bottom of the door plus a small crack that ran down part of the framework. He went over and stood there not really knowing what to do next. Should he knock or should he just enter? There was fear in those hands as that touched the doorknob to open it, he trembled even more as he turned the knob and pushed slowly, he then put his head through once again just in case he didn't want to enter.

There lying on the bed completely naked was Megan, she had covered her face with thick makeup and her beautiful, luscious lips were immersed with some awful dark red lipstick which had been so badly applied that in some areas it touched under her nostrils. In her right hand she held a very large cucumber and to David's abject horror he noticed there was quite a large amount of blood on it. Then he noticed that the entire area around her vagina was also heavily smeared with blood. Looking at the rest of her body, that below her breasts there was some bruising, he wondered if she had been punching her own breasts. There was a nasty somewhat ammonic smell within the room. At that point he saw that the bed sheets were completely soiled. She had noticed him but didn't really react to him standing there. Cartier, now standing in a very rattled indecisive stance opened the door to its optimum. Still slightly shaking from head to toe because entirely of what sights beheld him. He made the first sounds to speak,

"Megan! Christ woman, what have you been doing?"

Megan looked in his direction with now a glimmer of recognition showing in her countenance.

"Doing, me doing what?"

She looked puzzled as if what had been asked was an inane question.

"Why darling, I have been here all the time quietly waiting for you to return."

Then her eyes brightened as the obvious thought came to her mind, "It's time you shagged me again. I need you to enter me in every orifice."

Then giggling a little and added as an afterthought,

"Maybe you can find some other holes to fill, at least you can try, can't you?"

And then her eyes quizzically looked at him and then carried on in a very matter of fact tone of voice,

"That's what you were always there for! Now you know I don't lie, so you know that's the absolute truth, don't you?"

Before he could say anything to the sentence, she continued,

"I have been laying here keeping it all wet and warm for you. I want you to drink me up, put your very large knob in, put your hand in, climb in if you want to, why you can even pull things out, I don't care, I just don't care at all, everything you do is wonderful, and I want and need it all."

At the end of that sentence, she scratched her sharp fingernails down her two breasts bringing immediate blood to the surface. Then she wiped the blood on her face and said,

"But do lick my clit with that wondrous tongue of yours. I want you to make me come again and again and again. In fact, it mustn't stop!"

Towards the end of that last statement her voice had risen in volume and tempo, this accentuating her Welsh accent so much so that David wondered if the neighbours would be listening to this extremely erotic conversation.

"Shussssh! You don't want the people upstairs to hear you, do you?"

"I don't give a tinkers cuss who hears me."

Then at the top of her voice, she exclaimed,

"Get your bloody prick inside my crack before I burst from frustration. If anyone else is listening they will just have to wait their turn, then anyone can fuck me! In fact, more the merrier"

David was shocked to the core; he gulped and strained his ears to hear if anybody else was listening to their very private conversation. How the hell he thought he would hear people hearing them, this was just too much so-called nonsense, but he listened anyway.

He was nearing the end of his tether, anger and worry stirred within his frame but unfortunately, he wasn't quick at grasping the situation thus really didn't know which way to turn or what to say. He had decided one fact for sure, once out of Megan's grips he would be gone forever. As nice as she had been, history was what she was going to be.

"Look Megan, we need to talk. Things have happened quickly, and I need to tell…!"

Her eyes said it all, anger welled within her,

"I told you I want your cock! Now get it over here and be bloody quick about it."

Her eyes were staring wide and bright red, her veins stood out on her neck. For the first time since they had met David was more than a little frightened with Megan, to him there was something rather demonic about her whole demeanour.

"I want your tongue licking me all over and then you can stick your todger anywhere you like. Just do it and right now, and I do mean now!"

She paused, her eyes filled with water and were already red from her continuous sobbing. Then at the top of her vocal range she screamed,

"When I say now, I mean fucking now, not in your fucking time. Get over here and do your duty."

Young mister Cartier was truly amazed and the turn of phrases that Megan was coming out with, he had never used any bad language in front her. David was never going to be a saint, but he despised crude language and would often disown someone who he had known for their constant use of four-letter words. 'Where did she learn this language?'

As her voice continued to crescendo her pitch became almost inaudible, there was also a gurgling sound that was also coming from her throat. It was obvious that she was gradually losing her voice and to David's chagrin, this was a small bonus in a sea of ill-tempered obvious unhappiness. He was just a little relieved to hear her decibels lowering from the strain of bellowing, it had finally affected her throat.

'At least the neighbours will hopefully lose interest in the goings on in this basement.'

Cartier moved closer to the bed hoping now to pacify Megan down to a tolerable level where they could hold a reasonable conversation.

As he leant over the bed to plead something quietly into her ear, she grabbed at him pulling hard on his clothing, bursting his shirt from the buttons holding it together. He was pulled on top of her, his head banging quite hard into hers. Megan's lips lunged at his, she almost bit his lower lip off. As he gasped with pain and indignation, she thrust her tongue deep into his now open mouth. While doing this, the hand that held his shirt and jacket pulled at them with a very strong ferocity, the seem on his jacket split completely up the centre back, his shirt already sprung of buttons now came under exerted pressure to detach itself completely from his body.

Her other hand pulled at the fly buttons on his trousers, once again relieving them of the cloth that had held them. After doing this deed she thrust her hand deep into his crutch and pulled at the one thing she most wanted. As these three things happened at the same time, David in a state of shock could do nothing but firstly try and remove her tongue without actually biting it off. Then at the same time remove her hand from his penis, which was starting to show signs of enlargement. Everything was a complete blur; it had all happened so quickly. He was shaken by the entire incident, but it had not entirely aroused him, but it did in fact hurt him.

He could do neither of these two things to make her cease, he was completely overwhelmed by this sudden unforeseen attack on his body, the strength of this demure Welsh lady beggared belief.

It was the sort of event that pretty well all men would have dreamt of, if they were honest with themselves. This onslaught was the dream fantasy of most normal manhood, the reality was degrading, painful and overwhelming. All he could do was to struggle a little, while all the time Megan got deeper and deeper into what she desired.

He knew that if he hit, or bit her, he was going to be in trouble and as things in his life were now turning out for what might be an interesting future, he knew he didn't want any scandal occurring that might unsettle things.

Eventually he managed to recover enough strength to dislodge her face from his, this was his chance, and he had to take it quickly before any further damage happened to his clothing.

"Megan stop, stop! Listen, let me take what's left of my clothes off, then we can make love. Don't worry my sweet, I err, really want to do it. You are so sexy and desirable. But first let me go and do be quiet."

She went almost completely quiet immediately, removed her hand from his genitals and waited there on the bed lying in her our blood, faeces and urine. Finally in desperation he got off the bed, looked at his tattered shirt and jacket in the mirror. Sighed with a deep long sad heart felt escape of air, his face dropped in sadness and annoyance at what looked back at him. He then put his hand down to his fly buttons, noted that she had in fact torn them completely away, ripped his underpants at the front so badly that one leg part was hanging off.

'Oh shit, these clothes are going to have to be binned. She has now cost me some serious money. The stupid bloody bitch!'

David had never been in love with Megan, the age gap always spoilt that. The fact that she was also somewhat frumpy, especially in her dress sense, not always but at times and sadly it was always those times that he now remembered. Also, because she could be extremely bossy, something he always rebelled against in everyone that showed those traits. But most of all because she now threw herself so wildly at him and he had totally lost respect for her. He now looked at her in an angry, piteous way, sorry for her, but despising her at the same time.

He knew the only way out of this mess was to firstly appease her, which meant raise an erection and do the bidding. Secondly to somehow afterwards explain how things were going to be. It meant no more mister nice guy, from this moment on he had to be cruel to be kind.

Going back to the bed he once again looked down on the smouldering naked figure of the Welsh Dragon. This quiet reserved lady who went to chapel on Sundays and had done so all her life, never swore, never drank and would always be a virgin until marriage and if that was not going to appear, then a virgin she would stay for ever. But then that was before she had met young David Cartier, now she had met him and she had lost her virginity, never went back to chapel, drank and swore like a Welsh washer woman. Megan had completely lost to those decent ideals of goodness and righteousness.

David got out of his clothing and as he did so, tried to talk some reason into her.

"Megan, we will make love, but afterwards must talk. I have many things to tell you, very exciting things, and its very imp…"

"Stop your pissing about, I'm not interested in your waffle just your sperm, thrust that weapon now, get on top of me."

Those eyes which for a moment or two had calmed themselves, once again turned dark red in colour. There was a demon within her spirit that David just didn't recognise, but he knew he must perform if only to save his own neck. Megan was once again getting herself roused, either by the simple expedient of raising her voice or, more fun for her, once again grabbing at David's member.

He fell heavily onto the bed, she at the same moment slid down so that she could get his penis into her mouth. David yelped at the suddenness of the attack, but this time didn't fight back realising that he must in fact accept his fate, a very strange state of affairs when a man accepts his fate but not the woman! This to David was turning out to be some sort of almost voluntary rape, but upon him!

It wasn't long before he was starting to become sexually aroused, there was no point in fighting it, it was what he was there to do, so do it is what he did. His size increased until it filled her mouth, but Megan was greedy, she sucked very hard and pushed that penis deep inside and down her very throat, soon it felt like his member was almost touch her tonsils. All the time caressing his testis gently with her right hand, her left hand was firmly pressing the cheeks of his bottom apart. Soon she had extended three fingers up his anus and was searching to see if she could place in her whole hand. The pain quickly became immense but strangely interesting and that in itself worried Cartier. David started to wonder if he was actually a pervert, surely, he shouldn't be enjoying having his rectum filled with her fingers. Though it was impossible for her to put any more digits inside of him, she never stopped trying. She then shifted her attention to what her mouth was doing and made sure that this huge penis was pushed in far, then quickly drawn out again, then making it touch hard against the inside of her cheeks she would thrust it back into the very depths of her throat. Five minutes of this punishment was all Cartier could take. Eventually his penis was filled with semen and there was only one way for that to go, down Megan's very accommodating throat.

She breathed deeply as she drank all that there was to be given. David lay back in a state of utter exhaustion, his eyes were streaming with some pain and some pleasure, he didn't know what he had experienced, or what he liked the most.

What had happened to him, what day was this, what month, what year and who the hell was this creature trying hard to kill him through pleasure and lust?

He knew now what it was like to be ravished, this sort of thing is what happens to women on a daily basis, and it was degrading and humiliatingly sad. Suddenly, he felt sympathy and pity for womanhood as a whole, all that is except this one, the Welsh Dragon.

Megan though had only just started; she withdrew her fingers from his arse. He gave out a huge sigh of relief as he consciously relaxed from the pain of having three fingers firmly implanted there. The pleasure of having them removed was almost exhilarating, which made him realise that he liked having them being there in the first place.

Making sure that he could see everything that was happening and going to happen, Megan raised the offending hand to her mouth and proceeded to lick it. She was determined that he should experience all that she was now doing for him, or was it too him? One by one, Megan proceeded to stick each finger into her mouth and clean it with her spittle.

"See what I do for you, I am prepared to eat everything off you. Watch me suck each finger clean. That is, you I am eating, and I love it."

David was revolted by this action and made sure that she wouldn't try and kiss him again, or even breathe in his direction. Next she moved down to the nether regions once more, again taking his penis in her mouth, this time though much more gently. She licked and caressed every inch of the surface, somehow tenderness had crept back into her life, albeit temporarily. She once again pulled his foreskin back revealing his hardening crown, this her tongue gently licked and flicked at. She had only just started on satisfying what her needs now were, but without him being aroused it would be hard for her to be pacified and appeased. She needed to get some further response from his member at any cost. But David could never keep his ardour from showing itself, soon he was once again breathing heavily with a huge member sticking proudly into the air like a sentinel.

Once erect enough Megan made him lie on his back and climbed onto his penis. She too was breathing very heavily and felt the satisfaction that once again she was in control of the situation. She leant back and then forward, she was finding the best position for depth and feeling, once obtained she started slowly at first to rise up and down, all the time making him penetrate deeper and deeper into that dark warm wet cavern. After a matter of minutes David was once again close to ejaculation, but Megan was up to all his games and tricks, so she slowed then stopped, this allowed him to relax and then cool his ardour down somewhat, thus relieving that awful feeling of coming prematurely she was going to savour every second of this session.

When it was clear to her that he was indeed breathing in a more relaxed and normal way, she started her rhythmic pounding once again.

It was this second bout that became different, whilst she was moving up and down, moaning slightly and getting wetter by the second, something happened that made Cartier pay special attention, a change had occurred. He felt something very hard touching his penis, but the sensation came through her lower intestine. At first it startled him, then quickly he realised what was indeed happening.

Megan had taken the cucumber that he had noticed the moment he first entered through the door. She had forced an entry into her own bottom and plunged that vegetable deeply into herself, this was happening at the same tempo as she was pounding herself on top of him. Soon both of them were almost screaming with self relief. David because this might mean the end of being out of control, Megan because she was once again climaxing with her beloved David Cartier.

They both burst in a gush of ecstasy as sperm and body juices, which ran together within her body. After this joint climax, they both sank back on the wet, slightly ammonic smelling bed, their breathing rising and falling now in unison, giving them both time to recover.

Now Megan was, except for the sound of breathes being taken in and out again, silent. This was finally David's chance to extricate himself from this impossible situation.

Megan lay there panting quietly, her eyes firmly fixed on the ceiling. Her breast heaved up and down. David had always loved those breasts and as he looked, he realised that in fact he would miss those beautiful mammary glands, also that deep lush Venus mound, which now with absolutely no pubic hair was a delight to look at and explore.

David sighed and not for the last time that day, but he was resolved, his mind was well and truly made up, this was the last he would see of Megan. What he yearned for was not the lady, but what the lady had between her legs and if he was ever going to become a better person, he knew that sex alone was not ever going to be enough.

"Megan, I really must tell you what has happened. Since I saw you last Friday, I went to the coffee bar at

Clockhouse, I did some jamming with Steve Preston and one or two other musician friends."

David paused, giving himself time to think out what next to say. "You'll never guess what happened next?"

Another pause for breath, then as no answer came, he added,

"I was approached by an American impresario, who invited me to join his troupe working for the American armed forces. It is a world tour, and I will be away for at least six months."

Megan thought a minute or two and then it was as if grief of a departed loved one erupted from her very soul. At first her eyes misted up, then a small whimper sputtered out of her closed mouth, lastly, she exploded like the eruption at Krakatau.

She looked at David in total despair, then burst out crying, more than just crying she started to wail, at the same time she rolled backwards and forwards upon the bed. David now jumped back, he wasn't going to be drawn into any more orgies, or anything that might mean touching her anymore.

He knew that this was not going to end with him patting her on the head and offering a lump of sugar. The best thing he could do was leave immediately, but not before he finished what he had to say.

"Megan, you made a great mistake in doing my work for me, I wanted to pass or fail all be myself. I am and always have been since knowing you grateful to what you have done for me. But you have become possessive and jealous. You know I am my own person; you cannot own me or possess me. I must be allowed to come and go as I wish."

He was about to continue when Megan broke into the rhetoric with her own version.

"I made you, without me you would still be nothing. You took my virginity, and you debased me in your sexual fantasies. Now you have had enough you want to leave me. There is another younger woman, that's it isn't it? You are shagging a younger girl!"

"Stop right there. Yes, you helped me get onto my feet, which I shall always be grateful for. As for the sex, you were very ready to lose your virginity, and you know that's the truth. As for sexual depravity, my yearnings are very normal that I am sure of, we have done nothing but experiment which is what all couples do when they first come together."

David stood tall once more, it was with a certain indignation that he continued in the same vein,

"If anything, it is you that have become somewhat depraved and that includes your many sexual fantasies that I wouldn't have ever thought of until you pushed them my way. You should remember Megan that until you, I too was a virgin."

Now on a roll he added,

"I never asked you to give up your religion and I most certainly never taught you the bad language you now speak. What on earth would your mother and father make of the way you have become?" At this point he once again watched as she cried and banged her fists on the bed. He now knew whatever he said about the future, he mustn't tell her about tomorrow's audition or anything to do with the Royal College of Music. She is dangerous and she might try to ruin everything, and he knew that she was indeed capable of spoiling any future that he might make for himself. She possessed that sort of power and influence. She was still crying heavily when he took pity on her and tried to reason one last time.

"Look Megan, I don't want to fight with you."

Then added with a slight laugh,

"After all we have just finished a massive exhausting sex session."

He tried but failed to get her to lift her gloom. In a softer and warmer voice, he tried again,

"Look you are many years older than me."

First mistake,

"But that hasn't bothered either of us. But I must be allowed to do my own thing. I need the experience of working with other professional musicians, I also need the money."

Second mistake, and many more tears,

"Look, I will keep in touch, and I will see you before I leave the country. Think about it and you'll realise that after all six months is nothing and if we care for one another, then what is six months? Only one hundred and eighty odd days, that'll soon pass, then I come back, and we could possibly continue where we left off?"

Third error of judgement, a stupid and obvious lie,

"What do you say? Wish me well and let's part as friends, pals that can continue in just four thousand three hundred and twenty hours from the moment I leave these shores."

Final mistake, the crying had not managed to be controlled, but it had abated a little.

She looked at him in desperation and said,

"But what about your future A-level exams?"

Nothing but extreme pity showed in her downcast eyes.

"You need me for your studies, don't you?"

No answer came from young David, he couldn't possibly tell her that in fact he didn't need those exams, his position within a music college was going to be entirely down to his own playing ability. Now David was completely spent. He once again returned to the mirror and looked at his body, there were bruises everywhere and as he noticed them, he became aware of pain coursing through his being.

He ached and felt somewhat nauseas, that sick feeling was also for what had happened here, but he knew that he wasn't going to throw up. But Megan wasn't finished yet, she turned towards him, smiled demurely and asked,

"David, come and sit next to me for a minute."

He smiled back thinking that he was now just being nice and that just maybe he could soon escape Megan's clutches? He sat down and turned slightly towards the door with his back almost facing towards her. She grabbed his neck and pulled hard on him, as he fell backwards onto the soiled sheets she managed to climb up onto his face and rub herself all over him. He was once again completely overwhelmed by the suddenness of the situation, but it didn't end there, Megan had one last move to make. With a huge effort she managed to urinate all over him. The hot wet liquid went into his mouth, down his neck, in his ears and thoroughly drenching his hair. Before he could react, she finished, climbed off and stood by the door.

"Fuck off! You are a liar and a scoundrel, I hate you. Go on, get out of my life, fuck the hell off!"

David now in a complete state of shock, not saying a word he picked up his clothing or what remained of them. He knew that he would have to be careful how he left the building, if he was seen people would immediately know that something untoward had occurred in that unearthly basement.

He discovered that he couldn't do up his trousers, so he tied them up as best he could.

But he didn't want his privates to fall out at the wrong moment, as they had once when he was an early teenager. He now saw that memory coming to life through his thoughts, he turned sickly grey.

He had been running to catch a bus and became aware that he was getting an erection, which was not helped by the simple expedient that he was wearing very tight trousers which rubbed provocatively against his penis. These had somehow come undone with the zip coming down and as he climbed onto the bus, the driver and all the front passengers could see that he was indeed very well endowed as his old one-eyed trouser snake was protruding out of his drainpipes at an angle of ninety degrees.

Chapter 4

He then proceeded to try and do a temporary repair to his shirt and jacket but conceded defeat knowing that they were utterly finished as best clothes. David gave up and just put them on to cover himself up as best as possible. Looking at himself again in the mirror he was angered to see the state of his clothes. This attire that had taken a great deal selection and thought were his favourite set of clothing, he felt ashamed at the very loss of such a fine set of dress ware, then there was simple fact of how much money the items had cost him.

He had spent many weeks' wages on obtaining these clothes, and for what! Just so that Megan could write them off in a single orgasmic melee. Money that had been extremely hard earned. The more he thought about the vision within that bloody mirror, the more annoyed he became.

"Ah shit Megan; look what you have done to my clothes. They cost me seriously hard-earned money that I don't have, what are you going to do about it then?"

Finally, having stopped bawling again and looked at him with a stare of almost hatred, loathing that actually sprang from love and desire.

"I have fifty pounds in my purse, take the bloody lot. I don't care! I just want you to fucking well suffer, just like I have suffered over you. To me you are nothing but a face full of piss, take the money and fuck off."

The purse was laying beside the bed next to the bedside light. He felt absolutely no shame as he went over opened it and withdrew the fifty pounds. 'Serve her bloody well right!'

One thing about David Cartier, he never ever flinched from taking money from anyone. He put pound notes into what remained of his pocket and was about to turn away, when Megan said her last words to him that day. She opened her legs, showing her plump Venus mound, putting her hands down there, she pulled the lips apart, showing a lot of blood-soaked pink inner flesh with his semen dripping from it. Then with a sneer in her voice she said,

"See David Cartier, this is what you want and will never get again. This is now what I think of you!"

To his abject horror and more disgust, she once more squirted urine in his direction. But she was right about only one thing, he would miss that very tasty vagina.

He made it back to his digs with only his landlady realising that he had been in the wars. He went straight to his room and fell into a pure of heart dreamless night's sleep. His last thoughts were not of Megan but of tours and music college.

Dead on two o'clock, not a minute earlier or later, David presented himself at the Royal College of Music. He felt confident as over the last six months he had worked extremely hard with technique and sight reading. He had the Bartok concerto well in hand and could feel the warmth from what the maestro was trying to convey within that work.

He was dressed in his brown three-piece silken mohair suit with a smart tie and shirt and the shiniest shoes that he had even managed to bring forth with real hard hand lustre.

He felt once again a Jack the Lad, and he was there at those famous portals to show just what metal he was made of. Looking up at the red bricked Victorian building, in which so many famous musicians had passed through, he felt pleased and fortunate for getting this far. He could hear the sounds of practicing coming from many rooms, some sounding wonderful, many that could do better. He lifted his chest out again, breathed in deeply, gripped harder on the viola case and then climbed the stairs.

He went directly to the door marked office and introduced himself to the secretary, Miss Janet Church.

Somehow Janet had dressed differently that day, she wore a bright dress with a decorative flower motif printed on it. It made her look younger and much more feminine. As a top she had on a very close knitted cardigan, only buttoned up at the top two buttons, this matched the dress perfectly. On her head she wore a beautifully coloured ribbon, which went under the back and over the top.

When she arrived that morning, most people took her for yet another student, she loved and enjoyed that thought.

She hadn't thought about dressing up for that particular day, she just allowed herself to believe that it just seemed like a good idea at the time.

Her heart missed a beat, she gulped twice and felt the saliva dry in her mouth. Within the framework of her thoughts, Janet again refused to accept any reasonable logical idea as to why on shaking hands with this youth, she felt her knees go weak.

"So, you are David Cartier! I do hope you are well prepared?" Then she smiled a bright lovely warm smile and added,

"Of course you are. You wouldn't have wasted our time or your own now, would you?"

She already felt a little silly, she was not a baby, or even a young girl, why then all this flustering about?

"Err, David, might I call you by your first name?"

She didn't give him time to answer,

"I will tell the principal that you are here. I believe Steven Mundane will be in on your audition too."

As she walked off, she finished with,

"Don't be nervous David, I am quite sure you are going to do just fine."

The audition took place in the double bass room as no contrabass player was using it. The principal was dressed in a coffee-stained tweed jacket with trousers that had the look of something that should have been worn with spats. His hair was untidy and looked as if what was left was about to fall out of his scalp and all over the floor.

The first thing that David noticed was the smell that exuded from that unlikely formidable figure of a once great musician, now rather a decrepit shadow of his former self.

Steven Mundane was in his early forties, he looked casual and comfortable in grey coloured slacks and a check shirt which had been ironed so often it shone. It was open at the top and had both sleeves rolled up showing quite hairy arms, he was endowed with muscles that might have suited a bricklayer more than a musician, he was as he looked extremely fit. He was one of England's most respected viola players and made a very fine living playing in sessions with advertising, film music, or backing for pop musicians.

He was also the leading viola of the English Chamber Orchestra, and one must not forget, a professor at the college. He made sure that he sat as far away as possible from Sir Archibald Sanders whom he thought of as a sad individual who had come to the position of principal more by the simple expedient of being a friend of the royal family and surviving two world wars. It was Steven that opened the proceedings.

"Well David, what are you going to play to us?"

"Well sir, I would like to play the opening movement of the Bartok viola concerto."

There was a small intake of breath as both the principal and Mundane heard him say the Bartok concerto.

"What about an accompanist; do you have one?"

Then the principal added,

"I will play the piano part if you don't have anyone here?"

"Fine sir, that would be fantastic. I never realised that I should bring an accompanist with me. If you don't mind then, here is the music."

Sir Archibald took the score and went over to the piano.

He looked at David then started playing the introduction and it was miles to fast. David felt his first notes coming at a rate of knots, then he was playing. He had to listen really carefully as the principal's tempos were not good and he would either run away, or slow down to much. It all seemed somewhat bazaar to young Cartier thinking as he played. 'How could he be so erratic?' But David followed him anyway, he was really enjoying playing and this sound that he was making was hardly perfect, but very satisfying anyway.

It was very strange to David as this was in fact the first time that he had played this opening movement with a piano accompaniment. All too soon it was ended, he put his viola down, rubbed his fingers together and waited for what was to come next. He didn't have to wait long.

"Who has been teaching you David?"

Steven Mundane was showing real interest.

"Oh, I was lucky enough to be introduced to Charles MacFlatten, he has been fantastic."

Mundane nearly sputtered with amazement.

"Is that old bugger still alive? Well, well, he has done you proud. Are you going to play us something slow?"

"Well, I haven't prepared anything, and I have no extra music, but I could play the slow third movement of the Hummel viola concerto if you wish, I think I can remember at least most of it."

Once again he picked up his viola, made sure that it was in tune and then started to play. Of course, he remembered it from start to finish, he had been playing that concerto since he began on the instrument at school.

He had even given a rather poor performance in his early teens with the Catford Symphony Orchestra, with one very nervous Barry Green conducting. It wasn't that David had been so bad, it was more that the orchestra were sloppy and undisciplined and with his technique not so good in those far off days he had struggled through the concerto. But today was a different thing altogether, he played like his very life depended on it, he swayed with his eyes shut and could hear the Berlin Philharmonic Orchestra in his head following him and between the orchestra and himself, they were both doing a pretty good job. At the end of that movement both Sir Archibald and Steven Mundane looked stunned. Outside in the corridor miss Church was rubbing her hands together in glee. David Cartier and Janet Church were both going to be winners this day!

Some sight reading was presented to David. First the solo from Berlioz Harold in Italy. David hadn't played it before, though of course he knew it well as did all viola players. Then came a fast section from Bruckner's seventh symphony, once again it was not too hard, as this was an expected normal sight-reading part. They asked him to play scales, in major and minor keys, all this was bog standard and created no problem. Then the principal asked if he had a piano piece that he would play to them. At this question, David's day started for a moment to crumble.

'O, shit. I have forgotten to bring any music, that bloody Megan woman has made me forget!'

"I am sorry sir, but I have to admit that I have forgotten to bring any piano music with me. Can I be allowed to play something from memory?"

"Memory! Why of course. What are you going to play?"

Even Sir Archibald sounded saddened by the fact that maybe this wasn't going to be so good.

"Err, what to play?"

He said under his breath.

"Oh, I know, can I play part of Beethoven's Moonlight Sonata?"

It was Sir Archibald who reacted first, there was a distinct frown arriving on his brow and in fact his whole face, his eyebrows had dropped, and he looked somewhat like a boxer dog which had just heard the news of the onset of world war three.

"I er, could find the part for you if you want."

Sir Archibald had real concern in his voice.

"Can you really play it for memory?"

But David knew he had them both in his hands and he wasn't going to loosen his grip, so with a nod to the principal he moved over to the piano.

He had played this sonata since being just knee high, so remembering was not the hardest part of the day. He sailed through with hardly having to take stock of any point within the music.

After he came to the conclusion, he was asked to just stay there, while both Mundane and Archibald left the room to talk. They had been gone less that one minute when Norman came back in the room with a smile as broad as his mouth would spread. He came over to Cartier holding out his hand to shake.

"Well done my boy, that was quite a show you put on there. I am happy to say that the college would like to offer you a full scholarship and you can start in September of next year. What do you say to that then?"

"Oh, Christ! Oops sorry, I mean Jesus! Oh dear. I am very happy with that. This is the college that I have always wanted to be a part of. This is probably the best day in my life so far. How can I ever thank you enough?"

"I'll tell you how!"

Said Steven, with that grin still stretching from ear to ear,

"By being a good student, work hard and try not to get involved with shagging too many of the girls that you will find here."

"I have never been interested in girls anyway."

What a lie, but an understandable lie.

"I shall work hard and not let you down, that is a promise."

"Mmm! Okay, I believe you, thousands wouldn't. By the way how is Nevillia? I heard she got married to some bloody awful Mexican conductor."

"What, really! That's the first I have heard of it, then I haven't had any contact with any of the family for well over a year now." David then thought to himself. 'Maybe I should take a trip home and see what is what.'

Steven Mundane was physically shocked by what he had just heard, not because the boy hadn't seen or heard from the rest of his family, but because,

"Have you really got this far down the road without your parents of Nevillia's help?"

"Is that a problem then? I don't really have much to do with the other members of the Cartier clan. I was expected never to do any good by all of them including Nevillia, but I am a very determined person, and they never understood just how determined I can be. I have bought my own instrument, it's not great but it is a good starter. I have earned my own living and paid my way through life. I expect nothing and never got anything from my family. But you know what, I really don't care."

Steven stood there looking at him for a couple of seconds and then slapped him upon his shoulder.

"Bloody well done!"

David made his way back to the office to thank Janet Church for her help in getting him the audition. She blushed and told him it was nothing and that she was extremely happy for him that he had not only gained an entry place but won a scholarship to boot. She took all his particulars and then informed him that there would be a formal proposal within the next two weeks. But not to forget that he can also get help with a council grant, and he would need that extra money just to live a meagre life while studying. They once more shook hands, Janet reddened yet again at his touch and yet again her knees went weak. She steadied herself then wished him luck until they meet again. As he left the building, she sighed and commented.

"David, keep the practice going, work on your intonation and scales, these are areas that all new students seem to have problems with. Have a safe tour and we will all look forward to the next semester when you join us."

Then with a flurry she concluded,

"Bye for now!"

Two weeks past and David Cartier was just a little worried that he hadn't heard a peep from the college. He had told MacFlatten who then promptly took him out for a few drams of Irish whisky. He for one was going to miss the lad, he had become quite fond of him. He was also pleased that he going to do this tour for the Yankee's as he colloquially called them, the experience and the extra money would be a godsend for him. Plus, it would give him the chance to do extra sight reading and get to grips with improvisational techniques.

David used the money that Megan had bequeathed him at their last encounter, this being for paying some of his bills such as rent and the food and general living expenses.

He had now quit his job at the school library, and he really didn't want to have to work while waiting until the tour was to get under way.

Anyway, there were the concerts that would have to do at the various airbases around East Anglia and the first was coming up within the next two days. He had received his contract and though he would be paid for each performance plus extras for any rehearsals that might be deemed necessary, plus all expenses and a generous living allowance. David estimated that he should clear around five hundred dollars each week, which would translate to somewhere around one hundred pounds of real money. Even here in England he would be paid in dollars and not pounds, which seemed a little strange to him, but his thoughts were, 'Who cares anyway, money is money'.

He hadn't seen or heard from Megan in the last two weeks, and he guessed that she was recovering from the experience of knowing a Cartier, but he had decided that he would visit her just before he left for the Far East. He excused himself with the thought that it would be a pleasant goodbye not another torrid sex lesson. The truth was in fact he knew he was kidding himself, but better to want to believe that he would visit out of a caring nature, a simple need to put the record straight and not out of a desire to enter into Megan's knickers once more!

The truth be told his guilt was getting the better of him.

He had also decided to go back to Tenterden, there maybe and hopefully to receive some well-earned praise from mum or dad, but also to get any news of his older sister Nevillia. The family home was quite close to the railway station with plenty of land to hide it from prying eyes and nosey noses plus nostrils that could be offended by any lingering smells of drying cowhides.

David had long since given up his keys to the home, so it was a certain amount of trepidation that he finally got back there and knocked on the front door. The rain was falling hard, it was cold, and he was very wet. His raincoat hardly kept out the wet, and it certainly didn't keep the cold winds that came rushing down the slight slope to their property. So, as he stood waiting for someone to answer the door, he stood there and shivered, but not just from the inclement weather.

"My god, look what the cat has found, a drowned rat. And what do we owe this dubious pleasure for?"

It was his father and as he spoke to his youngest son, he didn't even offer him shelter from the rain but kept him standing on the doorstep along with all other traders and scroungers.

"Well, are you going to make me stand here all night? I am cold and wet, and I have come a long way to see you and mum. Can I come in or not?"

A voice from the kitchen rang out,

"Who is it John? For gods' sake come in and shut that bloody door, its getting cold from the draft. Who is it?"

"The prodigal son has deemed to visit; shall I allow admittance?"

"What, who? David is that, David. Of course, bring him in."

"Well, you heard your mother, you had better come on in. Don't get the carpet wet, it's just been cleaned. Better take your shoes off, watch where you put your raincoat."

David was already shell shocked by this display of open friendliness by his father, he smirked to himself, no change there then. So much for coming to see ma and pa, he knew it was already a huge mistake. Still, here he was it was best to make the most of it, anyway there was much to tell.

"Hello mother, it's nice to see you. How have you been?"

"As if you cared! I might have died and gone to heaven, or I might have been lying dying in hospital, do I ever hear from you? Of course not."

"Oh dear!"

Joked David,

"Are you dying in hospital then? Is this just a hologram image of you, meaning the real you is close to meeting your maker."

"Don't come here and be sarcastic to your mother. She spent a lifetime of worry and toil looking after you and what thanks did, she ever receive? You've just been a total waster and a nuisance."

His father looked as if he was about to clip young David around the ear once more, maybe just for old time's sake.

"Have you been in prison?"

"Look!"
Said David,
"Please let's start again. I have come here today to tell you about my plans and career moves, I thought, or better still, hoped that you both might be curious and interested enough to listen to what I have to say."

"Of course we are son. Sit down in that chair and tell us what you have been up to over the last year or more."

His mother stopped for a sharp intake of oxygen.

"By the way, did you hear that Nevillia is going to leave the Birmingham Symphony Orchestra, she has been offered the leaders job with the London Symphony Orchestra. She starts in, oh, I think in early January. She got married to a Mexican conductor, Joseph Beckarier. He is principal director of Orquesta Sinfonica del Estado de Mexico, such a grand title. Of course, they have both been so terribly busy, so we have yet to meet him. But I am led to believe that he is quite a catch, worth a fortune in Mexico. She has done so well, if only you could be a little like her."

Another large intake of breath again,

"So, what is so important that you made the journey over to us?"

"Well, to tell the truth,"
His father interrupted with,
"That'll be a first!"
"Oh, for God's sake dad, give it a rest!"

And Janet nodded in agreement and then frowned hard at her husband.

"To tell the truth; I don't know quite where to start. I have had a job in a night school as librarian, while doing this job I studied for two four O-levels, all of which I got A passes."

David looked towards his mother looking carefully to see whether there was a glint of interest in her eyes, none really showed.

"What you also don't know is that I have been having serious viola lessons with Charles MacFlatten and through his expert help I have been given a scholarship to attend the Royal College of Music, I start next September."

David looked for some sort of acknowledgement but found nothing stirring from either parent and with a huge sigh he continued,

"And the other news is that I shall be going away for six months with an American forces entertainment group."

Once again David paused with the hope that there might be some sign of interest from either of them, again there was nothing at all showing.

"I shall be earning some good money, maybe even enough to buy a fine Italian viola when I get back. So there in a nutshell is what I am all about. What do you think?"

"Are you saying and doing this to undermine your sister?"

"Dad please! I am telling what is happening that's all. Why should I want to undermine Nevillia?"

David stiffened and once again got defensive.

"Like you two I am extremely proud of her for her achievements."

That wasn't a lie, but he wasn't entirely happy at the thought of that stuck up cow being his bigger sister.

"Anyway, would it be that easy?"

A deep frown had appeared upon David's brow. 'Why the bugger did I bother to come here at all? I can see this is almost certainly going to be the big split in the Cartier family, they don't care, they never really have, and I must stop worrying about it.' Young David tried to continue one last time.

"Look, please listen. I came to see you both in the obvious wasted hope that you might hear what I have to say and maybe feel a little pride in what I have achieved and am in the throws of getting together for the future."

"Proud you say. I will be very proud of you son, when you actually achieve something that's for sure. You have done nothing in your life, and you have always been a waste of space and to be entirely honest, I see no difference now than from before. You come here expecting us to fall on our knees to you the mighty tank of all knowledge, the wondrous righter of all wrongs."

He almost snarled out the next sentence,

"And what's all this crap about you playing the viola, where, Royal School of Music! You are not capable of making entry into a can of beans, let alone a school of music. David, I see no change in you at all, just one continuous lie after another. You show no interest in us or your sister and haven't done in well over a year."

Then John smiled broadly and looked towards the cracked plaster ceiling within their lounge as if it was a painting by Leonardo da Vinci in the Sistine Chapel.

"Now there is someone to be proud of, Nevillia is a genius, she is going to turn the world of music upside down. Whereas you David, either you will end up in prison or worst; join some gang, kill someone and bring nothing but shame to the very name of Cartier. Really, I see no point in you even being here."

John now pointed towards the door.

"Just go please!"

At this last remark by John, Janet burst into tears, not because she was once again losing a son, more that she thought John was probably right, David has indeed turned out to be a complete waste of the very air that humanity breaths.

David left the house for what he hoped was the very last time. His head was held high, and a self-righteous sneer stretched across his face, he showed absolutely no emotion to either of his parents, what would be the point, that was until he was out of view, then he burst into tears, floods of tears for parents that would never understand or appreciate anything he would do or achieve.

He sat at the end of their driveway, on a kerbstone head in hands and the worries and torments of his now eighteen short years gushing forth. Everything was already wet, so it really didn't matter and in fact crying did some good, it made him now completely independent of any future emotional needs from his family.

Chapter 5.

The first concert that David had to perform in was tomorrow the twentieth of November; it was at an American base not far from Norwich. It was in aid of a special dinner party for the Colonel in Chief of the entire base. Colonel Martins had worked at this airbase for the past twenty years, in fact when the Americans first joined in the European conflict of thirty-nine to forty-five. He was now sixty-five years of age and this was going to be part of his swansong. Retirement, something that the Colonel dreaded, it meant going back to the U.S. and setting up home as a civilian and he hadn't been one of them since early nineteen seventeen when he was drafted into the newly formed United States Air Force.

He was with the first contingent of American warriors to reach Europe and help bring the downfall of the Kaiser. He always hoped that his fellow pilots and himself were instrumental in bringing the Great War to a conclusion, though he always went along with the remarks the General Pershing trumpeted, 'Armistice, humbug! This is just a temporary respite; we should have pushed the Huns right back into the Fatherland and taught them a very salient lesson'.

He had enjoyed his work with the forces and having survived those two world wars, actually coming through without so much as a broken fingernail, it somehow always seemed like a jolly wheeze. Both wars had been fun and from the first as a simple air mechanic, to the second as a flight sergeant, to the end of the war, when he made wing commander, then through this period of the cold war, when he had picked up the running of this important nuclear base.

Now that America was embroiled in an unwinnable scrap with the red menace in the Far East, he had been waiting patiently expecting a posting to Vietnam, the fact is that he had even volunteered to go, but no, the hierarchy had decided that to go to Nam, as if was became known through the grunts that served there one had to be under sixty year of age.

So the end of work was coming to a man that had enjoyed serving the flag, one who had become incredibly good at organisation, taking it from a skill to an art form, at least in keeping the men working under him on their toes.

His wife Clement was the only one who was glad of this forthcoming retirement, she wanted them both to have that little place somewhere in the prairie, with shutters on the windows, two sleepy hounds resting on the porch, and rocking chairs for the both of them to laze on. Even the men on the base were very sad to lose their Colonel Martin, after all, better the Devil you know than the Devil you don't know.

It was two o'clock in the after of Saturday the twentieth of November nineteen sixty-two. The weather was extremely cold, in fact when David got onto the train to London Bridge, this being where the coach would meet them it had started to snow. This was a little early in the year and no one seriously expected it to lay and thicken. The wind blew hard and cold, this lifted the snow and swirled it everywhere. And when he looked out of the train windows, he couldn't see anything but white fluffy powdery snow coming down at an angle of forty-five degrees. The train though still arrived on time, David alighted and made his way to the coach park area. There already waiting was an orange American school bus with everything being on the wrong side of the road. With his viola tucked under his arm he climbed on board. Every seat was taken, somewhere in the dark recesses of his mind he thought it was going to be a very intimate affair, but here were forty-five American musicians almost all over the age of forty and all looking at him wondering who he was and what the hell was he supposed to be playing?

"Hello David, I'm over here."

It was Stuart Holstein, and he was seated near the back talking to two other men. He stood up and walked down the bus to where David stood. Shaking his hand, then not letting go, he hailed to all on the bus. He lifted David's arm high into the air.

"Men, your attention please. This is David Cartier, he has taken Louis place which as you know died from peritonitis, so young David here has volunteered to take his place on the tour. David is a second pianist for us, just in case and he also plays the viola, which is what he will be doing today. Treat him well and kindly, he unlike the rest of you reprobates is just a boy and has a future ahead of him, not like you lot where it's all behind you now, in more ways than one."

He looked at David, smiled, lowered his arm and then informed him,

"Sit next to me, there are still some more forms that you have to complete, waivers and such, just in case someone takes a pot-shot at you."

He laughed at his own joke, David didn't, for he had already realised that where they might be going, the USA was not always welcome.

"Oh, and I shall give you the music you will be playing tonight."

The bus started up at three o'clock sharp to hopefully arrive at the camp not latter than six in the evening, but the journey turned out to be a very nasty experience for all on board as the un-seasonal inclement weather turned from being a nuisance to becoming sheer dangerous. Snow started to settle in the roadways, fortunately there was only light traffic on this occasion, but the further they went into the flat areas of Essex and Norfolk, the windier and more serious the snow, it was actually starting to drift. The worse it got, the more the bus slid and careered this way and that. Six o'clock was looking very dubious, they were going to be late.

The dinner was supposed to start at seven-thirty sharp, at the same time as the intimate dinner the main band were going to be holding a concert come dance in one of the aircraft hangers.

That was just a gift from the Colonel to his men.

When they finally arrived at the closed gates of the camp it was seven-forty-eight and everyone wondered if anything was going to happen or if they would be just turned around and sent on their way, back to the metropolis. The driver flashed his almost snow bound lights and tooted his horn. A very bedraggled guard wearing woollen clothing up to his neck, a heavy scarf wrapped around his neck up over his mouth almost entirely covering his head and on the top of his head, he was wearing a winter arctic afghan balaclava type head warmer.

Someone should have told him, (This is England mate! Snow today, gone tomorrow!) What is more he carried a rifle which he was now pointing at the coach in a very threatening way. The driver briefly opened the door to address the suspicious and extremely weary guard.

"It's the musicians! Put down that bloody gun you fool, you want to hurt someone? Now open up and tell us where to go."

The driver then leant back from his seat to tell the rest of us.

"Don't mind him folks, that's my brother, he's always pulling his gun out at me, it's his friendly way of greeting me…I hope!"

The dinner and the dance were still going to take place even though it meant that we were going to have to be ready to start in fifteen minutes. The bus drove over to the hanger that housed the dance. Lights were blazing and bunting was hanging everywhere and much to the collective amazement of the band members, it was also swinging gaily over the side of one of a Boeing B-52 Stratofortress, which looked as if it was still carrying its deadly payload slung under the bomb bay. People were milling around in a very casual way. There must have been at least fifty military men cleaning and preparing things for the fun to start. There were few women on the base, but certain selected local girls who over the time had been vetted and approved were allowed to attend, their boyfriends being usually members of the establishment and not your communal young Englishman.

There were trestle tables around the wall areas, and one was covered with food, proving that austerity was not present at American airbases. And much to David's surprise as he had been watching and mentally noting everything, the other tables were covered with barrels of beer and bottles of wine and all manner of liquids.

David went over to Stuart Holstein and said in a very quiet voice, so low Stuart strained to hear what the young Englishman was trying to say,

"Stuart, are they allowed to drink alcohols on this base?"

And not waiting for an answer, he added,

"Isn't that one of those nuclear bombers? And is that a bomb sticking out the bomb bay?"

Stuart smiled thinking to himself before answering: 'Nice boy, but a real green horn.'

"Yes, that is a B-52 and yes I believe it can carry a couple of nukes, or fifty tons of conventional bombs. Bit of a beast that one."

He was pointing to the tables, then concluded in a slightly higher pitched southern drawling tone of voice,

"You don't want to worry about these boys, they can all handle their liquor, leastwise up to their mouths, but from then on it's anyone's guess."

At this he burst out laughing, he always saw himself as a real comedian, sadly he was in a minority of one.

The bus unloaded the main body of the band and then drove off for about half a mile to where the main watchtower was. This was an enormous building that housed most of the advanced radar receivers, all the flight plan rooms, collection rooms for pilot briefings. There were kitchens, dining rooms, lounges with televisions and all manner of guest sleeping quarters, most underground and out of the way of prying eyes. And of course, on the top floor was the actual control tower, making sure that the planes came and went with the minimum of fuss.

There were never less than one hundred people in this building at any one time. There were B-52's flying in the sky's twenty-four hours a day, three hundred and sixty five days a years and that took planning and great organisational talents, skills that had kept a nation on permanent war footing without actually pulling the trigger.

One of the side anti-rooms was big enough to accommodate one hundred people sitting and dining. This was going to be the banqueting room for the Colonel.

The five remaining musicians got off the bus and really had a hard time to even see the door to enter, even though lights were blazing, the snow was so fierce that everything now was being covered with a layer of fine wet powder, some places already drifting up against building and other obvious collecting areas. Once inside they were shown to where they could change into their concert clothes. These comprised of dinner jackets and trousers, white shirts and black bow ties. All the other musicians sported very close-cropped hair, David though looked like the times, longish hair and long sideburns. He was quite obviously not an American and for an absolute surety, he was most definitely not military.

In the large room the tables were arranged in two long rows with the head being on a small table, seating just six at the far end. The walls were festooned with photographs of planes and important military people.

The stars and stripe hung on a pole beside the head table, next to it hung the Union Jack, but this was somewhat smaller and next to the flag of Great Britain hung the base flag with its glaring golden colour of a fighting Hawk show much clearer than either of the two national flags. The tables were awash with decorative silver and glass, the cutlery was all sterling silver, except for the head table which sported gold knives and forks and spoons.

Flower displays cascaded across various sections of the tables, giving an enormous array of colour and cheerfulness, also there were candlesticks using five candles to each holder, these were dotted along all the tables amongst all the decorative arrangements; with their candles having already been lit this again was giving a warm cheery atmosphere to the completed party room.

It was the centre piece that really shone out though, it was a solid silver model of a B-52 bomber standing almost two feet in length, and there were even nuclear bombs hanging from the undercarriage.

This to David was the height of extreme bad taste, plus it somewhat frightened him knowing that the USA held the finger to world annihilation.

In the far corner furthest from the head table was a small dais, on it a good German upright piano stood, then four chairs in a semicircle, each with its own music stand.

The five musicians comprised of violin, viola, cello, clarinet and piano. David had been given the music but hadn't had a moment to even look to see what was going to be played. He had been told by Stuart that the music was actually in order of playing, so don't mess around with it.

As the time had moved on faster than had been expected, there was absolutely no time to do even a sound check let alone rehearse. Stuart was there, just to sing the American anthem, plus sing along if requests were asked for at any time, he would introduce the pieces and players and sing the odd song or two, but only if really necessary. In fact, Stuart's real role within the troupe was one of master of ceremonies for which he was exceedingly good at.

But there sometimes came that moment that all the band members always dreaded, that was the moment that Stuart might decide to sing as his voice gave a lot to be desired. He was liked, feared, and respected, but everyone agreed keep the silly ass away from the mike if he is going to sing.

The five of them once dressed and finished prettying themselves; having one last look in the mirror, slicking down blondish light-coloured hair, well only in David's case on the head, the rest tended to brush and slick down their eyebrows. The three strings players tuned their particular instruments, quickly followed by yet another last look in the mirror and then onto that small, raised stage area.

As they marched out David remembered that he had in fact left all the music with his normal clothing, rushed forward nearly tripping up Stuart Holstein, placing his viola on the chair, he then ran back to the dressing area that had been allotted.

Once back on his seat he was informed that even though there was no one within the vicinity they would start. Anyway, this was a good chance to get to grips with ensemble and self intonation, plus once again, in David's case a chance to view for the first time the actual notes written on the music. The clarinet tuned to the piano and, then the three strings did the same. David luckily endowed with perfect pitch and quickly realised that the piano though in tune with itself was in fact a fraction sharp to normal tuning, that was going to mean careful listening all the evening if ensemble was going to happen.

"Right boys."

A cough, a smile, then,

"Let's start with the Schubert's Trout Quintet. I know it's out of the order, but it is a very difficult piece so it's good for us to try and get it together and as no one is of yet in the room mistakes can be kept amongst friends. Okay!"

Having finished speaking, Stuart pulled up a spare chair and then sat himself by the side of the piano.

It had been previously decided that the clarinet would play the cello part and, the cello would in fact play the contrabass part.

One more chance of an A all round. Then on your marks, get set, go!

David knew the viola part, so for him all was easy and relaxed. He was personally making a very respectable sound and that hadn't gone un-noticed by the five other players, this in turn made them relax and start to enjoy their own playing. Towards the end of the first movement the doors burst open and in marched all the various chattering officers and wives. The noise was enormous. After that fine start to the playing, they could have now been scratching out some squeaky gate music by Stockhausen for all anyone there would have been able to tell.

They finished playing the first movement and were well into the second and then once again the doors burst forth, in marched a trumpeter completely ignoring the small ensemble he blasts out a fanfare. Everybody within the room went silent and stood to attention, this included the five musicians, this didn't include the sixth as young Cartier was absolutely stunned by the surprise of this entry. He was nudged to rise to his full height by a frowning Holstein, who made sure that he understood this was already the first black mark against him and then he smiled and winked.

Then when everything was completely silent, in paraded Colonel Martin, on his arm was his wife Clement, then in came the Adjutant, Major Larking and his wife Ethel. Then much to David's surprise came a mayor in all his full civic finery and hanging on his arm was his wife Daisy and poor old Daisy couldn't have looked more out of place if she tried. David later found out that this was indeed the Mayor of Norwich.

They went over to the head table, lackeys pulled out their seats but they didn't sit down. David watched this all in fascination and again was taken by surprise when the other musicians broke into the American national anthem, this time with Stuart Holstein taking the reins and singing out in a very loud voice. David immediately picked up his viola and started to busk as he didn't know or have the music. Then the sound of Holsteins singing hit a particular ping in Cartier's brain. It wasn't that he was singing out of tune, no, in fact it was almost there in intonation. It was that in order to project his voice he shouted instead of singing the words. Anyway, to David, he now understood and was with the rest of the troupe from now on, no more Holstein singing please.

When the anthem ended all the regaled company within the room lowered their hands from over their hearts and sat down. The Colonel still stood; silence still reigned supreme.

"Ladies and gentlemen, there is good food, good wine."

And then pointing in the direction of the small group of musicians. "Good musical entertainment; at least I hope good?"

There was a ripple of laughter from around the assembled guests, which pleased the old leading warhorse.

"But most of all, there is really good fellowship from all of you. Enjoy this evening, I know I will."

He then sat down to thunderous applause.

This was the cue that Stuart needed to get the music going again. It was decided that instead of Schubert, it might be a better bet to do a medley of pieces by the Strauss family. The music would be light, airy and yet refined, not to heavy on the ears, but with a certain panache thus stylishly sophisticated. Waltzes, Polkas and old-fashioned Gallops, they were the pop music of the nineteenth century, yet at dinners they were exactly what was required. Clever but not taxing on the brain to much, after all for once husbands might just have to talk to their wives.

After all the guests might not actually be going to dance at this time, they didn't even have to listen, but as a background noise Strauss was infinity better than the sound of aircraft, though having said that, the vast room they were in was completely sound proofed so unless the plane came through the door no one was going to hear it.

"We'll start with the Blue Danube. Got it? Right, one, two, three."

Stuart waved his hands more or less in a three four-time rhythm, but none of the five even looked up to view his beat. They played for roughly one hour when they were given a break. Some of the audience did notice the end of one piece and the start of another, the notice came in the form of spasmodic clapping. 'At least one person has been listening.' thought David, as he turned over the music for the next piece.

Generally, the noise from the audience drowned out most of the sounds of music, but nevertheless, their sounds were crafted and pleasant even if it was just the six of them that really noticed. David's sight-reading was standing the test of time, he had no problems reading what had been written, and in many ways, he was within that first hour making sure that he was directing the group, by keeping the tempos even from the viola. Neither the violinist nor the pianist were what one would term as great musicians.

Well to be nice, they were rather poor players, or maybe just bored, it was hard to say which within the constraints of this sort of concert.

They left their instruments on the stage and went outside from the huge dining room. They followed a leading airman to another area; it turned out to be the main kitchen that had prepared this sumptuous feast for the Colonel and his invited guests. As they entered the head chef smiled in their direction and without saying a word, he led them to a quiet corner where a table was laid out for them.

It was piled high with plates of beautifully displayed culinary wonders, and it was specially only for the six of them. All six appreciated the gesture very much. Their own special feast, 'Nice touch' thought David.

The first course was a delicious bowl of lobster and crayfish soup, it was light brown in colour and carried plenty of small prawns within just in case the taste of lobster and crayfish were not enough. This was followed by some of the chefs special titbits, little croutons filled to overflowing with such things as Russian Caviar, though how they acquired that might just take some explaining. Some were covered in a paste made from Greek olives mixed with Italian Balsamic vinegar. The combinations went on and on. All these small delicacies were mouth wateringly wonderful and probably enough on there own but there was much more to follow. They were then brought a huge rack of lamb, slightly pink and beautifully tasty and tender. This was served with some seasonal vegetables. By the end of this all six were, to put in politely, stuffed!

But more was yet to ensue! Next came a lemon and elderberry sorbet this was just to clean the pallet which it did very well. Then came the sweet, this to David was the best thing he had ever eaten in his entire eighteen years of life, it was baked jam roll and lashings of vanilla custard.

David sat back on the chair and contentedly rubbed his stomach, not in fear of any pain just in contentment, this meal had been fabulous. To the others it was what they expected, okay not special.

A couple of beers later and the same leading aircraft man came to find them and take them back to work again. This time they discovered that the beautifully planned and decorated tables had all been removed, now they had to be a dance band.

All the guests milled around the walls of the room waiting for something to happen. They were not to be disappointed.

As the ensemble entered the room a small but distinct cheer went up. Drinks were returned to tables or just laid down on the floor, couples went into the middle of the area supplied for dancing, many already with their hands joined.

"Right, number thirty-one on your list. The Sinatra song, California mine. Up the tempo to foxtrot."

Holstein then looked at Cartier and smiled, mouthing with his eyes raised,

"Ready?"

Then once again tried to conduct a four-four tempo.

The floor was full with couples all swinging here there and everywhere, as they say in old colloquial American lingo, The place fairly hopped!

This went on until just before eleven o'clock, everyone was having a really good time. David was making sure that he understood these standards that were being played. Familiar to the Americans, but not to him, it was a good example of a learning curve, and he made sure that he was on top of it.

Most of this music was typical US, dance music. It was either taken from shows or from crooners such as Sinatra, Crosby, Ella Fitzgerald and Louis Armstrong.

"Right, number fifteen please, give them a cha-cha-cha. Do you know this style of music David?"

"Err, no Stuart, I have never heard of the cha-cha-cha. What is it?"

"Never mind what it is, it's a dance form, that's all. Just follow my conducting! Ready?"

But before he even raised a hand, a bell rang loudly, a red light started to flash, which the members of the band understood, the male guests completely understood, sadly though there was one person who just didn't have a clue, David. The floor cleared immediately of all the men, members of the band where quickly packing up their instruments. Some of the ladies knew what the light and the bell meant and where rapidly getting their personal things together, other lady guests, possibly the local English girlfriends knew just about as much as David, they stood there startled and starting to look worried.

David turned to the violinist and asked in a rather shaky voice, "Trevor what the hell is going on? Why have all the men left the room?"

Trevor was looking somewhat grim; he had packed his violin into its case and was now hugging it close to his chest.

"Well David, this is your first gig, it might well be all our last performances, our so-called swansong. I suspect that that red light and the rattling bell indicate that the balloon has finally gone up."

"What balloon? What the heck do you mean?"

But there was indeed a trace of panic in his voice.

"I mean the damn Ruskies are coming. This sounds like World War Three. Look my newfound friend, after all, since when has two World Wars been enough! My mother always said, bad, good, all things come in threes!"

At this point a guard appeared dressed in battle dress and armed with a rifle which was quite obviously loaded. This he casually pointed in nearly everyone's direction, that alone caused a certain amount of consternation.

"Right, you peoples listen up to what I have to say, listen well there may not be much time. I have a bus outside waiting. I shall be taking you to the outer perimeter of the camp where a bomb shelter is located. We are all going there currently, that means right now. I want no running and no panic, you all must abide by my law and that is military law, better know as martial law. Right, ladies and mayors first, then the musoes!"

And then the soldier really barked out his command,

"Come on fast walking please."

Little was said the seven men and twenty-eight ladies all followed Corporal Jenner through various corridors out into the cold evening to the waiting bus.

It took the bus a good seven minutes to board the people then close the doors and then start up the engine and get to the place of safety. Much to everybody's surprise the snow was indeed extremely deep and was still falling very heavily. So much for the theory that winter only starts after Christmas in Blighty.

David was peering out of the window trying hard to focus on what was happening outside, but by the noise alone he could tell. All seven of the B-52's, were already taxiing along the various runways. There were jet interceptors, some already in the air, some flying fast down the runways, all scrambling to meet the foe. People in battledress and armed to the teeth were running hither and dither, all with some sort of purpose attached to their movement. David had turned pail, and it wasn't from the cold.

'I am only eighteen, for God's sake! I don't want to be fried by some bloody nuclear bomb, or being stuck in a bunker for the next fifty years doesn't sound like a bunch of fun either.'

He looked around at all the people on the bus, it was then that he spied a young woman, very pretty, obviously American. He smiled at her and she blushed deeply. 'Well now, maybe fifty years with her, mightn't be so bad!'

By the time they had reached the shelter nearly all the planes that this base held, were now in the air. The noise from screaming jet engines was tremendous and the smell of kerosene even permeated through the locked door and windows of the bus making many to feel a little nauseous. But it was the roaring sounds that got into your very bones and David imagined what this din was doing to the neighbours one could only hazard a guess. But he wondered if the locals realised this might be the end of the world. With each jet running down the runway, it was akin to minor earthquakes happening, everything and everyone shook a little.

The shelter was an extraordinary building, it stood not more than ten feet high, with flowers and plants growing all over it, it had a very slightly sloping concrete roof, which looked as if it was no more than several inches thick. There were no windows and only the one wooden door, just big enough for one person at a time to enter through. From a distance it had the look of a very large garage, but as there were no portals for a vehicle to actually pass through, being so, made the entire construction redundant as a shelter for transport.

As the various party guests alighted from the bus their eyes focused onto this edifice, first in amazement at the very thought that this might well be their last resting place, then the penny fell into place and they all understood why it was camouflaged. But the real shock came when that small insignificant wooden door was opened.

First, the door itself was al least ten inches of thick steel, with just a veneer of wood on the front to fool any passing individuals. What they thought of as the roof, was also a ruse. The entire building above ground was just one huge block of concrete, reinforced with steel. The roof went another twenty feet below ground making just the top part of the shelter at least thirty feet thick. The door led directly down a flight of tight stairs and, every ten feet down they had to pass through yet more thick steel doors. Twenty feet below the surface they entered a large room which was at least twice the size of the area of the topside. There they found that there were more stairs plus a lift, but that elevator was only capable of handling ten people at a time, so the majority would always have to use the stairway. But getting to the next level down meant passing through two more steel doors and walking down a further twenty feet into the ground. Once down that flight it brought one out into yet another room which was almost double the size of the previous room. Here were two more lifts, each capable of transporting twenty persons at a time and both would go down another ten stories beneath the Norfolk countryside.

At the very bottom, or at least the core which people went into, that proved to be more than one hundred and fifty feet below the surface and below that finally stage, was at least three more floors which housed, water and cleansing units, so that all water was re-cycled. Another floor piped filtered air, from the surface, then as it descended, the air that one breathed was cleansed yet again, nothing it seemed was left to chance. No harmful bacteria or radiation would pass through these filters once the steel doors had all been closed, nothing was going to pollute the atmosphere down there at the bottom. The last floor was where all the electrical equipment was stored, only special people ever got down to those three hallowed areas. All walls even at the very bottom of the construction were at least twenty feet thick and then a membrane of lead sheeting encircled the entire structure. The only thing that might upset the applecart was a direct hit from a nuclear devise. Though there was only one way in, there were three alternative exits just in case the shelter was hit. But who would want to bother to try to escape? If anyone saw a drawing of what this bomb shelter looked like, their description would be that the whole structure resembled a giant carboy, except this one held human being, not acids.

Once they reached the very bottom they were met by a Sergeant. He went over to the Corporal and obviously asked under his breath if anyone had caused any trouble. And as the negative had been the answer, he looked at the unwanted refugees with a contemptible sneer of his countenance.

"Thank you, Corporal Jenner, please return to your normal duties."

David wanted to choke. 'What the hell were normal duties if World War Three was being played out above ground?' Then the Sergeant turned his attention to the rest of them.

"You will all follow me. An explanation is in order, but you will have to wait until we know exactly what is going on. So, please be patient, I am going to take you all to where, firstly you won't get in the way and secondly you will be with the rest of your friends or colleagues. This way please."

Then at the pace that only Sergeants in the forces know how to walk at he was gone, leaving everyone there to try and work out which way and at what sort of speed they should travel.

There were so many very large rooms, this one nuclear bunker was capable of housing for up to four hundred people for up to twenty months. There were sufficient dormitories both for men as well as women. The kitchens, that seemed to be on every floor, were large enough to cater for one and all. There were planning and meeting rooms, communication rooms, obviously with some way of dissemination and knowledge of what is going on topside. There were hospital wards on every floor, and they were graced with the very latest and most modern apparatus and up to date operating equipment. On one floor there was even a fully equipped operating theatre, quite capable of taking care of the worst disease or injury that might befall any luckless person down there. Then of course there was the obligatory morgue and disposal unit, just in case that disease got out of hand and the dead had to be cleared completely out of the way. Nothing seemed to have been overlooked.

When they trickled into the main congregating area, the Sergeant, who had got there ahead was silently watching and waiting, with his cheeks reddening in frustration. His first thought was: 'Bloody civilians, should have shot the lot, not waste time and resources bringing them down here.'

The trouble was that the civilians just couldn't keep up with his turn of speed, but very gradually they all appeared. Fortunately for Stuart Holstein, deliverance was at hand, and he gave a huge sigh of relief as he discovered the other members of the troupe, there they were waiting patiently and looking somewhat bored. 'Didn't they know there was a war on?' He may have been glad to see them, but he still shook his head from side to side. 'Bloody fools!'

A young Lieutenant was standing there waiting with his clip board already in hand.

"Thank you, Sergeant Rose, I will take over now."

He moved himself into the middle of the throng so that he could be overheard by everyone assembled there.

"Thank you for being so patient, it must be a real trial for you all. The truth is that we don't know what is happening yet. But one thing we do know, Norfolk and Norwich are still there above ground."

He smiled but quickly realised he was the only one.

"A huge attack loomed on the radar, this automatically triggers the alarms, sadly for all of you, or maybe lucky for all of you, you happened to be on the base when this happened. Once you are there one of two things can happen, either we throw you off base and you must take your chances, or as we have done, we rescue you from the possibility of annihilation."

He had tried to make his speech light and amusing, after all there can't be anything much funnier that a nuclear bomb dropping on one.

"Anyway, you are our guests. If the game is afoot, then we are all going to be down here for several months at least. But if it's another false alarm then we will know for sure within the next hour or maybe two. But assuming the worst we are allotting you all with bunks, though they might change as things progress."

He looked around to see what impression he had made and then he concluded.

"In the two rooms over on the right there are bunks for one hundred people. I suggest for the time being that you all select a bunk and then make yourself as comfortable as possible under the circumstances and just wait and see."

Gradually all the refugees from reality drifted into one of the two dormitories and then selected a bunk for themselves. David saw the pretty girl that he smiled at on the bus, he made sure that he would bunk down next to her. She must have been his age and boy she was so attractive and with such a beautiful figure. He laid his viola on the bunk and turned to face the young girl. He felt more than a little self conscious, but he was determined to talk to her.

"Err; excuse me for asking, but what is your name? I noticed you on the bus and in all the confusion I could do with someone to talk to."

She smiled sweetly and in a broad southern accent she answered.

"Why my name is Sally-Lou Greenache, I am here as a guest of my father who happens to be the Executive Office under Colonel Martin, where he is now I haven't a clue. I think him and mum must be in one of the other bunkers, so you could say I'm on my own here like you."

She smiled warmly to him, showing a lovely set of teeth.

"What is your name?"

David felt himself start to flush and that annoyed him as it always seemed to happen when he spoke to a beautiful girl or woman.

"Oh, I'm err, David Cartier and as you can see, I have been employed to play the viola with the band. I am supposed to be going on a world tour with them, that is if there still is a world to go on tour too."

"I love music, mainly country and western. Do you like country and western? What about Elvis Pressley, do you like him?"

Then her conversation changed to the matter in hand.

"Do you really think the Ruskies are on their way to bomb us? We could be stuck down here for months. I think we might become very good friends. I am seventeen, how old are you?"

Which question to answer first,

"To tell the truth, Sally, I don't really know your western music?"

She interrupted,

"I said my name was Sally-Lou, I really don't appreciate being just one part of the whole."

"Oh, sorry, er, Sally-Lou. Elvis, yes well everyone knows of him, but again to be honest, I really don't know his music. I was brought up to play classical music, once this tour was supposed to be over, I was going to become a student at the Royal College of Music, though that must be in doubt now."

He lowered his voice just a touch after all he didn't want everyone to hear.

"I am eighteen years of age."

"So, you want to play that caveman music eh! You should come to L'Oreal, it's a little backwater in Louisiana, which happens to be where I come from. The boys there play banjos and guitars, we call it duelling banjos."

She stopped talking, he could see that her eyes were misting up just a little. He thought she is going to burst into tears, but she didn't, instead she just added,

"I like that sort of music best of all. Those good ol' boys really know how to knock out a tune, it's all very exciting."

Then looking up at him straight into his light blue eyes, she reminisced about Louisiana.

"Why mum and me, we would listen to those ol' boys playing, we would eat a mass of crawfish, drink some cola, watch the sun go down over the swamp and in the background you could hear the frogs croaking and the birds singing, the only things you had to fret about were the gaiters, oh, not to forget the snakes and spiders."

David knew she had said enough to stop him ever wanting to go to that place.

"It is always either hot or warm, not like this Goddamn country where it either rains all day or starts snowing when the sun should still be shining. I am sorry, I know this is your country, but I hate it here. Anyway, I never get a chance to go out or meet locals, I have been here over a year now and I have only been off base a couple of times, once to go to Norwich and once to Ipswich, boy were they ever great days to remember."

Her sarcastic tone annoyed David, but he kept his smile, and he kept his good manners.

A voice came over the loudspeaker system asking all the guests of the base to assemble in the main area that they had just come from, also to bring all their belongings. The hubbub and confusion was tremendous, some people were afraid to go back, there thoughts being that they might yet be thrown off base. He heard one nearly hysterical woman crying into the arms of another. She either thought that Armageddon had happened, or the military were going to have her put against a wall and shot. After all, in her befuddled state of mind, her thoughts was of the old wives tale that it is a fact that American's eat human flesh, so they must be short of meat. Sadly, the very thought of being entombed down there had already unsettled her sanity. Nobody rushed back but ambled in their own good time. When about thirty people had got there, the smiling Lieutenant who had introduced himself earlier was waiting to orate to the guests once more.

"Ladies and gentlemen, I have some extremely good news. We are not all about to die. It seems that a very severe heavy weather front appeared on the radar looking like a flotilla or a Russian armada. The good news is that they are not on their way and that all our planes have now been recalled. But it does go to show how efficient we are and now you know where to come if the real thing does one day crack off with a bang."

This time he did receive a smattering of laughter and a smattering of applause.

"I have been told by Colonel Martin that because the snow is still falling hard and starting to drift, plus it seems to be blocking all road across the south of England, no one need move a muscle if they don't want to. He has informed me that you can all stay just where you are for the night. The kitchens are going to be opened, and you can be the chef's first guinea pigs. Blankets and sheets and pillows will be brought, and you can all have your chance of experiencing an Arabian night within this Ali Baba cave."

Smiling broadly and offering his hands to the heavens he concluded with,

"Who knows, it might just turn out to be a very romantic night indeed."

Cartier looked at Sally-Lou and winked at her. She smiled broadly and then winked a knowing wink back. 'Who knows, the Lieutenant might have the right idea there. She is very pretty, and I am as horny as a dog on heat, well truth be told I guess I am on heat. It would be a crying shame not to follow up after those prophetic words. Oh dear, mine is a hard life, or at least I hope it gets hard.' He was smiling to himself from ear to proverbial ear.

An hour later everyone was laughing at the ridiculous situation they had been thrown into. Now the battle was over, and the right side had won everyone was a war hero and the topic of conversation was generally one of denial, such as, I never believed that we were really at war. Or, we would have kicked the shit out of those red bastards, thus it might have been for the best anyway. And so on.

Then came the very welcome food.

David made sure that he sat next to Sally-Lou, he then acted the perfect gentleman. If she only knew what he was thinking. They talked and laughed together and gradually they got closer and closer. After what must have been another hour, which made it almost dawn outside, they were in fact now holding hands. It was Sally-Lou that made the first move.

"Listen David, I don't usually get interested in you limeys, but you are different, I like you and what is more I know you like me; I have an intuition about these things. Though I will give you my name, address and telephone number, it will entirely up to you whether you contact me again, but it might be nice. In the meantime, why don't you find somewhere for us to go where we can screw, interested?"

Her forthright manner blew David's preconceived ideas right out the window, er, sorry, there were no windows. Once again in his life he felt shaken to the very core of his being. But the thought attracted something within him, after all he was a horny old British Bull Dog and definitely on heat. He knew it was true, that being on heat, after all he had heard himself think that earlier and he knew he couldn't possibly be wrong.

"Wow! Now you do surprise me. But yes please."

He heard himself say that word please. He knew he sounded a complete inane imbecile and then thought, the more he said the worse it was going to sound. After all she might come to change her mind and that would never do, would it. He came close to her side and then whispered into her ear,

"As some people have actually left and there are plenty of dormitories that are not going to be used and it seems that most of the military are now back topside, probably snug in their own beds, lets just find an empty dorm?"

With that agreed, they left the dining area and retraced their steps looking for a likely place to consummate their new found friendship.

Every room they came upon had the odd person or two already settled either asleep or reading something within. No privacy presented itself very easily and this was after they had already explored two floors. The third floor was also used as sleeping areas, but there were other things like communications and forward planning rooms, it was quite obvious what these rooms were going to be for! Sure, enough on next door they came too, it had the words, **Executive Officers Only** in large letters printed on it, these rooms could never have been misread or mistaken. There was a small window that one could look through and into the room and showing before them was a bed, alright it was only a single bed, but it was a real bed. Then there was a dressing table and chair, then there was a small side room that presented itself and that would obviously be a toilet come bathing area, all very Spartan, but it had the essentials and in time of war that was just what was needed and would do the job nicely.

"In here, this is perfect. Is anyone around?"

"No, I think its okay. Are there any curtains to pull back over the window?"

David looked inside.

"No curtains, does it matter?"

"No, I guess not, I will just have to be quiet, which for me is not easy."

They entered the room and carefully looked around. There were no curtains as there was also no lock on the door, why would you need those things for down here.

Privacy was not an issue that would be contested after a nuclear war, only survival, so it was better if everyone was indeed seen and seen to be seen.

They went over to the bed and though no light was blazing within that small space light was coming through the small window, light enough to see what to do anyway.

They both sat down and before David could say anything, Sally-Lou was all over him. She kissed him passionately and then started to lick deep into his left ear, her hands were already exploring possible entry points into his trousers and at the same time she was trying hard to kick off shoes and start to remove her own clothes, she seemed to be some sort of expert in the art of clothing removal. 'Removal of said clothing must be an American thing, by the cringe, she's bloody good at it!'

David very quickly responded in kind and his enjoyment was heightened when as he touched her she started to moan. At first quietly but soon quite uncontrollably, then as the interest grew so did the decibels. But things were starting to get difficult, removing clothing and trying to please someone at the same time, well to say the very least you needed to be a contortionist, plus maybe with an element of genius to show how things needed to be managed. 'Oh dear, removal of said clothing, not a good British sport, as far as I am aware, this isn't a athletics competition, though being an athlete just might help!' With one arm out of his shirt and the other stuck up her dress David was quickly tying himself up in knots. Both were panting with early signs of fatigue and plus getting very close to reaching some sort of climax, David called a halt to the proceedings.

"Woo! Wait a minute, there is no rush; let's at least get out of our clothes."

Very quickly David removed all his garments, naked he crept over to the window and was happy to report that there was no one in the vicinity of their room, then he looked around once again in the direction of the bed and to his utter amazement there lying prone, with her legs wide apart was not a surprise to David, was a wonderfully delicious sight of Sally-Lou. David's smile now turned into a full-grown grin as he noticed her middle finger on her right hand was crooked and beckoning him hither.

His erection which had already been standing proud now pointed the way that he should go, it was if he possessed a divining rod on his torso and it was directing him right into her vagina. But as he started to climb onto the bed, he noticed her tummy was full of wrinkles. Nice as it was, he had never seen anything quiet like this before. Stroking those overlaying pieces of skin gently with his hand he asked,

"What happened here then, Sally-Lou?"

"Oh, that's nothing. Just stretch marks from when I had my baby at the age of fourteen."

His erection started to go the way of all dejected members on hearing bad news, it went a wee bit limp.

"Christ, a baby! What happened to it?"

"Oh, she's back in Louisiana with aunty May. That's my mother's sister, she brings Cheryl up as her own, after all it was her husband who screwed me."

Then lying with her hand behind her head she concluded,

"I liked him, he was a great lover!"

"Bloody hell! What did your dad say about all of this and what happened to the father?"

Now she frowned a little and then looked out across the small room, then in the direction of the window, her eyes had misted somewhat.

"Dad blew a fuse, that's why I am in England now, he said he couldn't trust me anymore. As for Derek, he just sort of left, but the strange thing is that he left without taking anything, no clothes, no personal belongings, not even his passport, he just sort of left."

A worry frown came across her face and then quickly disappeared. "Some of my friends reckon that he just became alligator dinner. That sort of retribution happens to a lot where I come from, people just go never to be seen again."

Then she laughed.

"I tell you what though, the alligators are big and fat around our abode."

David's penis was as wrinkled as Sally-Lou's stomach, he felt about the same as if he had just come out of a cold shower. He sighed and looked at her, then looked at his member. 'Well Sally-Lou, alligator dinner eh! That might have just put the mockers on our little flight of fancy.' But before he could say or do anything else, she pulled him once again down towards her.

"David, a girl might come to think that you have lost interest. Now let me get hold of this. Got you, oh dear! Needs a little work. Ah, there he comes, growing in stature all the time." Sally-Lou gritted her teeth and almost snarled the command,

"Now, stop talking and start earning your keep. Get that, ah yes, rather big knob of yours into this."

Both of them gave a smile as finally he entered her, but David's was tinged with a certain amount of consternation.

"That's better. You limeys sure take your time. Now work!"

Cartier was of course the perfect gentleman and if a pretty young lady gave an order, it was his duty and sometimes pleasure to perform the dreaded deed. While he was pumping for Queen and country, the thoughts and images coming from within his brain were of fat overfed alligator's and though he tried to eradicate that image it was indeed hard, that thought, and image was firmly fixed within his brain.

Sally-Lou was indeed vocal, her small moans gradually turned into almost a roar of pleasure. Sadly, for the two of them the noise started to attract attention. For a moment the room went dark as light was blocked from entering, then the door burst open and there stood a Sergeant with his red face blazing with fury.

"What the blue hell do you think you two are doing? This is a nuclear bunker, not a knocking shop. Get off that woman, get into your clothes and report to me immediately outside this officers' quarters. And I mean now!"

Then as a second thought he added,

"And make sure that everything is clean and tidy before you report to me."

Both David and Sally-Lou had very nearly climaxed, but not from the front, more from the back areas and from the shock of being caught. David leapt off and grabbed his clothes and started to dress just as quickly as he could. Sally-Lou was more casual about it. At first, she went as white as a sheet and then as the situation started to show itself for what it was, then she started to laugh. She rocked backwards and forwards holding her stomach all the time, then while laughing she kicked her legs into the air making bicycle motions. She had turned bright red but not from the terror of being caught in the act, she just reddened from her overzealous sky riding motion.

Sally-Lou didn't do shame or embarrassment, she just saw the funny side of this interlude and maybe not for the first or last time either. To this your lady, after the shock had subsided, she quickly realised that this had to be the funniest thing that had happened since arriving at this goddamn limey base.

Once David was dressed and decent again, he too started to see the funny side and started to laugh along with her, just not quite so loud. After about ten minutes, but to David a time that seemed like hours, they left the room. Outside still waiting for them and still in a fury was Sergeant Wilson.

"You two took your time! Thought it prudent to finish what you started eh? I do hope that room is in a good clean, tidy order? I shall be inspecting it in a minute. Now young lady, what's your name?"

"Oh no! Don't tell anyone please."

Sally-Lou was putting on an act of shame and surprise, it didn't fool David, but the Sergeant was something else.

"My name is Sally Anne Fielding; I work in Norwich and was brought here as a guest."

All the time she spoke Sergeant Wilson was making notes.

"And you young man, what's your name?"

"Er, my name is George Brown, and I was invited here by Colonel Martin, my father is the mayor of Norwich, and this lady is my fiancée."

Sergeant Wilson once hearing this started to calm himself down. He then looked at the two of them as if he was scrutinising the fuse on a bomb, then without any real feeling in his voice, he said, "Well, okay then. Let this be a lesson to you both. Don't get caught!"

He then proceeded to tear up his so-called report.

They walked casually back to where most of the people they had been with in the beginning of the panic and still should be waiting. No one that they knew was there, just the odd lady that had found herself still down in the shelter having probably fallen asleep in a dormitory. David looked around to see if any of his colleagues were there, not one remained, what was worse, his viola and case with his change of clothing had also disappeared.

Then the alarm went once again, but this time in not such a persistent way and then a loudspeaker crackled into life and a New Yorker, with his rough Yankee drawl blurted out the following,

"Now hear this, now hear this. Would one David Cartier please report topside immediately? Your coach is waiting to depart for London. Cartier, please report topside, if you want to get home!"

David looked at Sally-Lou and smiled sweetly, stroked her pretty face and said,

"Look, you have given me your number, but if I call and I still have a couple of weeks before we leave will you come down to London, maybe stay with me? Can you in some way get your parents to let you out for a couple of days?"

"Ol yea, I guess I could manage that. Anyway, you have some unfinished business to perform. Give it a couple of days and then call me. Bye sweat thing and I do mean sweat."

Sally-Lou leant forward and gave David an extremely passionate kiss on his lips. It was just enough to do two things, firstly start another erection, secondly make him realise that he would miss out on a lot if he really didn't get on that telephone to her.

Chapter 5

Right outside the bunker one orange school bus stood with its engine idling and waiting. He looked in through the windows but could see nothing as all the side glass had steamed up and that was because everyone on board was gently snoring, thus blowing out yet more and more American hot air.

They had been waiting thirty-eight minutes for him, but no one had become anxious just bored and tired. It had been Stuart who had brought up his things, then squeezed them onto a luggage rack. Just before the bus left, David looked around. He laughed out loud, 'Typical English weather, snow to end the world, freeze all human life, then the next minute gone, nothing left but memories.' All that snow last night, all the trouble that the snow had caused, where was it? Good old England, one thing you could always rely on was the complete un-reliability of the weather. The day was really quite warm, and the sun was shining bright albeit low in the sky and all the snow on the base had completely disappeared and outside there was little or none to be seen either. What a beautiful start to another day. He looked at his watch, 'Bloody hell, its eleven o'clock.'

The days passed quickly and fruitfully for David Cartier, he played four more concerts with the troupe all within the East Anglia region, plus he got offered a chance to play with Kent Opera for a week. This he enjoyed immensely. The opera they were performing was at the old cinema at Tonbridge Wells, it was by Leos Janacek, a beautifully evocative work called Jenufa.

The music is wonderfully powerful, and the story line is typical Czech being in some ways depressingly sad thoughtful and yet provocatively understanding the plight of the well down trodden peasants. The musical score is wonderful and difficult for all the instrumentalists performing, but between the music and the singing the story gives an insight to the peasantry of nineteenth century rural Czech existence.

The story is one that evokes the feeling that the provincial yokels would accept their lot as a matter of fact, no matter what happened to them.

The story unfolds around a water mill, a young girl called Jenufa falls in love with a local man, they consummate their friendship with a fling. Before she knows it, he is called away to the army. She has become pregnant, but she has no chance to inform him of her condition. Some time later he returns with an unexpected wife. Jenufa is totally mortified but doesn't show her concern excepting the situation as if it was exactly as she expected.

While various scenes are happening the grandmother to Jenufa takes her child and drowns it in the mill pond but blames the disappearance on a band of wondering gipsies, saying that they stole the infant. But sadly, for all concerned the babies body surfaces during a celebratory party around the mill. The abject horror of it all is the simple expedient that everyone accepts this nightmarish situation as if it was the norm, it is the karma of peasantry to expect and except the worst in their rather short miserable lives. The grandmother confesses to the crime, and she is taken away by the police. Everyone has accepted the appalling situation that has occurred, this trouble was obviously written in the stars, what will be, will be.

This very loosely was the plot that David saw unfolding itself before him on the stage each and every night. Almost all the stage is in viewing position for the viola section they all got to know the plot, and all cried in the appropriate places. David loved the challenge of the music by Leos Janacek and watching the scenes coming together on the stage were magical to him. Every night the entire viola section, being six middle aged men plus David and one young lady broke into almost uncontrollable tears from what was indeed occurring in front of them. When in one break David spoke to the principal viola player, one Steven Shakeshaft, he asked him,

"Steve tell me please, do all operas move players in such a way? Nothing in music before has reduced me to tears and who would think that this could happen every night as well."

The answer which came should have been expected.

"Viola players don't cry at any operas, it's just the dust in the air, it gets in your eyes. All that jumping up and down on the stage stirs everything up."

Of course, he said it with a smile and all listening knew he was joking, they all cried at the end of each performance and that applied to anyone that could actually witness the action on the stage.

"But Janacek is always thought provoking and emotionally draining. Tears...Baa humbug!"

Then he winked and went back to his beer.

This had been a wonderful experience for David, and he was very pleased to find the standard of the orchestra and conductor plus the soloists and chorus were of the highest quality. He was sad when he shook hands with the viola section for the last time. He told Steven Shakeshaft, known to his closest friends as Steven Shagnasty, to please bear him in mind if any other work for viola player was going to be needed in the future.

Then it was over, and he returned to Forest Hill feeling a little empty.

Next stop Germany! There was no work now until the tour starts.

The story about Sally-Lou became a little frustrating and disappointing to David. He did telephone her a couple of days after the bunker incident. He asked her if she would come and stay with him, he would book a double room at the local hotel in Bromley for the night and they would at least have a couple of days together. She agreed and said that he would have to meet her at Liverpool Street Station which he did.

They spent that day in London sightseeing. He took her to Madam Tussauds to view the waxworks figures. There they stood next to President Eisenhower which didn't much favour his appearance to either of them, they visited the dungeon of horrors, saw the murderers Crippin and many others.

But somehow Sally-Lou's heart was not in it. He then took her to the Tower of London overlooking the Thames. They wondered around the castle for an hour and that didn't hit the spot either. David then suggested that they go back to the hotel, then change clothes and he would take her to a jam session at the coffee bar at Clockhouse, after all it was Friday.

By the time they reached the hotel, there was only time to change and go out again. Both of them were hungry so David bought them both a round of roast beef sandwiches from room service. But they had to eat as they went on their way.

The coffee bar was almost full to overflowing, but David who was now some what of a celebrity, because it was there in that bar that he obtained the chance to tour with the military troupe of entertainers. He managed to get the owner to arrange another table near where the band would play. They both seated themselves and drank some of the favourite tickle, muddy looking frothy coffee. Sally-Lou thought it was quite disgusting in look and taste, so she stuck her hand in the air and demanded a coke instead.

By now David was more than a little upset with the day's proceedings. It had become a matter of the best laid plans of mice and men. Well Sally-Lou was not even a squeak from a mouse, she was dull and bored and made sure that David was well aware of that fact. David started to wonder if maybe better the vague memory than the actual reality of some people was best.

He got up with three other musicians which included his great friend Steven Preston the flautist. They played various tunes and pop songs of the time, but by now David's heart was most definitely not in the evening's session. Every time he looked at Sally-Lou she was either looking extremely bored or flirting with anyone who might come into contact with her. And the real bad news to David was when she desired some more refreshments her southern drawl could even be heard above their playing. After only one hour had passed David told the others that he was in fact going home. He packed his viola grabbed Sally-Lou by the arm, waved goodbye to some of the folks he knew and proceeded to retrace his steps back to the hotel. All the way to Bromley very little was said. By the time they reached the hotel Sally-Lou was in one huge strop and this fact alone left Cartier getting more and more irate as the seconds ticked by.

When they got back to their room, David put down his instrument turned towards this spoilt Southern Belle, he was going to give her a tongue lashing she would not forget in a hurry. But as he went to open his mouth Sally-Lou pounced on him like a hunting leopard.

Within the space of less than a minute, both sets of clothing were spread all over the room and both were now spread-eagle on top of the bed. They had sex three times that night and what occurred couldn't be thought of at any stretch of the imagination as love making, it was raw bone crunching sex each time. She bit him, scratched him, hit him all over his body. He had become a willing and somewhat bemused victim of her depravity, but though it left him sore and even bleeding from the odd deep scratch, he enjoyed every second.

The downfall came after their third session, both now in a state of complete exhaustion they decided enough was as good as a feast and sleep might be the next possible avenue to explore. Sleep, what sleep! David had been a pleasant companion all that day, he had escorted her to places that he thought might be of interest, he wined her and even dined her, he tried to entertain her at the jam session and what had he to show for it? A Louisiana lady that snored and devastatingly loud too, so noisy that the moment it started he was woken and never managed to get back to sleep again. 'Oh no, Sally-Lou, you are not the belle for me! It's back to Liverpool Street Station for you and straight after breakfast.'

The next morning when they had showered and dressed, they went down to the dining room for the obligatory English fried breakfast. Much to Cartier's abject horror, on the next table a couple were complaining about the noise that came from the room next to theirs.

"It was obvious that two people were engaged in sex romps, but the screaming that the girl gave off and then the bloody sounds of anguish from the boy, it sounded like he was being torn limb from limb, this seemed to go on all night. Of course, it didn't end there either, when the bloody sex was over, all we could hear was terrible roar of snoring. We are going to ask for our money back. This has been terrible heart wrenching experience for us."

David's head went down, and he got stuck into his breakfast. Sally-Lou once again spoilt the almost calm of the situation, by shouting out for more coffee in her southern accent. David, to his despair heard the voice from the next table,

"That must be them!"

David was happy when the train pulled out of Liverpool Street Station, relief of not having this awful noisy, spoilt Southern Belle, with her bored expressions and lack of any real conversation or interests other than of Elvis bleeding Pressley.

Right from the moment she arrived he suspected that it was going to be one huge mistake, he had not been wrong and now there she was looking out the train window waving to him.

Her last words to him had been,

"I think we have a future David. Keep in touch, you have my address, I expect letters from you at least twice a week. Boy what a reunion we will have when you return to this shit hole of a country. You're the best, I can't wait until the next time!"

Then she was gone!

As the locomotive went out of sight and within a few minutes like that train, Sally-Lou was out of sight and out of mind.

David now had no more concerts; it was the twenty-fifth of November and there were just a few more days until he was on tour. It was now time to do plenty of practice. His friend Steven Preston always said,

"If you can manage it, practice your scales and arpeggios, then your sight-reading pieces finishing with your concertos, not the other way round."

Steven had become a true friend, and David was extremely fond of him. David smiled at Steven as he carried on with his pontificating,

"This should be done over the period of twenty-five hours, on an eight day week, it will help your playing."

David swore blind that the idiot was quite obviously born with a silver tube sticking sideways from his mouth. Whenever he tried to contact Steve, he was indeed always practicing and the strange thing was, to David anyway, this was a player who was amongst the best players in the world, surely, he didn't need to work that hard, did he?

Having thought all this out, David Cartier had to admit to himself that he really didn't know many other flautists only those from recordings, but he did know Steven was really good, what one would think of as an honest-to-goodness musician with a flare for genius concerning his instrument, but this was a genius that was born for extreme hard toil. Anyway, he would take Steven's advice and do some hours every day. But he hadn't acquired Preston's love for work and usually always found any excuse to stop and do something else.

"Steve, I want to ask a big favour of you!"

"Yes, and what's that, not money I hope?"

"No, you old fart, not money. I want to move in with you until I can get to buy a house, I will pay my way and even give you a retainer for holding my gear while I am abroad. What do you think?"

"Yea, why not! Bring your stuff around today, I will get a key cut for you. Just keep the place tidy and don't bring home any old scrubbers before I get a chance to vet them. Agreed?"

"Agreed! And thanks, I owe you one or two. In fact, I shall go to the digs right now and give in my notice and collect my stuff, which should take all of ten seconds. See you in an hour or two!"

It was Sunday thirtieth of November, just one more day and then the adventure starts. David thought that he should in fact do the decent thing and contact Megan once more, he had promised to do just that, so he thought it was time to fulfil his promise.

He waited until lunch time just in case Megan had gone to church, she would be back at her flat by twelve at the very latest. He thought better of the idea of dressing up, so just wore his polo neck sweater and his rather worn-out jeans. He had a sporty denim type raincoat over the top of his sweater. It was cold outside but not cold enough for Cartier to worry unduly, he always thought of himself as being impervious to cold and subsequently always wore less than more. And, that dear reader was why he was always catching colds, not enough clothing being worn in the cold and damp of English autumn and winters.

Years of living in a cold house with his parents had taught him not to worry about a small drop in temperature. His father was quite rich but would never spend money on such things as heating, so often the house was almost icy cold with damp walls from condensation. There was installed a central heating system, but the temperature had to be below zero with the water pipes almost freezing up before it was ever lit. But these extreme forms of torment had toughened David and now to him, cold was just a state of mind, but his flu type colds weren't.

He walked all the way to where Megan resided, the wind blew quite hard and what was left of the leaves on the trees started to come down, they swirled as the wind lifted and chased them around the roadways and paths. There was either snow or cold drizzle of rain in the air and that just went to make life more uncomfortable for any member of human race who might happen to be outside walking.

When he arrived at her abode the front gate was open, and he could see by the light that shone from the basement window that she was indeed in. He knocked on the door, only silence answered. He knocked a little louder and then he heard footsteps approaching. The door was opened and there stood Megan, she was so shocked to see him standing there that they stood and looked at one another for the best part of a minute.

There was something about her looks that surprised David. Somehow, she seemed very bright, slightly pinkish in colour, she was somewhat heavier in her face, maybe rounded would be better terminology for her countenance. She was dressed very casually, with a flowery light brown smock of a dress, hanging freely but also rather sweetly, he liked her attire. She also wore bright green fluffy slippers, they hardly matched any other part of her clothing, these he thought of as probably being very warm and comfortable, but never should be seen by anyone other that oneself.

Her hair looked somehow darker, but he knew that Megan was not the sort of person to ever dye her hair, it just sort of glowed with radiance, there was bounce to it, what is more it was much shorter and had obviously been well styled. Megan had spent money on herself, and it suited her. It was very nice to see her looking so good and so positive and his heart started once again to warm towards her. The silence was finally broken by Megan when she said,

"Well, you are the last person I ever expected to see, you had better come in."

He entered and looked around that familiar flat, except it was no longer familiar to him. The four walls had been redecorated and not before time. Three of them had a floral-patterned wallpaper hung extremely well and the forth by simple coat of purple paint, though rather gaudy in colour somehow it worked against the paper. The whole ambiance was one of warmth and friendliness. It seemed strange to him, he never thought that Megan would ever re-decorate. He wondered what her bedroom looked like, but he wasn't going to ask to see it, not after their last encounter.

"You look great Megan, and I like what you have done here in the flat. How are you? How's the job going? I hope you don't mind me being here, but last time, er, we met, well I did sort of promise to come back to see you before I, er, went away on tour. I only mean good things; I haven't come to make trouble in any way. I really…"

But Megan interrupted him from carrying on. She raised her finger to her mouth to indicate that silence was the best words he could speak, and she could hear. She looked at him hard weighing up in her mind things that might have to be said. Then just when the silence had become deafening, she spoke,

"David it is nice to see you, though I never thought you would return. I have personally never been better, I feel absolutely great, never better. The job is okay, though if I'm honest it didn't seem quite the same after you left. But I shall be leaving in March and going home to my family in Neath, then who knows?"

A proud sort of smile crossed her mouth, it was if she was now just addressing a younger pupil.

"I redecorated so that I can sell the flat easier when I go. You probably didn't know that I bought a leasehold on this flat and as it's now fast becoming a popular area, I expect to do quite well out of the coming sale."

She smiled in a tender sweet unassuming way that now completely disarmed David, then continued in the same way,

"You look good yourself though somewhat scruffy, but then you were when we first met. So, when do you go on tour?"

"Well, tomorrow. But if you want, I can keep in touch by letter? Our first port of call is Germany we are there for about a month in various camps and then it's off to the Far East going to Panmunjom in Korea, Hong-Kong, that's just for a jolly and then it's on to Tokyo Japan and then of course Vietnam, finally ending in Alaska. After that I fly back to Blighty, the rest of the band all stay in the good old US of A. But the good thing is I should in theory, earn roughly one hundred pounds a week and as I get a living allowance too, I hope to have enough money to buy a house when I get back."

He looked her up and down once again and then added,

"Megan I can't get over how good you look. Why you actually seem to radiate and glow with health. I hope you don't mind me saying, but you look so much more feminine and pretty. It would seem that getting rid of me was the best thing that could have happened to you."

There was a moment of embarrassed silence and then Megan asked in a very demure way,

"Would you like a cup of tea; I can even offer a cream puff pastry if you would want it?"

"Well yes that would be nice, are you sure that you want me to stay?"

Megan had already walked across to the kitchen area of that room; she was filling the kettle and was in the process of placing it on the gas oven. Having done that task, she turned around quickly and looked at him again, hard and long. He really wasn't sure if he was being scrutinized for either slaughter, or what? All he knew was that her penetrating stare was unnerving him more than just a little. Finally, the spell was broken and Megan smiled at him, there it was that old friendly smile that he experienced when they first met.

"Tea first and then we will talk. But I have something special to tell you."

"Oh, what's that then?"

"After tea don't be so impatient."

David was intrigued, what was so important but still she had to have the tea first. Maybe, just maybe he knew, she was getting married to someone else! 'Yes, that's it!' And at that thought he felt just a little sad, after all she had been his first and visa versa, surely that meant for something? 'Yes,' he thought, 'it meant tea first.' At this he chuckled inwardly. They drank their tea and then they ate their cream puffs, finally David was unable to contain himself any longer.

"So, what is it that you have to tell me then?"

"Are you comfortable? First, please wipe the cream off your mouth, it's a little off putting."

This he did with reddening cheeks.

"Right then I shall now tell you."

A long pause, a deep breath and then,

"I am expecting your baby."

It just hadn't occurred to Cartier that this was the secret and to this shock he had jerked badly and dropped both the remains of his tea and cake all over her clean floor.

"Aren't you getting married?"

"Hardly, you haven't asked me!"

With this sentence Megan burst out laughing.

"Oh, you bugger, you are joking, aren't you?"

"No David I am not joking; the baby is due around the third of May. I intend to have it at home in Wales. My parents now know about the baby but not about you. So don't look so sad and upset. David, I don't intend to let anybody know who the father is. You are far too young, and I am far too old for you anyway. It's true that I fell in love with you, but it takes two to tango and I knew exactly what I was doing when we first had sex together. And as I know that it was your first time too, I don't blame you in any way what-so-ever! You were as big a virgin as I was, you probably never knew anything about condoms and such like."

So, Megan's words were exactly what he needed to hear, that would be his excuse and way out. David once again reddened, of course he knew about condoms, he had always known, but never liked the idea of them, so he had never ever bought any.

On visits to the barber and generally when he was leaving the hairdresser would lightly nudge him and ask in a whispering voice, "Would sir like something for the weekend?"

He always answered in the negative. He just didn't like the idea of ever wearing something on his member.

Like most men's inane thinking, contraception was the area that became the woman's prerogative. So maybe he is going to get away with absolutely no responsibility for this baby, nor any financial commitment, great news! Then he will make a very good wayward father, maybe seeing the sprog once or twice as it grows to maturity, or maybe not! 'Yes,' he thought, 'we will see! But what a time to hear this news, off touring the world tomorrow and now I am to be a father!'

"Megan how do you feel about having a baby? Is this something you want? I am earning money now; we could find a back street…"

She stopped him once more.

"Don't finish that sentence, of course I want this baby, it might well be my only chance to have kids. I am not so young anymore and being honest with myself I think I always wanted a child with you. At first it was that crazy dream of suburbia and domesticity, but as I got to know you more and more, know how completely and, I hasten to add, wonderfully immature you are, how could I ever have imagined you as a husband or a father. No David this is something for me, not you, just me. I expect nothing from you at all, there is no financial expectations."

She paused frowned ever so slightly and looked directly in David's eyes.

"You don't even have to see our baby if you don't want to that will be entirely up to you. Either way you have nothing to fear from me."

Megan looked hard into his eyes yet again, but this time her own face went reddish as if embarrassed.

"It's funny David, but I now feel very secure and fulfilled, I expect to be a very good mother, and I expect to enjoy ever aspect of motherhood. So, thinking these thoughts I suppose I should in fact feel some gratitude towards you and you know what? I do."

David was quite overcome with emotion; he hadn't expected any of this. He wasn't sure that she would keep her word concerning him, but he couldn't worry about that now. In fact, he just started to lust over her again, just like the first time. He casually strolled over to the windows and drew the curtains. Then he returned to his chair, sat down and thought how he would approach his lustful feeling.

"Megan!"

He started his sentence with authority in his voice, but then immediately softened his tone.

"You have been on my mind a great deal lately."

He was lying and felt a little ashamed of lying and what is more he thought Megan knew when he was telling a fast story, he wasn't at all good at it, but once starting there was no stopping, lust must be concluded in a satisfactory way.

"Oh, I don't know what to say. The truth is I want to make love to you again before I leave for the foreign shores. What do you say, any chance?"

Megan burst out laughing, she was half expecting this, after all she knew just what a little randy blighter he could be. It didn't offend her in any way, this was David Cartier after all! But the answer was easy to give.

"Not a chance, you could damage the baby. Sorry, it might have been nice, but no."

David was almost distraught with frustration. He already had acquired a very large erection, one that showed itself plainly to Megan through his trousers.

"Can you do anything for me as I am so horny now! What about giving me a blow job, that wouldn't hurt the baby?"

"Oh, I'm not sure."

She said slowly and deliberately, but to David, he knew he had her, not sure meant probably and probably meant okay!

"Well maybe a blow job, but just for old times sake. But will that be enough?"

"It will if you take all your clothes off and let me look at every part of you. You know I always loved looking at your bit and pieces, will that be, okay?"

She smiled,

"Well, I guess so."

There, an ace service, he had won and no one else there but him to enjoy the victory!

They retired to the bedroom, this too had been completely re-decorated but in a very girly fashion not really to Cartier's taste, but then he wasn't in there to admire the walls, he wanted to admire her figure, body and private parts.

David instantly removed his trousers and underpants but leaving everything else on, after all it was a little cold in there and he was bone idle when he was this horny. Then he waited on the bed watching Megan gradually remove all her clothes, in his eyes she looked as if she was there to be eaten. 'Now there a thought, she might enjoy that. Maybe they should partake in a sixty-nine, again that won't hurt any babies.'

She got on the bed next to him and waited, what was going to happen next? David took the lead, he caressed those two larger than normal breasts, in the dress her breasts had seemed as he remembered them, in the nude he could see the reality, they were filling with life juices for the baby.

Then he made her open her legs, but on the way down he could see that her tummy was slightly bigger than before, there was the bump that depicted a living human life form growing within. He stroked her tummy in a very caring tender way and Megan responded by almost purring.

He then came down to her vagina, he once again cupped that mop of pubic hair. His immediate thought was, 'Shame she hadn't shaved once again for me?' He opened it up to view the pink flesh inside her, he gently inserted a finger, just enough to give her a little excitement, but not enough to worry her. Then he climbed between her legs and opened her wide enough so that his head could get there and then his tongue started to work its magic.

He licked her clitoris very gently at first, just enough so that she would become aroused. Megan groaned a little and moved easily from side to side, sadly for David ever time she did that he got a mouthful of pubic hair. 'Bloody hell I shall have fur balls in my stomach after eating this lot.' He then noticed that her clitoris had stiffened just like his member, it stood out from her vagina by almost an inch; 'Wow, motherhood does some exciting things to the body. This is fun exploring these new little novelties.' He got quicker and slightly firmer with his licking. Megan groaned and moaned, rolling and rocking, all the time her breathing quickened and grew shallower, then as if Megan was about to expire and depart this mortal coil she jerked and arched her back, her final moan sounded more like a gurgling sound then anything else. She had a long and pleasing orgasm. Afterwards when the stars had once again disappeared and she was back in her bedroom, she just lay there quite still and very replete.

He raised himself from between her legs all the time trying to remove and cough up pubic hairs. Cartier didn't have a clue as to how many he had actually swallowed, but he knew it was more than just a couple and he was still pulling them from his teeth. Gradually Megan started to come to, she hadn't experienced anything like that for a very long time and she had missed it. She knew that she now had to please him, it was time for her to go to work.

He was lying beside her and obviously waiting for some sort of action to occur to him, she wouldn't let him down.

She touched his leg which lay beside hers, ran her hand up into his crutch and took hold of his penis. She didn't have to do much; he was already standing to attention and ready for the coming battle. She tickled him around his testicles and did this until she heard him breathing very deeply, then she went down to explore.

His member was huge, she had forgotten how big it could become. Gently at first, she placed her lips around the area, licking various little spots that she knew he liked having touched. Then without him knowing what was going to happen, she pushed the entire penis deep into her mouth. She went deeper and deeper, it was touching the back of her throat, and he loved it. She pulled it in and out making sure that it always touched the inside of her cheeks, that rubbing brought on climaxes usually very quickly, not that she wanted it all to end, no she too was enjoying this moment, maybe this was going to be her last session of sex with David, so she had already decided that she was going to go out with a bang.

This pounding only went on for several minutes and then he started to explode. He puffed wildly and then grunted as he could no longer stop what was going to happen and happen it did. David Cartier gave up a vast amount of semen and all of it went down Megan's throat, she swallowed the entire load much to his blessed relief and satisfaction.

He had loved every second of it and then as he was trying to recover, she lay there licking up any drops that might have tried to escape.

They lay there together both breathing heavily, both being pleasantly exhausted. David was still trying to remove the odd pubic hair from a tooth at the same time Megan rubbed her cheek, as she realised that both now sported blisters. 'Ah, what we give up for the acts of pleasure!'

"Megan please forgive my crude attempts of love making, I must be truthful with you. The shock of hearing the news of our offspring and the wonderful sight of you in all your pregnant glory, well to be entirely honest it was all just too much for me. I didn't come round here to take advantage of you, I wanted to do the honourable thing and for once in my life be a nice guy, but the truth is you made me randy, and I lusted after what we once had."

His head hung low, and his eyes blinked in a continuous way, just like a naughty baby would.

He then concluded with,

"Please forgive me!"

Megan laughed out loud and in a very pleasing way. She turned over to look directly at him and then said in a low but pleasantly loving voice,

"David, dear boy. I fancied you first, so who led who on? Do you think I would be lying here naked if I had minded? You didn't seduce me, let's say it was a nice way to say goodbye, if you like a mutual search for lost pleasures and what's more we both enjoyed it very much. Now get dressed and go home, tomorrow you leave to go abroad, there must be many things you have to do before you go, so go and do them. Anyway, I want to sleep, then I want to bathe, then who knows. But before you go, I shall give you my Welsh address. If you want to see me and your child, just write and let me know. And if while you are away you wish to write to me, that would be nice too. No pressure, no fuss. Okay?"

"My God! Has anybody ever had it easier? Right Megan, I shall leave, you are right I do have a great deal to arrange before the off. I will miss you and, in my way, I have always loved you. You are special to me, and I will keep in touch. Have a good life and look after our child, though I know you will! And I will try and write."

Then he left the flat for the very last time. Would he ever meet his child or see Megan again? Well for one thing, young David Cartier didn't know the future, but he sure hoped for the best and to an extent expected only good things to come from the future, as he always thought that the past wasn't worth trying to remember to much!

Chapter 6

All the troupe were to meet at Northolt airfield at twelve noon sharp. Though this was primarily a British airbase, some US freight planes used it because of its proximity to London. And for this military entertainment group, travelling with cargo and other military personnel was fine if not though a little uncomfortable.

It was a very large military Boeing that was waiting for them there. All the instruments were loaded unto the plane and in front of the cargo there were just enough seats to accommodate all military personnel that were indeed on their way just like the troupe of musicians to Hamburg.

These planes carried everything from people to cargo which might be extremely bulky, or as small as pins and needles. That was because everything was being brought primarily from America. For some curious reason, the military in their wisdom thought it prudent to ship everything that they might need from the United States, as apposed to buying it in the country that they resided in, thus bringing a little comfort and money to that countries economy and just maybe help that country with extra employment and thus boost their economics, also creating a small amount of good will which was usually lacking badly as America and Americans were deeply despised and distrusted in most occupied European Countries.

It was strange for David to show his passport, even stranger was the simple fact that he actually owned a passport. Now going through the British customs, he had to show it and he also had to prove that he would only be taking out of the country no more than twenty-five pounds sterling, which was the absolute limit, should he be in need of sterling when abroad he would have to go through the embassy and the British banks abroad, not easy and extremely long winded. What he didn't tell the customs men was that he carried two hundred US dollars which was some of the money that the troupe had already paid him.

They obligingly went through both his cases and then his viola case, they made him get a customs form cleared via an agent, telling him that if he didn't have that form stamped, there may be problems coming back through British customs with a viola in the future. In theory he could end up paying duty for something he already owned. To Cartier and Holstein, agents were just another way of taking money from people, he felt sure that customs men and agents were in league together probably sharing the spoils of the fee, which for something that took no more than thirty seconds, still managed to cost twenty-five pounds. A strange large sum of money, which had a certain ring to it.

So the troupe paid for his agent, got the relevant paperwork stamped with the appropriate little rubber stamp, the paperwork was carefully stowed away in a scruffy old leather briefcase that Holstein carried and David was also allowed to board the plane.

There were no seat allocations, it was a matter of first come first served, that was the order of the day.

Fortunately for David, he was one of the first to clamber aboard, he was shaken by the cathedral size of the plane, it was completely devoid of anything resembling comfort, just masses of freight, spaced in order to balance the craft, then seats here there and everywhere. He grabbed a seat that overlooked the port wing, he reserved a space for Stuart Holstein who seemed to have taken a personal shine to the British lad. Anyway, just maybe he recognised the potentially good musicians in him and if nothing else

Stuart liked being around people who he visualised as potential winners.

They landed in Hamburg at the US airstrip just thirty miles from the centre of the ancient medieval city situated on the river Elbe. It was early evening, and the night sky showed itself clearly. The weather was crispy cold and snow had for several weeks now been falling everywhere, or one could say almost everywhere, but as the German people never let a small thing like snow slow industry or commerce and apart from some fields everywhere else was clear, plus it was continuously kept clear, no one wanted the fluffy white stuff to be falling on their city, possibly slowing down traffic and commerce which is and was so vital to the very life blood of the nation.

Nevertheless, walking had to be done with some considerable care, as the snow might not be lying on pavements or roadways, but the night frost did and that could be treacherous underfoot.

David knew his modern history and was quick to marvel at the way the autobahns were once again looking pristine and clear of debris, there was no scarring to be seen anywhere along the countries trading routes. But that was not to say that there were no signs of the destruction from the devastating bombing that came from the direction of England during the small, elongated troubles of World War Two.

All major sites of destruction had been cleared immediately and replaced by good architectural constructions, firstly for the good of the forthcoming trade and after the money started to reappear, housing was re-established, good, clean well built comfortable dwellings, especially made to house the new workforces that were once again going to introduce wealth to the economy of that once beautiful city.

Once on the bus that carried the entertainers to the city, there were faces that looked out of the bus with amazement, seeing how quickly fine new buildings had replace those appalling scars left by the infamous Bomber Harris when he ordered carpet bombing of cities all over Germany.

In one raid alone more than one thousand bombers were used to devastate the city of Hamburg, and more than forty thousand civilians were killed either by the explosions of the ordinance or by being burnt to death by being sucked into the firestorms as those resulting fires whirlwinds ravaged the city.

Yet in just a few years those scars were replaced by new exciting developments, most designed with efficient modern techniques. A new renaissance was appearing and that was something the Germans could teach the victors with remarkable insight and understanding of the needs of the populace.

In nineteen sixty-two London was still pock marked by Germany's bombs and those bomb sites were destined to linger for many years to come.

In Britain as a rule, people thought of it as a country of many qualities, but sadly not in the rebuilding of devastated homes and factories caused by the German Luftwaffe during their many bombing raids on the Britain's towns and cities.

Where are those houses fit for returning heroes. The British answer to rebuilding was get something up that would be cheap to build and be damned to anyone who complained that the structures were poor in design, quality and comfort. Builders and architects were there just to make a good quick profit either for themselves or the companies they worked for, not leave lasting well proportioned and designed building that would show out as a beacon to Britishness, a landmark to development through forward thinking. No, it always seemed that most new developments just became a blot on the landscape, something that would sooner or later have to be replaced at much more expense.

They journeyed into the port area where their hotel was situated, once again this new hotel was not a big establishment, but beautifully designed and built. It only had sixty rooms, all doubles, but the way that it had been built was a marvel to German ingenuity. The entire edifice was made from glass, but not ordinary glass, oh no! The Germans had developed a special glass that could darken when too much sunlight shone upon its surface and then in darkness it cleared once again. And even if a small car was to run into this front of building, it might do damage, but the areas that would be damaged could and would be quickly replaced.

All the rooms were light and roomy with on-suit facilities which always included a shower, toilet, sink and bidet. The rooms all with a small honesty bar, coffee facilities and a black and white television that showed at least five channels, though the reception of the programmes was often quite snowy, but they did have the American armed forces channel which to David was the most biased nonsense he had ever seen. The propaganda was so poor and biased against the Eastern bloc countries, that on watching these programs could see that the Yanks thought of the Ruskies as evil people and individually all made pacts with old Nick himself.

David was utterly astonished at the corny attempts of anti communist propaganda, did anyone ever really fall for the nonsense that was spouting from those awful government run programmes? Now having known a few Americans, he thought, well, maybe!

The restaurant was spacious clean and warm both in temperature and ambiance. The food was very basic, plentiful and nourishing, and suited the pallets of American and British very well. They would be staying there for just two nights and then they would be staying on camps. So, the order of the day became, eat, drink and have pleasure, for tomorrow you will not have the same chance to get any of these sorts of pleasantries. Camps, he was told were notoriously basic.

David was given a room with the next youngest musician of the troupe, that was Roger Mills and Roger played the clarinet and saxophone and very well too. He was twenty-one years of age, married at the age of sixteen, hated married life so joined the entertainment section of the army, this he did quick enough not to be in line for drafting. Roger didn't fancy being a grunt with a rifle in Vietnam, anyway he rather admires the Asian races, so he didn't fancy the idea of having to shoot them.

He came from a small Midwest town called Westville and that small pimple of a town is situated in Missouri, his accent gave him away every time. But he was nice enough and David appreciated his slow logic and weird form of common sense. He was the only member of the troupe that received letters every day though sometimes they appeared in bundles, always from his wife. He told Cartier that she pleaded everyday for him to get out and come home again. She loved and missed him terribly, sadly for Olga, Roger bragged that he had never answered one of those letters. As far as he was concerned, the quicker she asked for a divorce the better, in the meantime this would do just to mark time.

"I want the bed nearest to the door."

Roger threw his cases onto the bed then went over to the windows and opened one of them as wide as possible. He wanted some fresh crisp cold air to enter the overheated bedroom. He never thought to ask David as to whether that was fine with him, but then fortunately Cartier didn't mind a jot, he was easy and accommodating.

He stood there throwing out his chest and breathing in the polluted air as if it was the cleanest newest oxygen having come direct from the North Pole. The truth was in fact, it came from the slaughterhouse, which was situated just down the road, almost to the entrance of one of the dock gates. But from this window one could just make out part of the river Elbe, a part that twisted out beyond the city. On it, at that point, was at least a dozen large ships all waiting to come through to various docking areas to unload imported cargos, then re-load with Germany goods that were being exported all over the globe. In fact, the nearest part of the river was not more than two hundred yards away, but it was completely hidden from view by warehouses, factories and ships themselves. But Roger already loved this city and had secretly decided as they had a certain time now to recuperate and that time was supposed to be used by all the musicians, to prepared themselves for the onslaught of work that would happen once they reached the camps. But Roger had already decided that he would use the time to explore this city. He had never been to Europe before, so was determined to see what treasures remained and also to get to know the people and find out what a World War did to them as individuals.

These next two days was there for the use of practicing and studying the sheets of music that had already been given to the players, but to Roger he knew he didn't need to even open a sheet of music, he could get around anything by first sight. No sir, this was exploring time.

"David what about us two going on a sightseeing trip tomorrow morning, or are you going to practice like a good little boy?"

David Cartier was not going to be put off any adventure by the thought of having to work.

"Yep, that sounds like a good idea. After breakfast, okay? Food, now that I think about it, I feel extremely hungry, coming down to eat?"

"I'm a jump ahead of you there. Come on unless you need to unpack or something."

"Unpack! What for, we are only here two days, it really doesn't seem worth it. Come on let's find the restaurant and while we are looking, I will tell you an old English joke."

They left the room and proceeded to wonder down the corridor picking up stragglers on their way. It seemed that everyone had the same idea. So, David raised his voice so all could hear,

"In the north of England there is a valley that has a huge dam built within its area. The dam had filled with water, and it was dangerously close to flooding and maybe taking the entire village away that just happened to be situated in the valley along with its mass of water. The small town that was in that valley was quickly evacuated, that is all but one stubborn priest that wouldn't leave his Catholic Church, as the water rushed over the top of the dam and into the village swirling and crushing houses everywhere. Soon it reached the church, at first the water swirled around the outside of this temple to God and the priest laid some sandbags to ensure that the water didn't get into the church, that was with a view to stop the flooding of the crypt. But gradually with the extra high winds and heavy rain, more and more water came. A boat appeared around from behind a submerging house and the pilot haled the priest."

By now David had the men's complete attention.

"We are here to save you father. Grab the rope and we will pull you aboard. The priest answered in the only way possible being a man of God."

Again, David was aware of the complete rapped attention, he continued,

"Thank you, my son, but I must save Gods house, he in turn will save me, that I know for sure. So the small boat went away, leaving him to his devises. The wind and rain became the worst gale in memory and the waters around the church rose and rose. Eventually the priest was left with only one place to go and that was on the roof. A little while later another boat came and the people on board once again haled to the priest. Come on father, its time to leave the church and save yourself. The answer was quite obvious too. God will protect me my son, just save yourselves. God is almost here with me now; I can feel his presence. The boat went away again. The water climbed even higher, and the priest was last seen hanging onto the weather vein and then with a final rush of water he was gone."

David now standing perfectly still with all the troupe standing quietly listening to every word,

"Then father Ted, which was the priests name, made his way to heaven, but he was more than a little upset. He stood in front of his maker and crossly asked, God, maker of all things, I have always been a loyal and truthful servant to you, why didn't you save me from drowning. I was there trying to protect your house, and you didn't save me."

David now paused for effect,

"What do you mean didn't try to save you, I sent two boats, and you ignored them both!"

There was a ripple of laughter, but nothing from the Catholics.

The restaurant was roomy, clean and patiently waiting to be used. The staff were plentiful in number and attended them without being obtrusive. David ordered roast pork with roast potatoes and sour kraut. The food was brought to him on platters, these were filled to overflowing and even when he had taken his fill, there was still a Mundane of spoils left over. He thought it was okay, though he wasn't sure about the kraut.

Maybe he will omit that next time.

For dessert he ordered apple strudel, this came with very thick cream which reminded him of Devon clotted cream. Here he could have eaten twice as much as was brought, which just went to show what a sweet tooth David had acquired since being alone and catering for himself. Coffee came in large ewer type jugs, and it was really too strong for Cartier's taste, so he left most of it.

After the meal had finished, he felt the day close in on him, he looked in the direction of Roger but saw that he was laughing and chatting to Anthony Flossing, the oboe and alto-saxophone player and so he didn't like to interrupt. He was tired and decided an early night might just suit him more than the possible drinking and talking that he expected the rest to be doing until the early hours. Travelling was tiring, he imagined that the day had worked out more like a day's labouring than just sitting on a plane and bus.

David washed and changed into the new pyjamas that he had bought for the tour. Climbing between the sheets and it took all of thirty seconds to fall into a deep dreamless sleep. He was suddenly woken by a noise; in his mind it was the family cat starting to climb onto the bed.

"Shoo, shoo."

He vaguely heard himself say, but in his mind the noise became persistent. Then as he started to wake, he heard the distinct voice of Roger Mills saying in an extremely low whisper,

"Keep quiet, I don't want to wake David up. And don't turn on the light I will open the curtains. Best put your clothes here on the chair with mine."

Now David was awake but quiet, he was listening to what was being said. As he had heard Roger speak and knowing he was talking to someone else he realised that he was not alone.

'Bloody hell, Roger's a queer. He's got one of the other fellows in with him and they are going to do some awful bloody poofter thing. I am not having this.'

David spun around in the bed and flicked on his bed side light before anyone could move. There was Roger, naked as the day he was born, and there was… 'Oh! It's a half naked girl.'

"What the hell! What's going on? Am I missing out on something here?"

David lay there wiping the sleep from his eyes. Gradually he was coming too and analysing the situation that was indeed exposing itself to him.

"I dreamt you were just about to have a session with one of the guys in the band, boy am I relieved about that! I really am glad you are not a bum bandit poofter."

Roger was quick to retort, he stood there not bothering to cover up his embarrassment, it didn't bother him that his very small penis was not going to impress any young ladies and when he looked in the direction of his female friend, he at once noticed that she was looking down at his member with her lower jaw drooping in a very sad expression.

"It's not the size baby, it's how you use it."

Then turning to David he added,

"David my old mate, as you can see clearly, she is not a he. How could you have thought I was a faggot? Christ man, I am a married man."

He said with a wink,

"Anyway, if I was to fancy any of the guys, it would be you sweaty!"

Cocking his arm up and taking hold of his own hip, he concluded with,

"You don't have to miss out on anything here, there is enough here to satisfy us both."

And then pointing towards the girl he said,

"Satisfy us both, yes, my boy. In fact, this young lady is big enough to take us both at the same time and that is for surely true."

He was now rubbing his two hands together in a smug self-satisfied way.

"Roger, Roger, Roger! I came to bed to sleep, this day has completely knackered me, I just want to sleep. Give me some of that cotton wool that I saw you with and I will push some into my ears then try and go back to the land of nod."

But then he looked in the direction of the girl, she was young being no more than sixteen or seventeen years of age, she had very blond hair, which was obviously natural, she was sort of pretty, but her pretty looks were somewhat spoilt as she wore to much makeup, and the makeup went to make her what she was, a tart! Her top was off showing rather large well-rounded breasts, but Cartier could tell by the look of them that they had been well mauled over time and even at this tender age were beginning to droop. Her mini skirt was open ready to be removed, and he could see that she wore very brief knickers underneath. Her legs looked slightly lumpish and showing signs that again that in the not to distant future she was going to have very un-shapely walking pins.

In fact, the more he looked at her the more sorrow he felt for her. This was a very young girl, probably taken from her parents and placed into the oldest profession. Even at her tender age she was already looking worn out. How long would it be before she was too fat, too plain and too diseased to carry on with her way of life? David speculated, 'not long!'

As that thought permeated around his brain a carton of cotton wool smacked against the top of his head and landed on his pillow. While he put some into his ears he watched with some fascination as the girl took the rest of her clothes off. Then he turned over and went straight back to sleep; Roger could hardly believe his eyes or ears.

The next morning at about six thirty David woke, he remembered that he had been dreaming about Megan and now he wondered how she was, after all it had been all of three days since he last saw her.

Taking a deep breath, he was horrified to smell the stale air. The windows had been shut tight and the hotel as of yet didn't sport air-conditioning. The room stunk of sweaty feet, dragon's breath, and stale alcohol, but worst of all other more dramatic familiar aromas.

He clambered out of his bed, scrambled to open the window and then took gulps of fresher, if somewhat polluted air. But the cold of the morning soon overtook the smell of rancid bodies, and he was forced by expediency to once again close the window.

He looked around the debris of the room, it seemed obvious to him that Bomber Harris had sent yet another calling card while he had slept. There was rubbish, clothing, empty bottles and all sorts of nasty rubber things that David was very cautious about touching, they seemed to be spewed all over the floor and the chairs, dresser and even hanging across the television. His eyes had now accustomed themselves to the dim of dawn and on looking around further, he saw half in a half out of the other bed one young girl and one extremely rancid smelling American. Both were completely naked. David's eye caught sight of one thing that really bothered him, there was considerable blood on various parts of the sheeting.

"Roger, wake up. Roger, come on rise and shine!"

David pushed and pulled at him a couple of times and he gradually roused himself.

"I hope someone has died, because I wouldn't want you to have woken me for anything other than dead bodies everywhere."

Without trying to waken the young girl, who he considered might well be dead anyway. David got Roger to climb back onto the bed and then to sit upright and then seeing that he was once again compos mentis he pointed to the blood.

"What is all this about then? Is she okay? You haven't done anything that you are now going to regret?"

Roger looked at the blood then frowned deeply plus he looked closer at the spilt life juices, then looked at the young girl. His heart was now pounding, was she still asleep? He put his head towards her prostrate body, listening for the sounds of life. Realising that she was indeed still taking oxygen on board, he consciously sighed with relief.

Then his thoughts turned to himself. He jumped out the bed and started looking for wounds that might be leaking on his being, none showed themselves. He looked puzzled; this riddle was indeed an enigma that must be solved.

"I'll have to wake her. Can you speak German as her English is limited to jiggy-jiggy and then role her fingers and thumb together as to indicate a price? That I believe is the extent of her knowledge of planet earths only real language!"

"Sorry pal you're on your own, I had difficulty learning English, so saying that there was no chance that I could manage another tongue."

Roger looked crestfallen, then he looked at the girl again and nudged her gently, nothing happened, he nudged her a little more violently, to this she started to murmur. She licked her lips a couple of times and then her eyes opened. She looked at Roger, smiled and then looked at David. Her right leg was still dragging outside the bed and along the floor, she realised this fact so then lifted herself onto the bed. Not at any time did she try and cover up her modesty but lay now on top of the bed looking bloated and tired. She half got up at least onto her right elbow and then she scratched her hair hard, as if there were mites crawling over the entire area. Roger had been watching her the whole time, when she had finished her grooming he asked,

"Are you okay? Are you wounded somewhere, anywhere? If I hurt, you I didn't mean to honestly."

As he spoke, he raised his voice decibels all the time, so much so that by the time he said honestly he was almost shouting. She looked at him as if he was an imbecile, then maybe that thought wasn't such a bad one, perhaps he was.

It was David which finally took matters in hand. He pointed to the blood stains across the sheets. The lass looked down and then understood, she too looked over her body, then in an understanding moment a light bulb exploded within her brain. She opened her legs to reveal a very hairy vagina, she rubbed her hand over the area and there for the three of them to see was the answer, her period had started.

Once again, the German lass showed no compunction for shame or embarrassment, just one of those unfortunate things that happen on a monthly cycle.

Roger got her dressed and out the hotel long before anyone was going to notice the fact that there was indeed one extra person within those hallowed walls. He came back to the room, got out of his clothes then went and had a bath. While Mills was in that tub soaking gently and trying to get rid of the evidence of the offending blood by having the sheets in there with him. Roger suddenly burst out laughing. David was still a little shaken by the whole experience and was extremely glad that he hadn't given a serious thought to getting involved as well. He called through the bathroom door to Roger,

"What was her name?"

"That's why I started to laugh; it had occurred to me that I didn't have a clue. She spoke no English, me no Kraut, it rather put a scupper on us having a meaningful thoughtful relationship. Hungry?"

"Bloody hungry now!"

Just about everyone went on a city sight-seeing bus, those that were staying at the hotel were either recovering from alcohol poisoning or just too fatigued to be bothered to go out, preferring their own company and that of the bed.

Not one of the troupe was doing any practicing and that simple fact surprised no one. The hotel supplied the old coach which had one window missing and a small hole in the roof, this was just to let rain into the vehicle and that way get the pleasure of soaking the last four right hand seats at the back plus all the people that sat in them.

The broken window had been done in one of the rare dock workers union rally's which had occurred a couple of months previous. On that occasion the coach had been used by the police. What the general public didn't know was that the police broke the window later that night when most of the local constabulary got blind drunk and their poor behaviour was because sixty burly police managed to stop a rally of twenty-five Dockers who were in fact only being addressed by their leader.

The police had been told that it was a communist plot to undermine the entire fabric of the working docks. This would then bring down the industry of Hamburg, affecting the whole economy of Germany, this in turn might lead to the fall of Democracy in the western free world and the subsequent takeover by Communism throughout the entire globe. No one would be spared!

The fight had lasted roughly thirty seconds, twelve of the Dockers had to be hospitalised because of their appalling wounds. But most astounding and even somewhat confusing tactics used by the constabulary, plus the very bullying way the police handled the entire situation shocked all that witnessed the incident. It made one wonder why the police were even there?

But one good thing came out of this melee, the bus was now air-conditioned. Great in the summer but this was December and to cap it all there was no working heater. But when you are having fun, who cares about such trivial things as comfort.

So forty musicians from the US military entertainments corps were shivering from being freezing cold, or worse if you sat at the rear, freezing cold and wet.

The first port of call was the magnificent Cathedral in the city centre. The coach pulled up in front of St. Michaelis (or St. Michael's) Cathedral, close enough to the portals so that not all of them would get soaked by the insistent raining. It didn't work, they all got wet. But to the delight of the bus driver everyone did alight and start to look around this Baroque inspired place of worship.

It had scaffolding over most of the edifice as ongoing repairs were taking place. This was essential restoration that was badly needed since the allied bombing had taken its toll. As they all gathered around the entrance, a middle-aged woman rather large in stature, wearing very dark dull peasant like clothing which didn't make her look at all official, came and approached them. She was tired and aged looking, though probably no older than middle forties. She sported completely white hair which was also showing devastating signs of thinning. She introduced herself as the guide and asked to be paid in Dollars. This one tour would make her a tidy few dollars plus tips, this was a fine chance to make enough money to finally pay off her new television.

Margaret Stein was her name, at least this is what she told them along with a large part of her life story. Evidently, she had lived in Hamburg all her life, living a very middle-class existence with her mother and father who had been a trader in jewellery, specialising in diamond and gold artefacts.

When the Nazis came to power her parents were two of the first to be deported in Hamburg, there were sent to Treblinka, neither lasted more than a couple of weeks. Their fate had been sealed as early as the beginning of nineteen thirty-eight. Margaret informed the assembled American musicians that her parents were taken probably because of her father's possible wealth, which the Nazi party wanted for their own means.

Her father's cause had not been enhanced by the simple expedient that he was also the local Rabbi, thus getting rid of him meant that the rest of the Jews within the area and as a whole, wouldn't be hard to round up and deport.

Margaret had escaped persecution by fleeing just at the moment of her family's arrest. The plucky young Jewess had run from her home to a wealthy neighbour, fortunately for her that family was entirely anti-Nazi and anyway had always liked and respected the Stein family, so they took her under their protective umbrella away from prying eyes and Jew hating locals.

Her Protestant neighbour had saved her life, and she lived for five years in the basement of their building never seeing the light of day, which was until the building took a direct hit by an American bomber during a daylight raid. Her two saviours had been instantly killed and she was buried for almost a week, but when the rescuers finally dug her out of her tomb, they mistook her for the lady of the house, thus she took on a completely new identity. This she told the now awe-struck Americans, saved her from being deported to an extermination camp.

After the story was completed most of the musicians were still wondering why a Jewish lady was guiding them around a Protestant Cathedral. The rest realised from the start that this was going to be a way of getting better tips, out of sympathy for her plight in life, but most of the gathered assemble actually heard the story and really did feel pity for this sad luckless lady, so she was going to do rather well from these soaking American musicians.

Margaret started the tour by pointing to the steeple and explained that though this high tower had been seriously damaged it had survived the worst of the raids. It is a fact that it was decided at the SS headquarters to demolish it as they thought it was a beacon for the bombers to take bearings from, but that never actually happened. The height is and was always one hundred and thirty-two meters high.

"Gentlemen, as you can see on places around the outside there are several gargoyles, many of these date back to the seventeenth century to the first church that was built on this site. There have been three churches built here, the first was in sixteen forty-seven, and that took until sixteen sixty-nine to complete."

She took a deep breath, then looked around to make sure that she had indeed captured their imagination, she smiled inwardly knowing now that she had,

"It was improved and built upon up until sixteen eighty-seven, this was the time that it became the main church of the district of Hauptkirche and was then enclosed within the city walls."

Margaret stopped to make sure that her charges were still following her and not lagging behind too much. Once they were all gathering around her yet again, now all dripping from top to bottom from the very persistent rain, she continued.

"Eventually the then main part of the structure was sadly destroyed, this happened because a freak storm that appeared from nowhere. The steeple that was then sticking skywards was struck by lightning and the subsequent fire brought the whole building down. The locals blamed the Jews on that occasion too. Their complaint was that God had shown his wrath because Jewish traders had taken up commercial residence within the proceeding limits of the church. Many got stoned to death and several others burnt at the stake. All their property and chattels were shared amongst the looters."

She looked questioningly at Stuart Holstein,
"Sound familiar?"
Her eyebrows raised and she still looked towards Holstein in an expectant way, she got no response,
"Now I will show you the statue that symbolises the fight for good over evil, if you will please follow me back to the main entrance."

They all walked back once again to the scaffolding and waited for the guide to inform them of what, how and why?

"As you can just see there above the portal there is a fine bronze statue of Archangel Michael, he has just conquered the devil."

As she said the next sentence, she made a sound of Humph!

"So it seems we will all be going to heaven."

With this sarcastic remark, there was a good babble of nervous laughter that came forth, it seemed to clear the air a little. Margaret smiled knowingly.

"Now we will all enter, please follow me and I must ask for a certain reverence and quietness as there is a private service going on in one of the side chapels, I wouldn't want us to disturb their prayers."

They all moved into the main body of the Cathedral, but most of the troupe were rather disappointed by the austere plainness of the fabric of the church.

There were several statues and half a dozen biblical paintings, but there were no gold or elaborate carvings to be seen.

To David it didn't hold a candle to St. Paul's Cathedral in London.

All in all as a building to base a tour around, it was all a rather big disappointment, one might say a very damp squib, that was until Margaret having shown them most of the inside, suggested as a final treat, maybe some of them would like to climb the steeple to a viewing platform, there the brave people that climbed could get views of most of the surrounding city area, but most of all the dockyards. A dozen brave souls ventured the steep stairs to the platform, this was extremely dangerous place to be standing. There was absolutely no rails or fencing to stop an unfortunate person from falling off and plummeting to their destruction.

Margaret waited by the door with her outstretched hand holding a plate, just so that they could all drop in some more dollars as they left the Cathedral.

Forty wet and cold American musicians scrambled once again onto a coach, which should have been condemned once the Ark took rest spite on Mount Ararat.

The rest of the day's tour was taken up in seeing Hamburg football club stadium, which meant nothing to anyone on the vehicle as Americans don't understand or appreciate European football or soccer as they call the game, but strangely they all decided to see the stadium and subsequently paid their buck each to enter. They were then transported to the old, damaged opera house and the new concert hall where the Hamburg Philharmonic gave their great performances. This interested David immensely but not anyone else. They travelled around the new housing estates and the new factory sites.

Finally hunger and sheer boredom got the tour cut short and they arrived back at Hotel Splendour in time for a well-earned meal and rest. Everyone of them was soaked to the skin, this would be one tour that would go down in the annals of the participating persons personal memory, one of abject misery from the continuous cold soaking that they all had acquired.

David Cartier was pleased to be back in the dry and warmth of their haven. He vowed that tomorrow he would indeed do as bid, and practice scales and arpeggios until either his arm dropped off or anything better might just come along over the horizon.

On the fourth of December at exactly ten past nine in the morning, a military bus appeared at the front of the hotel and all the musicians packed into it with luggage and all, it was indeed time to start work. And Cartier was actually pleased to be getting down to the nitty-gritty of work, plus earning that money that was promised.

The camp that they were taken too was a very large airbase that also housed the tank corps. It stretched for well over a mile in length and though it was camouflaged within a large forest complex just about everyone including the Russians knew of its existence.

There was also a very big chance though supposedly kept quiet, that it housed nuclear missiles, all being aimed at the Soviet Union. That meant somewhere within the East Bloc was a similar facility that had missiles aiming straight back here should the whistle go up.

So much for Hamburg and the surrounding countryside, in fact the whole of Germany was going to be one huge graveyard. If the so-called balloon was ever to go up, the force of the destruction would make World War Two look like a Sunday school playtime mixed children's melee.

As they drove through the entrance of the base two highly armed guards came on board to firstly to scrutinise all passports, then go through the passenger's entire luggage leaving absolutely nothing to chance.

An explanation had to be given as to the reasoning behind a Limey being there with the ensemble. But after the guards read the report given about Cartier, then checking with a superior office they quickly lost interest.

The base was just three parallel long airstrips, between each runway were many young pine trees growing, this being to give some sort of camouflage to what was going on within the complex. On each side of the two outer runways were the storage facilities and hangers for the aircraft, all very low lying, it was deemed better to have buildings with low profiles. They had all been built especially to house certain kinds of aircraft, so the height of a building was in accordance with the size of the said plane. Every now and again roadways ran off into dense forest, these led to the tank's maintenance stores and the fuel and just about everything that this base needed to run competently and smoothly. Then within the trees were the various accommodation blocks that housed the troops of airmen, they all looked the same being just one storey dwellings. But looks could always prove to be deceptive as they all stretched a further three storeys below ground plus an air raid bunker leading even much further down. Everything was painted grey and green, and all these buildings looked extremely sad and depressing. It was later thought by psychologists that the colouring had a lot to do with the high suicide rate that went on in American bases within Germany.

Considering that the whole place must be housing several thousand personnel, very few people were to be seen anywhere.

As the bus drove down the left-hand side runway the overall silence was quite deafening to all on board, it had a ghostly eerie effect on all the troupe that were aboard the bus and voices automatically lowered themselves almost to a whisper, as if the passengers of the bus didn't want to disturb the reverent dead from the past, or the future.

To David this camp reeked of death and misery, and he had only been inside it for five minutes. Near the end of their particular runway there was yet another turning into the forest and this road was going to be their road and, at the end of it stood two very large spacious bungalows, they were the sleeping dormitories for the entire troupe plus their practice rooms. Just across the way still hidden by trees was a large old flat roofed plane hanger which now showed that it needed a great deal of repair, it was quite obviously a left over from the Nazi's. It looked abandoned and most certainly it had seen far better days.

This was going to be the concert hall. This hanger had not been in use for the past twenty-five years, it belonged to the Hitler's war machine and had housed the experimental rocket planes that Germany had been experimenting with towards the end of the conflict. Had they tried with their investigations two or three years before, the allies wouldn't have stood a chance. Now it was a rather dilapidated structure that had known better days. The troupe on hearing of its former use had the collective thought that good old

Adolf would not have been at all pleased at the idea of an American band playing in his building.

The two low bungalow type buildings, which were going to be their accommodation areas turned out to have a very big surprise in store. It was two nuclear bunkers but joined into one complex. The bunker was somewhat designed after the same pattern as the airbase in England. Both entered one huge hole in the ground, this disappeared down at least ten floors. It came with the most up-to-date facilities and services that US money could buy.

The amount of Coca-cola vending machines that stood proud on every floor did to David sum up the entire American dream, making it more of a wet dream than anything superior to the rest of the world.

David started to sum up his thoughts concerning this particular American base, he was hugely disappointed, but not surprised. This was a race of people, highly prejudiced towards so many other races of people, yet they call the United States the great big melting pot. Truth be known, those melting pots were to do just that, melt down various races of people and while thinking these negative thoughts, much to his disappointment he noticed that there was always someone buying a drink or two from those cola machines, it just added fuel to his dissenting negativity.

There down in depths of cold war hell, all the areas buzzed with activity, the personnel that would have been expected on topside all worked below ground. To Cartier this was a place for moles and to the people had in fact now turned into those pointed nose mammals. They looked pale and drawn and young men looked well beyond their actual ages being on constant alert, waiting for the very moment that World

War Three was going to become reality and that sort of stress always takes its toll.

They were all taken down just three storeys to a huge dormitory where they would all bunk for the next week while entertaining on the base.

Stuart Holstein immediately called a meeting to order.

"Tonight, as you should know, if any of you have read your schedules, there is a small party going on for some of the officers and I want a small ensemble of just ten musicians to play chamber music. Its just a dinner so no real pressure, should be easy and pleasurable. So, I want just two first violins, one second, one viola, cello and bass, plus single flute, oboe, bassoon and clarinet. The rest of you, I want you to rehearse some of the standards with Charles Warner leading."

Holstein stiffened ever so slightly bringing to bear a more serious face.

"Though there were no complaints from anyone, I thought of the last show being that it was sloppy and tired, was something where we all could and should do better. Please remember that it may be all old hat to you, but to the people we are playing too, it must be nothing but your best efforts."

He sighed deeply, looked around to make sure he had their full attention then carried on,

"They need our help, and entertainment is important to them, for they have very difficult task that they have to perform, something that none of us would ever want to be involved in. So please don't forget at the end of the day these people pay all our salaries. Remember and keep always in the back of your mind, we perform for them, not ourselves."

He looked around again where they all were gathered, he still had their undivided attention.

"Now, there is enough space in here to manage a rehearsal so no excuses. Stow your gear in the lockers provided and keep your keys safe. I am told there is a certain amount of pilfering going on within this base, so keep your keys close to your hearts."

There was a moments silence while Stuart thought about the next sentence, then he concluded with,

"As you can see there are several vending machines on each floor, if you must drink, keep it to just root-beer or cola. Anyone caught intoxicated will be fined a day's money. Is that understood?"

There then came a small but distinct groan from some members of the troupe.

"Now there is also a well-equipped canteen, it's on the bottom floor. You can obtain food at any time of the day or night, but and please listen carefully, outside of proper dining times you will be charged. So, as we now have several hours to kill, there are television rooms and also a games area all of which you are entitled to use. Lunch can be from twelve until three, dinner from six until nine, eat early and give yourselves time, but don't be late. I want the rehearsal to start at seven thirty sharp and I reiterate, don't be late! The chamber ensemble must meet me topside at six thirty sharp. Now bugger off and annoy the locals. Charles if you will follow me I will give you the music I want you to rehearse!"

The rest of the day dragged slowly and as there was very little to entertain oneself with while being underground. Most of the men played games such as pool and darts or partook in various schools of poker, the rest watched I Love Lucy, which starred Lucile Ball, or Sergeant Bilko, with the indomitable Phil Silvers.

Though those television programmes were aging rapidly there was still something very funny about them and thus still good entertainment to be had by watching them. Of course there was the usual CNN news channels, spouting there propaganda everywhere, then there were always the military advice channels to view, these could be hilarious to the observer, as the advice given was usually the most biennial garbage that was ever likely to be screened.

To watch listen and learn from them, you really needed to be between the ages of two stroke four years of age to gleam any real knowledge of value. But between wiping the tears away from one's eyes, because of the dribbling which occurred after bouts of laughter either intentional or un-intentional there were moments of sheer and utter boredom. Possibly the best way to get through the waiting periods were to snooze, it could and often did spoil your nights rest, but it went to help pass the time quicker.

Six o'clock came, David had eaten and was changing once again into his dinner jacket. He didn't have a clue what the music was going to be, but the thought of sight-reading a concert certainly didn't faze him. At six-thirty sharp he was topside with his viola. The darkness was the first thing that struck him. No lights appeared anywhere, and it took a whole minute to accustom his eyes to the gloom of a cold, sleety December night and because there was so much cloud cover there were no stars to be seen.

The next thing that became obvious was the smell, there was a distinct odour of pine mixed with kerosene, but it was quite overpowering, nothing nice about that oppressive whiff.

In fact, once again the eyes came under attack, this time from the smell of the actual plane fuel. Out here he had hoped for clean fresh air but that was a delusion that he would very quickly be dispelled, this was the sort of aroma that he was going to experience from now on.

As he stood there waiting for the other members to arrive, the lights of the nearest runway went silently on, it gave a very eerie strange glow that surprised him, in fact it reminded him of the Blackpool illuminations for a brief minute, but then the noise came.

At first there was a high-pitched whine which was obviously being muffled by the surrounding trees, then that whine turned into a roar as a large jet plane landed on the runway. Even though he must have been at least a quarter of a mile away from the runway, the noise made his ears hurt and he had to cup them both with his hands. Then the plane had passed, and the lights went out, all of this took less than two minutes.

He turned around as he heard the sound of other people approaching. His ears were still hurting when Holstein spoke to them all.

"There should have been a coach here waiting for us, but I guess it will arrive in a moment or two. I want you all to enjoy this concert, it won't be heavy. I have some Haydn early symphonies; some Hummel chamber works and some Gershwin and Bernstein. The whole thing should be done and dusted within a two-hour period and our reward will be I believe, a feast that will be waiting for us all afterwards."

The evening went with a splash of splendour. The dinning room that they had to perform in was just big enough which meant that the acoustics were more than somewhat dead on the ears. This meant that each player had to listen very carefully so as to stay in tune, intonation was not swallowed up as when they played in large rooms or auditoriums giving some sort of echo. It is always the distant resound that helps intonation melt within itself.

David personally liked this sort of exercise, it was good for his ear training, and he was once again determined to play to his ultimate potential, not for the good of the ensemble but purely for the good of his future playing abilities.

Young David Cartier had now long acquired ambition, he knew that if he progressed the way he was doing at this time, within four years, after finishing the Royal College of Music he would be good enough to get a good position in a major London Orchestra and that's what he now wanted. He was determined to show his family that he was indeed a success and not the total failure that his father and mother had always predicted.

To that end he worked hard when he played, his feelings were, take what you can from this experience, but not to forget to get as much money too from the playing of ones instrument.

They played Haydn Symphony number twenty-eight, this worked well with a small group as they were. Then came a medley of Strauss dance arrangements, followed by a string quartet by Hummel, after that some Gershwin arrangements. The evening ended with a rousing chorus of the Stars and Stripes and then sadly for David, who had enjoyed the experience very much, it was all over.

The audience was made up of forty officers of various ranks, no wives or sweethearts, just men. All the musicians could see that their efforts were indeed being appreciated as the entire assembled men just loved the whole ambiance of the occasion, even though none of them were particularly music lovers, but they did appreciate the standard that was showing itself to them.

Eating well, drinking good wines and aperitifs, smoking their cigars and cigarettes, all went to make a very special night for every officer there. It seemed strange to David, watching these American officers seemed to copy all the same sort of rigmarole that their English counterpart did. He felt as if he was actually watching a bunch of toffee-nosed Hooray Henry Chelsea types, the sort who's great-grandfather fought alongside Wellington at Waterloo. The only difference was there was no toasting to the Queen only the President. But the port was still passed to the port side and this little throwback to a once colonial past really made him smile.

But the evening was rounded off nicely for all the musicians with a sumptuous meal, a repast that will stay in the memory for a very long time.

The week was a great success, they played several concerts for the entire base and all the serving men enjoyed these home-grown musicians who could turn the hands to anything that might be requested. There were also two more private dinners one of which included a special evening for just ten officers of quite high rank. All these men were in their late forties or fifties, and they had personally commissioned a small jazz band to play at a dinner for a Lieutenant Colonel Summers. This entailed a great deal of organisation from the base and part way through the evening a huge cake was brought in and as the music reached its crescendo much to the excitement of all attending, including the musicians, out sprang a young girl, she was of course completely naked. Once let loose, she then proceeded to prance around trying hard to dance in the most provocative way. Her role was to titillate, and her technique didn't go amiss to the men assembled or come to that the musicians.

She was the entertainment, and the young girl had absolutely no qualms about doing things that would not have necessarily make her mother proud. But the officers loved it all and by the time the evening was over the poor unfortunate lady had been passed from officer to officer, each practicing their own special moves with her.

During the days while awaiting the nights work, all the musicians became bored. There was no chance of leaving the base to visit towns, there were so many restrictions as to where one could wonder around the confined areas. Very fierce guard dogs patrolled all the perimeter fencing, all trained to kill if intruders crossed into the US territory. The entire base was one huge top-secret establishment which the whole world knew about. But it was a fact that the military who worked there really didn't know what the left side was doing, if they happened to work on the right.

Soldiers or airmen knew better than to talk about anything or to anyone, which also meant musicians too. So outside of concerts there was no fraternization between the grunts and the entertainers.

Bored musicians have a tendency to gamble and gambling can often lead to angry confrontations and fighting. This happened on the last night at the camp. The concert had been organized as a dance, a chance for the military to say goodbye to the musicians and visa-versa. The problem started but the simple expedient of poor attendance less than one hundred soldiers and airmen turned out. The reasoning was really very simple, there were no women to talk about. The entire establishment employed fewer than fifty women and most of those were married to other base workers. That meant that there were actually more than twenty men to any one woman. That constituted to a very unhealthy environment for harmony, especially at a dance.

To be fair to the few un-attached women, they tried very hard to even the score and make every man feel that at one time or another there was a girl for him.

Those sassy girls were very quick to spread their loving feelings to as many men as possible, this spreading applied to their legs too. That was a proven fact and because of that simple truth there were many posters and condom machines for the use of contraception dotted all over the base and the reason these machines and notices were everywhere, was because of the great amount of infidelity that went on between the unattached women and the men that were there.

It was very depressing for forty musicians to play in that cavernous old hanger to just less than double their own number. So, in his infinite wisdom Stuart Holstein did a roster for the players so that some could have a break and either join in the fun, or at the very least have some drinks, maybe even two.

It was just before ten o'clock when the two saxophonists were told to take thirty-minute break. Bret Jansen and his pal Anthony Glenchurch went out to mingle with the few soldiers that were there. As none of the soldiers were in a very communicatory mood the two musicians decided that a dance was probably the next best thing. They approached two youngish ladies both standing by one of the walls drinking, they asked for a dance which was gratefully accepted.

The four of them hadn't been out on the floor more than one minute when three airmen came up and tried to muscle in. This didn't go down at all well with either of the two men or their new found dancing partners. It was inevitable that when Bret Jansen told one of the airmen were to go and what to do when he got there, that fists would soon be flying instead of nuclear bombers.

Bret swung a lively right arm towards the nearest airman who easily sidestepped then swung back. He didn't miss and Bret fell to the ground with blood pouring from what turned out to be a nasty broken nose. Anthony was much stronger and just as easily upset so he got hold of the nearest soldier to him and brought his knee up straight into the groin of that person. The poor soldier gasped as pain traversed from his testicles right up into his brain and he fell to the ground holding himself in a very peculiar place and way.

Anthony then swung at the other two clipping them both. If it had ended there, there might not have been too much trouble, but at that point some of the other soldiers and airmen thought that as there were no Ruskies to kick arse with, then crippling some crappy musicians was the next best thing.

Anthony was immediately overpowered and set upon. Within the space of twenty seconds there were five wounded men on the dance floor, had it ended there, things might still have been overcome.

The entire brass and woodwind players put down their instruments and leapt out onto the dancing area to do battle with the new found enemy. Soon all the musicians save for David Cartier and Stuart Holstein were tangling in the melee. Fists flew, arms swung, feet kicked and teeth bit. Still, it might have been forgotten had it ended there.

Holstein in a fit of panic, rushed over to the hanger door where and emergency alarm was. **Only to be hit in the case of an imminent invasion**. Taking off his shoe he smashed the glass and hit the panic button. Sirens rang, all lights went off and emergency red lights took their place. Within the space of thirty seconds the whole nuclear base was in a state of extreme readiness, was it true that the Russians were finally coming?

There had been a great deal of explaining to do, poor Stuart Holstein thought he was going to be placed against a wall and shot as a provocateur. It was only when the military police got involved that things started to come together and not necessarily in a good way. The three original airmen were arrested and were expected to be sent home in disgrace. Anthony and Bret were hospitalized, but off base in Hamburg, had they stayed within the perimeter of the camp the commander could not vouch for their safety. Holstein fined all members except Cartier one week's wages, then threatened anyone else who was to ever get involved in a fight, that he would be instantly sent home and fired from the entertainments corps. This was a threat to be taken very seriously, for being dismissed meant almost certainly the immediate possibility of being sent to Vietnam as a grunt.

That night while waiting for the morning and transfer to Mannheim that once again the gambling started, one trumpet player lost a packet over which person would appear through the door first and so what with the week's wages being withdrawn and now losing fifty dollars on the fact that it was a mere private instead of a Sergeant that appeared first through a stupid bloody door, enough was indeed enough.

That was why two more fist fights occurred and Stuart hung his head in his hands. 'Oh Lord, please get us to Mannheim in one piece!' Then without a moment hesitation he called out at the top of his voice.

"The bloody bus leaves at ten o'clock in the morning, anybody that is not waiting topside ready to board will be fined another week's wages. I suggest gentlemen that you all bloody well piss off to bed and try and sleep off the remaining couple of hours in peace and tranquility and woe betides anyone that is not peace loving and friendly to his colleagues from now on, don't bet on my peace-loving ways, you will lose your money."

Within the next two minutes there was once again peace and silence and harmony, friends were friends once again.

The camp at Mannheim was a complete contrast to Hamburg, it comprised of being a huge tank and armored weapons storage area plus a gigantic fuel dump. Also, it was a radio communications centre for the whole of Germany and of course everyone knew these simple truths. It was close enough to the firing line to hear all the messages being passed to and from the Russian side of the wire, but far enough away as not to be too obtrusive.

Supposedly another secret establishment which the entire world knew about.

This time the whole base was secreted within a large oak wood which also backed into an old Roman quarry. The perimeter fencing was nearly twenty feet high with rolls of barbed wire on both sides of the corrugated fence, also on the top. There were very open machine gun posts every one hundred yards surrounding the entire camp and these were manned twenty-four seven by extremely tough looking guards who would always shoot first before asking relevant questions.

Though in theory the camp was not supposed to be seen from the autobahn it was obvious to anyone with half a brain, as the main entrance bordered the south side with a huge sign saying in English and German, *Welcome to Mannheim, safer by the grace of the US Army Tank Corps.*

Tanks came and went twenty-four hours a day three hundred and sixty-five days a year. A very busy little place with everyone being kept on their proverbial toes once again because they were expecting that fatal bell to be tolled at any time.

The first thing that David and the other members noticed was just how many civilians seemed to be on this particular base. The entire place was buzzing with what appeared to be a German workforce, there were girls standing around chatting and laughing, men scurrying to and from here there and everywhere.

As the bus pulled into the camp the contrast between this establishment and Hamburg, showed Mannheim to stand out like Sodom and Gomorra with its obvious decadence thus creating damnation. This was the place that was going to turn all of them into Lott's pillows of salt, compared to the chaste Jerusalem that was Hamburg.

It was extraordinary how much difference there was between the perimeter guards and the rest of the establishment. Even the guards on the gates were relaxed with their rifle slung casually over their shoulders, one was even surreptitiously smoking which one felt if in Hamburg would have been a shooting offence. He was the one that briefly checking the coach driver's dockets with a casual glance, he didn't bother to completely enter into the actual coach and check everyone's credentials. He laughed and joked in a private way to the driver and then pointed down the way somewhat.

This was his instructions,

"Driver, take these good old folks down the main driveway avoiding the tank movement, if possible, er, tanks tend to come off best in a confrontation. You'll see the billeting areas roughly half a mile down on the right-hand side. You'll have a nice day now." He looked around smiling at everybody and then stubbed his cigarette on the busses floor and left.

The driver was laughing silently to himself as he drove off in the right general direction. Tanks were everywhere, there must have been a couple of hundred of the iron beasts and it didn't go un-noticed how sparklingly clean they all looked, there was absolutely no mud to be seen between the tracks everything shone. It was once again obvious to any onlooker that these tanks were new and virtually un-used, they certainly had never been driven off the roads over mud and slush yet, which is where one would expect tanks to scurry. But the maintenance crews were bobbing from one to another trying out this or that, or maybe just trying to impress any officers that might be looking on.

Then some of them started up, the noise was awful as was the cloud of black sooty smoke that exuded from their exhausts. The most amazing aspect of all the bizarre events that seemed to be unfolding around them was the array of different armory that was on display for practically everyone to see. There were two or three dozen beautifully kept M41 Walker Bulldog Tanks, M47 Medium Tanks, M103 Heavy, M48 Medium Tanks, M42 Self-propelled anti-aircraft Guns, M44 Self-propelled Howitzers. There were also many M113 Armoured Personnel Carriers, all bristling in bright wood green colour, several M60 Main Battle Tanks, with their one-hundred-and-twenty-millimeter armour piercing shells, this was an awesome very dangerous weapon. And lastly, standing proudly in the dull December sunlight were two M50 Ontos Tank Destroyers and one of them had six one hundred- and six-millimeter recoilless rifles mounted on the top.

It was an awesome display for all the musicians to view as they sped down the roadway. They reached the billeting area and were very pleased to note that everything was above ground, there were several dozen long billet huts all just one storey, behind them were the canteens and hospital facilities. Far behind them were the huge underground dugouts that stored the shells and bullets. Even further behind those main armoury bunkers were the many huge underground fuel tanks and they stretched way back into the old quarry with pipe ways leading off to their own loading and refueling places and these were far from prying eyes.

When David looked the other way across the roadway leading in the opposite direction, he noticed various playing fields and parade grounds, there too were the offices and officers' quarters. And standing above everything was the only building to be more than the one storey, it was what turned out to be the entertainments area, the very place they would have to work the next day.

When they had said goodbye to the bus and driver and had unpacked their various item of clothing, mainly evening wear which needed to be hung up to look good when being used.

While the men were preparing their attire for the next day, there appeared at their billet door one huge muscular sergeant, he was at least six foot four inches in his socks. What blond hair he once had, was cropped so close that he really gave the impression of being totally bald, his mouth was slightly curled and he showed several teeth through this grimace, the rest he had lost in various conflicts. His chest stuck out showing a very muscular torso, nobody had really seen him enter let alone become aware of his singularly perturbed attitude of what he was eyeballing. He stood there surveying in great disdain this collection of unruly undisciplined musicians, even though most of the troupe were in fact connected to the military, not many came under the same sort of discipline as normal soldiers, airmen or sailors.

It seemed to this particular sergeant that entertainers came with a set of laws that only applied to them, that was virtually none. Sergeant Robert Norris was what was known in the US as the TOPS, being probably the one man that rules the entire establishment, but sometimes allowing the Colonel to believe that he was in fact in charge.

"I am Tops Sergeant Norris and while you are on my base you come under my military law. I have just read a report that while in Hamburg some of you were in fact involved in a scuffle."

He almost snarled the next sentence,

"That under no circumstances ladies,"

Again, a glare from his eyes, a deep breath and continues,

"Will happen here."

He paused so as his words could sink in, his scowl had worsened. "Two of your units are in a hospital and I have been led to understand that they will not make it here today but will arrive tomorrow in time for the concert. The concert or concerts are being divided into two sections. The first is..."

"Just a minute Sergeant."

Stuart Holstein interjected quickly before the Tops could say any more.

"We come under our own jurisdictions not yours. If any of my men cause problems, you may indeed deal with it in so far as murder or thieving may be concerned, any minor misdemeanors I will deal with and usually where it hurts most, in their pockets."

Holstein was not exactly seething, but he was very annoyed at this overbearing welcome.

"This is no sort of welcome! We have come a long way to entertain you, we are not here for trouble, so forget what you heard in Hamburg this is a new day and a new camp for us. Anyway, for the record I out rank you as I am a Major in this man's army. For your personal information I just choose not to wear a uniform or come the old soldier. And lastly, not all the men here are military, why we even have a Limey with us and there is nothing that you or I can do about him, so maybe you would like to go out, come back in and start again?"

Tops Sergeant Norris looked like a raging bull about ready to stampede through the billet and maybe trample a few bodies on the way.

"I, er, sorry sir. I didn't know that you were an officer. I guess I was a little hasty at that."

He started to turn from crimson to a shade of pink as he visibly calmed himself down.

"Yes, er, welcome to fort Clements here outside of Mannheim. I do hope your stay will be a pleasant one and I am sure the, er, two concerts will be great successes."

It was truly amazing how quickly he had changed from a domineering oaf to the friendly good old Sergeant that everyone wanted to see and hear.

"Now, there is a canteen open for you I am sure you are all very hungry after your long tedious journey, so please feel free."

As each moment passed Tops visibly relaxed, he then concluded with,

"I must warn you about one or two things though, I wouldn't be doing my duty if I didn't. Please do not fraternize with the locals that work on base. God knows why we have so many civilians working for the military as we are hardly short of soldiers to do anything that may be needed. But Colonel Masterson believes in employing local civilians, he says it creates a good relationship between the conquerors and the vanquished. Though for the life of me I don't know which one of us is which!"

This caused a small ripple of laughter amongst the men.

"The second thing is please don't get in the way of any work that is going on with the vehicles. These machines are extremely dangerous, and things can and do go wrong, so please stay clear of any of my armour. Lastly, beyond that perimeter is the armoury and fuel bunkers, these areas are completely out of bounds. I must emphasise that there are armed guards patrolling all the time and there orders are to shoot first then ask questions later."

This sentence was said with a smile.

"Gentlemen, once again sorry for my initial outburst and welcome to our little home from home. Enjoy your meal and enjoy your stay."

He then stood to attention and saluted Holstein and then turned on his heels and was gone.

"Bloody hell, I didn't know you were a bloody officer?"

Said Steven Higgins, who was a very fine cellist and guitarist. Holstein looked at him and winked.

"Well, there you go then! So, you don't know everything about me, do you? I'm going for a meal, anyone coming?"

That night after the meal had been consumed and just as quickly forgotten about, some of the musicians decided to go over to where the concert was going to happen, they had been told that there was a pool table that they just might be lucky enough to get a game on it.

David Atkins was the bass trombone and bass saxophonist within the group, he was a very fine player and had he not been called up to do his national service he would now be playing with one of the major orchestras within the United States, everybody liked him, he was without a doubt the clown and the funniest musician but he also inspired the other players around him to perform at their best. But more important to him and his fellow conspirators, he was also something of a real dynamo on the pool or snooker table.

Four of them accompanied Atkins, mainly because they knew of his reputation for playing pool. There was one soldier playing already but as the five musicians gathered around, he was persuaded to give David a game, just you understand for a bottle of beer. David wiped the floor with the young man and got his free beer.

While all of them were talking and drinking another soldier came up and having seen Atkins play challenged him to a serious game, er, twenty dollars serious. By the time it was agreed, and money had been handed to a second, at least forty other soldiers gathered around sensing some serious competition was about to happen. It was agreed that it would be the best of three games.

David broke to start. The soldier, who was known as Corporal Bryant managed to clean the board on the first game, he was good. The next game was much closer with Atkins just winning, by the time the decider happened there was a great deal of money floating across the table as bets were being placed by most of the crowd of now nearly one hundred soldiers. There must have been the best part of one thousand dollars being played for and both men were feeling very vulnerable and didn't want to lose their friends money.

Several mistakes took place by both players but finally the game was won by David Atkins. He got his twenty dollars but was astounded to see the actual amounts that had been gambled by the others. The Corporal was a fair-minded man and allowed David to take the praise without showing any reproachful feelings. In fact, he admired David and the way he played so he bought a round of drinks for all five of the musicians.

And after the fracas that had happened the night before there were indeed one or two sighs of relief.

Back in the billet Stuart Holstein was now giving out instructions as to the two concerts that were going to occur. One would be a quartet of two violins, viola and cello, this was for a special supper that was only for several very important guests of the Colonel in Chief, no more than ten diners in total. The music was nothing serious, again just some light music from various shows on Broadway and then some Waltzes and Polkas of the Strauss family, it was only going to last an hour, so it was an easy night for the four string players of which David Cartier was yet again the viola player.

The other concert was a proper variety show, lots of various variety acts were coming to the camp and it was the band that had to accompany everything, no matter what the performers were going to do. The person responsible for coordinating everything was Stuart himself. But then he loved to stand in front of an audience and hear his own voice. The musicians might not be enamored with Holstein as a compeer, but he was something of a raconteur, or so he thought. He loved nothing more than telling jokes, all of which he was generally the only one who thought they were funny, but his shoulders were broad, nothing would upset his arrogance when it came to believing in his own ability to be a comic.

Whenever there was a chance of standing in front of the audience, he was there like a shot, these were always going to be his moments of glory, they were his public and his alone. But he was popular and liked by his troupe, so nobody really minded, they all understood and accepted that every man has his dreams, standing in the limelight was Stuarts. He felt smug about his role within the ensemble of gifted musicians, but he knew he was appreciated by all his boys he just didn't understand why they didn't like his jokes.

But at the meeting he had decided he wasn't going to name all the band yet as he wanted to know what was happening to Bret and Anthony first whom he hoped they both would be in a fit state to play.

The variety concert went fine, one could hear the cheering all over the camp. The dinner for the officers was not so good, it had a problem that comes back to haunt the musicians, something that does occur on a very regular basis all over the world.

The evening started well enough with canapés and drinks being served to the guests, but one friendly and slightly drunk Captain decided that it would be a nice gesture to give the quartet and bottle of champagne, in fact before half an hour had passed, he had given them three more.

David had never been a serious drinker and had only drunk bubbly a few times, but he definitely had the taste for it but unfortunately it went straight to his head. The first violinist one Simon Ward never drank as he was a reformed alcoholic. That was he had never drunk anything alcoholic on tour before, until that particular night.

Sadly, he allowed himself to be teased by the captain to just take a little sip, at first he refused profusely, but the frustration of one being teased, two being there watching his friends enjoying the drink, it soon became too much for his body and soul to take. And as the Captain was if nothing persistent, so after a while it became, well maybe one small sip just to be sociable, then two more sips, as it was obviously okay to indulge a little, then the entire bottle disappeared, and all this happened inside of three minutes.

It was Stuart Holstein that realised what was happening, he knew of Simon Ward's affliction with alcohol and when he realised the amount that had been consumed and how quickly he knew immediately that only trouble could ensue.

"Simon put that bottle down! Who was stupid enough to allow him to drink? You are supposed to keep an eye on one another. David, for Jesus' sake, how much have you been drinking too?"

David was indeed feeling a little merry, but not so much as not to be able to play. But it was Stuart's remark that made him look towards Simon. Ward had a distinctly glazed look in his eyes, he leaned forward ever so slightly, but just about enough to make the other three think he was going to fall over into the music stand. Someone had to do something and quick. David took the bull by the horn.

"Right! Let's play the Blue Danube!"

The music was quickly placed onto the music stands.

"Right, in three…"

David, Joseph Skabinski second violin and Charles Lambest, all started with the waltz by Strauss, sadly

Simon decided that he would play the Washington Post.

Three musicians played in three four time and one very noisy violin playing in two four, fast, furious and loud. Within four bars, the entire entourage of guests had stopped whatever they were doing and looked towards the band in open horror.

The noise was awful, but to the four musicians it soon became incredibly funny. The first to stop was Cartier as tears streamed down his cheeks, he could no longer play. Instead of playing David was almost peeing in his pants, he was bent forward and crouched in an almost fetal position having hysterics. Next was Charles Lambest, at first in amazement with the mess that was indeed coming to bear, but then he too lost complete control and burst out laughing, this laughter finished off Skabinski who had tried hard to bring some sort of semblance of respectability to the proceedings, but now failed miserably.

He also started to laugh at first behind his violin and then as the tears flew down his face, he lost any sense of propriety and gave in to mirth.

All the time this went on Simon Ward carried on playing the violin part to the Washington Post, it got louder and noisier then more out of tune, poor Simon was competing with laughter and a general distraction from what he was meant to be playing, then he very gradually started to lean forward, still playing. At this point Holstein came to the rescue, he gently took the bow from his hand and then the violin. That was the only cue needed for Simon to fall into his music stand and then lay prone on the floor with the music stand lying gently by his side.

All the time this was happening the audience were looking on in total silence and abject horror, but with the laughter coming from the other three players and the way that Stuart rescued the violin everyone thought this was pure pantomime. Then as Simon hit the floor there was a tremendous round of applause along with whistling and cheering, this sadly made the other three laugh even louder.

The evening had finished hardly before it had started, but none of the guests seemed to mind very much they just carried on drinking eating and enjoying themselves.

"David I can't say that I am pleased with you about yesterday. I look to you as a guiding light in a dark forest of depravity, you Brits are supposed to be more educated and civilized than us, your cheap white cousins."

"Oh, come on! Stop all this flattering bull shit."

Chuckled David but knowing what was going to come next. But before the tirade it would be better to get his two pence worth. "Stuart I cannot be held responsible for what occurred last night, and I really didn't know that Simon had an alcohol problem and before you ball me out for getting tipsy myself, remember that it was that bloody officer that forced the bottles on all of us. There was no way that he was going to take no for an answer, so we all drank some of the Champaign."

He smiled broadly and then continued,

"I tell you what though, it was bloody good stuff. But like I have already said, don't hold me responsible for the way Simon behaved."

Then once again smiling broadly, he concluded,

"Mark you, it was hilariously funny."

"Well, maybe I can say a word or two now? I was sad to see Simon fall so easily back into bad old habits, but he is his own boss, I shall just fine him and make sure that he is kept well away from booze again.

No, it wasn't your drinking or the fact that you showed your lack of knowing when you have had enough. No, it was the way that you decided to take charge and suggest a piece of music to play, that is not your job, that is mine and if you had really been on the ball you would have noticed that the Washington Post was indeed the next piece to have been played. That and your immediate fit of giggles is going to cost you a day's pay. Understood? Okay?"

"Stuart, I don't know really what to say in my defense. I thought I was doing the right thing, but I guess you are right. A day's pay you say…mmm!"

They then looked at one another and smiled and then the smile turned into a broad grin followed by both laughing out loud and then shaking hands.

"Oh, go on then! Piss off, but please keep playing well, don't get cynical like the rest of them, or come to that me! I was sort of serious about looking to you as a guiding light, you are the youngest by far here, yet you are a very fine musician, what is more you are also untainted by years of playing badly and without the real appreciation of the audience. I really hoped that bringing you along would raise the moral and interest within the entire band."

Once again that extended grin came,

"So, my young Limey friend, there you are absolutely no pressure."

Neither Bret nor Anthony, the two missing musicians came back, at least not that next day. But they did appear a week later in Berlin smiling and unabashed and both still sporting two black eyes.

The next day they left Mannheim but not before one more small problem occurred, though it was not directly involving any of the entertainers.

They had all congregated at the canteen, some were still finishing their breakfasts others just drinking coffee, but all the talk was about poor old Simon and the debacle that had ended a very eventful evening at the officer's dinner.

Stuart came running into the building and started shouting out very loud,

"Quick move everyone. Some maniac has grabbed a tank and there is hell to pay going on outside. I suggest that we try and make it back to the barracks, because as far as I am aware the bloody thing is heading this way."

At that moment there came several cracks as small arm fire went off. Then a proper rat-tat-tat as a machine gun erupted. Everyone in the canteen started to run in different directions, it was something straight out of the keystone cop's routine.

But then the whole building shook, windows broke and fell in, light bulbs shattered and fell along with their fittings. Then one long heave as the entire building started to look as if it was coming down, but instead, the wall on the left-hand side of the main door cracked and started to collapse and to everyone's horror and amazement in came a M48 medium tank smashing its way through walls, windows then furniture. Its weight made it go through the floorboards, crunching and grinding as it went. Wood splinters were flying everywhere, and many people were in danger of being impaled by large sharp pieces of floor boarding which the said tank was now churning up badly.

By the time it was in the centre of the canteen nearly everyone had managed to get out, either through the main door or jumping out of the side windows. Bullets were flying everywhere, but all coming from soldiers and aimed at the tank.

It was soon obvious that the intruder was a German youth who had conned his way onto the base and found the tank ready for use, with a full tank of diesel and a full turret of shells and bullets. As the vehicle had actually stopped it quickly became apparent that the young man was indeed intent of causing more than a minor problem.

He had now shifted his bulk from the driving position into the turret for the firing position. The people that were still within the canteen threw themselves down onto the floor, or what was left of it. At the furthest corner of the building one table with four chairs still stood erect, there sitting drinking his coffee was one very tired looking violinist, Simon Ward. It was obvious that he was indeed sporting one huge hangover, and he looked awful.

He brushed off the dust that was starting to settle on him, picking up his coffee cup he got to his feet and then deliberately ambled in the direction of the M48. 'How could anything be so bloody noisy; how dare they make such a racket when I feel so shit awful?'

As he walked over, he tried to take a sip of his drink, but only managed to spill most of it over himself, this made him even madder.

As he strolled over, the turret on the tank moved in his direction. Was the young fool going to blow Simon away with a huge shell, would he even know how to fire it? But the turret still followed Simon.

"Get down you bloody fool, he will blow you to pieces, get down!"

Whomever shouted certainly wasn't inside the building. But the small arms firing was still going on and bullets were flying everywhere, all around Simon and all over the tank, bits of metal were ricocheting all around the place. The turret still followed methodically until Ward went directly underneath it. He carefully and gently placed his cup of coffee down on the metal of the lumbering beast and then delicately climbed on top, he walked up to the turret hatch and pulled it open. Still bullets were bouncing off the sides of the tank, going through the walls of the building, smashing into the ceiling and breaking anything they happened to touch.

Simon was good and angry, his head ached, and his muscles strained, but he was intent on one last deed. He thrust his arm inside and then after a second, in which there was one almighty struggle he dragged out a young man who in turn was now screaming in abject terror.

The firing now had finally stopped and several heavily armed soldiers were once again entering what was left of the canteen. They grabbed the young man and pulled him and Simon Ward off the M48.

It was then the cheering started.

Simon looked around, the first thing that came to his mind was the green colour of the tank matched the green colour of what was left of the wallpaper, he looked to where his cup was, went over and picked it up, putting it to his lips he was disappointed and taken aback at how cold the coffee had become, he looked down into the cup and looked at the swirl of brown liquid with dust that was settling upon its surface, he then looked up to see a similar brown ceiling at least the parts that didn't have burns from bullet holes. Casually putting the cup down once again on top of the front of the lumbering giant metal M48, he turned and then as if for the first time noticed that there were now in the region of fifty to seventy soldiers all looking at him in a very bewildered way, smiling he looked at the ceiling and then at the floor as it rushed up to meet him.

There he lay, dust, sweat and heroism all clinging to his now very dirty grey suit, with his white shirt and flashy highly coloured Mickey Mouse tie that was lying across his chest in a half-undone fashion. He was indeed finally finished, tired of life and yet scared of death. He lay there in the dust, wood fragments and ceiling plaster, waiting for either the doctors or angels to come and rescue him, instead he was picked up by half a dozen soldiers and lifted out of the building to a hero's welcome, or was it sayonara.

Simon Ward spent the rest of that day sound asleep on the bus that now was taking the troupe to Nuremburg.

It was later estimated that more than two thousand rounds of light ammunition and three heavy caliber machine gun shells were fired at the M48 medium tank, yet amazingly no one was hurt, not a single scratch.

As for the seventeen-year-old German master terrorist, he was taken a hospital for a psychological examination, declared to be suffering from a form of schizophrenia and transferred to a mental institute for further study, then after just six months he was released with no charges being preferred. The hierarchy in their collective wisdom thought it prudent to keep the matter as quiet as possible, but to make sure this didn't occur again, the security of the base was immediately updated, with a new TOPS Sergeant being put in charge.

The road to Nuremburg was straight and cleaned of snow, though there was very little traffic the going was slow as ice was everywhere. Most of the troupe were sleeping their journey away, enjoying the chance to either sober up or just rest tired weary eyes having been tested from the previous night's merriment. The entertainment that the alternative musicians had played in had been a roaring success, probably because they had been left to their own devises, giving the drummer one Charley Stannery, a chance to shine as a compeer, thus allowing gags and japes to happen that were enjoyed by the audience as well as the musicians, after all, the troupe hadn't heard them before.

The only person who was enjoying the scenic beauty of the countryside was Cartier, he had his nose well and truly pinned to the window and was watching the various contours of the landscape unfold themselves before his very eyes. He had to keep wiping the window with the sleeve of his jacket as his breath steamed up the view every few seconds, but the action had its value as it kept him awake.

As all the roads that they drove on were autobahns the coach hardly ventured into any towns, but as the light faded in the late afternoon another small flurry of snow started to drop from clouds that could hardly be seen in the fading light, but it twirled and drifted through that scenic pastureland like a picture postcard of a Christmas Panorama. Then amongst that swirling fluff of white there were twinkles of fairy lights revealed themselves, showing the location of small towns and hamlets within the hills and valleys. For a while that backdrop played out a small melodrama within his mind, as he tried to remember what it was like to have a happy Christmas festival with his family, but nothing really came to mind only stories that he had heard from some of his friends. But then he thought of Megan, wondering how was she and their baby doing? Would he ever get to see the child? Did he even want to see the child? He shuddered slightly and quickly went back to wiping the window clean.

David was not slow to imagine the tanks and vehicles of Hitler's army rolling down these roads, he could almost hear the roar of their engines, smell the burnt diesel, see the black escaping exhaust and see the flashes as the guns sent their wares across this beautiful panoramic spectacular picture postcard that was Germany.

As they crossed over from the rolling flattish countryside to the grander views of large hills, with their woods and then forests, there in his mind's eye were the gun positions, the machine gun nests. There at the back of that forest in his thoughts he saw the landing field of part of Goring's Luftwaffe, with its Messerschmitt and Junkers all waiting for the order to go forth and attack, they were awaiting an order that was now twenty years too late.

As the coach got closer to Nuremburg the snow got deeper and now the vehicle had to drive extremely slowly, but the lights of the town lit the night sky in such a way that the entire terrain was bright white and sparkling, a fairyland of past hatred now trying hard to be forgotten by the allies and their past enemies alike.

As the bus got within a short distance of the camp, they passed by the famous arena that Hitler had held his rallies. David could almost hear the incredible rhetoric that the German leader spouted, hypnotizing with his mesmeric way of speaking.

The Nazi parties flag waving approach to the crowd, inducing a seductive collective hysteria, the incredible display of touch light parades along with the marching goose stepping feet, all went to work his followers into a frenzy so fierce that while he strutted on that dais with his head held high and his arms beating at his own chest, he could have demanded the people be made to eat the person next to themselves and to do so would have seemed perfectly normal. His power of speech and his use of words, all stirred up with pseudoscience invoking racial hatred and that was entirely mixed into the demonic approach that the

Nazi party had towards the Jewish faith and its people. This just went to show how easy it was to seduce a populace, anyone that stood there would have almost certainly been immediately allured by the Fascist ideals, even though in the deepest recesses of their souls they must have known that they were just lambs being led to the slaughter.

Thus, the strength of a great orator.

David Cartier was no idiot, he understood how history has always shown that a clever orator can and does start wars, just as easy as the self-same speaker can win those self-same wars too. The mass is so easily seduced by a fine discourser of words and history has time and time again shown that a few clever men who were great at oration seemed to always to get most people to do their bidding. David felt the chill of that particular devil run up and down his back, he realised that this was indeed Nazi territory, and he was in the middle of it.

The camp was a rather dreary place and after such a long tedious journey all the weary travelers wanted were hot drinks and warm beds, anything else can await the morrow.

The concept of the establishment was twofold, firstly Nuremburg was one of the centres of the Nazi party, so it was important that America was being seen to keep any possible resurgence of fascism well and truly under the Yankee heavy marching boots. People didn't become Nazi party members just to drop their personal beliefs just because they lost the conflict that had incurred. Underground membership to the illegal party of National Socialism was still running rampantly straight and true and in fact to their now deceased leaders' ideals, his tenets were still part of the Germanic psyche and it was going to take a long time and patients to change views and creeds ingrained deep within each Aryan citizen.

The second reason for the base being where it is was, was even simpler to define. Nuremburg is not so very far from one of the worst of the eastern bloc countries, in so far as their oppressive regimes went. Czechoslovakia was considered by the free west to be one of the major threats to world peace, mainly because of its alignment to Russia and the oppressive ways that the government had with its own people, plus the simple expedient of keeping rife the hatred that the Czech folk had towards Germany and its people, mainly because of the invasion by the Nazi's which took the world once again into war.

American presences had to be considerable, they were there to hold back the Russian hoards as they swept across from the east taking the west to its doom. All along the Czechoslovakian border were many US bases all armed to the teeth and waiting for that special day when they could once again fire their guns in anger. This all meant that the camp in Nuremburg was basically the headquarters for all the outlying camps facing the Czech tanks. It was the staging post that would inform the free world that death was once again coming on four white chargers.

It was a dismal place, but that exterior was kept that way to fool all simple-minded communists that really there was no importance to this American base. Never mind all the electronic surveillance equipment with the aerials and radar all pointing towards the east.

The perimeter fencing was almost twenty feet high with barbed wire topping the steel and wire barrier, it ran in a very large semicircle for nearly one mile, with watch towers that were manned with soldiers all armed with heavy caliber machine guns and each of these watch towers were positioned every two hundred yards. Mines strong enough to blow up any advancing tank were situated in very obvious positions, but those mines were placed along the track ways where those tanks would almost certainly be coming from. All this firepower was to protect the facilities that were held within the compound, roughly one thousand people worked on the base, most being involved with spying on the cold enemy at least one way or another. All buildings had the words, *Access only to those personnel that work within, identity cards must be shown at all times.*

And many buildings had guards posted outside all armed with sub-machine guns and side arms and this meant to any young fool that whatever was inside was indeed top secret.

There was only the one theatre and that was next to the canteen which was huge by food serving standards.

The troupe ate their breakfast greedily, enjoying the rashers of bacon along with French toast and maple syrup. The chattering that went on was extremely noisy so much so that Stuart had to bang two plates together to attract attention.

Both the plates broke.

"Quiet, quiet please!"

Gradually the noise abated to the degree that Stuart could hear himself speak and think, even if no one else could.

"As by now you have all read and digested your schedules, you will know we are here for the week. I know none of you ever look at your schedules or read the notice board, so I feel I must tell you like a teacher talking to small children. Somehow, I must drum in the facts into more than empty heads."

As he said this sentence his own head shook from side to side, he was indeed talking to little tots.

"We have three performances to deliver, three good, no, great performances."

Stuart paused, looked at his charges than smiled inwardly and carried on speaking as if to small children,

"I don't want any debacles like Mannheim ever again."

He looked crestfallen as he thought about the tragic events that occurred.

"I know Mr. Ward was almost forced to drink the Champagne, but it must not happen again. Understood?"

He waited to see if there was any reaction, none came, just the sound of men scratching their plates with knives and forks as they consumed their early morning meals.

"There is scheduled a rehearsal for tonight in the theatre at seven o'clock sharp and to those of you who are blind as well as stupid the theatre is just next door."

That caused a small ripple of laughter.

"Then tomorrow will be our first show and then the second two days later and the last two days after that. The program might alter from show to show, but that will only happen if some requests are being bantered around either by the audience or just for fun by any of you. So, your wondrous ideas just might be approved, who knows? I have been told that all three shows are a complete sell out, so my guess is that the officialdom is bussing in troops and such, from the outlying camps. Actually, speaking entirely for myself, I think these shows are going to be very good, I am told that variety acts are coming from all over Germany and no expense has been spared."

Once again Holstein waited on a response that never came.

"So, my boys. Today is a free day you can go into town if you so wish. But please mark my words well, make sure you are back here for six o'clock so that we can at least eat our dinner together then go onto the rehearsal. So, children, off you go. Go on, shoo!"

He waved both hands in the air as if he was trying to scare birds from a newly plowed field.

"There is a camp bus that goes to town every half hour for those of you that wish to take advantage of your free time."

David looked at his friend Roger Mills, they had become friends since the first night that they shared a room. They had agreed that should either of them have to share again then they would try and make it together. 'Anyway, Roger doesn't snore, and I would hate to be stuck with a bloody snorer.'

"What about us two going into town? Are you up for it?"

Roger nodded in agreement and that day's tour was confirmed there and then. Curiosity had gotten the better of them both, they wanted to see where all this Nazi stuff came from and what better way than to view and discover together.

But first a journey into the marketplace within the towns centre, then maybe a trip to see the cathedral, they both knew it was being repaired from bomb damage during the British raids in nineteen forty-four. This building which in many ways was Gothic in design was considered to be a masterpiece in Bavarian terms and Hitler thought of it as equal to anything that the Romans had built during the great classical periods of antiquity.

Both David and Roger needed a break, it was the tenth of December, and they needed to view human beings other than just the blasted musoes from the Americas. German men and women started to sound like a fine idea to them both, even if it was just a few hours. Anything to get off camp and anyway David did like the company of Roger Mills. David last thoughts as they got onto the camp transfer bus was, 'Who knows, we might even meet some girls?'

The bus took just twenty minutes to reach the heart of the town, luck was with them that day, market was up and busy, the stalls buzzed with trade, flower sellers, cloth, clothing in general, fruit and vegetables and nicely placed near the middle of the market were sculptures and painters all showing their works of art and all at affordable prices. This was obviously a Christmas market as well as the normal farmers produce, there was so much Yule tide festive trading going on, so colourful and cheery it warmed the cockles of the boy's hearts.

"Roger, I know that America was never bombed or invaded, but you have seen the damage still in London, look how much rebuilding has already been completed here in Germany. You would hardly think that this place had ever been bombed, would you?"

"Well, you know why that is don't you? The west has sunk millions of dollars into this country. Germany may have lost the war, but they have made up for it by winning the peace hands down."

Roger pondered on his statement and then added in a more serious mode.

"This is the new front line if there is going to be a heating up of this cold war, Germany will be first in the firing line, that's why we are here and why we will stay. Hitler was right about one thing, Russia is the biggest menace to the free world, Bolshevism is the curse that the Nazi's did understand and that is why immediately after peace had been declared General

Paton kept a whole battalion of SS elite troops armed and ready to fight the new cause, but Eisenhower vetoed his actions. But and it's a big but, had we have used those troops along with ours and your countries, we might have had a chance to change history, that is before it has the chance to alter us."

"Wow! What a speech! Who gave you that information?"

"David my boy, I am not just a pretty face, I can think for myself and anyway my dad was a Major working in Paton's team during the war, he loved the General and believed in all his ideas."

Roger feigned shame and then concluded in a more bored voice. "Come on, let's go and see this church then."

The main church was not more than a three-minute walk across the square that held the market. Both boys were surprised yet again at how much damage had already been repaired. It was a true Gothic masterpiece with its façade showing like a pyramid with little turrets sticking high into the sky and at the very front, was a very beautiful clock tower that had been very heavily restored.

Before going inside to view the treasures that might be there, the lads looked at one another then both agreed that a cup of coffee was in order as the café they had just passed sported two very beautiful girls sitting at a table close to the window.

Both the ladies were dressed in modern western cloths and had obviously been on a shopping trip. Neither of the ladies were more than twenty years of age and both had that Aryan look with pallid whitish skin and long blond ponytailed hair. Luckily for the lads the café was close to being full so as Roger ordered the coffee David approached the table where the lasses were seated, and he asked if they didn't mind if they could join them. Both the girls looked at David, then looked at one another and then giggled, they didn't speak a word of English. But the gesture with the hands indicated that the other two seats were indeed free for the boy's use, at least they had understood his gesturing. Roger returned and informed David that coffee would soon be appearing. He then looked at the nearest girl to himself and in a smooth American drool stated.

"My name is Roger Mills, this is David Cartier, as you can hear I am from the US, but old Davy boy here is a Limey. We are musicians with…"

An out of tune cord must have struck home, the word musician must have done it.

"Beetles!"

The girl asked with very bright wide opened eyes. She then thrust her hand into her bag and produces a forty-five-playing record with the words, *She Loves You*, and Beetles written on it. Roger was not slow to miss an opportunity.

"Yes, we know and work for the Beetles."

He then went on with more bull,

"John Lennon is a good friend of mine."

And then pointing to David to added to the bull with,

"We have both worked for the Beetles and the Rolling Stones. I play the saxophone, and Davy here plays the guitar and various other instruments."

Again, the girls looked at him and then giggled once more. 'This is going to go nowhere,' thought David, 'how could it, they don't speak a real language like good old English.' David paused thinking hard on what he had just thought and, then in his mind he added, 'Come to that neither does Roger.' For a whole minute there was a pregnant silence, which made all four of them at the table feel a little uncomfortable.

The quiet was shattered when an elderly man seated with his wife on the next table broke the silence having overheard their previous conversation.

"Excuse me gentlemen, I couldn't help overhearing what you were saying to these two girls. Is it true that you are musicians? And have you really played with the Beetles and the Rolling Stone? Or is it just that you want to enchant our ladies here in Germany?"

Roger took up the mantel in a more subdued tone of voice.

"Yes, no and yes. We are musicians, we both play for the military and will be working here in Nuremburg for a week, which is at the main US base. Yes, you were correct in your assumption concerning the girls, we were both hoping to be able to talk to them but our German is just about as good as their English which makes it a non starter. And lastly no, the bits about playing for you know who, was total bull shit. Sorry, I guess we show ourselves up at times."

Both the man and his wife burst out laughing as what they had guessed turned out to be true. Both the young ladies were looking completely confused and the one that Roger had originally spoken to, turned to the old man and asked in German what had been said. When she was told the truth both the girls laughed too.

David at this time wished the ground would open up and he would gladly have jumped into the vacant space. But to his pleasure, the girl nearest him placed her hand on his arm and rubbed it in a friendly gesture smiling as she did so. But those two girls weren't interested in two boasting foreigners, plus the fact that they were considerably older and wiser than a couple of lads who they cannot communicate with. So, they said something that was an excuse to the old man and he conveyed that the two young ladies had prior business.

"They said, to wish you well and hopes that the concert is a success. She then added that you should give their good wishes to John, Paul, George and Ringo and who, oh yes, Elvis Pressley."

The man smiled a warm and pleasant smile, at least his jesting was not vindictive in any way.

"Can my wife Helga and I come and sit next to you both. It is so nice to be able to speak English to someone again. Please allow us to buy you both another coffee each and maybe, what about some strudel? Have you tried the wonderful Nuremburg strudel yet?" Then without waiting for an answer he called over the waiter.

"Four coffees and four strudels please."

The waiter looked at him in a rather stupefied manner, at that the man realised that he had spoken the order in English, he smiled to himself thinking how easy it was to forget. He then repeated the order all over again but this time in German. He held out his hand so as to shake the young men's, and then added,

"My name is Joseph; may I know who I am talking too?"

Introductions were made and soon David and Roger were enjoying the conversation that they were having with Joseph. It was all trivia and niceness itself, then Roger dropped the bombshell.

"Tell me Joseph, what did you do in the war?"

David, Helga and Joseph were completely taken aback by Roger's forthright questioning. At first Joseph just pondered the answer he was going to give and then he answered with,

"What do you think I did? Do you think I was a member of the Nazi party? I might have been, or still might be, I suspect that nine out of ten men in this café are still quite active. So what do you think?"

"You are old enough to have been in the war somehow doing something. The reason I ask is that I am truly curious to know what it was like. We are told a great deal but just like people here, most of what you hear in your own country is just plain propaganda, I never take what I hear seriously. I wouldn't blame anyone who was drawn into the war, after all what choice did anyone have? And even us Americans can be hypnotized by the oration of Adolf Hitler; he most certainly had the magic tongue. I was telling David that my father was in the army and achieved the rank of Major, he worked with General Paton and Paton had great admiration for the German people and dad always said that Paton probably thought that America joined the wrong side."

Joseph thought about all he had just heard. Then in a slow deliberate voice, he said,

"Your father may have said that about Paton and if it is true, then Paton would have been wrong. America fought a just and proper war against a ruthless foe and enemy, this was an enemy that would have wiped out all the Jews, gypsies, Russians, Slavs, homosexuals, deformed and un-Aryan like peoples around the world. He would have created slavery again, with the Baltic and Slavic peoples as their surfs. Almost certainly he would have waged war on all black people and so many other types of people around the globe, in fact anyone he thought was un-Aryan."

He was almost spitting with indignant outrage; his fists were clenched, and his countenance was showing more than just slight annoyance.

"Had Germany won the war I must wonder how many of us would still be alive? O yes. You wanted to know what I did in the war."

He pulled up his coat sleeve to reveal a long number tattooed on his arm.

"I would be one more of the many dead. I am so lucky to still be alive, I thank God for every dawn that breaks, you see I am a Jew and I spent my war shoveling the dead into furnaces in Auschwitz. I took beatings on a very regular basis, I watched my own father being taken to the gas chamber and yet didn't have the courage to warn him, anyway what good would it have done. I had to allow sadistic Yugoslavian prison guards to fuck me for an extra piece of bread. So, David and Roger, that is what I did in the war."

"Oh, please forgive my stupidity, I really do feel ashamed of myself. Please I meant nothing nasty or sinister, I was just very curious that's all. History is fascinating, but we all need to hear it from those who experienced it, don't we?"

Roger had gone as red as a beetroot, but he was contrite, and Joseph heard and saw that the young man had meant no disrespect.

"Both David and I were born at the very end of the war, we can only listen to what people who were involved have to say. Anyway, we are now here right in the centre of the National Socialist Parties territory, we must wonder. So surely you can see that?"

The Jewish man had now calmed to an understandingly quieter tone of voice, he now understood these young boys' curiosity towards the venom that was preached in the name of National Socialism and on thinking about it he had to admit that the devil did have a smooth tongue when orating.

"Yes, of course I can see that. There is no need for apologies, you are right to be curious! But remember, learn from history, it always seems to me that people just repeat history. Dwell on this as we now leave, there has never been a time when somewhere in the world a war is not flourishing and that means warmongers, and warmongering make lots of money."

He smiled warmly at two novice foreigners, then stood up saying,

"We have to go, it was our pleasure to meet you both, do enjoy your stay. You are both very young, make sure that you are allowed to grow old. Goodbye and good luck!"

As Joseph and Helga left the establishment David turned to Roger and said,

"Christ man, I nearly crapped myself there. I thought he was going to go nuts at first. Well, what do you know, a Jew ah, I never would have guessed it. I imagined him as a SS General or some such. A Jew ah! Well, well."

Roger looked shaken, he then sighed a long lingering sigh, maybe one of utter sadness, for he realised that what Joseph had said was entirely true, there was always war, from the beginning of time and until humanity is wiped off the face of the earth, war will exist.

He sighed again.

The two lads decided that probably prudence was the best way out of what had become a rather embarrassing experience for both of them. Other clients within the café were looking at these two foreigners and not in what one might term as a polite welcoming way.

And it hadn't gone un-noticed by either of them that they might have just spoilt the day for Joseph and Helga, what will happen if they come back to this café, will they be welcome as good German customers or would they be cast as just the surviving Jews, only the good people of Nuremburg could answer that thought?

"Davy, old man! May I suggest that we make a rather hasty retreat from this rather haughty establishment? It seems to me that we are getting more than our fair share of stares from the locals and who knows they may be just waiting for the chance to get even after our lot destroyed their beautiful town. I rather think it is time to view the inside of the church, Cathedral or whatever it is over there."

"Good idea! And I have an even better one. You got us stared at; you pay the bill."

The Cathedral was an extraordinarily beautiful building to the eyes of both the boys, how it survived the appalling raids of World War two was mind boggling. The two eighty-meter-high towers that stand pointing their cold stone construction high into the sky, lift the very souls of all who take the trouble to view their magnificence. And the SS were probably right in thinking that those towers must have been the beacons that led the planes to the town. Even as the two lads viewed these towers the clouds rushed by on that cold but bright day and as they passed it made the two transcending pillars to the heavens look as if they were in fact growing and shaking. Walking up to the main entrance David noticed a brass plaque that had been newly placed there, on reading what he could by translating the easy readable parts. It stated that the Cathedral was dedicated to St. Lorenz and the first stones were laid in the year twelve hundred and fifty. The rest just went over his head.

"Wow, its kinder old. Then I guess it's been remodeled many times. But look at those stone carvings. Such beauty, as I have always said whether it be painting, sculptures, music or architecture, God always got the best of it all."

"My goodness, you bloody Limeys do wax lyrical don't you! Who would have guessed that someone your size and age could be so profound."

On entering the first thing that surprised them was that a mass was being performed and holy sacrament was being given to the faithful. David was not a religious person but erred on the side of caution, just in case God does exist. Roger on the other hand was a real Catholic and immediately went to the font placed his right hand in the holy water and then crossed himself and then bowed towards the alter. Roger was indeed transfixed with awe and wonderment and as he walked up the aisle his mouth had dropped open, and his head was pointing heavenward towards the arched ceilings so high above them.

David became more fascinated watching Roger than viewing the beauty of this religious house of worship. Roger's eyes had misted up and David was quick to notice that lines of tears were running down his friend's face. This sight made David think much better of his colleague than ever before, it showed to Cartier that Mills had a soul, and that pleasant thought was a good thing.

Roger Mills walked down the aisle in a very somber yet inspired manner right to where the congregation was queuing to take their individual sacraments. Roger had obviously made up his mind to do the same, as it had been quite some time since he last indulged. He had not been inside a catholic church within the last two years and coming here today, meeting Joseph and Helga, then coming into St. Lorenz was the final straw concerning the young Mills soul and he knew it needed to be cleansed.

Finally, the priest came to Roger who was now on his knees giving the sign of the cross, a wafer was placed in his mouth by the priest and the sign of the cross was then administered by the holy man and then another younger priest came and gave a sip of red wine. Thus, the body and blood of Christ had entered Roger Mills soul once again renewing him. Roger was once again in the fold of his religion and it showed, but in a harmonious pleasing way.

For the very first time in David Cartier's young life he felt completely overawed by the experience he had just witnessed. 'Maybe there is a God after all?'

That evening back at the camp, both the boys were still in a state of grace. They both went along to the rehearsal with high expectations of giving their very best to the troupe. Both Roger and David played their collective hearts out most of the way through the practice.

There were various acts that came together to make a variety show. Local singers, dancers, one or two minor American comics that like the musicians do the rounds of US camps entertaining the troops. A juggler and tumbler were there having come from the Nuremburg area, though how they got through the security is anyone's guess as the two men looked more like SS refugees than entertainers, neither had the smell of troupers about them.

The other thoughts that went through the minds of many of the musicians were that these two locals were in fact Russian spies planted there to do their damnedest to create mayhem, and strangely enough they managed just that one night and were not seen again after that. So, it was now the duty of the band to accompany these motley ragamuffins, their entire week was to be sitting within a pit under the platform within the pit and not for once on top of the stage.

It had all the hall marks of being a very good entertaining week with such a variety of talents.

As for the two lads, their personal state of grace came to an end when an exotic dancer appeared on the stage and the band had to play Richard Strauss's suite Dance of the seven veils from the opera Salome. Through the entire short piece of erotically evoking music, the girl removed various shades of different coloured veils, at the climax when the girl took off the seventh veil, she should have been wearing a body stocking, but this young Fräulein decided that her American audience was old enough to experience the real thing. And as the last veil did in fact fall to the ground there was a huge cheer from the musicians that continued for several minutes, as there for all to see was a truly stunning naked German lady.

No blushes were spared, it was this moment in time that God left David and Roger to be replaced with a warmer, redder deity, one with a tail and pointed horns. At that moment they both lusted and imagined themselves between the strong and shapely thighs of this woman or come to that any woman.

The week was indeed a fine success, each night was full to the rafters with cheering soldiers, those lucky enough to have been bused in from all corners of the Czechoslovakian border and the grateful troops enjoyed this show and especially Francine Gottler, the exotic dancer.

The free days were spent looking around the Nuremburg area. The two lads visited the actual arena where the National Socialists held their huge rallies. Both David and Roger stood on the supposed spot that Hitler strutted while reviewing his black suited troops. David could visualize those goose-stepping feet as the storm troopers did their own version of the Nazi salute.

He saw Leni Riefenstahl, dressed in her long tight fitting black woolen dress taking photographs and newsreel film of each occasion. Standing next the Adolf was his so-called trusted friends, Himmler, Goebbels, Goering, Hess and one must never forget the Fuhrer's architect Albert Speer, all standing erect sporting extremely wide smug grins. Hitler with his right arm extended to his loving devoted followers in the Nazi salute, looked to all the world like Mussolini his Italian friend. He also took Benito's stance, sticking out his extended chest with his arms akimbo on his waist, nodding his head in that pompous knowing way.

The colour of the spectacle, the grandeur of the event, the thrill of being a member of the master race there watching as their destiny was unfolding before their very eyes.

Then that grandiose moment suddenly passed as a snowball hit David straight in the face. So much for peace and friendship, war was once again being declared, but this time it was between the United Kingdom and that egotistical puppy from over the pond, the United States of America. England of course won the war as there was a great deal more snow to throw where Cartier and Hitler stood.

On another free day they went to visit the Palace of Justice, this was where the trials of the war criminals took place in nineteen forty-seven and eight. They investigated the faces of the allied judges as they were escorted through the huge area that became the court room. Then they were shown the prison cells that held the Nazi criminals. They saw the actual cell that Goering committed suicide in once he knew that he was going to be hung for his collusion in the war. The building was menacing and grandiose all at the same time and they discovered that it was one of the few buildings not to be badly scarred from the bombing that took place, very little damage had actually occurred to the edifice.

Both boys were indeed warming very strongly to one another as their time together continued and Nuremburg had been an exciting and fulfilling week for them both.

Chapter 7

It was nine o'clock in the evening of the eighteenth of December, and the bus that had brought them from Nuremburg was just skirting around checkpoint Charlie, this time there was no camp that the troupe of musicians were to be staying in while spending Christmas in Berlin, no just a five-star American re-built hotel, now re-named Hilton Hotel.

There was to be several concerts, mainly officer's dinners plus dances, but before they left Germany altogether there was to be a final huge dance out at an airfield that had once housed Goering's finest, but now housed NATO's nuclear bombers all armed with their own brand of deadly warheads.

Since arriving in Germany with the entertainments band David Cartier had now become fully aware of how dangerous the world situation was and he had now achieved a very cynical mode of thinking concerning American policing and policy towards NATO and Europe in particular, it was as if the USA saw Europe as the acceptable bombing place of the world. In his mind's eye, Germany and Europe was a good testing place to see how far Russia could be pushed and it also seemed that Russia was doing much the same. To young Cartier it didn't bode well for peace everlasting. But he also admitted to himself that his knowledge was now prejudiced by the time being spent with red necked Yankees, showing all their vitiations towards other human beings.

It was now time for the band to be broken up for the Christmas and New Year holidays. It became a lottery for those who got a ticket home for a week and those who stayed. As David had nowhere to go it had already been decided with Holstein that he would forfeit his place on any plane home for someone with a family. The need to fulfill the program could be achieved with single strings and woodwind, that was the minimum to suffice and even then, there would be chances for individuals to have proper rest periods. David soon came to realise that having a rest period was going to be a must, as after they left Europe there would be no rest for the wicked. Anyway, David did want to spend time just practicing, as he knew his technique was suffering a little, so scales and arpeggios were the order of the day.

Roger planned to stay around with his new found Blighty friend, instead of getting a plane back to the States. For this David was very grateful, it meant that any spare time they could explore Berlin together, after practice that is. They had been warned on the coach that to roam around on one's own, was tantamount to courting trouble and possible major disaster.

On the whole Berliners despised Americans, thinking them as shallow worthless un-intelligent, chewing gum munching oafs that knew nothing about diplomacy or tact, had little culture and brains to ever understand arts, history or any form of aesthetic accomplishments.

To the people of Berlin this was clearly shown when immediately after hostilities had stopped, on trying to reform the Berlin Philharmonic Orchestra and the setting up of the first program, ideas were set before the American representative within the newly formed board of directors. The suggested program was immediately put a stop to, it had been decreed that the orchestra were not allowed to perform Wagner's overture to The Mastersingers, because the American governing body thought that Wagner was a possible attribute towards the Nazi ideal, thus the general consensus was one of complete disgust towards people that had such small, closed minds.

Over the prevailing years nothing much had changed to alter the German prejudice towards the US occupying forces, the greatest insult being to the elder generation, those people that actually fought during the war, many of the older population were terribly insulted when Elvis Pressley was sent to join the American forces within Germany, most would have preferred Leonard Bernstein to Pressley, but then Germans had a thousand years of history and culture, America has only Jazz and Rock-n-Roll and coca-cola and burgers, lots and lots of burgers, in all their various fatty shapes and sizes, so to any outsider one might just agree with those Berliners.

They arrived at the Hilton just in time for some hot supper, a few warming tots of whiskey and a hop and a jump into a large warm bed. The sharing of course was obligatory, and David once again housed himself with Roger. They had a twin-bedded room on the fourth floor, but glory be, there was a lift and it worked. Their suite was just large enough to house two twin beds, a large closet for clothing and an armchair and table, plus an extra bonus of a large comfortable settee that looked directly at an old television which showed nothing but CNN news and cartoons. Then adjoining the sleeping area was a small bathroom. Within the bathing area there was a compact cubicle shower, next to that was a very petite toilet, the décor if nothing was bijou. The whole toiletry space was decorated with light blue Italian tiles depicting areas of beauty and ancient sites around Rome. It made sitting on the throne an historical eventful journey, but to the boys more hysterical than archival. The nicest aspect of the hotel was that it was clean, warm, friendly and basically full of foreigners, plus if wanted there was a bar and restaurant open to order twenty-four hours a day.

Once explored the lads went to bed and slept the whole night without any disturbances, a silent night. But then they were woken by the appalling noise of trams and vehicles banging and crashing on the road below and worse than anything, it was still dark and only five o'clock in the morning. David looked at his watch, saw that it was indeed only five o'clock, sighed, turned over and tried to go back to sleep. All his dreams until finally rising were of either, being run down by trams, trains, lorries or cars.

A sad end to a night full of what promised sexually fulfilling dreams, in fact so much so, that he realised that he would have to wash his pajama trousers yet again.

The food in the restaurant was good and plentiful, not that they had been any going without. But this hotel catered for the entrepreneurial American businessmen and Germany certainly attracted the basic instincts of greed within the would be buyers and sellers from abroad.

Labour was good and it was cheap and the rebuilding that was going on meant that many foreigners could come over and introduce lucrative money-making schemes. Thus, so the food had to be what the hotel thought its clients would be wanting. Eggs abounded, fried, poached, boiled, eggs with bacon, eggs with toast, French toast, come to those good old English fry-ups.

Kippers, raw fish mainly pickled, just about anything that one could desire was there to be eaten. And something very new to the German folk that ventured into this home from home American style, cereals! Cornflakes, oatmeal, rye, barley, all there to be had either with milk, yogurt, cream, honey and any combination that the customer could ever think up.

To David this was a true Aladdin's culinary cave. After breakfast Stuart Holstein called a meeting of the musicians.

"There has been a lottery for all those who wish to return to the States for Christmas, the list is pinned to our notice board. You know the one, that flat piece of wood with padded cloth glued on to it, that's the one that is called a notice board, which I post notices that none of you ever read on it. Well, if you wish to get a family vacation, better start reading."

Stuart sighed a long-depressed sigh, one that told the listener that he was fast approaching the end of his tether concerning them all. "But for the record, those of you that are staying here in Berlin, there are only four events that we have to attend before the New Year concert, so all those that want it can have a ten-day break. In fact, I guess that's most of you, I shall not need you back before the fifth of January, but once again look on the board. If you are going home, then you need to be at the hotel entrance for two o'clock this very afternoon where a bus will be waiting to take you to the airfield. Have a safe journey and rest plenty, come back safe and in the sort of spirits that will carry you through till the end of the tour."

Then strangely with an almost contented smile, or maybe one of relief, Stuart added,

"Happy Christmas to you all. To those few of you that are staying here with me, as I have already said there are only four concerts, all easy-peasy stuff that you know by heart. We are going to spend our entire Xmas jollies here in the Hilton and I have been told that it will be very special, so I have agreed to play a small concert of jazz to the staff who will be joining us on Christmas eve. I hope this arrangement meets with your approval?"

There was a small cheer, obviously by those who knew or thought they knew that they would be returning to see family or friends.

It became an odd sensation for David, as people that he had now got to know and overall liked, started to disappear; most going home to America for the Christmas rest period. He smirked to himself as this new feeling of loneliness crept over him. How could he be lonely, he still had his friend Roger staying on with him, but seeing familiar faces, most beaming with the thoughts of family and friends now brushing passed him as if they didn't even know him, he felt something like the onset of a melancholy depression invading his being.

Why didn't he have a family to spend Xmas with?

The hotel was so quickly dissipated of its residents, leaving just the diehards and staff to jolly things along. This spacious, light airy hotel now seemed just that little darker, stuffier and somewhat dismal. Hotels need people, the more the merrier. It wasn't enough that there were fine restaurants, waiting for one to eat their fill, or a games room to pass the time of day and the waste of having a small swimming pool in the basement, which came with a sauna and gym equipment to help trim the body and muscles, with no one to use it.

It quickly became a ghost ship with bright lights, bar tenders and porters, all dressed in their best dress clothes and with no one to serve, all waiting there in expectation of guests who might appear but instead seeing the hopelessness of a hotel that was fast becoming a Mary Celeste in a bright newly rebuilt city, for the people that they housed had already disappeared going back to families and friends, knowing once again the warmth of their own homes. But that feeling was soon to pass.

The next morning Stuart called a rehearsal for the next evenings officers' dinner, which coincidentally was going to be held within the confines of the Hilton hotel. The interesting aspect of this particular evening was that all the officers were going to come from all four sectors of Berlin, that meant Americans, English, French and Russian. When Holstein told the gathered few of what was going to happen, there was quite a gasp from the diehard Americans.

"Ruskies! Are the brass insane?"

Well of course, they already knew they were!

David just thought the whole idea was going to be an amusing event, one for the old age book of memories.

The program was going to be very varied starting with a string quartet, playing very light arrangements of many composers. After this and then throughout the dinner, there was a jazz nonet which was going to attempt variations of Glen Miller themes and re-visited solos. To David Cartier, in his own eyes this was going to be a serious trial as he really didn't think that the remaining musicians were good enough to pull off what was going to be extremely difficult ordeal. Then if the officers still wanted more entertainment, they would round off the evening with old war songs, such as: It's a long way to Tipperary, Pack up your troubles, Goodbye-ee and so on. Even Russian Generals knew these old war horses as most of them had sung them within their own particular trenches. As David was only playing in the string quartet, it was going to be a comparatively easy night's work for him.

The rehearsal took three hours to complete, and David was nicely surprised at how good the string quartet sounded. His big fear was always that the intonation would be hard to keep on a straight even keel, as the other three players are all good wind players, who rarely double on strings making them their second fiddles, such is the pun.

But the tuning was perfect, as was the sight reading and interpretation of the musical works that the musicians very proudly performed.

The other three musicians were professional soldiers, all seconded from other branches of military life, all being saved from the possible fighting going on in Vietnam. With the extra money and the relaxed lifestyle, being a professional musician in the American army, navy or air force could be a very rewarding way of life to follow. David was always surprised at how lax the troupe could be, for a starter, none as far as David knew, ever acknowledged the simple fact the Stuart Holstein was indeed an officer, thus they treated him with the same deference as any other member of the musical society and this meant with total indifference, but also there was a sort of warm apathy that had a sort of family feel about it.

He was popular in so far as it went, which wasn't very far.

But like all musicians that were regular in a musical ensemble, the familiarity that abounded was in many ways warming and had a certain understanding tender warmth to it. No one ever called him sir or saluted, he was Stuart or other less flattering adjectives.

But Stuart never tried to lord it over anyone either, he saw his role as being one of the boys and left it at that. David had never seen Holstein get really irate and even when he did get somewhat angry, he rarely used it against the offending person. One guessed that his simple philosophy was, Don't rock the boat; Let sleeping dogs lie; If it's not broken, don't mend it, and so on.

Generally speaking, David liked his fellow musicians and he especially liked Stuart Holstein and recognized that he was a fine organiser and a diplomat of the highest order, especially when it concerned his boys, David was sure that he went overboard to protect them when they got into any sort of trouble.

He might not have been the best musician amongst the ensemble, but everything else that he was and did, made up for that fact.

It was perfectly obvious to anyone that could see further than the end of their noses that Holstein's life involved entirely around this touring group of entertainers. These were his charges; he was the father to them all even those older than himself of which there were three.

Interestingly, truth be known, just about everyone in the musical ensemble respected and understood completely how much Holstein loved his band of troopers, though like many petulant children they erred and defaulted, generally speaking they all treated Stuart with deference and respect and of course careless disinterest and like children, a certain disregard, that all applied to the man not the officer.

When David's part of the rehearsal was over, he decided to stop and listen to the Glen Miller tribute. The standards were easy having been played many times before, the band sounded good and tried hard to make up for the lack of numbers within their group. The trouble started when they tried to revisit the solos that accompanied the standards.

Cartier's fears were soon realised when Johnnie Miller the lead trombone stood to perform his solo, he just wasn't good enough and the struggle that occurred appeared as frowns and lines on his face, showing just how much of a problem it was to him. The difference between Glen Miller's musicians and this band of warrior troopers was a cavern wider than the Grand Canyon. He squeaked and slid through the notes and was almost a beat behind all the way through, the intonation was slippery, and the entire thing just sounded awful and nervous. Stuart stopped and took him aside.

"Johnnie, are you going to be able to get this solo together by tomorrow night?"

"It's so bloody difficult! I think the solo idea is just going to be too hard for all of us. I am quite prepared to stay and practice all day and night if it will help, but the guys that performed these solos were world class players. Me, I'm just a Sergeant in the marines. I know I play a mean trombone within the group, I can even make a good sound at my own sort of solos, but these guys were virtuosos, it came second nature to them, but not to me."

He was crestfallen, and it showed,

"Sorry Stuart, I guess this is a long-winded way of saying forget it, try something else."

Stuart sighed deeply, frowned and looked towards the floor, stroked his nonexistent beard, sighed again and then looked towards the band with a wry smile that said it all.

"Have I made a mistake, should we forget the solos?"

This was spoken in general to anyone who might be listening, then a very un-expected voice answered his vague question.

"I agree with Johnnie boss, these are never going to sound like anything better than cheap imitations. May I suggest that you let us improvise our own solos?"

The voice was that of Roger Mills.

The next evening true to form, the ensemble quartet gathered to play in the guests at the Four

Nations Officers Dinner, with some light melodies from Lehar's - The Merry Widow.

Ten topflight officers and partners had been invited from each Country, the host for the evening was General James Thomas Shute, a hero of World War One and Two. He had spent this last war working closely with General Eisenhower, but on several occasions managed to find himself right in the middle of firefights. Possibly the most famous being the defense of Bastogne where he commanded a small contingency of marines that had been cut off from the main part of the town but managed to hold off the German tanks for four days until they were re-supplied from the air. For this brave and courageous deed, he won the Congressional Medal of Honour.

His role now was to govern and lead the American army of occupation in Berlin. This stout seventy odd year-old war horse was dressed in all his finery, he was sporting medals that could have dated back to American War of Independence for what anyone knew. He was as sprightly as he had been on leaving West Point Academy as a cadet just before the First World War.

Though he had little hair to talk about and what he did have was snowy light and cropped, just as it would have been all those years ago. He must have been several stone overweight, but he carried those extra pounds with a grace and elegance that would have been hard for a man half his age to have bettered.

He was used to playing the diplomat, so when the Russian contingency arrived James and his older wife Margaret were charm personified. He sported a side arm of a nineteenth century colt pistol. It was reputed to have been owned by Wyatt Earp though no one really believed that it did. That pistol sported beautifully hand carved ivory handles and also a finely engraved barrel and chamber that must have taken a craftsman many hours of hard work and skill to do. Fortunately, it had no bullets in the chamber so was considered quite safe, but he always had to explain to the gathered guests that it was just a trinket to show those damn Limeys that they didn't have a monopoly on formality and pomp.

Anyway, the display was special and General Bruzchenski was immensely impressed and offered to buy the pistol from Shute there and then. But old Shute knew how to play the crowd, so he let the Russian General handle the weapon and pretend to be Billy the Kid much to the amusement of all the fellow officers and their wives that had gathered around admiring the US trinkets.

Eventually all the guests appeared, four sets of national anthems were played and everyone sat down to their meal. As things were still hard to get in post war torn Europe and various food stuffs were nonexistent the meal started with a soupcon of Caviar which came on thin wafers, the amount that was placed on each plate would have satisfied an entire football team, but there it was in plenty for all the officers and their spouses. Served with the roe was the finest pink Champaign and this came from the nineteen fifty-eight vintage and by the bucketful. To this course of food, the quartet of musicians played a Mozart quartet, after which some arrangements of Beethoven's symphonies. Not that anyone heard them play as the guests were enjoying themselves, gorging on food and wine, and spouting the usual nonsense to one another, each officer obviously had personally won each and every war know to man and also probably many that weren't.

This was not going to be an evening of culture for them. The second course comprised of a very clear thin oxtail soup and by the noise that this generated by the sucking and slurping showed that everyone loved it. That was served with a very delicate subtle semi-sweet rosy French wine. Now the string quartet accompanied this course with some arrangement of Borodin, primarily for the pleasure of the Russian officers; yet again heard by no one.

The third course was a light carp course, the fish had been poached and placed in an individual flaky pastry pie, this came with some baby asparagus. This was served with a very fine Chablis wine, again of the fifty-eight vintage. So much of this wine was consumed that they ran out and had to use another vintage not that anyone would have noticed or even know, but by now practically all the guests were quite drunk.

After this feast of gluttony, the guests were offered a sorbet to cleanse the pallet, though the Russians thought it was a desert and asked for several more each. All the time that this was going on the musicians were working their fingers to the bone and suffering from all the delicious smells that were transcending across to them from the various tables. By the time the main course was to appear all four of them were drooling from the mouth.

As for the main course, wow, the various chefs outdid themselves to impress. Various meats were on offer, plus more fish should anyone want to forgo the carnivorous showings that were taking place before their eyes. Beef Wellington was on offer. Lamb cutlets, cooked in white wine and simmering in their own juices and flavoured with pine nuts and cardamom and fennel seeds. A suckling pig had been roasted along with the old proverbial apple crunching between the jaws of the small beast, its eyes staring in a white glazed empty expression, which was now matching most of the drunken officers.

The accompanying vegetables were either roasted in the ovens or lightly steamed, they all looked beautiful and mouthwatering. The piece de resistance was when two chefs marched in carrying a roasted swan, this brought a spontaneous applause from all the gathering. With this main course there were several fine red wines on offer, which to be fair, most of the officers managed to try all of them out, or at least gave a heroic attempt at trying them all.

But the best was a superb vintage Burgundy, which was served only to the various Generals, or the head of the various tables. This incredible experience was appreciated by all that tasted the nectar, they were the last four bottle of nineteen twenty-seven vintage possibly the very last in the entire world.

David was to get his wish with the selection of the music for this course. The music was a quartet arrangement of Edward Elgar's Pomp and Circumstance, though sounding somewhat thin with just four musicians, it pleased David Cartier who played his heart out and put a smile on Stuart Holstein and the other three player's faces. Yet again it was just those five that heard the music, so they could have played some old Nazi tunes for all that the gathering there would have been aware of.

After a further hour of music for the main meal, the desert course was eventually brought forth. For the English contingent a very strong sherry trifle was made and served, this was presented with a very sweet wine which disappeared as quickly as the trifle.

Finally, a cheese board appeared with some fine vintage Port and once again the American General Shute mimicked his British counterpart, all Port bottles had to be passed to the left which meant they all ended up on the Russian table and there they stayed until they were emptied.

By now the quartet were aching from fatigue and hunger, but they still managed to end their stint with some light Strauss music and, this final flurry of notes did get the notice of the audience who clapped along as they recognised various melodies. Not that anyone was sober enough to appreciate the effort that the musicians had made, but they themselves felt they had performed well under very difficult circumstances.

As the tables were cleared and drunken men and women lurched around, a small resolute clap appeared in the air, this turned into a larger clap which became clapping, then the odd,

"Bravo,"

appeared, and finally the complete entourage burst forth with cheering and clapping and this time it was for the string quartet that had spend three hours playing nonstop. The four musicians stood and took their well-deserved accolade, all were wet with perspiration tired and aching, they were famished having smelt the wondrous variety of foods, as the aromas drifted across to them from the tables it had sent their taste buds into overdrive.

What had been on offer for the assembled guests should now be there for them the musicians, but they got just the clap and the thought of what might have been if they had only managed to get all these heads of armies to talk instead of just to eat, after all there they were back behind the front line of a cold war zone and they were at least for that time no longer cold, but full of friendship and good feeling.

Finally, it was now time for them to get some of that well earned repast and to relax and catch their breath. They packed up the instruments and made their way backstage and into the kitchens. 'Oh, joy of joys, let me loose on that grub!' David and the others were not going to be disappointed.

Once the stage had been cleared and the quartet was busying itself with gorging the succulents that were on offer the jazz nonet was setting up ready to give their own personal renditions. This was going to be the real tester for the night, nine musicians were not enough to get around Glen Miller tunes and melodies, but Stuart was going to make sure that they gave off their best.

The noise coming from the floor was enormous, crashing, banging, shouting and laughter. Had anyone just heard this and not seen it, they would have thought it was the prelude to World War Three. The officers were having a wonderful time, they didn't need excuses to enjoy themselves. The French contingency was singing French songs at the top of their voices, mainly Edith Piaf tunes, the Americans were laughing at jokes many being extremely bawdy. It was General Shute himself that had the floor with many of his own officers standing around him listening when he told his most famous joke.

"Are you listening? Come in closer, I don't want the ladies to hear this one."

All the men closed ranks and crept closer.

"It was on a village green during the great depression, a traveling salesman was attempting to interest the ladies of the town in a new-fangled idea for washing clothes, it was a washing machine. 'Gather round ladies,' he said; 'I am here to startle you with our latest invention, one that will transform your lives from one of drudgery to a more refined, relaxed tempo of living. I want you to bring all your dirty clothes and I shall show you how easy and well they will be cleaned.' Eventually ladies brought him their personal dirty laundry, to which he loaded some into the machine and then switched it on. 'As you can see, they are all being thrown around in the frothy water.' He then acted out the following, 'Into the wash, out of the wash, into the rinse, out of the rinse, into the dry, and as quick as your eye, up to your nose!'

He then sniffed if as if he was trying to smell the clothing.

'Fresh as a rose.'

To this he got a huge applause.

He tried this on several occasions trying hard to show how wonderful the machine was. Then he had a brain wave; 'Is there anyone here with really stinking dirty clothing to really test the machine?' At first there was no reaction, then the ladies parted leaving a corridor for an old vagrant to come through the throng, you could tell he was dirty as two thousand flies followed above him closely. 'I have a challenge for you.' He shouted. He stripped of all his clothes and left them in a heap upon the ground and half the fly's descended upon them in an excited flurry. The salesman picked up the smelly rags with some tongs and the aroma made all the ladies take a step back. But the rep was not to be daunted. 'Into the wash, out of the wash, into the rinse, out of the rinse, into the dry, and as quick as your eye, up to your nose,'"

Once again, a huge sniff, then his face dropped, and he finished with,

'Into the wash'……"

A roar of approval came from his fellow officers though many were just being polite, after all this was the supreme commander of the American forces in Berlin, one always laughs at his jokes. But old Shute was content, this had all the makings of a great evening, and it was on his watch, he was going to milk the occasion for all it's worth.

The nonet was now ready to play their first piece of Glen Miller, and it was the task of Stuart Holstein to introduce the band and what is going to be played.

"Exalted ladies and distinguished gentlemen, if I may have your attention for a moment, please. As you can see, we have now changed tact, we have for your pleasure a dance band that are going to play Glen Miller arrangements and er, if you will be so pleased to accept my musicians, they will add their own improvised solos to the well-known familiar standards. The tables are now being moved back, so it will be our pleasure to play for you as a starter, In the Mood. Please feel free to use the space to dance."

There was a small clatter from the tables still being moved and then one or two people clapped Holstein after his introduction, other than that everyone was chattering away as if their lives depended on extra loud vocalisation. Stuart raised his hands to start conducting, but with the noise coming from the floor. He waited for a moment, then another moment, he looked around with a face that showed something like dismay embossed on it, he tried to "ssssh" the audience, no response, he tapped his foot a few times, but no one was taking a blind bit of notice.

It was then that he became aware of a different noise developing, it was the distinct sound of bagpipes and not one but many and all being warmed up in the next adjoining room.

Holstein face went immediately crimson, he was furious. He placed his baton down on a chair, stormed off the stage and went to investigate the sounds from the next room. He opened the door and to his complete and utter amasement there in lines of four were sixteen Scottish pipers, all dressed in ceremonial kilts and because he had opened the doors, this was their cue, up they started and marched in almost walking over the irate impresario.

This did stop the chattering though and an immediate spontaneous applause started up from all the guests. It had been the idea of the English General, one General Archer and his aide Colonel Spencer, but they had forgotten to warn General Shute and probably more important Stuart Holstein. In they marched playing Scotland the Brave at a quick tempo and a volume that made all sober members of the contingency place their hands over their ears. To this sound up stepped the Scottish officers from the British sector and started to dance a reel, this was just the prompt that the Russians needed, they just rushed out from behind their Vodka glasses to join in, but with their own version of a reel that being a Cossack dance. And not to be left behind, the French started to sing at the top of their voices the Marseillaise trying very hard to drown out all other sounds and frolicking noises and movements that were being performed on the dance floor.

In desperation Stuart rushed back to the rostrum, picked up his baton and started the band with their weaker version of In the Mood. The noise was so incredibly loud from all the participants that most of the kitchen staff appeared to listen and see what the heck was going on, many of them wondered over to adjoining doors to see for themselves.

The quartet of course not to be outdone, came in to view this incredible scene of infantile nonsense that was occurring, after all, these were people that could destroy the entire globe. There for all to witness was the band playing Glen Miller, the sixteen bagpipers belching out their Scottish reel, the French singing their National Anthem, the Russians now singing Glinka and dancing with their high kicks and yelling.

Then you had General Shute still trying at the top of his voice to tell yet more silly infantile jokes and all the women were laughing and dancing around to anything that had a tempo, beat or a tune.

David Cartier was crying from laughter, partly because he had been disturbed from the food, but also partly because he was witnessing a pageant drama from a painting of the Dutch master Hieronymus Bosch, this was a scene directly from The Garden of Earthly Delights.

Tears streamed down his face, his stomach ached from the laughing, this was indeed madness in all its glory.

'Jesus Christ, these imbeciles control the destiny of the world! They don't have more than ten brain cells each and nine of those they sit on.' As he thought these thoughts he shook his head from side to side in a certain resolve. 'Death, where is thy sting?' He sighed again and wiped the tears from his eyes, decided it was time to get back to the food and the last thought that entered his head before the feasting started up again was, 'And to think we get paid money as well!'

It was the band that quit first, no one could possibly hear their arrangement of the great late Glen Miller and Holstein quickly realised that he was only making things worse by competing. He sighed and thought, 'what the hell!'

The pipers had marched backwards and forwards many times, and the audience just loved their sound, so they had quickly become the main attraction, not the band. After they finished Scotland the Brave, they continued with Highland Cathedral, though much slower the guests were now in a state of high euphoria and each Country was doing its uppermost to outdo any of the others and all to the wailing of pipe music.

Eventually after several other pieces being played the pipers departed the floor, the guests cheered and clapped as they left, they had been a great success. It was then that the brandies and whiskeys started to flow. Stuart sat on the edge of the staging area with his band, waiting patiently he tapped his fingers on the floor. His mind was racing for what was going to happen next.

Should he stand up and try again? Should he give up completely? Anyway, everyone was out of the skulls with alcohol, nobody but nobody was aware of the band anymore.

Finally having made a decision, he stood, got the band once again ready to perform, raised his hands to give the down beat, then on bringing his hands down instead of his band picking up the beat and getting stuck in, all that came out above the hubbub of the officers and wives was the sound of an piano accordion and it was playing some Russian dances, then two or three violins could be heard, and finally two or three balalaikas. In desperation Holstein lowered his baton once more. With his head practically hitting his stomach, a sigh and a look of despair made him look twenty years older at that very moment, he sat down on the side of the stage once again.

Almost in tears of frustration, he concluded that yet again he had been made to look and feel a complete and utter fool.

The doors to the next room were literally thrown open and in burst, like an eruption of Mount Etna, ten Russian musicians, four balalaikas, four violins and two accordions, all dressed in traditional costumes playing their colourful hearts out to traditional Cossack music. Once again, the Russian officers abandoned their standard hobby and on putting down their drinks, they as one rushed out onto the dance floor.

The noise was incredibly fortissimo in volume but their quality for endurance was truly magnificent. Officers were spinning on one leg, kicking almost to the ceiling, leaping into the air giving scissor kicks as they did so. Then swords appeared and were placed on the floor to which two officers leapt and sprung around them. This display was thrilling and professional in its execution, it was perfectly obvious that these men were born to dance as well as fight. Very quickly a circle of guests had enveloped the entourage of Russian musicians and dancers, everyone clapping to the rhythm of the electrifying musical sounds that were swelling throughout the room. Even General Shute was transfixed with wonder and admiration to this band of would-be enemy soldiers, how he wished his own men could perform something along these lines. The excitement generated was enormous, just about every one of the guests was now up and trying hard to move to the rhythms of the music. Why even the Generals and their aides were trying out their own interpretation as to what a Cossack dance was meant to be.

The food had been great, the alcohol had flown freely throughout the entire evening, very few pompous speechifying had been done, not one person thought of anyone else that night as potential enemies, only good warm friends.

That was with one possible exception! Stuart Holstein now hated deeply all the guests that attended, but like all the Generals aides and other ranking officers, they would have to keep up with Reveille and all this nonsense would be quickly forgotten, that applied for him too, tomorrow was going to be yet another day.

Stuart decided to minimise the embarrassment by taking his musicians off stage and to the area set aside for their food. 'Yes,' he thought, 'that's probably the best and easiest way out of this situation. Anyway, I am hungry for one'.

He sighed deeply, being an honest sort of man Stuart only wanted to give of his best by his men, he sighed again and thought, 'Those bloody bastards!'

No one noticed them leave, even the clatter of instruments being packed away was drowned out by the tremendous yelping and baying as each officer be it Russian, French, British or American, as they tried to kick higher, wider, and more often to the music, thus outdoing the fine Russians who had started this melee.

All the time this went on General Shute was in a corner and had a small, dedicated gathering of sycophants hanging on his every word as he told more and more stupid and somewhat dirty jokes.

There was one bright spot that came to Holstein that day, as the evening drew to a close and a very successful evening it had been and gone, General Shute called for Stuart to attend him. Officers were leaving and all were laughing and acting extremely merry, but a couple had held back, it was General Bruzchenski with his rather large wife and his aide and his wife. They had asked Shute if they could meet the band leader, firstly to apologise for taking over his evening's entertainment, secondly to see whether he would bring a small contingency of musicians to play for him at a very special birthday party. It was the aide that spoke almost perfect English who addressed him. Bowing quite deeply and graciously and then offering a hand in friendship, he stated,

"General Shute has kindly given us permission to ask a favour of you."

Stuart looked puzzled his eyes and mouth showed a frown developing and it was quite noticeable to all there.

"I understand your name is Stuart Holstein and that you are also an officer in the American army. The request that I ask is this, General Bruzchenski is having a special party for a very few selected guests as it is his seventieth birthday next Friday. He would love it if you had a small ensemble that could play some good modern jazz at his special occasion? Would that be possible?"

Holstein nearly jumped for joy.

"Wow, that took me by surprise, modern jazz you say. Any particular style of playing, I mean any particular persons influence that takes the Generals imagination?"

"Well, I know that the General loves your Charles Mingus, and I believe he thinks highly of Thelonious Monk, could you make arrangements around those two, say as a starter. He will of course be happy to pay you all for your time."

"You tell the General that it would be our pleasure to perform for him and his guests and what's more, I think we can make some arrangements to suit his likings. As for payment, a decent meal and a few drinks will suffice. My men are paid a good salary, and they don't have to work too hard for it either."

Stuart winked a knowing wink at the aide,

"An extra evening will do them good. I will ask though if you can supply transport to and from the venue? I presume that you know where we are staying? Anyway, maybe you can come over to the hotel yourself, say lunch tomorrow and we can plan the entire show over a meal, how does that sound?"

Shute puffed out his chest with pleasure. He patted Holstein on his shoulder.

"Well said Major Holstein."

The Russians left happy with the entire evening's goings on. When all had departed, Shute offered Stuart a very large shot of very fine aged malt whisky.

"You have done your country a great service tonight. What this shindig has done, is better than diplomacy at the United Nations, we have bonded tonight just like during the war and this goes to make more lasting relationships between east and west. We Major have made a few strong ties, created new friends and all because of some good food and copious amounts of booze and lots and lots of fun." It was amazing to Stuart how obviously General Shute had in fact managed to stay stone cold sober, when everyone thought he was paralytic with alcohol like the rest.

"I am sorry that you lost out in the playing stakes, but there you are, after all is said and done it was really a small price to pay."

He smirked to himself, then added,

"Who would have thought that a very aging Russian General brought up with left wing ideals and Stalinist doctoring would love American black jazz? I am presuming, that what's their names are black? And the only way he can get to hear them is to ask for our help, or better still, your help."

Shute smiled broadly and patted Stuart warmly on his shoulder.

"How about that!"

Shute put his drink on the table and then added as a final offering. "You realise that next Friday is what the Limey's call boxing day. I will give you a special present that you can present to ol' what's his name on or after the party, it will be from me to him, and I know it will seal a bond for both of us."

Stuart Holstein got back onto the bus with the musicians, now a huge smile had appeared out of the tired gloom. 'That Shute is not such a bloody fool after all! Old what's his name, silly bugger! And after all the booze he had consumed he seemed absolutely stone cold sober!'

Christmas Eve came, and the hotel had more or less closed down except for the remaining musicians and the staff. So, it had been decided that a party was to be held for everyone.

The management, chefs, waiters, porters and even the cleaners all gathered in the main dining hall, all dressed in their own personal finery, all looking a little sheepish and embarrassed at mixing together with guests.

Soon the drinks started to flow and then inhibitions dropped, and fellow workers mixed with one another, they then started to enjoy themselves. Stuart decided along with two of his of closest chums that everyone should try to do a little entertaining, so a few more drinks quickly went around.

Stuart selected four of the younger musicians to perform as backing, four players that could busk easily and well thus giving accompaniment to the poor people that had to perform. It was meant to be fun, but as nerves showed themselves it was never going to be entirely fun for those who had to stand their ground and face the enemy and sing.

Fortunately for Holstein there were four young musicians available that could improvise most tunes, they had grown up in the Rock-n-Roll era. They knew the Bill Haley songs, the Little Richard screaming tunes, Buddy Holly and of course Elvis Pressley.

Of course, like most people they were turning their considerable attentions to the new English groups like the Beetles and the Rolling Stones. Then, if necessary, they could even sing along with whom ever to help the party go smoothly. These were talented boys that were quite capable of doing just about any type of song.

The first person to come up and sing their song was a young girl, her name was Louisa Young, and she was in her early twenties and came originally from Malaya. Her job in the hotel was of a maid come cleaner, yet there was something about her demeanor that showed that she had brains, but as her background was not German, life was always going to be tough for her.

Even intelligence would not necessarily get her a decent job. It was obvious that she had European and Chinese blood within her frame. She was beautiful with a great figure, sporting petite slight breasts, not big but there for all to notice, her looks were the sort that men dribbled after, yet her beauty was stunningly Oriental and in a fragile china doll sort of way. Girls like Louisa were easily exploited in all European countries, yet they always seemed to come across as nice to all those around them. When she smiled Louisa showed beautifully white perfect teeth. It was then that David felt his heart go a flutter as she crossed over the floor to the quartet. She bent down and whispered something into the ears of the pianist David Leonard. He smiled in return, stood up to address the audience.

"Louisa Young is going to sing a traditional Malayan song, er, so I am sorry to say we have been made redundant, she is going to go it alone. Please put your hands together for Louisa Young."

A small ripple of clapping broke the otherwise silence that had prevailed. Everybody was looking at the sweet young lady, with either a certain trepidation, or hopeful expectation.

Louisa didn't let anyone down. Her song was beautiful even though no one had the slightest clue as to what it was about. She had obviously had some sort of training as her intonation was very accurate, in fact the whole experience was captivating and surprising to all there. As she sang Louisa started to move in time with the music she was producing. At first slowly, but then as the tempo picked up so did her movements, her arms were raised and lowered in a very rhythmic fashion it was if she was painting in the air, then her legs moved, one in front of the other with her toes pointed out very carefully. Her song and her dance were a joy to behold and that was shown when she finished, they clapped and cheered. Louisa was going to be a hard act to follow. She bowed sweetly and then made her way back to where she had stood. David Cartier had anticipated this and was there waiting too great her.

"Hello, that was really fantastic, can I get you a drink? Oh, by the way, my name is David, David Cartier."

"Thank you, David, yes you can get me a drink, some white wine would be nice. Though I rarely drink alcohol, but let tonight be an exception."

David went to the bar and ordered two glasses of white wine and then presented Louisa with a glass.

"I thought your singing was very beautiful and your movement to the singing was just exquisite. Where did you learn to sing and dance like that?"

"My mother was Chinese Malay and my father was Austrian. He worked for the consular in Singapore, but he was killed during a local insurgence just after being released by the British from internment at the end of the war. My mother brought me to England where we lived in Birmingham for some years, there I went to school, then having left school and not able to get a grant to go to university we come to Germany to live, here in West Berlin." She smiled a sincere smile that warmed young Cartier through to the very marrow.

"So, David you see before you a young lady who is Asian-European, who has had a fine education with three A-levels and eight O-levels in England and what is more I speak four languages fluently, yet all I can get to do as a job is working for an American company in a hotel as a maid."

"What happened to your mother? Is she still alive?"

"No, sadly she died. After I got my job here in the Hilton, she too managed a job within the kitchens, mainly washing up. But about one year ago she got her finger cut in a bread slicing machine, not serious just a small nick, but a nick that soon became infected and as we never had medical insurance no one would attend her when she became extremely ill, she died about one month after the cut." Tears welled up in her eyes.

"Had I known that all she really needed was a course of Penicillin I would have worked day and night to get it. Instead, she died, and I had to bury her in a pauper's grave. Since then, I have had to work off a loan that I borrowed just to get her interred."

David had immediately become strangely attracted to this young girl who now worked seven days a week so that she can just live. Her story moved him, he felt a real compassion for the sadness of her life, it put his own miserable being into perspective.

He might not have had an ideal life, but it had been safe one and he never went short of anything, for that he was extremely grateful.

They finished their drinks and David got in another two and, while he was doing that Louisa went and got two plates of food from the buffet.

The band was accompanying a would be singer who was trying hard to sing the words to Elvis Pressley's Hound Dog, fortunately the quartet played louder in tune than the poor unfortunate chap could sing out of tune, so not to many people heard him, not that it would have mattered as it was all done in the name of fun and everyone was indeed having that served up in high exhausting doses.

The next performer was one of the local chefs within the hotel complex, a half Italian, half English man who had studied his cookery skills in Ramsgate in the south of England which is not far from the main port of Dover. His name was Franco Tomlinson and dear old Franco specialised in Oriental cuisine, not that there were the ingredients to produce authentic dishes, or the enthusiasm to eat what was served on the plates as either Chinese or Japanese food. He tried hard to please with his culinary skills but generally failed miserably, leaving nothing but problems and complaints lying on only half empty plates, these being the only tips that the management earned from his meals. Franco was very much the caricature of a comic book fool, he was extremely red faced, obese and this corpulence made him an overweigh buffoon of a person.

But Franco had aspirations, he imagined that he was a natural comedian, except he really wasn't funny at all and when people didn't laugh at his attempts of japes and jokes, he would become very annoyed blaming the audience instead of his jocular attempts.

When people did laugh it was usually because they didn't want to upset him, sending him into a distinctly unfavourable unsavoury mood, unsavoury not being a word that should be banded around a chef.

So when this clown came onto the staging area still dressed in his whites with a towel thrown over his shoulder, the mood within the room changed from one of merriment to one of gloom and foreboding.

"Oh dear! Here comes trouble!"

The under manager was talking to Stuart Holstein and he held his hand to his mouth and had lowered his head as he did so.

"What's the problem? Why all the silence, is there a problem?"

"Well, this chap is a bit of trouble. He has been close to being fired on several occasions and only kept his job because one of the top American brass likes his cooking. But he is a difficult nasty bit of work, a person that only ever thinks of himself never interested in anything anyone else has to say in life. And what is worse he isn't funny, but may I suggest for the sake of a quiet evening we all laugh and clap like mad."

Chef Tomlinson spoke to the pianist then turned to the audience and in a broad American deep south accent, he said,

"Thank you, ladies and gentlemen, for my first song I would like to sing the great ballad My Way."

Holstein turned towards the under manager.

"I didn't know he was actually an American?"

"He's not, he's a limey from the south of Blighty somewhere."

Stuart looked completely baffled and all he could respond with was.

"Oh!"

And then a shrug.

Franco Tomlinson Oriental chef of the new Berlin Hotel Hilton started his bellowing of the great Frank Sinatra song. All the sound was forced and rather shaky in substance and when the melody slowed so that the words…

"I did it my way…" the entire song went flat and not just the intonation, the whole thing just sort of petered out, the attempt of producing dear old Frank Sinatra's song sizzled to nothing.

He came out trying hard to sing with that ridiculous phoney accent, David Cartier and Louisa Young could not contain themselves any longer. David started to laugh, at first under his breath and then as the pain increased so did the volume of laughter. Louisa was not going to be left out either, she had good reason to dislike Mr. Tomlinson, he had tried very hard one night to seduce her, even to the extent of threatening her, saying that one word from him and she would be out on her ear without a reference. She was lucky, she called his bluff and when he became more abusive the hotel main porter just happened by, he nearly knocked old Franco out giving him a very sore black eye and that did nothing for his ego.

So Louisa decided that David was right in his assumptions, there was a rather obese stupid person trying hard to sing what is considered a classic great song but very, very badly.

Laughter is a strange thing, once started it is very hard to stop, but more to the point it is a very ferocious disease that spreads from person to person at a tremendous rate of knots. Once the person in front and beside David and Louisa heard the laughter, they soon became embroiled in the mirth and then next to them and so on. Before Franco had reached the end of the first verse, half the audience were laughing out loud, so loud that everyone could hear the chortling, which meant even mister Tomlinson. The band were trying hard to hold it together but in the end Franco and the band decided that enough was indeed as good as a rest and stopped. For a moment Franco stood there shaking with rage but then the mood changed and so did his temperament.

"So, you want something good to laugh at do you, right!"

He was still irate from being stopped dead in his crooning mode, but after all a chance to tell a joke or two, one cannot turn away from a captive audience.

"Right then! Two ministers of the cloth were playing golf together. Both were playing quite well, when the Protestant Vicar hit a really bad ball that flew off into the rough, he was so angry with himself that he said, 'Oh, buggeration missed the bloody green.' The Catholic Priest, who was his opponent, looked at him with a certain amount of dismay. 'Please don't swear, God will punish you if you persist.' The Vicar smiled, then swung his five iron at the ball and missed it completely, with that he said: 'Christ almighty missed the bugger!' The Priest quickly crossed himself and then told the Vicar off once again. 'God will punish you for sure.' They carried on to the next hole and then the Vicar swung his club again and then he missed once more. 'Shit, buggeration and Christ almighty, missed the bloody thing yet again!' Before the Priest had a chance to warn the Vicar, the clouds parted within the darkening sky and a bolt of lightening came down and struck the Priest stone dead, then a distant rumble was heard all over the golf course and a deep voice was heard to say... 'Jesus Christos, Shit, buggeration, I missed the bugger!'"

At first there was complete silence and then one or two people realised that he had finished and also that the joke was indeed quite funny, they then started to laugh and then once again laughter spread throughout the entire room. Franco had his first success and maybe his last? Sadly, Chef Tomlinson now had the bug, he went on to tell another four long rambling so called funny stories that left most of the people puzzled by either not understanding them or being slightly offended by the crude content of the story.

But it was proving hard to get him to leave the staging area. Eventually Stuart went over shook his hand and thanked him on behalf of all there, then quickly ushered another would be singer to take the stage and perform.

"Louisa, would you like another drink? I really want to try their whiskey, fancy one?"

"Sorry David but I never drink strong alcohol. To tell you the truth, I have a small headache coming on mainly because of the smoking. I fancy getting some air, would you like to walk me around the block?"

Cartier looked up at the ceiling as if searching for the heavens, he smiled broadly to himself and thanked all the Gods if any were listening to his thoughts. 'Thank you, God!' This was just the remark that he wanted to hear, not the one that Louisa had a headache but just the fact that they could be more or less alone together. As the party was in full swing no one would miss their leaving, anyway what would anyone say?

"Can I get your coat for you, there is some snow outside I wouldn't want you to get cold?"

David felt good with himself, the chance to escort a beautiful woman and to act the gentleman as well, it certainly made a nice change, a warm glow descended upon him like dipping very slowly into a warm bath.

"Thank you, David, but my coat is up in my room, I shan't be long, maybe two minutes."

She walked to the elevator and David's eyes could see nothing but her form, had his life depended on it he would not have been able to survey anything other than that beautiful creature, it was an impossibility for him to look anywhere else, he followed every wobble of her beautifully formed bottom as it made its way to that lift. Two minutes later to the second Louisa re-appeared wearing a heavy woollen coat of a pale green colour, a woollen matching hat and knee leather boots. David looked at her with a broad smile expanding across his countenance almost from ear to ear. She looked lovely even though her clothing was maybe ten years out of style. 'Who cares, she would look good in sack cloth and ashes, whatever that means?'

They walked outside the hotel and were immediately hit by the extreme cold; the temperature must have dropped to at least minus ten centigrade and that was enough to take both their breath away. It was a cloudless night and as electricity was still limited to various times of the day there were no streetlights spoiling the view to the heavens. The roads and pavements had been cleared of snow and frost, so it was quite safe to walk.

Once again David thought about how efficient German manpower was. England would have long come to a complete standstill with this sort of extreme cold. Once again, he thought about the old saying… 'Germany and Japan lost the war and quite convincingly, but they both won the peace even more convincingly…'

They walked for about one hundred yards down the road and then a huge lorry carrying metal trunking for some new building being erected came down their road lighting up everything. David instinctively took Louisa's arm and brought her closer to himself. She didn't resist, instead nestled even closer, the lorry passed, but David still held tight.

"This country is truly amazing, Christmas Eve and yet they are still working on their building sites. England would have declared a six-week national holiday by now, especially in this cold. Well, I might exaggerate a tadge, but not much!"

They both laughed which brought them even closer together. David now in a state of euphoria let his eyes transcend to the heavens, at that moment a flash of light crossed the sky as space debris crashed into Earths atmosphere.

"Look Louisa, a meteor hitting the atmosphere, can you see it. Oh, it's gone now, did you see it?"

"Yes David, I saw it. Just think, that light was made by something not bigger than a small, tiny pebble hitting the upper atmosphere, probably thirty or forty miles upwards. What would it be like if something the size of a car hit the Earth?"

For a moment she stopped walking, so did David.

"Have you even heard of Tunguska? I think it was the 30th June 1908, at seven-seventeen in the morning, an object was seen glowing and falling at a tremendous speed. It hit the ground in the very remote part of Siberia hence the name Tunguska. When it finally smashed into the ground it went off like a nuclear bomb and it devastated an area more than one hundred miles across. The crater area was more than one mile across. More than fifty odd years have past yet still nothing grows there, and the devastation is still to be seen, fallen rotting trees lie everywhere all pointing outwards from the blast. Scientists believe that whatever hit the Earth was probably no bigger that a rock the size of a man, weighing far less than a ton. Sooner or later a bigger piece will hit the Earth and then man will not have to worry about wars, racism, trade, world affairs, mating or setting up homes. There will be no life left on the planet to worry about. Earth will be able to start again, this time without the most devastating creatures that could ever have been imagined, man!"

"Well, if it's the end of the world, I had better start living now not much time left."

He stopped dead in his tracks, swung Louisa towards him and kissed her full on the lips. He felt her body shudder gently and then thought he heard a small gasp as their tongues met for the first time. That first kiss might have been very disappointing, but it wasn't, it might have been their one and only kiss, but it wasn't. David felt very strong feelings overwhelming him, he didn't like the word love it sounded ridicules and that very thought made him blush inwardly especially as he had only met Louisa Young for the first time a few of hours ago. But this feeling that was escaping from his heart and invading every nerve end within his being was something completely new and it was so very exciting, he liked this new sensation.

He eased her away from him and investigated her face. He could just make out a thin smile in the starlight. He smiled deeply into her eyes, there was no mistaking either of their strong feelings and they didn't have to say anything to one another it was quite an obvious show of affection and trust manifesting itself between those two people. But then on reflection, words must be said, time is of an essence, feelings had to be spoken about, it was David who eventually broke the silence.

"Louisa."

David stumbled badly at what he wanted to say, but he tried again, "Louisa, I know we hardly know anything about one another, but I sense that you feel as I do and that is a great bond developing between us. I am not going to use the normal flirtatious worn cliché's, I won't embarrass you or myself with words of love etc, but I feel some sort of bond quietly and quickly developing between us and I for one like that feeling very much. I am not a here today gone tomorrow sort of person, but as you know we are only here until the New Year and then we are off to the far east for a few months. But between now and the time we go I feel I want to get to know more about you and hopefully, you will feel the same."

David blushed but neither of them were aware of that, it was too dark even to see features let alone colours.

"I am younger than you, not that that matters to me, but you should know that I start Music College next September and my studies will last at least three years, so if something is going to come from our relationship it is going to take a great amount of patience on both our parts, it also doesn't help the fact that you live in Berlin and I live in London, or at least I will when I get back to old Blighty, er, that is England."

David stopped to take breath, and then concluded with,

"Christ Louisa, maybe I have already blown my chances with you."

Once again in that darkness David blossomed with a bright shade of pink,

"I rather guess I have said too much too soon, in which case I am very, very sorry."

Louisa smiled back at David, but this time he could not see that smile as most of the sky had once again clouded over and snow was once again starting to fall in a gentle but rather determined manner, fortunately for them both the grit on the pavement and roads would not let it settle yet.

"David, yes, I like you too. I don't know what to say, I have always avoided contact with men as all they want is to try and get me into their beds. I hasten to add that I am still a virgin, but I am also not a child, I know right from wrong, and I know when someone is special, and I think that maybe I have found that special person here and now in you."

David could not see how red faced she had become. Louisa had never spoken like this to anyone before but somehow it seemed so easy with David, yes, she liked him, and she especially liked the feeling of liking him.

"Please take me back to the hotel, give me half an hour then come to my room."

And then in a more demure voice she continued with,

"Though I must ask you to be especially careful with me and very gentle too."

When they arrived back at the door to the Hilton with its lights blazing away, they laughed at each other as they both now looked like snowmen. They were both covered from top to toe with a fine showing of white powdery fluff, this they brushed off one another before entering the building.

Having been given a key to Louisa's room David went and had that whisky he had promised himself earlier, though he would loved to have just followed her upstairs to her room but as she had asked him to be thirty minutes, that's exactly how long he would be.

When he went back into the main room where all the fun and games had been happening, the first thing that he noticed was that the live music and singing had now stopped and people were laughing and some were dancing to the blearing pop music coming from a transistor radio, it was perfectly obvious that it was beaming from Radio Luxemburg as the strength kept fading in and out, not that anyone fretted about something as mundane as actually hearing what was being broadcast.

Most people were very drunk, and the rest were well on their way to reaching nirvana, but not quite the way that Buddha hoped they would reach it. Food was still plentiful, and it was by the table with the buffet that David fell upon his friend Roger Mills. The latter was yet again tucking into a huge piece of pumpkin pie. David smirked to himself, he looked like a naughty boy having been caught raiding the larder, there were bits of pie all over his face and some even in his hair.

"How the hell did you get pie in your hair? Have I missed a food fight?"

"What ho, Limey friend of mine. Us Yankee bastards never learnt good manners like you Brits. When you left us after the war of independence, you took manners with you, it was very unfair on the part of your ancestors, very unfair indeed!"

Roger flicked the offending piece out of his hair and then stuffed another piece in his mouth.

"Where have you been, I have been looking for you. I think I have a hot date tonight, see that rather large blond Fräulein over there, well she belongs to me, I own her from the waist down and I intend to take what is mine tonight. Er, are you going to use our bedroom for a bit?"

"Well now, what's it worth to get rid of me for the entire night? What about a bottle of Champagne for your old and only friend in life, then you can be assured of peace for at least twelve hours, otherwise your arse belongs to me. Deal?"

"I don't trust you. Have you already got something lined up? You're on a promise, aren't you? Come on, come clean who is the poor wench? Which of these lovelies is going to suffer a humiliating experience with an Englishman?"

As a truth incentive he added,

"Come clean and the Champagne is yours."

"Okay, okay, no more torture please I can't take the pain, I will tell all. I am seriously afraid that I may have fallen for that Chinese Malaysian girl who started the singing, her name is Louisa Young. We seem to have really clicked together. But and I do mean this is for your ears only and no jokes, to me this is really serious."

"Well, you could blow me down with a feather, you sly old dog. Wow, she is gorgeous, well done you. I shall want a full report in the morning though, a blow-by-blow account. Okay you win this round."

He raised his right hand to gesture to an imaginary waiter.

"Waiter, a bottle of your best Champagne and two glasses please."

Although David had been given a key, he felt it was probably prudent to knock before entering, as he did so, the door opened and there before him stood Louisa Young dressed in a small slip and covered by a very heavy dressing gown. Cartier smiled warmly as he crossed the threshold, the glasses clanked a little because his breath had been completely taken away by her beauty and the nerves were starting to show themselves. She glowed with rouge on her lips, as well as reddening naturally from the slight shyness and embarrassment of being half undressed.

The truth is that Louisa really didn't know what to do, she was naturally sexy, but not when she tried to be, and her idea of sexy nightwear was really not quite right. But David didn't care as his heart was circling the moon and then tailing off to Jupiter for a quick jaunt. He felt nothing but warmth and tenderness for this woman and the fright of it all to him was, that they still had only known one another for less than five hours, yet already in his subconscious he was planning a lifetime together.

He walked towards her placed the bottle and glasses on a small table, and then took both her hands in his.

"Louisa, you look divine."

With that, his soul was chasing his heart around Saturn. She smiled once again taking the compliment as it was intended.

"Without doubt you are the most beautiful woman I have ever known."

Then remembering the bottle and two glasses, he added,

"Look I managed to con my friend Roger out of a bottle of bubbly, wouldn't you like a drink with me?"

"Oh, David, are we doing the right thing? It is all too soon! But, but yes, I will have a drink with you, I understand now why people take alcohol, it is to calm the nerves, am I right?"

"Well yes, well maybe sometimes Louisa."

Cartier reddened in the face once again and with his red cheeks glowing and white teeth sparkling from his warm smile, he melted Louisa's heart away there and then.

"You are right; both of us feel nervous about what is going to happen, I am no lothario, I too feel unsure about what is happening so quickly. All I know is that though I might be an amateur in the courting stakes, I have never felt anything like this with any other woman I have ever known and though we are both young, I feel very sure that I don't want to miss out and let what I think might lead to a wonderful relationship just pass me by."

He managed to gleam a twinkle that showed clearly in his eyes, that at least what he was saying now was truly sincere.

"Actually, you are by far the most beautiful girl I have even been lucky enough to clap eyes on, how would my street credibility stand if I allowed you to slip through my fingers."

"Please David, kiss me, and show me that you really care. I am yours and as this is the first time I have ever entertained a man in my room please be gentle and show me what to do."

David carefully placed the bottle and glasses down, went over to Louisa, took her in his arms and kissed her full on the lips allowing his tongue to explore the inside of her sweet tasting mouth.

A shiver went through both of them, Louisa clung to David almost as if a deathlike grip was upon her. David then picked her up in his arms and carried her over to the small bed that stood in the corner furthest from the doorway, it was as he did this that he noticed just how squalid the room was. One bed, one wooden chair and a bedside table, there was a sink with just one cold water tap hanging over it, beside that was a singles old fashioned plywood wardrobe. On the floor which had rough sawn floorboards with just one well worn threadbare carpet to help protect the feet from splinters, the entire room was a very depressing place, but for tonight David couldn't give a damn.

Once they both lay precariously on the single bed, David leant in towards Louisa, he then kissed her once again but this time he undid her dressing gown and put his hand inside to feel her breasts. Louisa didn't refuse his advances but breathed deeply and more often, he then bent down slightly to kiss her right breast, then his gentle kiss turned to sucking the nipple which sent her into a rocking motion with her breathing now in a frantic state of panting. It was then that Louisa had her very first orgasm, but not the last one that night.

Gradually David worked his way down her body and in doing so managed to remove all their clothing which ended up in a very untidy heap on the floorboards. Unfortunately, this interrupted a woodlice as it made its interminable way across the floor in the direction of the wardrobe, had the small creature understood what was happening on the bed it might have thought better of leaving this area as the heat that was going to be generated would have lit up its life for all its time left outside of woodlice-heaven. Maybe it did understand and had decided that it was time he searched for a lady woodlice to generate their own heat.

As Cartier caressed Louisa's vagina, first with his index finger which gave her orgasm number two, then lowing himself even further number three was quick to ensue as his tongue managed to enter that area too. As this was completely alien to young Ms. Young, she was lost in feelings of euphoria and panic, as explosions of new experiences flowed through her being, each sensation outdoing the last one and the more that Louisa enjoyed her faltering attempts of sex the more David wanted to please her. After her fifth scream of delight, Louisa now in a near state of collapse said,

"David, David, please stop for a while, these emotional feelings that your touch is inducing is becoming too much for me. I think if we don't rest, I shall have a heart attack and then you will have killed me with love."

She smiled towards him wondering if he even noticed her look of delight and some slight panic. Now she wondered if he was disappointed with her as she had done nothing to try and please him and she fretted knowing that he hadn't yet penetrated her, but how could he, she was showing the signs of being close to complete ecstatic collapse. Her breathing had become ragged and uneven, her eyes had lost their sparkle, and she looked tired and drawn. Her small but firm breasts heaved almost doubling in size as they lurched up and down to the rhythm of her heart.

David of course stopped immediately, got up to the top of the bed once again just stroked her hair and around her brow.

"Louisa I am so sorry, I just got carried away. I guess we were going a little too quickly after all we have all night and beyond."

He smiled warmly at her and realised that he would indeed have to show her everything if he wanted more from her.

"When you feel ready, I shall make you wet once again then we will really make love, and you shall feel my penis enter you."

They lay there together and within two minutes both were sound asleep. David only woke because he knew his bladder had filled and he needed to pee, in fact he was already overly desperate to relieve himself. The light was still brightly burning, and Louisa was sound asleep with her head tucked nicely into the crook of David's right arm, somehow, he had to quickly untangle himself. He gently lifted her head off his arm realising that his upper appendage had actually gone quite numb with the shortage of blood being able to circulate around it. He sat upright and rubbed that arm until the feelings came back and then he wondered about the toiletry arrangements. Seeing the sink there with nothing in it, he knew he could wait no longer, he stood on the wooden floorboards and placed his member in such a position as not to make any noise when he released the flow. He sighed a long loving deep seated sigh as the water exploded out of him, though he was on tiptoes his body relaxed noticeably as urine gushed forth.

"Er, David, the toilet is just next door."

The shock of hearing Louisa soft demure voice made him jump backwards, but he was too far gone to stop now, and pee squirted almost everywhere. It was too late now, he got back quickly into position and finished what he had started.

"Louisa please forgive me, I am not usually that crude, but when needs must and believe me, the needs really did must, I had to use whatever was available. I didn't know where the toilet was, had I known I would have slipped out to use it."

But Louisa was laughing gently she was not angry.

"I have used the sink too which is why it is almost falling away from the wall."

Louisa laughed a little nervous like squeak as she too realised what she had just said.

"Why don't you wash yourself than come back to bed then maybe we can finish what we started."

And that was how young Louisa Young lost her virginity and David lost his heart.

The next morning was Christmas day. Arrangement had been put in place for the hotel staff to once again join the troupe with a real Christmas turkey dinner, then a string quartet would play for the staff as a thank you.

Stuart Holstein looked out the window of the lobby and was overjoyed to see that there was at least twelve inches of snow lying everywhere. 'What ever happened to that German efficiency? No one was coming to clean this area this day,' but then as he thought this, a noise of a diesel engine could be heard and shortly a snow plough came into view pushing all the snow from the road onto the pavements. Holstein shrugged and thought once again, on how wrong ideas of German folk were so easily assumed, this country and its people were an enigma, you assume one thing they do the other. 'Oh, what the hell, it's warm inside this hotel, the staff are friendly and the food and drink and very acceptable, all's well with the world, at least as far as I am concerned.'

David cuddled up close to Louisa once again, he had just awoken realising that his bottom was sticking out from underneath the blankets and that in fact his posterior was freezing cold, he looked around the room and saw frost on the inside of the window and even the walls had moisture dripping slightly showing just how cold the room had become. As he nestled in, Louisa responded with a grunt and a snuggle of her own.

Once again, his right arm was dead and needed a little revival time, as he tried to retrieve his arm her bottom snuggled itself nicely against his penis which instantly went hard, that in turn aroused Louisa and even in her sleep she pushed her bottom against it to give room for entry into her vagina. David obliged willingly and once more they experienced the joys of one another's body parts coming together.

As David and Louisa reached climaxes David forgot to withdraw and managed to squirt his semen into her. It was only as he relaxed that he knew it was already too late. 'Women don't get pregnant from their first sexual experience; pregnancy has to do with being in the middle of their cycle or something like that. Anyway, it's too late now to worry, what will be will be, as that crappy song goes 'Kay Sara, Sara.'

David then promptly turned over and pushed his bottom into Louisa's midriff, this woke her instantly and she pushed him hard, so hard in fact that he felt the pull of gravity and hit the cold floor.

It was almost ten o'clock in the morning before everyone descended to be greeted by Stuart with,

"Happy Christmas!"

Followed quickly by the said person's name, this always amazed David as he knew that the turnover in personnel was quite large and for someone to keep learning all their names was quite a feat. David greeted Stuart back with the same, but David looked alive and bright even though his sleeping position had been somewhat fraught. He had been revived with the power of sex and lovemaking to a loved one. This today he learned was an exhilarating experience that lifts the cobwebs away from fatigue.

He stood there looking at Stuart with a widening grin planted firmly upon his countenance and then while there up came this beautiful Oriental girl who tucked her arm into David's. All the while David stood grinning at Stuart.

"Stuart, may I introduce this beautiful lady to you, her name is Louisa Young and you are looking at two people, who are firmly as one now."

"What? Well, it's nice to meet you Miss Young, I remember you from last night, you sang and danced gloriously for all our entertainment. I truly wish my boys could be as exactly precise as you were."

The polite grin left his face, and he said in a very matter of fact way,

"Now David, what's all this firmly as one stuff? Are you still suffering from alcohol poisoning?"

"Oh, nothing."

Said David as an answer and he grinned even broader.

"It's just a wonderful day and I for one am extremely happy. Why I might even be persuaded telephone my mother and father to wish them greetings from Berlin! On second thoughts I probably won't do that, maybe not such a good idea. Come on Louisa now you've met the boss, so let's get some breakfast inside of us."

Stuart stood there stroking an imaginary beard. 'What the hell was all that about? To my dying day I shall never understand Limey's.'

David found his friend Roger Mills, went up to him as he had his back to Cartier, he was eating his breakfast cereals, he didn't see David until he was tapped on his shoulder.

"Roger, I want you to meet Louisa, Louisa this is my pal Roger Mills. Be nice to Roger he has a terrible inferiority complex, mainly because he is a Yankee Doodle Dandy and wishes he was from Blighty and belonging to a real civilized country."

"So, this is who you had to have a bottle of bubbly for? Well Davy old son, she is most definitely worth the cost of Champagne. Louisa what on earth do you want to associate with this awful reprobate for? Anyway, he is just a baby being still wet behind the ears, this is probably the first time he has left his mummies pinafore before, but I guess though."

And he pursed his lips.

"He is kinder pretty and what's more he doesn't smoke or drink, at least not like a fish."

Turning back to his breakfast, he then made a statement of intent, "I intend to eat, drink and be merry today and maybe that should be your objective too? After you have played that is."

"Oh, crikey, I had forgotten. Louisa you will have the great pleasure of hearing me play my viola, because we are entertaining all the hotel staff that are left here to one or two light music quartets. I do hope you like them?"

"Well breakfast first, after that I will be happy to talk to Louisa while you do your eight hours of scales and arpeggios."

"Don't listen to him Louisa, I can't remember the last time I did any serious practice, though I can't say I am proud of that little fact of truth."

David paused for a moment thinking, then as if coming to a light bulb moment within his life he said,

"Actually, I will do some work on my technique but not today. Sweetheart what would you like for breakfast?"

Christmas day was spent lolling around that watching CNN on the television which had been strategically placed in the dining area. Louisa had to do two hours work after breakfast, mainly making the beds for the musicians and then she was once again free to relax and enjoy her first Christian Christmas with a person she was quickly falling in love with.

The dinner was served at four o'clock in the afternoon. Not one person had ventured out of the hotel, it was far too cold just looking out of the windows. All the staff and the musicians were having a great time. Friendships that were being formed would stand in good stead for a long time to come. There was merriment and laughter from everyone, games were being played, people were singing, dancing, drinking and eating.

The Christmas dinner had been fine, even the chef himself came out of the kitchen to eat with them all and afterwards he was cheered and carried shoulder high around the dining room, then promptly pushed back into the kitchen to produce the expected plum duff. All in all, a wonderful great success.

An hour went by after the food and then Stuart called the four musicians to come and produce their own brand of magic. The first pieces were a medley of Strauss waltzes, set for just four string players, they were fun to play but to the purist listener they came across as rather weak in sound. Then a selection of tunes from the films, including Casablanca, Wizard of Oz, African Queen, The flight of the phoenix and lastly Little Caesar. The quartet ended its session with some Christmas Carols, which everyone was made to sing along with after which the under-manager stood up and said a short prayer of thanks. It had become a very special time for everyone.

All the time that David Cartier had been playing Louisa Young just sat there on the edge of her seat with her back bolt upright and her concentration extending only to David. She didn't hear a note, just watched her new man playing an instrument that she knew nothing about and that was enough for her, now she felt extremely proud.

After David had packed his viola away, he asked Louisa if she would like to spend an hour in his room which was bigger, warmer and a darn sight more friendly. Anyway, his bed was bigger and more comfortable. She smiled and nodded, and they then crept away from prying eyes had there been any.

They made wonderful sex together three times, by which time David was almost incapable of any more movement. He suggested that they sleep for a while and then go down and join in the fun and games, that is if either had any more strength left in their bodies to even get back down the stairs. They slept for nearly three hours and by the time that they awoke it was quite late in the evening. David took a shower and then pulled Louisa in with him, which after a little squeal of delight she nearly crushed him to get there, this would be the first time that Louisa had taken a shower in over two years, she only got the chance for a bath, then usually only once a week. He leathered her down with beautifully smelling soap, when she looked at it she exclaimed to David as if it would mean something to him, that it was of course French that's why it smelt so nice. After rubbing soap into every possible orifice on her being and enjoying the sensation of exploring, she was just about ready to drop in a dead faint, but instead splashed hot water over both of them.

They kissed and then tried once more to make love, this time standing up in a doggy fashion, but to David Cartier's dismay, he could no longer keep an erection and after what seemed an interminable length of time he gave up, got down on his knees and proceeded to bring on another orgasm for her with his tongue. After which he invited her to dress up to the nines and then accompany him to the next meal as if it was to be their last banquet together. Once they got downstairs the first person they met at the bottom was Holstein.

"Oh, David, I'm glad I have bumped into you both again. David you will not forget that we have a date in the Russian sector tomorrow. I want you up, dressed and ready for breakfast by nine o'clock. I don't know yet what time the bus will come to pick us up so an early rise please. One thing for sure it will be a long day for us all, but it should be an experience, and it will create goodwill, so it's over the top and up and at 'em. By the way you are playing piano tomorrow, how's your jazz reading?"

David's face dropped almost to the floor.

"Stuart, I'm not sure that my reading is good enough for jazz, especially modern jazz."

David cupped his hands under his chin, he stroked the stubble that was starting to form, he then imparted with,

"Surely you have a better choice than me?"

"No, you are my only option. Don't worry too much, if you flop you will end up in a gulag in Siberia, so absolutely no pressure."

This no pressure phrase was fast becoming his catchphrase.

Then he walked away leaving David wishing the ground would open up and swallow him whole. This news spoilt their plans of a special celebration together, so David went and looked for Roger just to make sure that he wasn't going to use their room tonight. When he found him, he was chatting to a German woman almost twice his age, but he seemed to be doing well.

"Roger, sorry to interrupt, are you coming with the band tomorrow?"

"Why yes, is there a problem?"

"No not for you, but Stuart has asked me to play the piano and to be honest I haven't got a clue about reading jazz on the old plonker, I think I shall take my viola just in case I do bomb. Now the other thing I want to know is can I have our room for tonight without you bursting in spoiling a good night's sleep?"

Roger turned to his lady friend, looked her up and down and then asked,

"Glenda my lovely creature, can I sleep with you tonight and can we shag ourselves to death please?"

The answer was forthcoming,

"Why of course darling, but you must be good, no five-minute wonders please."

"So, there's your answer! In half an hour I shall be up to my neck in this lady's love juices, I hope you will be too?"

"Not tonight, we both just want a good night's sleep."

David now feeling a little happier about the room situation but was more worried about the piano playing that he might be forced to do. He went and found Louisa once more, she was talking to that fat oaf Franco Tomlinson, or he was lecturing her, wagging his finger up and down as he spoke. He went quiet when David approached, but the damage had been done, Louisa had obviously been crying and that immediately incensed David. He looked directly into Franco eyes and then in a very rough voice asked, "What have you been saying to Louisa? Why has she's been crying, what is your game mate?"

"Mind your own business you little squirt, what is said between me and this lady has absolutely nothing to do with you."

"I know your name Franco and I know exactly where to find you. If anything, that you have said is in anyway unpleasant about Louisa, I shall be coming after you and I have a lot of friends that will back me up."

Franco coughed and moved a step back; sweat was streaming from his forehead and the smell from his armpits was almost overpowering. He was no longer someone who could create a problem in a scrap, so his reactions were now becoming one of complete self preservation. Sweat was now flowing almost by the bucket load, a very unpleasant state for anyone within proximity to be aware of.

There had been a few people that had been aware of the slight fracas between Louisa and Tomlinson and now were quickly concluding that Mr. Tomlinson was an incredibly nasty bully that only picked on women that were small in stature and unable to verbally defend themselves. Those onlookers seeing that

David was standing up for Louisa were now siding ostensibly with David. One trumpet player called Billie Joel was the first to stand next to David.

"Listen you big tub of lard."

He jabbed Franco hard in the ribs with his finger.

"Louisa is David Cartier's lady not yours, I heard you making snide remarks to her, so if you don't want a good beating and then your job being taken away from you, I suggest you leave now and never ever let any of us see you even talking to Louisa again, understood?"

"Okay, okay, I'm going, but you haven't heard the last of this mister Cartier, oh no, not by a long shot. No one threaten Franco Tomlinson and gets away with it."

David stamped his left foot hard on the ground and Franco nearly messed his whites, he then quickly turned and was gone.

"Thanks Billie, I owe you one."

David then turned to Louisa.

"Sweetheart let's go to bed, you can stay in my room tonight, Roger has gone for the night. Go upstairs and get you night things and washing stuff and I will meet you in my humble abode. I will make us a nice cup of Rosy Lee."

"What the heck is Rosy Lee?"

It was Billie Joel who was still fascinated by the Englishman's way of speaking.

"Why Billie boy, you really must learn the Queens English."

David took a large breath, then said in a knowing arrogant way,

"Rosy Lee is cockney rhyming slang, it means tea."

A massive smile came over both of them and then as an aside as if talking to no one in particular, David said,

"Oh dear, I fear the worst for you past colonial boys."

David then turned towards Louisa once again, but she had already gone to get her attire. David smiled to himself then started for the stairs, but as he passed Joel he brushed and stroked his shoulder in a gesture of thanks, Joel responded with a,

"You are welcome, David, but watch that heaving tub of lard, he seems to have something over on that Chinese girl that you like so much. I somehow don't think you have heard the last of him!"

He then wrinkled up his nostrils and added,

"Christ, he smelt so bad anyway. Good God man, is it possible that we have eaten some of his food?"

Joel wrinkled up his nose again and then made the gesture of shaking from head to toe as if in disgust.

David laughed, but at the same time thought that his new friend was probably right. He decided to go straight to Louisa's room just to make sure that everything was indeed okay. He had to run up the stairs as the lifts had not worked since they had checked in, there was some major problems with all these pre-war lifts throughout Berlin and the company that made them had been bombed out of existence, so it was just a matter of waiting for the replacements, which didn't help the guests in the meantime.

It took a whole minute to reach the top floor, and David felt the pressure of being out of tune with his body, he knew he didn't do enough exercise.

As he reached the door into the corridor of Louisa's floor, he distinctly heard a small, muffled scream. Bursting through with new found energy, he could see that the door to Louisa's room was also open. There came a crash as furniture was knocked over and then another muffled scream and then a squeal that sounded as if a hand was placed over a mouth to stop any noise from coming out. David burst through the door to find Franco trying to rip Louisa's dress off, she was now showing her breasts and had an expression of abject terror written into her face. As Franco had already got his own trousers down to his ankles it was going to be easy for David to tackle this huge hunk of a man.

David grabbed him by the shoulder and spun him round, at the same time Louisa fell heavily to the ground and lay there in a fetal position. David was so enraged that he just kept pummeling Franco with blow after blow, his arms were swirling around like a windmill's sails, but every blow landed on some part of the chef's body or head. After about twenty seconds going on for what seemed like two hours Franco fell to the floor whimpering loudly, sweat and dribble were running everywhere. One last kick with his shoe into the side of Franco's monstrous belly did the trick, laying there winded he couldn't even cry.

"Right, Louisa here are my keys, take your stuff and get to my room and then use the telephone and say what has happened. Get the manager and anyone else to come up here now!"

Louisa scrambled her clothes together and nearly ran out the door. Just for luck as Franco was now starting to show signs of recovery David kicked him again.

"No more, please no more. I won't move a muscle. It was her own fault though, she teased me all the time promising me sex but never actually giving in to me. I'm not an animal, she shouldn't have pushed me that's all."

David kicked again, Franco gasped and lay mute and still. This time urine was running across the wooden floor and dropping out of sight probably to the next floor below. Soon running feet came up the corridor and in rushed the under-manager completely out of breath, utterly red in the face and like most people over fed, over drunk and feeling very much the worst for wear.

"What's this bastard been up too now?"

He panted with his hands on his knees almost bent double.

David explained what he found and the terrible state that Louisa was in. Charles Spooner, the under-manager looked at Franco with loathing and disgust, he then turned to David and asked,

"What should I do with him? I can get the police involved, but what happens if he cries fowl play and that he was led on. I can also sack him now, donate his salary to Louisa and have him thrown out the building within the hour, lock stock and sweaty barrel. It's yours and Louisa's call?"

"I suggest that you ask Louisa first, whatever she wants I will go along with, but he's ripped her dress and terrified her. But honestly, the thought of him maybe getting away with it is too much to bear."

David thought for a second before adding,

"Speaking for myself though, tell her I suggest that she just takes the money and let the bastard run across Berlin in his trousers still hanging down to his ankles."

"Well mister Tomlinson, you've gone ten steps to far this time. Take it from me whatever happens, whether we get the police or just kick you out it is going to cost you your month's salary plus Christmas bonus, and you will get no reference from us, not unless your next employer wants the truth."

He was almost bent over Franco and was pointing his index finger at him in an aggressive way.

"John, will you go with David and this piece of shit to his room and make sure that everything he owns is packed and ready for the pavement. If he tries anything, no matter what, kick him in self-defense and very hard! Franco I am off to talk to Louisa, your fate depends on what she says."

Franco was dragged to his feet; he was trembling with fear mainly because he didn't want to spend any time in the cells. He was soaking from sweat and urine, he now wanted more than anything to get back to England.

In his mind he was already planning to develop an idea which had been formulating within his brain about a special sort of burger, he had been experimenting for some time with various ingredients and now he thought he had the perfect idea for a chain of burger shops, once back in Blighty away from spying and prying eyes, all of which were after his formula, he would approach his local Lloyds Bank with his thoughts and they would advance him a couple of million Pounds sterling so that this new breed of burger shops could get well and truly off the ground. But first he had to break free from the shackles of work and the myriads of wanton women all chasing and trying hard to get his virtue.

He would make these two young people pay for their personal interference at some later date. After all it was Louisa that had tried to seduce him just like all the others, not the other way round. He felt he had always tried hard to be a gentleman and his respect for the fairer sex was plain for all to see.

Strange how some people can indulge in fantasies of thought when they are in some physical or mental danger.

As he finished packing his two small suitcases along came the under-manager.

"You are lucky Franco; Louisa is not going to press charges against you though I told her she should. So, you are officially sacked as from this moment, we have your English address and that is where we will send your papers. As for your salary and bonus, that is going to be given to Louisa, tax free. But we will be holding this episode over you, I personally will write the entire matter into a personal account of what you have done, then I shall ask all who know you to sign it, then if anything else occurs which we hear about concerning you, the document will be presented to the police. So, do you entirely understand, if we hear at any time in the future that you have been involved in any way what-so-ever, doing something against a woman and that means in any way or form against her will, this case will be re-opened. If you understand just nod as I don't want to hear your voice again."

Franco just nodded.

"I will carry out the threat that I have stated that you have my word on it. Now boys, instead of me calling security, you two can have the distinct pleasure of throwing this bum out where he belongs, onto the streets."

'What a strange Christmas this has been! I've met the woman of my dreams, I have enjoyed great fulfilling sex, it has had its highs, but now it has its lows too. I almost feel pity for this wretch, where will he end up at this time of night? Bloody hell it's teeming down with snow he could freeze to death out there. I think the security can do the deed, I have done enough, I don't want to have a hand in this fat pig's death.' David looked at the under-manager and told him what he was thinking, so security was called and one chef Franco Tomlinson was ejected onto the streets of Berlin in the snow on Christmas Day evening, maybe he deserved to be punished, but to David it seemed a strange time to pick.

David was developing pity, something new and novel for him to consider, maybe it had something to do with being in love? In love, was he in love? Was this the start of a new existence one that involved Louisa Young? Surely it was all too soon to speculate on such things, back to bed and Louisa!

Franco Tomlinson didn't die that night. Once on the street with his two suitcases bundled along beside him, he turned one last time in the direction of the Hilton Hotel and stuck two fingers up at the security man who had actually spilled him onto the street. Picking up his cases he legged it as fast as he could in the direction of the railway station. There he would spend the night and then got the next train back to England and make that new life and earn millions of Pounds, after all, it was his destiny, wasn't it?

The security guard rubbed his hands together and then smelt them, they stunk of urine and something else, whatever it was it was extremely unpleasantly pungent.

He smiled as Franco was last seen running along the road, then turned back into the hotel bent down and picked up a handful of snow and rubbed it hard into both hands, he then smelt his hands again and once again grimaced. He then closed and locked the doors of the hotel once more and then went to wash his hands properly.

David Cartier took Louisa Young into his arms and stroked her hair and wiped her eyes, this evening had been one awful ordeal but now it was completely over.

"Look Louisa, that awful man is now gone, you will get his salary and bonus, that could amount to as much as one hundred and sixty Pounds in UK money. Make sure that you save that money we will both need it for the future. May I further suggest that you nip into the shower and have another wash, at least to get rid of that mister Tomlinson smell."

He smiled at her, kissed her cheeks, then sat her on the bed, it was then that he thought about what he had just said, so had Louisa. She responded first.

"Do you really believe we have a future? I really love you, but I allowed you to make love to me because I just felt the time was right for both of us, it wasn't to tie you to some sort of promise or whatever."

"I believe we can make a go of life together, but you will have to have patience with me. Like I told you before, I am now about to go to the Far East on this tour, then next September I go to the Royal College of Music and that will last for three years. But my love even after that life might be precarious, musicians don't earn a fortune just a living if they are lucky. My plan is to make as much money as possible while on tour with this American band, then at the end of the trip, I should have enough money to put a deposit on a house. If there is a future for us I will hope that you will help support us both by working too. But let's take one step at a time. What about that shower, then bed and, I mean bed to sleep?"

Chapter 8

The next day David was up at seven o'clock in the morning, he had slept well though he dreamt heavily with many silly dreams flashing through his drunken mind. The dreams were mostly about playing jazz on the piano in a Russian gulag with Franco as the prison warder and tormentor. When he awoke, he found himself covered in a cold sweat and this was followed by a distinct feeling of unease. He went for another shower, one that was incredibly hot, this was mainly to wake himself from that awful drowsy feeling that is left, when you don't quite get enough hours of sleep under your belt from having a disturbed night with nightmares.

He came out of the bathroom feeling like a new soul had entered his body, so he proceeded to do some press ups, after just five he nearly collapsed from the ache in his arms. 'Boy,' he thought, 'this is going to be some new regime that I have to start, I am so unfit.' He jumped up and down on the spot, bent to try and touch his toes and after four attempts he managed to reach the floor, that pleased him a little but he knew that he must do plenty of exercise to keep fit. Everyone and anyone of his age, should be fitter than he was and he knew it only too well.

David dressed in his concert clothing so that the less he had to carry the better he liked it, he placed his bowtie in his jacket pocket and then looked in the mirror, there he was imagining that he was Humphrey Bogart in the Big Sleep, smiling to himself knowing that he would always be a small boy at heart, he pretended that he had a gun in his pocket and was just about to threaten a villain with the onset of death.

While he stood in front of that full length mirror Louisa woke finally from a dead to the world sleep, then seeing her man playing at gangsters she burst out laughing. This in turn startled David, who dropped his jacket which had now been slung over his shoulder straight onto the floor, that in turn startled a spider which as Cartier turned, lost its battle for life as he, young Cartier trod on it.

"You know I shall be working all day today, there is much cleaning to do so don't worry about me I shall be fine."

"Are you going to get up and come down and have breakfast with me? Or are you going to stay in bed for a while?"

"Darling, you know what, I think I shall stay a little longer than get up and start work. I will be here when you return home."

Both Louisa and David started at that word that indicated commitment.

"Home, that does sound strange to me. Anyway, I shall ask mister Spooner when he thinks I shall get the money promised, then tonight we can discuss some sort of plans. If you want, I can give you the money to keep? I shall do whatever you decide. But in the meantime, I must keep myself busy if for no other reason than to forget that awful man."

"Right then, I will see you tonight, but I think it will be very late. I'm off to eat, see you later."

David kissed Louisa full and deeply and then went down to meet the others and start a new day's job.

The Russian coach turned up to collect them at ten thirty, absolutely on the dot. It was so punctual that it made one think it had been waiting at the corner of the road, just so that they could time their arrival to the minute. The drive was interesting to all aboard, most had never seen or passed through Check Point Charlie before, none had ever entered into the Russian sector of Berlin before. The Western side of Berlin was one of development, new buildings springing up everywhere, fine architectonically wonderful old buildings from the 18th and 19th centuries that had been devastated during the blitz were once again shining out to mans engineering and ingenious brilliance. The madness of the war finally being swept away with rebirth of the old, fine and grand, the new birth of modern clever and free-thinking architects and developers, of these somewhat exciting new and extremely dangerous times, were in many cases a wonder to behold.

When they reached Check Point Charlie they slowed down, a bored American marine crossed over to inspect the somewhat rickety old Russian bus, he smiled inwardly to himself thinking how rusty and dilapidated it looked. The guard scratched his nose, then looked as if he was about to sneeze, thought better of it and instead looked at the passes that had been supplied for the enclosed musicians, in a tired sweep of his arm he indicated to his colleague to open the barrier.

The drive across that small stretch of no-man's-land was such that it woke everybody up, hard worn cobblestones, barbed wire encased both sides of the road, which also had iron tank traps to make any vehicle slow to almost a stop and then must swerve around them thus keeping the speed to nothing more than a crawl. At this point the passengers wondered just what they let themselves in for, everyone was silent and sitting bolt upright, a strange trepidation showed on most of the musicians faces, not outright fear but a slight alarm, all wondered what would happen if they got caught in the Russian sector and the proverbial balloon was to go up?

Reaching the Russian barrier was an experience in itself. The coach stopped and the driver got out and went to the main office that housed the guards, at least ten minutes passed before anyone appeared, then three fully armed Russian guards appeared as if from nowhere. Guns ready and cocked, they ordered everybody out of the coach and then lined them up in the snow and cold, this frightened all as it was as if they were awaiting the firing-squad. Then one guard held his automatic ready, while the other two went through the bus looking for what? They turned everything out onto the wet roadway; they went through all bags and baggage, investigated every music case, even the music basket. Were they expecting to find secrets, drugs, weapons? Who knows, it was never said, though on later discussions most thought that they were just being bloody minded, making them all stand in the wet and cold for what turned out to be almost an hour. Eventually they were allowed to carry on, everyone once again boarded the coach but not without a few sighs of relief and a little prayer of thanks to their individual gods.

The journey to the Russian barracks still took the best part of an hour as they drove very slowly avoiding cratered roads, they passed hundred and empty bombed buildings and piles of war-torn rubble. The people that they saw were moving in a very cold slow determined way, their well-worn clothing looking pre-war, drab and functional was the order of the day here. Nobody seemed to smile and the glares that the coach got for just being Russian was for the passengers quite unsettling.

It had started to snow once again and that flurry of white only went to ensure that feeling of gloom and doom, it was a depressing morose feeling that was brought that much closer to the forefront of all their collective minds.

Eventually they rounded a corner in a roadway, on each side of the street was lines of tenement housing, most grey and cold looking, made from granite blocks that had saved them from most of the bombs, but everywhere was pitted with shell, bullet and bomb fragments, many windows were boarded up with wooden shutters, but it was perfectly obvious that most of the dwellings were being used by the populace. Some had washed clothing draped on lines across the road to the opposite building. Generally, though the housing was in a dreadful state with little or no repairs having been done. The Russians were certainly making the populace of Berlin pay for the trouble they allowed the Nazi party to get up to.

Finally, there at the end of the road was the entrance to the barracks. The entrance had once been a very grand affair, made from granite and steel with statues covering the roof area, except it was now completely impossible to tell what these statues represented as all had been somehow smashed beyond recognition. This was the gateway to what had once been a huge nobleman's estate and park, sadly the grounds now housed tanks, guns and general armour for the army. The whole area was fenced off with twenty-foot-high corrugated metal barricading with a topping of curly barbed wire, this was there to either keep the local people out or the Russian soldiers in? Roughly every hundred yards was a watch tower manned with guards armed with mortars and heavy caliber machine guns. The once grandiose gardens and lawns were now covered with concrete or tarmac or had been allowed to become mud tips that became the natural haven for rats and other vermin. All along the side of the fencing were many temporary sandbagged cabins that were there especially to house the troops that resided in the barracks.

As the coach drove down the main avenue, which fortunately still had a few cedars trees breaking up the monotonous expanse, of grey tired looking buildings that had once been part of the estate, the musicians looked with growing feelings of sadness as all the barns, stables and outhouses had been allowed to fall into a desperate decline. But then at the end of the half mile drive through the barracks, the apex of Russian domination stood as a testimony of real communistic ideological stupidity, the main sixteenth century manor house, or castle as it really was thought of, stood looming out of the wilderness with all lights ablaze. This had been completely restored to its former grandeur, it sparkled and shone like a beacon of light in a forest of darkness. But the restoration that had been done was just for the comfort of the officers, especially the Commanding Officer within the occupying army. This was showing communism at its callous best, it completely smacked of George Orwell's Animal Farm. *All men are equal, but some are more equal than others!*

This was the way to show the German folk that under Russian rule their lives were much richer, brighter, healthier and so much more fun!

When the coach pulled up at the main front portal of the old manor house, two guards jumped smartly to attention, then three porters came out to help unload the instruments and paraphernalia that the troupe brought with them. They were ushered into a very large room towards the rear of the building, here pictures of Lenin, Stalin and Khrushchev hung with the latter being almost life size thus dominating all the portraits around it. David looked at Roger, smirked then through a tight-lipped grin said,

"Bloody hell! The old buggers gone and copied exactly the table layout that we had back at the Hilton."

"What a copycat. So, we are here to emulate that evening with American jazz as the offering to the communistic Gods. I just hope the food is as good that's all, oh, and not to forget the drinks, I hope that it is something other than just Vodka?"

"Roger my old salt, what the heck do you care, one sniff of the cork and you are anybodies, especially anybody."

Stuart gathered his flock together; he had a few words to impart.

"Men, I don't need to tell you that you now represent your government being here as guests of the Russian General, er, what's his name? General, er, Bruzchenski. No one is going to get drunk, swear, spit or do anything other than to try and play the best that they can. We are here as entertainers and thus one must think of it as a great honour not a chore."

He then stiffened and looked almost angrily at some of his troupe and imparted in a much sterner voice.

"Don't smirk I am serious!"

He looked around with an accusing look on his countenance.

"We will be fed, soon I hope, then we will do a little rehearsing."

He paused for effect, then continued eyeing everybody as if he was interrogating them as suspects for a murder.

"Then tonight we will play for the Russian officers. I want you to make them feel envious that they are not in the West, though I rather think that goes without saying. Ah, that's another thing."

He made the men close ranks around him so that he could almost whisper the words.

"No talking out of turn! I have just been too loud and said things that might be misconstrued, so say nothing that could ever be taken as offensive, even if you should be provoked in any way. Mouths tightly closed at all times, in fact say nothing full stop! Lastly, anyone arrested here for whatever reason I shall personally order up the firing squad."

Then looking towards Cartier, he added,

"That includes you too David. You might be a Limey, but that won't save you, I shall still personally pull the trigger."

A ripple of nervous laughter went around the men.

"Right get yourselves set up ready to start the rehearsal and I in return, will explore the food situation."

They ate a fine meal of boiled beef and various out of season vegetables, mainly out of tins, but the taste was good and that was all that mattered when hungry mouths take in nourishment to satisfy empty bellies.

Though it hadn't been that long since breakfast everyone tucked into the food as if their lives depended on it, after all many thoughts this might well be The last supper. Once they had finished eating the chef came out and told Holstein in stumbling English that they would all be fed with what the guests were eating, but it would have to be during one of the breaks, in what the Americans were fast thinking as a special jam session.

In fact most of the troupe were now looking forward very much for the chance to play and experiment in various modern styles.

So now David was not feeling quite so excited as the rest, to him this could become a nightmare if things went badly and as improvisation was something he didn't understand at all well, how could things go anywhere but badly. It was one thing improvising within the confines of the coffee shop in Beckenham, it was another when expected to be a top line professional.

Finally, Stuart called them all together for the rehearsal.

"David, I know you are sweating over this, but if your piano playing is anything like your viola playing it will be a complete doddle for you. Anyway, here is some of the music that you can work around. We will start with that old standard, Butterfly Ragtime, by Charlie Parker."

He handed Cartier his score which on scanning David wondered if he was a dead man? Then Stuart raised his hands.

"One, two, three, four."

To David, this was a starter's gun going off and he was in the race to win it. Before ten bars were up, he was at least one bar in the lead going for the tape. Holstein stopped looked at David and smiled and then said,

"It's okay son you were fine, just get the feel of the tempo and rhythm. Again, one, two, three, four."

Bang they were off again, this time David felt more confident and managed without a great deal of swing or feeling to at least reach the end along with the rest of them. But in less than two hours David was feeling very good about playing the piano, he was in fact getting on fine and making the right sort of feel in his playing technique. By the end of the rehearsal, he was wondering why he had never tried playing this sort of music before, it was wonderful, and he loved it. It was if just at the drop of a hat that everything clicked into place. He could keep the tempo's going well, he could improvise around a theme when solos were called for, it all sounded right in his head and his hands followed what the brain ordered.

Most of all David Cartier enjoyed the lilt and drift that people like Thelonious Monk and others just took as the norm within the melodies, listening to their ideas of jazz transformed David's feel on life there and then. 'This 'ere General Bruzchenski knows something about American jazz, but you have to ask yourself, how would a Russian General know and like Charles Mingus, Charlie Parker and all the other great musical innovators?' That was a question that would never be answered, at least not entirely.

It was a very sad fact that General Bruzchenski was the very next year recalled back to Moscow, he was considered to be to moderate. And as time passed it was noticed in the West that he seemed to have just disappeared.

At seven-thirty sharp that evening the band was ready and willing to play for their new Russian audience of army officers. The music had been selected, solos sorted, and breaks organized. No one was sure as to how long the dinner would last, but from common knowledge of Russian boozing should it still be going on when the musicians ran out of music, they unanimously decided that they were going to turn the scores back to the beginning and start again. Just as predicted, as the liquid flowed, so memories of what had been performed would be forgotten, that at least was the hope and desire.

As the officers collected and got themselves ready to sit at the tables provided, the band was instructed to play the Russian National Anthem something completely new to the troupe. Once over, the officers sat down and were expectant of something new from the band that was before them. Stuart got the nod from Bruzchenski, and one, two, three, off they went. At first there was absolutely no reaction, just open mouths and wide eyes from the Russians, as jazz circled around the room bouncing its swing off the walls and ceiling. But very gradually after a couple of minutes Holstein noticed that some men were tapping their feet or hands, nodding heads and generally moving to the tempo. The ensemble was beginning to win the campaign with yet no blood being spilt.

Then the courses were presented to the top table and gradually to all the other tables, along with the onset of food came the start of the babbling conversations. Stuart always the keen salesman wanted to make sure that the Russians were now responding to the various tunes and melodies as any band would desire. And to his eternal joy they were. Even while eating Holstein noticed that generally there was a very positive response from the cold war enemy. As the evening progressed so did the drunkenness of the Generals guests. To absolutely no one's surprise, the troupe discovered that Russian army officers like most army officers around the world, liked their drink and as the drink flowed so did tongues flap. So much so that it wasn't long before the band could hardly be heard at all. Stuart ended the rendition of Blue Monk and then called a break. It was now time for the band to try some of that fine smelling cuisine that had been wafting over to them.

Not one member of the band was going to be disappointed with the spread that was offered to them. They started with oysters and were told that these pearls of the sea, in fact came from the Thames estuary in England, how did Russians acquire trading rights to British sea food?

After these gems from Blighty came various fish caught in the North Sea, cut and boned, cooked very lightly by being marinated in vodka, along with this course came bottles of Russian beer to accompany the sea food, everything was developing nicely, and the musicians thought the presentation and taste a complete delight. But these two courses had already taken nearly one hour to be brought and eaten so it was deemed best to perform another session before eating the next course.

This evening had developed into a very special occasion for David, the music had tempted his taste buds as did the Russian food and it was a case of, so far so good.

He smiled at everyone and generally felt good about himself, he always thought he had potential as a professional musician, but now he knew he could make the grade. This music had opened his eyes to a new understanding of his own abilities, he now realised, possibly for the first time he really wasn't a bad music maker.

The second session was really good. By now all the performers were warming to their individual tasks with a relish, playing became more daring and the improvisation became cleverer and faster and much more polished. This was due to a combination of getting used to playing together and being relaxed as the audience were fast becoming completely and utterly intoxicated, mainly from Vodka, but some and this was a very pleasing aspect, were excited and pleased by the music, it was something new and unique to most Russians. Modern jazz, who would have thought it?

The second break came, and the band went backstage to eat what was to be served to them. Again, there were no disappointments, there was a platter of dried cooked meats, served with pickled vegetables. David didn't eat too much of this because he saw what was coming next. A huge plate of roast beef which was served with Mundane of mashed potatoes and Swede, plus a very tasty flat rye bread, which was stuffed with herbs and flower seeds, the bread was used to mop up any remaining food on one's plate. There was no cheese, or desert served, but instead a very strong dark red liqueur made from cloudberries, this came with very strong coffee.

All through the meal, either bear or vodka was being handed out to the appreciative musicians and in some cases, both were consumed by the same person. Truth be known, most of them there drank what was put in front of them. The old adage applied, when in Rome, do as the Romans do!

The third and final session of the evening went well but was finally broken up at around eleven-thirty when some of the officers became so rowdy that they tried dancing their own version of dance to the jazz that was being played to them.

Eventually General Bruzchenski stopped the band as it was becoming more than a little embarrassing to him. He stopped everyone in their tracks to make a small speech, this also included a section in English thanking the musicians for coming all this way to entertain them and he ended his oration when four soldiers marched in bearing enough small packets to hand one each to the band. Stuart Holstein bowed graciously to his host, thanked him in return and said how much they had enjoyed themselves, he then proceeded to inform the General that a special present had been given to him to hand over to General Bruzchenski.

Again Holstein bowed graciously and then picked up the parcel given by General Shute. To the astonishment of everyone there, it was the ivory handled pistol that was supposed to have belonged to Wyatt Earp. Bruzchenski was beside himself with emotion, tears were streaming down his face as he accepted this token of friendship with a slobbering dignity.

Then the room more or less cleared on the spot. They came they saw, they conquered, but only temporarily. Instruments were quickly packed away and the coach, already there with its engine running, waiting to be filled both with the men and their chattels.

Once on the coach, people started to open their little present from their Russian host. Each packet contained one bottle of Vodka, one half pint jar of caviar, one bottle of Lacha Liqueur, which was the cloudberry drink and a personal thank you from the General.

They arrived back at the Hilton at approximately three o'clock in the morning of the 27th December; they had one more dinner and dance to play for and that was to be on New Year's Evening. But somehow it just came and went, not a patch on the dinner for General Bruzchenski which had been agreed by all the ensemble, as being the best for many long years.

David's relationship with Louisa was now going from strength to strength, he now experienced a deep and very sound love for the girl, and he knew she felt the same. He felt that they could now be set for a lifetime of bliss and happiness and though he would soon be flying off to distant lands, he knew she would wait, and they would write to one another almost every day.

Gradually, on the 2nd January men started to appear once more; most having flown back from the United States of America.

It had been a delightful interlude for most of the troupe and yet somehow that feeling of excitement was starting to build within all the Americans and not to forget one Englishman, the tour was starting in earnest as from now.

Chapter 9

The flight to Bangkok turned out to be an infuriating nightmare and not the last on the tour. The first plane was an old DC10, fitted out to carry passengers and cargo, but the problem was that it was having to go via Nicosia in Cyprus, there it was to land at the British base and re-fuel then go on to Istanbul in Turkey, no one understood the route that it was taking and as the entertainers were the only passengers why couldn't the plane fly direct to Turkey it carried enough fuel to do so?

Such was the organisation that planned the tour.

But before anyone could clamber on board the first major problem occurred. For some inexplicable unexplainable reason the Russians had decided to play annoying war games over the Berlin air space, this put all the American bases on high alert so the ancient DC10 was kept waiting at the main airport until the air was clear of Russian MIG fighters and that was a delay of four and a half hours. Waiting inside a military terminal was hardly a bundle of fun. One small stall for snacks and coffee with very few tables and chairs for anyone to sit on and relax, so the air became very heavy with the irritation of discomfort caused by the Russian war planes exploring the American and Allies weakness for letting them get away with their foibles, it was like children playing games with one another, at first they play well together but then something silly happens and it goes badly wrong, that is the cue for one side to sulk and change the game and not let the other play.

Finally, when the Russians went home for their tea, the flight was called and everyone got on board. Snow lay everywhere though runways were clear, there was a storm brewing with high cold winds.

There was a collective groan of misery when the musicians clambered up the steel ladder and into the craft; to their abject horror all the seating turned out to be canvas chairs with an iron framework that stuck into everyone's bones.

This wasn't a promising start and the fact that all seating was squashed very tightly together, so as to be able to get away with just one airplane which made it an ordeal as opposed to any sort of pleasure.

There was no air-conditioning, no heating, no food or drinks and to make matters even worse the flight was due to take at least ten hours. The only obvious solution to do, was to try and sleep, but with cramped uncomfortable condition that was nearly impossible for anyone other than the very young and those who were still suffering from the drunken melee that had occurred the night before.

The aircraft finally got the order from the command tower that all was okay to take off, in fact they said in a very matter of fact tone of voice.

"That it might be prudent to get out now while the going is good as it was now just starting to snow in earnest and the forecast is for the weather to get much worse."

What worried the pilot was the lack of de-icing that had been applied to the wings of the craft. But there was no turning back now and these pilots were if nothing somewhat gung-ho, most having fought in the second world war, they weren't young men anymore, but they still had that devil may care approach to flying.

Everyone was strapped in, albeit uncomfortably squashed, then the engines burst into life, the cabin already smelled of fuel and they had at least ten hours to endure this suffering. The captain stuck his head out from between the cloth sheeting that separated him from the passengers, he smiled, waved for attention then stated in a very bored cavalier matter-of-fact way,

"Hold tight this could be a bumpy ride."

The brakes were let loose and all at once the machine started to roll forward, then very gradually it gathered speed, bang, it hit a rut, everyone held on to anything much tighter, knuckles were white, nerves already stretched were now set to burst. Musicians' eyes stared straight ahead never blinking, for most of the passengers that meant staring straight into the back of the neck of the man in front.

Cold it may be, but all were perspiring badly as if in a sauna and with the smell of fuel combined with the odour of body excretion coming to the surface through fear, the whole experience was not one of delight.

Then the plane got to a crucial speed and briefly lifted off the ground only to smack down again within thirty or forty feet. The bang once again made hair stand on end, but then another burst of speed was felt, and the craft finally lifted off the runway. But the buffeting didn't stop with the race down the runway, once airborne the winds threw the craft this way and that, up and down, side to side, that was until they reached their cruising height which for this plane was ten thousand feet, still well within in the storm area amongst black angry clouds and heavy snow.

Everyone understood the danger of ice forming on the wings and now eyes were averted to the windows, they were all looking at the outside wings and the increasing fury of the storm. The plane was now being shaken very badly, baggage was being loosened on the overhead string netted racks, the noise was appalling, what with the groaning that the hull and wings were making and the thunder that could be clearly heard from the outside, even above the roar of the twin engines. The men quickly thought that their number was going to be up, many were crossing themselves and praying.

David's thoughts went straight to Louisa, who he had left the night before with streams of tears flowing like torrents from her dark brown eyes. How she had almost begged him not to go anywhere but stay with her there in Berlin, this had been said in a tacit way, by looks and gestures alone, those two eyes pleading with love and tenderness. They made gentle love most of the night. Between sessions of intercourse, they just lay on the bed warm and cosy, wrapped in one another's arms. Neither slept that night, nor very little was said either, just caressing and stroking of hair, arms and holding on to one another's hands.

"I love you Louisa and after this tour I shall call you back to London where we will marry. I shall write to you most days and try and send them as time will allow. You can write to me via Stuart Holstein, care of, Army Band on Tour, P.O.Box 2590, Washington, D.C. I think that is all you need to get a letter to me, but even if that doesn't work, I shall telephone you from time to time. I shall think of you all the time and I promise I shall not even look at another woman."

"I will always be faithful to you, and I shall try and write every day too, though it will be hard to make the letters interesting after all, you know what it's like here in the hotel, nothing out of the ordinary happens from day to day. And now that awful Franco has gone there will be even less interesting things happening."

She looked into his eyes.

"Oh, darling please kiss me again."

David remembered every word that had been spoken between them, he recalled every action and every kiss and every caress and re-thinking all their conversations and tenderness's together helped take his mind off the foreboding of a plane crash, which prospect was going through the collective minds of just about everyone on that craft, each considering it a plausible possibility and in fact very likely to happen at any moment.

No one was screaming, no one was crying, but all were tense, ridged with the terror that loomed around them.

The ghosts of ancestors spun around and through the cabin like the electrical storm that was surrounding them on the outside, everyone was experiencing the nightmarish phantoms, all were seeing their wasted lives flashing before them.

The buffeting didn't stop for a minute, and they had been in the air now for over an hour, but in fact they were making good time as the wind was now pushing them, but the storm didn't let up for even a second all the time, it did seem to all on board that the storm was getting more and more ferocious. Quite often the plane would fall hundreds of feet in a second, as air disappeared leaving a vacuum to fall into, then an air current would lift the craft like a feather and throw it way into another place. But those aged DC-10 aircraft held together well. Another shake, another rattle, more heads being lowered into brown paper bags to leave the contents of their stomach.

While everyone was now praying for a quick and pain free end, the captain opened the curtain rose from his seat and proceeded to casually walk back through the aircrafts cabin. He struggled to walk as the plane jostled for position on the starting line. He smiled at his passengers, and then spoke.

"I'm bursting for a piss. I hope this little shaker isn't upsetting you guys. This is nothing to worry about, you only need fret if the engines burst into flames like it did the other day! The only other thing you should look out for is, if you see two parachutes descending through the gloom, then you can then start to worry as it will be the co-pilot and I."

He then burst out laughing, somewhat hysterical in sound but reminding all that their personal specters were there and chasing them to their doom. Then clutching at his privates, he raced to the single toilet in the rear of the plane.

It was Roger Mills sitting next to his pal David Cartier that mouthed what they were all thinking.

"Who is now flying the bloody plane? I bet that cretin has taken the only parachute and left us to our fate."

Stuart and others laughed at his banal and rather tense attempt at a jest, then added his own remark.

"He's so scared that he is cowering in that toilet, I bet he's just gone through his third pair of trousers."

Another flash came as lightning struck the fuselage and a crackle went through the cabin's interior as static electricity went harmlessly around them all proving the Faraday effect. A second or two later and the captain appeared again this time whistling a modern Elvis song. He was halfway back when, yet another crack came and this time a gasp came from the collective lips of all on board including the first officer. The port side engine had caught fire.

"Jesus, now this time it is not a joke."

The captain rushed through to the cabin and grabbed the controls. The fire was very quickly contained but in doing so they lost the use of that engine. He struggled with his second in command, both pulling sharply at the joy sticks trying to keep the nose high and not going down into a plummet. After a minute he turned to the third officer who was in control of the radio said something inaudible to anyone outside of the cockpit area, then went back to holding a course. By now everyone was just praying that their end would be swift and that when standing before their maker their individual actions would be taken into consideration, that being one of not having had time to scream and shout but came to death in a hopefully calm and serene manner.

Then the Captain looked out at them again and shouted out some encouraging words,

"There is no need to worry and fret, this old machine will go on forever with just the one engine, but it does mean that it will take us longer. The radio operator is searching for a convenient airport for us to land on, that is in the area. The trouble is that the storm is also affecting radio waves so we will carry on as best we can for the time being, but at a lower height and that means I am sorry to say yet more buffeting. But fear not my friends we will eventually get somewhere."

He then tittered to a silent audience, in fact everything within the plane was at peace, in a quiet mood of contemplation, or was that straight raw fear?

The noise only came from the screaming of the wind and sleet outside. The one thing that this emergency did was to stop that awful sickness, passengers were to now far to tense to be sick. Then above the noise of the storm, one smart foolish lad sitting next to David, in fact it was his friend Roger Mills spoke loud enough just to be heard by all the assembled.

"Bloody hell! I just understood what that bloody Captain said. If the closing of one engine means that this journey is going to take much longer, if the other engine packs up too, then we will be stuck up here all night!"

That just about did the trick, the entire passenger list let their pressure valves release with a burst of laughter. Another thirty minutes went by before the captain once again poked his head out to speak to one and all,

"We have been blown off course somewhat and we have picked up some speed through the wind prevailing in our direction. What do you think? I have now just been informed that we can land at a small airfield in Graz in Austria. But we might be there for some time. Either to fit a new engine or to get another plane in, either way expect a few days extra rest period."

He looked towards the radio operator then added,

"I have also just been informed that we will be controlled into the airfield by radio as there are also extreme weather conditions there too. I think another ten minutes and we should be thinking about hot food and drinks."

And then in a deep slow drawl he added as if he was talking to young children,

"Relax everybody, nothing to worry about, nearly there and you will all have a special drink with me tonight, or at the very least on the United States of American Army's petty cash."

Ten minutes came and went with the plane still shaking every rivet and weld loose with the weathers buffeting. After yet another fifteen minutes the passengers started to become aware that the craft was circling, not just one way but all over the place. There was nothing to be seen only more wind and more sleet. Then it became obvious that they were losing height gradually coming down lower and lower. The wings were flapping more and more with the variation in air pressure and though they came lower, every now and again an air current would whoosh them up again, yet there was still nothing to see. Then all of a sudden there were a few lights to be seen as they came closer to the ground, it was at this point that everyone realised how good a pilot this Captain really was as the plane was descending between two dangerously jagged shale sides of two cliffs, which now loomed menacingly on either side of this war time aircraft. Then bang, bang, the wheels hit terra firma, then it was up in the air again, then bang, bang, down again, up and down for another three goes until very gradually the aircraft came to a stop and the one remaining engine was switched off. Still the wind rocked the fuselage but now safely. Twenty seconds passed before anyone dared breathe again, then one of the saxophone players called out at the top of his voice,

"Three cheers for the crew. Hip, hip!"

And the required answer came back and so it went on.

Deep down within the very souls of all on board, that machine they that they had just flown in had aged them all by ten years, they had witnessed the face of extinction and come through it without a scratch, though maybe a few more grey hairs. Their individual skins was still pink and unblemished, but their spirit was exhausted and tainted by the experience, that was something that none would ever wish to go through again.

Everyone clambered down the ladder and out of the craft as quickly as possible, luggage was bundled out and the feeling of relief was so evident because the passengers were laughing almost hysterically.

It was David that pointed out just how serious their plight had been when he looked at the failed engine and noticed that steam was appearing from within it, showing that it was still glowing hot and that was despite the extreme cold weather. But now it was that very same cold that was now beginning to attack all their bodies, very, very quickly biting icy snowy conditions start to break down the very senses that the body needs to survive, so it fast became a race to the hanger.

The main hanger was only one hundred yards away, but it could have been miles, for as the snow gathered it became a seriously real chore to cross from the plane to the safety of the hanger, especially as they all had to drag their own instruments and luggage. By the time that they got into the chilled but safe environment of the hanger, several of the troupe including the captain of the plane were suffering from minor form of frost bite.

The snow was now totally blizzard in proportions with very nearly zero visibility. The crew had got the plane down on the ground by the grace of God and the skin of their teeth more than one hour ago, yet no one outside the crew and musicians had even managed to get to understand where the hanger was situated in connection with any other buildings in the vicinity, in fact there were no life signs around anywhere.

They stood around now out of the snow, but not out of the cold. They started jumping up and down and rubbing their hands together to get circulations within their bodies moving once more, cold was now, the serious contender for causing dangerous situations to seriously endanger life and limb. Most of the musicians were quickly realised that extra clothing was now the order of the day, so a frenzy of unpacking the suitcases and clambering into any spare clothing, that was to be found.

There was little light coming from the neon lighting system but most of the light was too high up to have any satisfactory effect on where they huddled around together and the wall lighting was really for the work benches that were dotted around the sides of the building and what shone outwards, was of little use for seeing anything, not that there was anything to be seen.

It was now totally dark outside, and the snow was drifting so hard that it was extremely unlikely that there would be any sort of rescue within the foreseeable future. Stuart talked to the Captain and it was decided that they would search through the hanger to see if there was any chance of maybe telephoning out to the tower and if that was possible, surely this part of Austria experiences conditions like this every year, in which case they should have good winter transport either to rescue them or to send in warmth in the form of heaters, food and drinks, plus maybe some bedding as this was not going to be a short over night stay as would have been hoped for.

They had no idea whether they were near a town with hotels, or if this was an isolated area with nothing but mountains and forests, lacking any basic facilities that they would need and expect to get by as just ordinary people.

Being untrained and un-experienced for cold winter conditions such as they were now experiencing, somehow, they must get by until they could continue their onward journey, though that now all seemed a light year away.

Stuart and Captain Harry Jenson started to walk around the vast expanse of the hanger. It quickly occurred to Jenson that this place was not for planes but dated back to the early part of the century when it was built for the housing of Zeppelin air ships. The size was cavernous, and it was this vast space that made it so cold, it had its own mini environmental climate and subsequently everywhere was dripping water which was now starting to freeze into drops of ice.

Eventually they reached the other end and there was a set of stairs, where it led to, they had no idea as yet again the light showed nothing. They both started up for at least fifty feet, there they came to a balcony, walking along this somewhat now rickety aged slightly rusting walkway they reached a door to what seemed like the outside, on opening it to their complete astonishment it was a control room with wonders of wonders electric light that lit the entire space. There were tables and chairs and a telephone albeit an ancient one. The lifted the receiver and clicked it several times and then came their first real bit of luck since landing.

"Hello, is that members of the crew from the plane that landed?"

"Yes, this is Captain Jenson. We have taken squatters rights on your Zeppelin hanger, what's the chance of being rescued before the spring?"

The sound of laughter came back, then a pause for roughly twenty seconds.

"We are hoping to get a snowmobile to you quite soon, but may I suggest that if you are in need of warmth as I am quite sure you all are, then get your people to retire to where you are now, being a small room body heat might warm the space for you. But please be assured that we will be doing all we can to make you all comfortable. Once we have the vehicle to get to you all, we will evacuate any that need to be, but we will also bring hot food and drinks, though it might only be schnapps. But then if you die of cold, you will at least die happy."

Once again laughter echoed from the receiver.

"Is it likely that most of us will have to stay overnight here in the hanger?"

"To be honest I suspect that is the truth, so I suppose yes to that question."

"Then can you send along some warm bedding in the form of hundreds of blankets, plus lots of food and drinks, maybe give us a portable stove to brew coffee."

"Please stop right there! Where the hell do you think we can lay out hands on portable stoves? Blankets, yes, food, of sorts, yes to drinks, maybe you must forget the stoves. Anyway, if things start to clear a little during the night, you will be taken out of there. Now please let me get all this underway. Just out of personal curiosity, was it a nightmare up there? Wait till you see where you have landed. To be entirely honest with you, we thought you would never make it, we expected a crash, so from us to you, jolly well done!"

While the Captain was talking to the tower, Stuart went back out onto the walkway and then screamed out a command at the top of his voice. The echo rebounded for several seconds, but no answer came back, he tried once more,

"Get your gear and come up this end!"

Still, no one answered, though he thought that he heard what sounded like laughter coming through the air and dark. 'O well, I'll just have to go down there again.'

When he arrived at the entrance of the hanger which was still wide open, and snow was drifting into the darkness giving off a very eerie light, he caught up with several of his team.

"John, couldn't you hear me calling? I told everyone to gather their belongings and come up to where I was, no answer except what sounded like laughing came back."

"Yes chief, we heard what sounded like – *great for beer, will have it sent.*"

The smile appeared again, and a ripple of laughter went along with it, at the same time everyone was hopping up and down clapping their hands trying hard to keep warm and cheerful.

"I said, get your gear and come to my end! Oh, forget it. Right, everyone, we have contacted the outside world and the long and the short of it is that we might be here for a long time. There is a small room that we can cram into to keep warm, but you must follow me with everything you brought from the plane, if you leave anything behind it will either freeze or be ruined by the damp. The tower controllers have informed me that at some time they will get a snowmobile over to us with blankets and food and drinks."

Stuart sighed deeply; he was entirely fed up to the high teeth.

"So that might just be the best we get, rescue might not happen for many hours and as you can hear the storm is getting worse not better. So come on follow me."

Gradually the musicians followed their leader through the huge hanger all the way to the small room up above the far end. On the way some bright spark started whistling Colonel Bogey and before long everyone was marching in step, laughing and whistling the same tune and dear old Stuart Holstein made a very good attempt as Alec Guinness.

Not many people slept while the storm was raging outside, but at least they didn't die of hypothermia as body heat did the trick. Though it did become a trifle stuffy and more than a little smelly, within the confines of the room with an area of forty by thirty feet. The idea of housing forty-nine musicians and three air crew within that area meant that many nerves were strained to almost breaking point, but they survived the ordeal with nothing more than cold exterior limbs and angry agitated brains from lack of sleep, also from continuously having to move to stay somewhat warmer than freezing.

It was three forty-eight in the morning when the engine was heard from the snowmobile. It came into the hanger and tooted its horn three times to get the attention of the involuntary guests.

Once again Stuart took the lead and went out to investigate taking with him the four closest to the doorway. Ten minutes later they returned with hot coffee, sandwiches and bread and cheese. Then the four other musicians, now smiling from cheek to cheek, brought in huge bundles of blankets, which were immediately distributed to those who really felt they needed to have them first. After that an Austrian man obviously the driver, stuck his head around the door and asked if anyone felt the need to get back to the warmth of the tower. Forty nine hands went up in the air along with a groan, then the odd laugh, it was decided by Holstein that the Captain and his co-pilot and radio operator should be the ones to get the benefits first, as anyway, they could and would contact the outside world and let them know at headquarters that this was not another Glen Miller story of an American band disappearing into the great blue yonder.

The food and drinks went down a treat, even though most were not particularly hungry or thirsty it just helped liven up the proceedings somewhat, the blankets once distributed gave a childlike security against the cold and the rather scary unnerving predicament that they found themselves in. Even though it had now been many hours since the forced landing, nerves had started to show their displeasure at being put through a horrible ordeal, grown men started to shake vigorously and teeth started to chatter loudly.

Knowing they were safe meant tense nerves relaxed, which brought on the ague. Yet again and not for the last time, Stuart decided on starting something up to keep spirits high. A jam session, with everyone that had their instrument in front of them taking part.

"You can all take this as a rehearsal and instead of you getting paid, you contribute a large, fixed sum of money to my pension as a reward for keeping you all alive."

A prolonged groan along with a very small grunt of almost laughter emerged from within the gathered ensemble. Gradually instruments were produced and on the count of four Stuart wanted them to improvise to the ballad Porgy and Bess in the key of G sharp minor. He wanted it to start with the clarinet and then it was up to whom ever wanted to break in. The clarinet started as asked, then gradually a flute appeared, at first slightly wispy in sound but as warmth took over from nerves the sound developed. A saxophone broke into the melody along with an accompanying trumpet then trombone, within the space of one minute twelve very clever musicians were improvising and developing up on the original theme. Stuart was elated at the standard of musicianship that his boys brought to the occasion, and he stood there beaming from ear to ear with pride and satisfaction, he knew he had picked a fine bunch of reprobates to be on tour with.

When it finally came to an end the applauding that the rest of the men gave was almost enough to be heard at the tower. This music went on for another hour and then another engine noise was heard and in came the snowmobile once again.

It tooted three times once more and this time the driver came with some good news for the men. A snow plough had managed to get through to the airport from the town, which was a little strange as it was the only snow plough in the district and it belonged to the airport, it had cleared a way through and was now in the process of scraping the snow off the runway to the hanger, rescue was indeed on the way and the men should get themselves together, for the journey into the nearest town that had a reasonable sized hotel. That just happened to be a settlement called Cretoria and it came with a hotel that had been built by Hitler for his Aryan workforce in the early forties for their rest holidays.

They could ski, walk and generally keep fit in the beautiful clean crisp air. Plus the fun that was once on offer, there was the mountainous scenic grandeur of this part of Austria to be seen and explored.

The hotel itself was now very rundown but it was warm and could house all the passengers of the DC10, while they were awaiting repairs at the old military airfield.

"Jesus, what a relief."

David's reaction was somewhat predictable.

"I really thought we would be here for many more hours, I for one could use a good meal and a bath."

Roger agreed with his Limey friend, and they started to climb back down into the main section of the Zeppelin hanger. As they reached the main entrance, they were aware that dawn was gently breaking in the east and better news, the snow was now a steady flurry, the storm had finally broken.

Youthful hearts took over from the cold and misery and a snowball fight developed, which spread rapidly to all America picking on poor unprotected little England. David was soon looking more like a snowman than anything else, but the laughter and jollity was great for morale and despite the extreme cold, most were now in a state of almost euphoria, rescue, hot solid food, hot bath, warm bed and the chance to get even with the British for dragging the US into Two World Wars, what on earth could be better for America than this.

The hotel was very sad and run down and they turned out to be the only guests. Wallpaper tended to be the original and came in one colour, dirty light green. The lobby and stairs were clean, but the carpeting was almost completely worn out, plus there were great gaps in the wallpaper where age had just allowed it to peel away. The bedrooms were small and once again somewhat tired, but they were clean and though the beds tended to be ancient and too springy they too were robust and came with very thick and welcome duvets, though old and tired, all the rooms had adjoining bathrooms and after several hours the water was once again hot enough to fill the aged deep baths and then heaven, utopia, nirvana, in other words, elation! No adjective could be good enough to explain the euphoria that a hot bath brought to their bodies and souls. The actual luxury of allowing the occupant to clamber in and let the warm water soak into the skin bringing life back to fatigued and weary, not to forget somewhat shell-shocked limbs, was a pleasure that only the musicians understood, having experienced that particular unwelcomed ordeal.

Down on the first floor was the dining room and as food was next on the agenda, it became a very pleasurable sight to all the men despite the rooms lack grandeur. Though the food was very bland, being huge chunks of pork, cabbage and potatoes, it was welcome and nourishing and of course the most important ingredient, it was hot!

Life was once again returning, jokes erupted, noise and laughter abounded. What was all the fuss about, nothing had really happened to them. This exuberance just went to show the resilience of the human psyche, humans can overcome almost any hardship and torment and then carry on just like before.

They were stuck well and truly in the Hotel Folkstadt, there was nothing to do but watch the weather come and go like a football being kicked from one end of the pitch to the other. One minute it was snowing the next the sun came out and the white powdery flakes were turning to slush and muck, this went on for an entire week.

A few paperback novels were being passed from reader to reader, chess was being played, but most of all out came the cards. Poker was the name of the game and most of the ensemble played at one time or another.

In one hand five players were playing seven card stud, the kitty started with fifty cents in the pot, all five carried on with a raising of two dollars, then the fourth card was dealt and the player next to the dealer raised the ante up to five dollars, all stayed in except the last player decided to raise it again to ten dollars, again all stayed with what was shown. The fifth card was raised to one hundred dollars, by this time most of the musicians that were within the vicinity came over to watch the proceedings. The sixth card started on five hundred dollars, matched by another five hundred, plus a gold Swiss jeweled watch, that went around with the last player throwing in the keys to his car back in the States. The last card and the first player next to the dealer offered his house, car and all his possessions, the next player matched what was on the table, but the third player had become so agitated that he pulled the cards out of the dealers hand and screamed obscenities, then with his eyes bulging and his mouth drawling saliva, he threw all the cards high into the air. At first there was complete silence everyone expecting fire and brimstone, then someone tittered, this caught on and within a second all around started to laugh loudly. It was then agreed that all cards should be gathered in, without anyone seeing what his opponent had. A general sigh of relief went around the table, and it was then suggested and agreed that there would never be a raise bigger than one dollar at a time.

Two whole weeks went by before the news came that the plane was once more ready to depart, but to everyone's dismay it was still bound for Cyprus.

The hotel owner was extremely sad to see his guests leave, he had made enough money to keep the place open for at least another eight months, so of course he was unhappy about the Americans departing, but facts were facts, and the time did spring forth at a rate of knots, but sad it might be, it did leave him with money and lots of it. But having departed the gloom did descend once more upon the owner and this was at the prospect of having an empty cold building once again. It is not the same sharing a huge building with just the mice and spiders, even Americans soldiers were better than them, after all, during the good old days, this hotel was full to overflowing with soldiers, all wearing either brown or black shirts, they were mainly attired with SS uniforms. The now very old owner sighed another long lingering sigh. 'Oh, for those good old days once more!'

The snow was much more manageable now, the plough kept everything down to no more than one inch in depth. The runway was practically clear, plus it being a bright day with no wind and no falling snow, it once again cheered everybody up.

To everybody's delight and there was the plane stood shiny and clean, refueled and with a brand-new reconditioned engine, at least it looked brand new, having been completely rebuilt after being rescued from a crashed plane that once carried General Eisenhower around the various battlefields of Europe.

It stood outside the tower, engines throbbing from the idling that it was getting, awaiting the arrival of its passengers. The loading took approximately one hour and then after its long break, it was ready for takeoff once again. The original crew were there, goodbyes and thanks were said, the three crew members had stayed all the two weeks with the original radio operator that had talked them down during the storm, they had all become good friends, pals that would always mean to keep in touch, but like most of these sorts of acquaintances, it would just never really happen. Finally, everyone was waiting for the Captain to pull on the throttle and get the old crate underway yet again, he looked around one last time. A vast white Mountain on either side of the airfield, the wonderfully beautiful forests and fields that could also be seen on the foothills, everything covered in layers of white powdery snow, the huge hanger that once proudly housed the Kaisers special great war attraction, the scourge of cities like London, Leeds and Liverpool, plus one must not forget Norwich and Scarborough where the giant of the air would usually drop its payload of bombs without much retaliation, that was until the incendiary bullet was developed, then the airship had had its day. No Zeppelins hovered in that building anymore and would never do so again, yet that simple huge structure was still something special to behold. Then there were the normal airplane hangars that were dotted around the field all housing small propeller craft for the new fledgling Austrian air force, of which not a single pilot had been seen the entire time that the Americans had been forced to land there. Lastly that old tower, which now housed reasonable radar equipment and good modern communication, with good well-prepared engineers and service men that never seemed to get stressed under pressure, they were all a credit to their uniforms. These men, now all peace-loving bipeds that only now wanted war with the Communists, plus all despots that still lorded over entire countries around the globe. It was true to say that the once indoctrinated extremely Nazi-fied people of the town and countryside of that region of Austria were extremely happy to take the American dollars from the saving of one DC10, plus its crew and passengers. They had bent over backwards to accommodate all the rescued passengers and crew and that simple duty, had won them the grateful thanks and praise of everyone in the United States of America, had they known about the incident!

Once the normal routine of checking all the planes components had been carried out, there was one last wave out the cockpit window and then something was said into his radio headpiece and off they taxied.

They reached Cyprus safely with absolutely no problems, but once landed they were kept waiting until an American member of the Embassy arrived. Something was delivered to him, a small parcel and a briefcase. No one knew what the parcel or briefcase were about, no one asked any embarrassing questions. No one was allowed to leave the plane, it was refueled and off they went again, this time to Istanbul.

It seemed that the only reason for going to Cyprus was just to deliver those items for the Embassy.

The tour of the Far East went quite well and most of the venues were a joy to work in, they were always popular and brought a great deal of joy and happiness to most people that witnessed their performances. The weeks past gradually, then turned into months. David wrote letters to Louisa almost daily, his ardour had slackened slightly as the old adage took hold, out of sight, out of mind. Sadly, most of the correspondence had become a routine, and was written more as a diary of events than a great declaration of love.

To Cartier his passion had waned somewhat, but why had it? It seemed to him that he had lost that vital spark and their great love affair, one to rival that of Romeo and Juliet had slipped to one of warmth, it had that very slight feeling of being scared of committing to the future. It was if dawn had broken on the simple truth, that was he really didn't know this Louisa Young very well and did he want to take a chance on making their lives together? Anyway, he had not received any letters from her at all, so maybe she too had also lost interest.

Taking all these things into consideration, he wondered if he should just stop writing as he wasn't getting any from her, though he had been told by Stuart Holstein that it was never easy to receive mail as they were always one step ahead of the mailman. David was clearly learning a truth about life and that was that love is a moment of passion and that incredible feeling that one gets from passion, like a fire needs fuel adding all the time to keep it alight. So at the end of April with the last two weeks coming up, meaning a tour to Indo China, or Vietnam as it was now known as, David stopped the correspondence and decided that his career came first. That had all the hall marks of meaning college then an orchestra, then and only then, maybe a wife.

They arrived at the airbase in Saigon on the eighteenth of April early in the morning, dawn was considered the safest time to land, being that the Vietcong wanted their beauty sleep like everyone else, meaning that they never rose for war before ten o'clock in the morning, or so it was thought and hoped. But the wrecked planes that scattered around the airfield told another story.

The weather was beautiful, warm, sunny and cloudless. Yet there was a smell that hung in the air, something none of them had experienced before, yet it wasn't normal airfield smells such as kerosene and the like, it had a burnt sweet smell yet distinctly chemical as well, it was the feeling that clawed at the back of one's throat, it didn't make anyone cough particularly but it did irritate and that sensation lasted all the time, it hung everywhere.

They were given the normal routine of going through the customs and the customs officers were all soldiers, basically children not older than Cartier, completely wet behind the ears. As they entered the hall they held their baggage, all one could hear was the Rolling Stones blearing out at full throttle. These youths were laughing and singing along with the records while the newly arrived passengers waited patiently for someone to acknowledge their existence and if needed to get on with their so-called search. Eventually they got around to the musicians, a very cursory search was held, though all they wanted to know was that no drugs were being brought in! Well not much anyway, possibly only the smoking variety, no hard stuff such as Opium, Heroin or Cocaine, which if they found they kept for their own personal use.

This was what had become typical in the bases, but this was fine as practically all the musicians under fifty years of age were carrying Marijuana, all except David and Roger Mills his friend.

Once outside the building a bus was waiting to take them all to one of the main army bases on the outskirts of the city. Just to get out of the airbase was a trial of nerves. They zigzagged their way through numerous armed barricades, were stopped on two occasions and heavily armed grunts made sure that their own personal frustrations were taken out on the passengers by holding them up for long periods of time, just being pedantic for the fun of it. It seemed that each guard had the sole rights of life or death against anyone entering or leaving the airfield and they all looked as if they were high on drugs or drink. To make matters worse when you sat there and these young American heavily armed boys came and annoyed you by re-searching the bus and everyone on it, you knew that their guns were loaded and ready for use, to these young fellows the enemy was anyone that got in their way.

They might have been privates, Corporals or even Sergeants, but even Generals could be and frequently were harassed and searched by them, they were the law, they judged and executed at will.

This man's army had taken ordinary men from ordinary jobs in the USA and turned them into killers, men that now had no conscience, or belief in human dignity what-so-ever!

On the road into the city of Saigon they passed many obstacles, mainly craters left over from the occasional enemy mine or shelling campaigns, often these holes were deceptively deep, mainly filled with water, some with dead animals floating in an ugly bloated manner thus creating millions of flies and disease, but also there were the remains of some sort of military vehicles that were too far gone with damage to even be bothered to be pulled out the various holes. It made all the musicians wonder if the dead were still sitting inside those trucks and cars, still waiting to reach their own particular destinations. The drive proved one thing to the entertainers and that was that pure bull shit was being broadcast about Saigon never coming under enemy fire.

The message that was being delivered home to the United States was one of the armies being in total control and thus winning the hearts and souls of this particular crusade, all being done for the good of the free thinking world, kicking the arse of those pesky Chinese advised communist terrorists with their Russian arms and money. The overall trouble was, that no one had told the rules of the game to the Vietcong, they were cheating and making up their own rules. 'Un-fair, un-fair!'

As they came within the outer perimeter of the camp, which consisted of World War One type trenches, masses of barbed wire, obvious mine fields, machine gun towers and of course plenty of howitzer gun emplacements, once again the guards were there to scrutinise their every move. The first obstacle was tank traps of huge concrete slabs that any vehicle wanting to enter must go around and that then faced all the incoming transport onto machine guns and yet more obstacles.

A wooden barrier was down, and an armed guard was waiting for the bus to stop. He boarded the old army coach with a certain but already now familiar show of arrogance and then demanded to see passports and travel documents, to which he scarcely even glanced at them, just yet again showing that he was the man with the power.

He asked in a very sarcastic way,

"I understand that there is an Englishman with your band, could he please stand and identify himself."

David now feeling somewhat vulnerable stood and showed himself, much to the cheer of his friends.

"So, Limey, here to see how it's done ah! We helped your people in two world wars, where are your armies now when we could use some support?"

David was suitably annoyed with this jibe.

"If you want me to answer your stupid query, all I have to say is, I hope they are all tucked up nicely in bed."

There was a small amount of nervous laughter, so David said what he was thinking,

"Fancy getting yourselves embroiled in all this political nonsense. No one believes that the world is destined to be red, after all if you know your history, all past regimes have crashed, so will communism and probably our own Democratic way of life along with it. God knows what will take its place though?"

But the grunt had long lost interest in what David Cartier had to say.

As he alighted there was a small but distinct shudder, this made everybody turn their heads to the starboard side of the bus. In the distance a large black cloud of smoke was rising in that time old familiar mushroom shape above the buildings.

"What the hell was that?"

Asked Holstein to the indifferent guard.

"O, nothing much! Just the 'Cong letting off some steam, shit happens here. Welcome to Gods Pleasure Dome! Never a dull moment to be had, this is much better than Disney World."

His indifference was annoying everyone, but they all kept silent, David had said more than enough.

"Okay driver take them into the entrance to building seven to nine. There Captain Travers is waiting for them. Gentlemen, enjoy your holiday here and watch out for those distant flashes, they probably mean you are about to die in an extremely painful way."

The guard immediately did a Roman style salute, this meant stamping to attention, placing his right arm across his chest, then he said in a stupid attempt at an Italian accent,

"For those of us about to die, we salute you!"

He laughed raucously at his own inane joke, nobody even smiled at him, as by now everyone was silent and pensive. The driver did his bidding, still chewing the gum that he had in his mouth since the moment they had entered the bus back at the airfield. He stopped the vehicle outside a building marked with a huge seven. David thought about what was there in front of him: 'Boy these Yankees sure know how to make things obvious. I guess we have arrived at building number seven.' Just as the Captain was about to board the bus the driver surprisingly decided to speak, and his voice surprised everyone. He was from the deep south, but his southern drawl was almost falsetto in pitch, and it was almost impossible for the passengers of the coach not to burst out with laughter. It was entirely understandable, as tensions had built up to fever pitch since arrival in Vietnam.

"You'll 'ave a great stay here in Saigon. I'm'mer comin to you'll concerts, so you'll better be good. You'll all have a nice day now, be good, be proud and stay alive!"

Then Captain Travers climbed on board and managed to break the spell.

"Gentlemen, welcome to Camp Ruby here in sunny Saigon. I hope your stay will be a joyous affair and that you take back our good wishes and good feeling and memories to the States when you leave. You are here for two weeks, and these three buildings will be your home for that period."

He moved slightly from one foot to the other, looked at his clipboard that he was carrying, adjusted his dark sunglasses perched precariously upon his nose and then carried on,

"I understand that there are three concerts and two dinners that you will regale yourselves in, I am sure they will be fine and that you will be a credit to the section of the army that you actually all come from. Er, that is except that I understand that we have a guest with you, a Britisher! Mr. Cartier, will you please stand and make yourself known to me! Ah, there you are. Okay Mr. Cartier, two things to tell you. First, while you are here in Vietnam you come under US army ruling and that means if you do anything wrong you will be incarcerated like any other military personage. Taking that into account, that means anything untoward, means you could face imprisonment or even the death penalty, that is if you commit murder or treason."

He grinned a long knowing grin and there was a distinct twinkle in his eyes.

"Welcome to our world boy. Oh, the second thing is that we have dozens of letters for you inside number seven building and boy do they smell sweet and feminine, I got a hard on just handling them."

This sentence got a huge round of applause and cheering from David's compatriots. David just went bright red and managed a smirky grin of embarrassment. The captain was grinning with the satisfaction of knowing that he made a bus full of men laugh out loud.

"Right men, enough of this frivolity, off the bus and into the barrack buildings. At the double now, you're back in the army and if you slack, we will hand out rifles and you can go on patrol rounding up the commies along with the real cowboys."

Again, more laughter, but the assembled musicians knew when to laugh but also when to move quickly. Once outside Stuart called for hush and then spoke to all his boys.

"Men, before we get drafted into different billets here, let's get one last group photograph. This is our last part of the tour before Alaska and for most of you that will mean going home and leaving the services, which I for one will be sad about. Overall it has been a great tour of duty, we, er, you have performed well, and we have given some good shows and concerts. But in case there is no chance to get together and thank Mr. David Cartier for standing in for Dennis Wilson, who sadly I heard has died back in Louisiana, evidently, he expired from Peritonitis! Anyway, I would like this photograph to be dedicated to young Mr. Cartier. It is true to say we have all become fond of him and he has been exemplary in his playing and his behavior. Strange really, as he is a bloody Limey that so being one of the boys of the band must have been difficult for him. So, gentlemen please leave your instruments where they are for one moment, you know the routine, tallest at the back smallest front. David, you stand beside me in the middle. Captain, if you would be kind enough to take the snap on my new camera."

There was a long pause while adjustments were made and then,

"Right say cheese!"

Then came the resounding retort, one that was always expected, "Bollocks!"

And then a huge, long lingering laugh. The word bollocks is not a word that is really understood in America, it came from David when he was upset or slightly angry, out would come the word. It had sadly for the English language caught on, especially when it was explained by David as to what it actually meant to the British. That word quickly grew on all the ensemble, and they all used it as often as possible, to the other musicians the word just rolled off the tongue.

David was given his bundle of letters which immediately revived his passion for Louisa Young. He then spent the next two hours lying on his bunk reading words of love from his lady.

The first week went extremely well with one officers' dinner and two shows, one a variety concert in which all the entertainers were American. The star of that show was the fantastic comedian Bob Hope, the orchestra just had to play Thanks for the memory and the audience went wild with enthusiasm. He really was very funny and even all the members of the pit were hysterical, almost dropping their instruments from laughing so much.

It all seemed so strange and bazaar to David looking out at the sea of faces. All those soldiers were so young, but they had that grey ashen drawn look of youth being old long before its time. Cartier got the impression that he was looking out at a generation of lost souls. Very, very old young men, lost in their own hell hole, all somehow waiting to die with only marijuana, heroin and alcohol and rock-n-roll to prop them up on their merry way, for ninety-nine percent of the grunts there in Nam, Saigon and the Vietcong just needed to be a thing of the past, something they would one day hopefully forget.

It was that over exuberance that made David wonder at them all, they were living for this very moment in time, Bob Hope was there past, present and future, it was here and now and so they crashed dived through every experience. None were expecting to be alive before the end of their tour of duty, they all lived for this very moment and that was what was etched on each young man's face, that patient in bed waiting for death look, with the only hope that it would be quick and not drawn out with excruciating pain and that also meant not being captured alive by the North Vietnamese.

The other show that Stuart's men appeared in was a dance for all ranks. That also went well and David in a moment of free time was picked up by a woman Sergeant who realising that he was not an American thought it would be fun to parade this Limey as a trophy, one of her sexual conquests that she could brag about for her period of duty there in Saigon.

"Hey! I have heard about you! You are that musician from across the pond in rainy England, am I right?"

"Well yes, I come from the south of England, and I was asked to fill in for a poor lad who became very ill and died. What's your name? Mine is David."

"Oh, don't worry about names, after all here today gone tomorrow. Dance with me, will you?"

"Yes, of course that will be my pleasure, er, Sergeant!"

"It could be your pleasure if you play your cards right. And forget that Sergeant crap, my name is Lucy. Now come on let's get it on with some rock-n-roll."

It had been many a long time since David had done anything as physical as dancing and he soon became exhausted, but even though his knees shook from fatigue and he developed a stitch in his side and his mouth was as dry as the Sahara Desert, he thought of his Queen and Country and carried on dancing, had he been on a battle field his gallant efforts would have earned him the Victoria Cross at the very least. Eventually having danced solidly for nearly ten minutes David looked at his partner Lucy and asked,

"Fancy a drink, Lucy? I could murder a Budweiser, what about you?"

"Yer, okay, some liquid might just put some spring into your feet and some lead in your pencil."

The music carried on and David fought his way to the bar with nice polite English phrases.

"Excuse me please... pardon... Sorry to disturb you... May I get through...?"

And so on, but it worked. Generally, the soldiers were so shocked to hear real English being spoken, they allowed passage for that particular person.

"God, I could gratefully sink a pint of bitter now."

"Bitter, what's bitter?"

"English beer, the difference is that we serve it warm and also alive, the yeast is still producing alcohol and that's the taste that us strange people like."

"Warm beer! Strange people, yes you can say that again. I've never been to Ingerland, in fact other than going across the border into Mexico down at El Paso, Nam is the only foreign country I've seen and Saigon is all I've seen at that and that is all I want to see of this God forsaken place. Now..."

She gently placed her left hand on his testicles.

"Are we going to get it on or are we going to talk about warm beer all day?"

"Blimey! I wasn't expecting this."

David looked Lucy squarely in her face, thought for five seconds, by which time she had removed her hand.

"I bloody well say so! Where do we go?"

"Oh, I have a billet on my own just about two hundred yards from here, think you can wait that long?"

"Not entirely sure, we best be quick, I am supposed to be playing with the rest of the band."

Being seduced was a new experience for David and the idea that some woman found him attractive enough to ask him for sex made him instantly forget that he once again had a lady waiting for him, but then she of course was thousands of miles away back in Germany.

'Never mind, what she doesn't know or ever get to find out, shouldn't hurt her.'

Lucy took Cartier back to her billet, this turned out to be a side room off one of the main barrack quarters for the army women who worked in an administrative capacity within the barracks.

The space that Lucy had was neat and tidy but bland, with just dark pine floors, walls and ceiling. The room was small, just enough space for one person, two made it cramped, but it was just as well that it was designed for one person as it was no more than ten feet by ten feet, in one corner was a single bed, against the opposite wall was a table and chair which doubled as her work area plus dressing table, then next to that was a sink with only one tap producing icy cold water, not much good for getting things clean, but ideal for waking oneself up with. Then beside the door was a steel closet which housed all her personal belongings and her rifle and ammunition. Once two people were in the open space there was no room left, but at this time it made the whole experience kind of cosy.

Lucy didn't waste time, she grabbed at David virtually lifting him off the floor and both of them crashed onto the small compact single bed. The fumbling that went on as they both tried to remove one another's clothing and kiss at the same time quickly became very farcical.

Eventually Lucy called time out, as she had almost managed to remove his shirt and get one sleeve caught into her own arm. Laughing loudly, she rose from her part of the bed knocking David off at the same time. Then she started to remove her own clothes, then standing there naked showing her large shoulder tattoo of the regimental badge, she carried out the same process for Cartier. After just one minute, but what seemed like two hours they both stood as naked as the day they were born.

"You better be worth all this trouble! If you don't come up with the goods, I will have your balls mounted on my wall, it needs something pretty for me to look at."

Once again David was thrown onto the bed and Lucy leaped on top of him. She clutched at his penis making it erect instantly, then looking at his face she kissed him hard on the lips and then equally as quickly disappeared from view as she proceeded to place his member in her mouth, as she sucked it got harder and bigger almost filling her entire mouth and throat. The trouble was that her enthusiasm got the better of her and she almost bit his manhood in half. David gave out with a huge gasp of pain, decided that it might be the time to reciprocate, that way she could feel some of that discomfort. Extricating himself from her almost death grip wasn't that easy, but when she realised that he might indeed get down to her she allowed it to happen.

He was so horny that he wasn't sure just how long he could hold out once he entered her, so cunnilingus seemed like a good way of cooling his ardour.

She opened her legs just wide enough so as to accommodate his approach. To his complete surprise she had an enormous Venus mound, this hung down like a sack between her legs and the amount of pubic hair could have filled a cushion had she allowed herself to be clipped. It was so dense that Cartier had some difficulty finding her clitoris with his tongue, but eventually he managed to feel her quite long g-spot stiffen as did her body. Her smell wasn't quite as nice as he would have liked and wished that they had not been in quite such a rush but spent some time getting to know that cold tap.

But tastes get better when one's tongue really gets to work and it wasn't long before Lucy experienced her first orgasm with David. Gradually he allowed her to relax and regain her breath, then when she was not expecting it, he slid up her body and push his penis deep into her wet vagina. The whole session of pumping lasted no more than three of four minutes by which time Lucy had come again and David could no longer contain himself and he let go with an eruption of pure venom.

As it had now been many weeks since he had last made love to Louisa, he was full to the brim, so now Lucy had it all. They lay there on the bed, Lucy with her back against the wall, David squashed up close to her with one of his legs supporting him by being on the floor.

"Christ! I meant to tell you not to inject me with sperm. I'm halfway through my cycle, just about the worst possible time to let go inside of me. Oh, well, what's done is done, not your fault."

"I'm so sorry, it never occurred to me that you wanted me to withdraw. What will you do if you become pregnant?"

"Why, get rid of it of course. I cannot stay in the army with a brat, can I?"

David gave a long sad but contented sigh.

"Well did I cut the mustard, or what?"

"A little better than, or what. But you can keep your balls. I think we might be better off going back to the dance."

After finally experiencing freezing water from that one tap, David got dressed and wished Lucy good luck and a long a happy career in this man's army, to which he got a very stern look. Having obviously spoken out of turn, David decided that retreat was probably the safest option at this time. He gently opened the door and looked outside, no one was there so he turned back to Lucy blew her a kiss, thanked her for having him and went back to join the orchestra.

Once outside the billet David leaned up against the door, breathed deeply lifting his chest high and let out a single huge sigh of relief, scratched his itching damp crutch and then adjusted his trousers once more and proceeded back to where the orchestra were playing.

'Better playing the viola with the band than playing music with her, what's her name, er, Lucy. I can't remember that last time I got that battered, but was it worth it, debatable. That female, she could suck someone in and blow them out again in bubbles.'

The dance ended at one o'clock in the morning and by all accounts it had been a great success, only two fights for the military police to deal with and neither were serious more bruised pride than bruised bodies.

Four other soldiers had been arrested for drunkenness and one for getting his penis out on the dance floor, which by all the various descriptions was a huge disappointment to all those unfortunate people who witnessed the incident, maybe huge was the wrong adjective.

The next morning being a Sunday, it was decided that some of the younger musicians would take the bus into the centre of Saigon for the first time. They would brave the reports that the Vietcong never fight on a Sunday being that most of them are Catholic, that being after the French influence, no one really believed that Sunday would make any difference what-so-ever, but being young gave them that edge on sense, meaning that they had very little. But they all exuded bags of nerve, not that having nerves would stop a bullet.

They were all dressed in the finest Sunday best that being suits and ties, though they could never disguise the very fact that they were foreign, in fact American, thus all six of them stuck out like sore thumbs. David walked with his pal Roger Mills and then there was the young and very talented pianist Bernard Sumner, the drummer David Simmons and two other saxophone players Tony Bruce and Glen Hardis. All of them were under thirty years of age, plus David Cartier was still in his teens. They all looked young, mainly because they were all young. Though they wore civilian clothing they still looked like military on the town.

They made their way to what they believed to be the centre of town and were immediately struck by the absence of military personnel within the vicinity.

Roger looked at the others and said what he was wondering,

"I think we may have inadvertently wondered into a no-go area?"

Tony stopped in his tracks and looked around, it was extremely quiet, just a few traders doing what comes naturally to them, trying hard to sell their various wears. But the six of them had been quickly noticed by many of those traders and instead of trying to sell them things, they rapidly started to cover their goods and make it look as if they were clearing everything away. Bernard was the next to get that shiver down the back of his spine, he stopped and looked around as if expecting to see a ghost spring out at him.

"You're right!"

Said Tony Bruce quickly looking from side to side of the roadway. "I suggest that we backtrack and find the touristy parts of this town. I want to find some of those beautiful ladies that I hear so much about."

Then he turned to Bernard and added in a not sarcastic but straightforward way,

"Don't you want to find some of those famous he-she's?"

Bernard looked casually back at Tony and replied with,

"He-she's, he she's you blithering idiot, they come from Bangkok and that's Thailand, this is Vietnam you moron."

Already with just two minutes gone, the area was a human desert completely clear of the locals. It was David that then took up the mantel.

"Christ you bunch of duffers, let's get the hell out of here. I think we could end up in serious trouble if we stay around this part of town much longer. Look how quickly the locals disappeared, they don't want us here and I agree with them I don't want to be here. Let's go down this road, it does look as if there are more people down the end there, anyway it's lighter, I mean bloody hell, eleven thirty in the morning and it's a ghost town, something's definitely wrong, please let's go."

They started to walk down this new road, and it was true, it looked as if there were more people down the other end, which was about four hundred yards away. They were walking more of less in a line keeping as best they could to the slightly raised pavement.

As they approached their goal, David heard the engine of what was obviously a scooter or moped down the bottom coming in their direction. There was a crash and then several screams. The scooter then turned into their street and headed directly towards them. David stopped dead, he knew something had happened and then he saw that the rider was just a boy of about twelve years of age and he had a baby of around one year of age strapped to his back, but in his right hand he was struggling with an automatic pistol, which he was finding hard to do as he was also riding at full speed.

The baby was crying fiercely, such a noise that would have attracted even the deaf. Transfixed, but knowing that danger was coming their way they all stood there silent and motionless. Still though, above the roar of the engine all the six could hear was the sound of that baby yelling. Very quickly the scooter was parallel with them and Roger realised that the young rider was trying to aim his pistol at the bunch of them and without much thought he cried out,

"Duck everyone, the buggers got a gun."

Everyone did just that, they dived and ducked, but the young man couldn't do the two things at the same time, he couldn't fire the gun and drive the scooter, so he did the next best thing, he pulled up and tried to aim in the general direction of the six of them. Bang, followed by another bang. But it hadn't come from the rider it had come from two local military police that had chased around the corner to catch the young terrorist, the first shot went through the baby on his back and knocked both off the scooter and onto the ground, the second shot nearly took all the boys head off. Blood shot everywhere along with gore and brains and the young man and his charge were both quite dead. The scooter lay on its side with the engine screaming and the back wheel spinning crazily managing to turn the vehicle around in circles. The two military police who turned out to be from the South Vietnamese army ran up to their fallen game, one raised his rifle again, poked the young man with the barrel then realising that he was quite dead smirked and grinned at no one in particular, as he thought any hunter would having just bagged his quarry, he then proceeded to search the boy thoroughly.

Blood was now running freely down the gutter and around the six musicians all of whom just stood their mouths agape and saying nothing.

Once again, the silence was broken by David Cartier as he leaned forward and quietly vomited into the blood and gore. This understandable act was expanded upon by two others. Still all six were transfixed to the very now bloody ground. But the mood was soon broken when the other military policeman came over to them, smiled and said in broken English,

"You, all 'merican soldiers?"

Bernard saved the moment and answered for them all,

"No, we are musicians, we are here to entertain the troops. What did this boy do to make you shoot him?"

The soldier frowned and answered in a more somber mode.

"He terrorist, he throw grenade at café, many people hurt. Him Vietcong. Never mind, one less now! You all go from here, not safe. Soon more bombs, more shooting, take that road to left then second right and first left again, that bring you touristy area, all guarded by 'merican troops, much safer."

Now all six were fully compos-mentis and all they wanted to do was get as far away as possible from this scene of carnage.

Half an hour later they were sitting outside a café where many US soldiers were frequenting and there for the delights of the musicians were the girls, hundreds of Vietnamese girls all very beautiful and all extremely desirable. They sat there in the sun, now a million miles away from death, but all were still shaking and all felt very queasy indeed. Roger Mills ordered six large tots of whisky with six strong black coffees. His senses told him that the quicker he and the rest got piddled, the faster they would settle down and put the past events to the back of their minds.

It seemed that the young man had lobbed a grenade into one of the local cafes that housed just native peoples, but he was unlucky on two accounts, firstly, the bomb exploded early and though it injured several people, no one was killed, secondly, he stopped to try and shoot some Americans, ipso facto the musicians walking down the wrong road, had he not stopped to take a potshot he might just have got away on his scooter. Instead, his luck ran out as the two local military policemen managed to have time to take aim themselves and because of that a one year old brother and a twelve year old son lay dead in the street. But what the hell, an almost daily occurrence in Saigon.

Three large whisky's each later, all six of the musicians were feeling a little braver and could now talk about the events that had so recently taken place. And as the sun shines down on the righteous, what had started out as a major tragedy started to become an almost amusing adventure.

As they got drunker, the ladies of the street closed in for the kill. Several had planted themselves on Roger and Tony, Bernard had managed to show his complete indifference to the female fraternity, but his eyes had settled on one of the young male waiters. 'Anyway, why worry, like the soldier said, they had just rid the world of one more Vietcong, one future potential terrorist.'

This was the general thoughts running through shaken minds. Drink quickly made those children into seriously dangerous war mongers, laughing off all possible dangers.

The ladies became very persistent and one very young girl, certainly not older than sixteen, came and sat on David's lap, the sudden move towards him made him lose his concentration and he spilled his drink over her and himself and then he dropped the glass which fell onto the pavement. It didn't break so the young girl bent down to pick it off the ground, it was this movement that made David realise that this particular girl was not wearing any knickers. As she sat back on him, he could feel the slightly wet warmth from her vagina rubbing against his trousers, this had the desired effect of giving him an immediate erection.

She asked for a drink of Champaign, but didn't wait for an answer she just waived her hand, and a bottle was instantly brought over. Champaign it was not, it didn't even look like that bubbly French drink, plus it cost twenty dollars, but no one was fooled, David and the others knew that the girls got commission from the bar for making customers buy this cheap rubbish. No one drank any, one or two of the men took a sip, but it was so sweet and chemical in taste, a sip was all anyone wanted.

The girls themselves didn't even touch the bottle, which made David wonder if it was deliberately poisoned? Not that David would've cared, this young slip of a thing was very warm and warming, so the more she moved this way and that laughing at the banal jokes that were being bandied around the warmer he got, in fact he was fast reaching boiling point.

His erection must have shown itself to the girl as she now moved more and more rhythmically making David perspire freely. His now dry mouth had dropped open and his breathing had become shallow and faster, at this point Roger realised that his pals, one-eyed-trouser-snake was indeed close to a climax and it would be a vast shame on his devil-may-care attitude to life in general if he didn't make sure that everyone present was aware of the eruption that was soon to take place, after all this could just rival Krakatau. Roger watched out of the corner of his eyes pretending that he was completely un-aware of the forthcoming event, when finally, David's eyes started to roll back and his breathing was more like panting he announced the following to all at the table and anyone that cared to hear anywhere in the area.

"Look fellows and ladies, our young Limey pal is just about to squirt venom in his trousers."

Gradually his voice rose louder and louder.

"O, too late, poor David! What's worse, you didn't even get it inside her. How are you going to get to the men's toilets, everyone will know what you have managed, or in your case, not managed to accomplish."

He laughed loudly as he concluded his oration,

"I'll make sure of that!"

It was not just their table that burst out laughing, but all around them on other tables, grunts who had taken residence in this café were falling about with mirth and quickly just about everyone knew that some Englishman couldn't hold on to his dignity. David realised too late what was happening and he squirmed with shame, not at being caught out but by the simple fact that this was a woman of the streets and the one thing that one never ever did in his own eyes, was fall for their charms.

Somehow, he had to make his way to the back of the café, take down his trousers and clean himself up as best he could. He had managed push the young lass off his lap and putting his left hand into his trouser pocket, he had managed to pull his member into a not so obvious position, but the wet was already starting to permeate through the cloth showing on the outside. He got up and moved in a very rapid way to try and extricate himself from the annoyance of being laughed at. No chance! Now everyone was aware of what had happened, and he became the object of the mocking, but by the time he got into the toilet, he too could see the funny side of the situation. He dropped his trousers, not worrying if anyone else was going to enter the urinal, then taking some very rough toilet paper managed to wipe most of the stain away, then seeing just one tap over a filthy sink he washed the affected area. At least he could walk around with wet trousers, not a big deal! He again laughed to himself but knew that had he not been so drunk this wouldn't have happened, at least not for all to see.

He was replacing his now soaking slacks when the big roar of another explosion occurred, this time it was not just the sound of the bang, the whole building was hit by the shock wave, and it was hard enough to make the toilet doors swing open. David like everyone else was in a state of shock, there was silence when the roar abated for some seconds, then the hubbub started.

There was huge confusion going on outside and military men were shouting the odds at this or that, all running around like headless chickens. Cartier rushed outside again to make sure his companions were okay; he was in time to see a scene of carnage. It was yet another café about fifty yards up the road on the other side that had been the target and this time there were many fatalities, mainly American grunts.

There was debris spread across the roadway, windows were shattered, tables and chairs thrown hither and everywhere. Two American Jeeps which had been parked quite close were fiercely ablaze from their fuel tanks, now with flames leaping skyward, this in turn was helping to catch the buildings on fire that they were beside. Bodies lay sprawled everywhere and even more parts of bodies were lying uncomfortably close to the musicians who were now either standing in a dazed state or lying where they had been thrown by the blast. Blood and guts were flowing freely and as the smoke drifted slowly skyward showing the surviving people just how lucky they were to escape the mayhem; the injuries were awful and it soon became obvious that the death toll had not finished yet.

As David's friends started to rise, he noticed that they were all holding their ears and in Roger's case blood was seeping from his right ear. David could see that each one of them was now in a serious state of shock. Fate had saved him from that. The girls that had congregated around them were now nowhere to be seen, immediately the explosion occurred, and they knew they were still alive, they also understood it was time to disappear.

No one was able to see who had planted the bomb and there was no evidence of anyone trying to flee from the scene before or after. Soon the fire brigade arrived and extremely quickly had the blaze under control. The army's special task force for dealing with these sorts of incidents turned up in less than five minutes. The extraordinary, strange thing to David was the absence of noise. After the initial shock of the explosion and the panic that ensued calmed down, there was only silence reigning supreme, the injured and onlookers just stood around observing and taking in all the ensuing events in almost total silence.

To David this was all very eerie. There was nothing that could be done and the talking would come later after shattered nerve ends steadied themselves.

"Roger, you others! We can do nothing here, let's get back to the barracks."

David had broken that silence with common sense.

When they arrived back at the camp, as they were actually witnesses to the carnage, they were asked to attend a de-briefing session. This of course they did, but as they knew nothing, it became quickly obvious to everyone that they really didn't want to be there, answering ridiculous questions to and from bored, tired looking MP's. The entire troupe of musicians were glad to see their colleagues back safe and sound, though the trauma of the events would probably stay with them all for life.

The concerts and dinners soon finished, and it was finally time to finish the eastern part of the tour.

Chapter 10

Only Alaska now and then for Cartier the long-haul home to Blighty.

They were now off to Anchorage, the capitol of Alaska. A largish sprawling city that had the sea on one side and the tundra all around the rest of it.

The first thing they all noticed was the midges and mosquitoes, billions upon billions everywhere they went. The heat was oppressively hot and very high humidity, and this only went to encouraged yet other sorts of insects to invade the privacy of the humans frame. Yet the beauty of the area was there for all to see, a wilderness with a frontier town come city.

There were going to be only two concerts, both in the small training barracks just outside of Anchorage on the sea. Both the concerts were a big success, especially for David as he was asked to play some viola pieces which he did and got a huge applause from the grateful audience.

David had experienced marvelous fellowship with these men, he had learned many things, not least of all that he liked the musical life, it suited his psyche, he jelled well with other musicians, and they generally liked him. He was not overly arrogant, cocky or bumptious, he could find good things about most people and thus enjoy their company.

Musically speaking he had gained an enormous amount from the tour. His sight-reading abilities had soared with just about every concert and generally they did have to be sight read. His sense of improvisation went from zero knowledge to a relaxed confidence that could and would stand him in good stead in just about any musical situation. Maybe his technique would need some fine tuning, but this he was well aware of, and he knew exactly what he would have to do when he got back to Blighty.

Back to Blighty! That was something that he really hadn't thought about as each day had been an experience, a chance to learn, so he just hadn't given England a thought. But now it was going to happen. It was going to take the ensemble just two days and they would be home. David was given a ticket that was going to take from Anchorage in Alaska, flying over the North Pole and finally landing in Heathrow. The complete journey would take just twelve hours.

On the day of departure, the entire troupe wished young Mr. Cartier God's speed and good luck for the future. His friend Roger gave him a bear hug and then kissed him on both cheeks, much to the amusement of all watching. Then Stuart Holstein came over, first he handed him a banker's draft for the money that he was owed, then clearing his throat he made a little speech.

"David Cartier helped us out in a time of need. I am sure I speak for all of us when I say that we are very grateful to him. He has been the model of politeness and friendship and speaking for myself I have enjoyed out talks and banter, plus I have enjoyed our games of chess, especially as I won them all."

He coughed and then smirked.

"We are going to miss you David. May I suggest you throw away your Limey passport and come and join us for good and all."

A pause was expended upon,

"Well, I guess your silence is a no, no! You will always be welcomed in the US, and I have here two items that you might like to keep. First there is the picture that was taken outside the barracks. There was no point in framing it so I have rolled it up so that it is easily carried. But when you look at it you will notice that everyone has signed their name to it, that is a good sign of friendship for you. The second thing is a card that once again everyone has signed and you will notice that all have put their addresses and telephone numbers on it, that means Davy boy, you will be an honoured guest at any of those addresses. This has been a very eventful tour, one that has generally been a great pleasure, and you have contributed so much for someone of such tender years. We all wish you well and do come and visit. Goodbye my Limey friend and good luck."

There was a roar of approval from all standing there. David was now in a state of shock and there was no way that he could keep the tears from streaming down his cheeks.

"Thank you all, this has been very special."

David was almost choking with emotion,

"Please come and see me too, I live in London, just ask anyone, they'll all know me. Goodbye to you all. I know it's a cheap stupid thing to say, but I love you guys. My very sincere hope is, like the song says, 'we'll meet again, don't where, don't know when'"

I paused to see if anyone recognised the song, not so much as a raised eyebrow,

"That was a wonderful song sung by Vera Lynn, a fabulous English wartime entertainer, a true example of why the word Great got put into Great Britain."

Still no response,

"So to briefly recap my words of pure wisdom, we will hopefully meet up again, hopefully by that time you will all have learnt to speak the Queens English?"

Then unable to contain himself any longer, through laughter and tears, he jumped onto the bus that was to take him to the airfield then on to London. The only sounds he heard as the bus pulled away was the cheering of the band, he had found friendship in these American army band soldiers.

Chapter 11

It was the twentieth of June the weather was typical for an English summer, raining, windy and almost cold, but at least it was truly British. David had been back in England now for ten days, yet he was still finding it difficult to adjust to the sanity of rural Southern England.

He had managed to get his old friend Steven Preston to put him up for the time being, that was until Steve was either sick of having him cluttering up the flute players small untidy one bedroom apartment, or he had managed to find a more long-lasting solution.

The cheque which had been paid to him in US dollars had now been converted into pounds sterling and deposited into his new Lloyds Bank account in Sydenham, which is in south London.

He had told the manager how he obtained the money and was informed that he might well have to pay British tax on the money, which irked David no end at the thought as he had already paid some US tax on his earnings, but had also been informed by his friend Stuart Holstein that any good accountant should be able to get the money re-paid as all the working time had been spent outside of America, Cartier was banking on this. But after all the money he had spent while on tour, he had still managed to save just under two thousand pounds. This is an ideal sum for buying his own first dwelling abode.

David had written several more letters to Louisa Young, but because he didn't have a permanent address of his own, he wrote to her saying that for the time being not to bother to answer any of his correspondence. He had even telephone her on one occasion, but telephoning Germany was prohibitive in cost and as it was quite embarrassing not knowing what to say after so long, the shyness of not really knowing one another came across, so all the talk was about trivia, not important things. But David thought about Louisa a lot and had wanted to tell her how much he loved her and how much he was missing her, but none of these things came out so he thought better of trying to telephone again.

So the letters went back to Louisa more or less day after day. David believed that he really loved Louisa, but it did bother him that he couldn't take his eyes off any attractive young lady that just happen to pass by. What played on his mind most, was knowing that he had already been unfaithful to her.

It was at a time when she was on his mind twenty-four hours in every day, but within his soul he knew these continuous thoughts didn't bode well for a future together. An age-old adage always came to mind whenever his mind dwelt on negative thoughts concerning Louise, 'Out of sight, out of mind' and there were so many things about her that he knew would become problems to them both. For one, she wasn't seriously interested in music, at least not the serious classical and jazz music that he liked and as music was his entire life, he quickly understood that could develop into an issue. Two, there was David's insatiable appetite for historical monuments, such as Roman and Norman castles. Three, since being a boy he had developed a huge interest in World War One. He knew that this was nothing to her, she made no connection between the Great War and the effect that it had on the rest of modern history, he doubted if she even knew anything about those incredible events. Should it matter? Maybe she would develop interests in his hobbies? Should it even matter if she did or didn't? The trouble was that it played on his mind, he wondered if their love for one another could survive without mutual interests.

July came and things started to happen very quickly, young Cartier knew that it would be easy to just waste the money that he had earned on trivia, but he knew that such a large sum was unlikely to come his way again so easily, he thought that being sensible might be the best option.

And the thing he needed most was his own house, so he decided that he would buy a property and somewhere that might be able to create wealth in its own right for his and Louisa's future.

He was about to start college in September, so he had to find something sharpish if he wanted to be in before winter came. With the help of his close friend Steve, they both combed the south London area for a cheap suitable property that young Cartier could invest and live in. They were advised and eventually visited a mortgage broker, but when the manager of the local branch heard how young David was, he told him he would never get the rest of the money in a mortgage, as anyway you needed to be twenty-one to get on the land registry. So, David thought long and hard about his age. He went for a walk up and down the road and then miraculously went from eighteen to twenty-one years of age. After all, if the payments were made regularly who would ever know, or come to that care?

They looked at properties in Forest Hill area, they looked at a small cosy two up two down terraced house in Penge, David liked this as there was no garden to maintain, just a concrete patio. But as now he was starting to understand pricing of properties, he though the price was a little more than it was worth. He did like the property though; it did seem to be maybe a fine solution to his needs. The asking price was three thousand six hundred pounds, so David made an offer of three thousand five hundred, only to be turned down and told that it was already under offer.

Then an estate agent advised him that a house in Beckenham was on the market in a road called Clockhouse Road, literally around the corner from the coffee bar that he liked and played in.

"Shall we go and see this one? It is a four-bedroom semi-detached house. Evidently it also has a long garden backing on to the railway. What do you think?"

Steve pondered the questions, and then said in response,

"What is the asking price?"

"It's cheaper than the house in Penge, it's only three thousand three hundred pounds. What do you think, should we bother, or can you cope with me in your flat for a few more years?"

"We'll go right now! The sooner I get you out the better! For one thing you are spoiling my love life. Oh yes, that's another thing, my girlfriend Patsy is coming round tonight, don't be in, go to the cinema or something."

The house number was seventy-seven and from the outside the semi-detached house looked in quite good condition, no cracks down the walls, though the windows and frames were original they would in the not too distant future need to be replace. And though the overall condition was okay with no apparent rot, the wood most definitely needed some tender loving care such as painting and maybe new putty here and there. The roof was of slate but again, though they could see a few cracked slates, overall, the entire roof looked waterproof and sound.

The owner of the house was not living there and probably never had, so he had let the top out as a self contained flat with the entire bottom of the building being left empty. Once again, the condition was not too bad, there didn't seem to be any dry rot or rising damp which could easily have been expected in a house dating back to nineteen hundred and eight.

These old Edwardian properties were in fact built to last and were built for the new upper working classes, or lower new middle classes, something that had been done for the first time in history, the workers could finally afford to buy their own dwellings and good housing at that, these properties were built quickly and comparatively cheaply, but they were built well and soundly, unlike the old Victorian terraced tenement type housing that usually abounded with the working class peoples of Britain, generally just renting, thus often those said properties were in a poor state of repair.

Getting the tenant to allow access to this flat was not easy and the estate agent an extremely affable man by the name of Denis Manger, insisted to the extent that access be allowed, he threatened the tenant with the landlord and the police, if he didn't allow access immediately, so he finally relented and allowed David to see over the entire building. It soon became obvious as to why the price was very reasonable, though the structure of the house was sound the electrics, water and gas needed quick attention.

The garden was long and extremely tidy, as the tenant had taken it upon himself to maintain and use it for his own designs. There were apple and pear trees and a small, grassed area, then at the top there was an extra fifty feet which backed onto the railway, this had been cultivated into a fine vegetable garden with potatoes, carrots and various other produce growing in abundance. Looking back at the back of the house David could see that once again the structure was sound, but it did need that work of sprucing it up, and very soon.

"Denis, er, Mr. Manger; would the owner be interested in an offer?"

"I wouldn't think so, you saw how difficult Mr. Brown was upstairs, that was because you two are the fourth lot of people I have showed around the building within the last two days. No, if you are interested then I do believe that you will have to pay at least the asking price."

"At least! What on earth does that mean?"

"It means that someone might come along and offer a higher amount. Are you interested in buying this place?"

"Well, yes, I guess so. I like this garden. Tell you what, I'll offer the asking price if the owner takes it off the market. What do you think of that?"

"I think he will go for that. How will you proceed, who is your solicitor?"

"May I call you Denis? This is all new to me! I have a large amount of the money but not all so I will need to borrow the rest, which might amount to a thousand or more. I really don't know what the procedure is, what should I do next, where do I get a mortgage from, or anything else? I am a complete novice in these matters. I was sort of hoping that you will help me by answering all these questions."

Denis Manger laughed heartily and then looked keenly at David Cartier. He lowered his eyes to a squint, stroked his chin for roughly twenty seconds and then said,

"I suggest that you apply for a council mortgage, Bromley council that is. Go and see one Mr.

Coursden, Joe is his first name, say I have recommended you to him. Now you know that you must be twenty-one years of age or over?"

Then he looked at David hard once again.

"But if you can afford the repayments, it sounds like you don't want to borrow much money, then I would think it would be a formality, but remember that you need extra money for moving, solicitors' fees, surveyors' fees, stamp duty and any emergency repairs that might need doing. So, David, if you think that to buy this property will be three thousand three hundred only, you are dreaming, you will need at least another seven or eight hundred pounds to complete. But first things first! I suggest your next step is to get the house surveyed, a good survey will cost you roughly seventy-five pounds. I recommend that you approach Mr. Author Mack he is a cheap and reliable surveyor, and I will give you his telephone number. You can feel safe with his knowledge, also he is a pleasant amiable person that will be honest and reliable, which is exactly what you want."

The search was made, mortgage agreed with Bromley Council, contracts were eventually signed, it was just a matter of waiting for a completion date and that was not going to happen before the end of December, probably around the twenty-second which was going to be a logistical nightmare.

Things were now moving fast, maybe faster than Cartier wished for. The first crisis that could be looming was the simple fact that on the fifth of September, this was going to be the first day of his new life studying at the Royal College of Music. But before then he needed to earn some more money and probably stay working until the New Year, thus allowing extra money for moving and the buying of some furniture also allowing for a little something for

Christmas. What sort of job could David get quickly he pondered? He decided that his first move should be to go to the local Labour exchange and ask for all possible vacancies, even labouring on a building site, if necessary, after all that was the career that David's father predicted for him.

"So, Mr. Cartier, what sort of position are you seeking?"

The lady that confronted him was a very voluptuous middle-aged woman with beautiful brown shoulder length hair, large bosoms and a round pretty face. Very noticeably she wore a wedding ring on her finger, which was the second thing that David noticed. And though she sat with her legs crossed opposite him at a large table, he could see that she sported nice, shaped legs, plus her figure clung deliciously tight to her dark blue one-piece dress. Her voice was somewhat severe but somehow not unpleasant at the same time.

"So Mr. Cartier, made up your mind? I do have other people that are looking for work too. What's it going to be then? I need someone to drive a taxi at a new car hire place not far from here in Croydon Road. The money is not so good as they expect you to make it up with tips. But if you apply for that job you will need to know your routes really well."

She paused briefly and almost fluttered her eyelids which caught David completely on the hop.

"The other job that might suit you is delivering bread. Ackerman's, which is just off Beckenham High Street are looking for a delivery boy. There the money is not bad, and you can earn extra by selling, I suppose extra products such as cakes and buns."

To this she laughed a little.

"But I do need to know if these are the sort of jobs that will suit you?"

"Look I shall be straight with you. I haven't lied, but I haven't told the entire truth either. I need a job realistically until Christmas, then who knows? Believe it or not I am just about to buy a house in Clockhouse Road, just around the corner."

She nodded with recognition, laid her chin onto the palms of her hands with her elbows spread at an angle of forty-five degrees resting on the table, she knew this was going to be a long speech. As the tension drained from her being, she smiled knowingly.

"This coming September I join as a full-time student at the Royal College of Music, though I have won a scholarship plus I will get a council grant, I will still need to earn extra to cover the mortgage re-payments. Basically, the best paid job wins my favours."

David relaxed slightly seeing this woman smiling and at ease with him.

"You can see I need some help! It would be a crying shame if getting as far as I have, I lost everything now, you can see that can't you?"

Flory McDownley smiled sweetly at this boy; what nonsense was he spouting? She could see from her records that he was only nineteen, yet everyone knew that you had to be twenty-one to buy a house, something to do with land registry.

"Mr. Cartier, what is your right age? I know you are not twenty-one, that's for sure, so please tell me how you can buy a house?"

"Do I have your word not to tell the authorities?"

Still smiling she nodded, but had her fingers crossed as she did so.

"I have lied about my age. I am close to already having all the money needed for the buying of this house, why should my age be my downfall?"

Flory thought that one out and followed up with,

"You know what! You are right, why should your age be your downfall? It is almost the same for us women! If I want to buy something that entails a loan, then I must get my husband's approval even though we are divorced. Sometimes the law is there only to make one's life more difficult."

David knew now that she was on his side. He now decided that it was indeed time to go for broke,

"I see from your name tag that you are called Flory McDownley; would you think I was being presumptuous if I called you Flory?"

She went quite red, thought for only a second or two and then in a quiet demure tone of voice answered with,

"Yes David, you can call me Flory. But before we get to palsy, palsy, what sort of job do you want? My own personal feeling is that you should take the bakers delivery boy, because the run up to Christmas might bring you in with some very good tips. You said you needed to earn some money to help pay your way into being a householder, which might just suffice."

"Flory would you be interested in coming out and having dinner with me?"

Now the pink look went bright red and then on to crimson, but without stopping to think it out she replied with,

"Yes, David that would be nice. Say seven o'clock tonight outside the cinema?"

"Wonderful, yes Ackerman's sounds like a good idea. I'll go for an interview; can you arrange that for me please?"

An interview was quickly arranged for the next day.

Seven o'clock arrived and David was looking a million dollars in his newish three-piece suit made from rather shiny brown pin striped mohair. He had managed somehow to get his blond mousy hair to do as it was instructed, so he felt positively booted and suited.

He felt as if everything was starting finally to go his way. He had completed a very successful tour with an American army band, he had not caught any nasty diseases, he had come back with enough money to pay a large deposit on a house in Beckenham and all of this had been achieved just before his twentieth birthday. His parents of course wouldn't give a damn, but he felt more than a little smug and quite proud of himself anyway and after all, self esteem matters most of all.

He was going to contact his Louisa Young by telephone at the weekend and arrange that she fly over for a long weekend, maybe the following week, but in the meantime he was going to flirt and enjoy the company of this older woman Flory McDownley, who he guessed who be around the forty to forty-five year mark. Not that David cared about age, after all she had a body to die for.

The sun which had shone brightly all day was now beginning to set behind the buildings, leaving streaks of yellow and golden reddish colours hovering in the sky looking for all the world like a Turner painting, except it was all done in an urban setting, but there wasn't a cloud in that sky and it was warm and yet fresh, as there was just developing a warm but obvious breeze.

David turned to look at the posters seeing what was being shown on the cinema. I was a showing of Ben Hur, that old story of right over wrong set against the backdrop of the crucifixion of Christ.

It was starring Charlton Heston, who David had seen in several films before but always thought of him as not a serious actor, just beef cake. There were various photographs of parts of the film, one being the memorable chariot race that killed two people in the making.

David got quite engrossed in that photograph wondering if he was looking at anyone who had died, when a very light tap on his left shoulder occurred, it was so light he for a second thought a bird had deposited a present on his suit, so he turned to look and there in all her voluptuousness was Flory. As David had almost forgotten why he was there in the first place, he was a little startled and almost jumped, but then getting his composure back he said,

"Wow Flory, you look absolutely gorgeous."

"Well thank you young David, but you might as well know I very nearly didn't come. I started to think, you a boy of nineteen! Nineteen, me a woman of forty-one, it just didn't seem right. So, this evening is just going to be a dinner as two pleasant friends. Agreed?"

Young Cartier was taken aback by this statement of fact and though he went along with it, now had other more determined ideas.

Together they walked up the high street towards the traffic lights and then turned right to go into Kelsey Park. David was a total gentleman and made sure that he walked on the outside just in case a car mounted the pavement, he would take the blow first like the hero he was pretending to be. It was a gesture that didn't go unnoticed to Flory and on crossing the roadway David would take her arm and show her some sort of full protection from the oncoming traffic, not that there were many vehicles on the road at that time. Truth be known, had one car come at them out of control, David would have been the first to jump clear. David's life had up to this point in time been one of self preservation, after all is said and done being a typical male of the species, he knows a thing or two about avoiding serious trouble even to the extent of leaving another person to take the fall.

When they entered through the gates and on into the park, David was nicely surprised to see such a welcoming sight as the various colours of the flower displays. On all his travels around the globe he always thought how beautiful the British park system was with its myriad of colours and varieties of blossoms there for all to enjoy, parks in Britain were for everyone not just the elite as in other so called westernised countries.

Germany might have a big edge on re-housing and general development of buildings and industry, but they didn't have the parks and colours that the British are justifiably famous for.

And the old adage, An Englishman's home is his castle, isn't just a saying as far as gardens went. They stopped on the bridge that spanned the small rivulet that was called the river Beck. Now the Beck ran through the town of Beckenham, which somewhere through past history must have meant, The village (Ham) on the river (Beck), thus Beckenham. They both leant on the railings and looked into the water. David immediately saw a small fish and pointed it out to Flory.

"Isn't our park system beautiful? I have travelled extensively but never seen parks that match our own. Look at the flowers, aren't they exquisite. I have never seen such arrays of colours, not even in Vietnam, in their jungle."

David was no fool he knew when to drop in the word Vietnam.

"You have been to Vietnam? How come?"

"Like I told you, I went with an American army band, they just happened to be short of a player when they came to Blighty. I got chosen and fitted the spot well."

He looked at her in mock shock.

"Flory dear, surely, I told you about my journeying around the world? How do you think I made enough money to get the deposit on a house? I earned it by my playing. As we get to know one another, I shall bring my viola to serenade you. That'll frighten the neighbours."

Flory looked at him and smiled warmly. 'So, it wasn't all bull shit then.' She looked a little sideways at him and saw him in a completely new light. This wasn't a young lad that was full of the stuff of life, he was a young man but had already lived like someone twice his age. Now she was interested.

"So, David, tell me about your music. Are you a pop or folk musician, what sort of music will you be studying when you go to college?"

"I am a classically trained musician; my sister is a very famous violinist and my father was a good amateur violinist and aspired to something better until he got injured in some way during the war. My love is for early twentieth century classical music, especially Russian. Composers such as Prokofiev, Shostakovich and so many others, I just love that style of music. It's powerful and dramatic, yet it can be tender and compassionate at the very next bar. I just want to be sitting in a good section of a London Symphony Orchestra. Preferably just that, the LSO that is!"

He was now dreaming that dream that was with him almost twenty-four seven.

"Don't you just love fine opera and ballet? To watch dancers and singers doing their magical stuff with a good orchestra in the pit! Oh yes my dear Flory, there in my mind is nothing finer on this earth."

David was now on a roll.

"I played all sorts with the band, which included jazz, traditional and modern, plus traditional folk, pop, swing, dance music, music for variety performers, even light classics and chamber music. It was such a fine grounding for my training and what's more I got paid a good wage and worked with friendly good musicians, all of which could and probably would aspire to better thing in the near future, when their tenure with Uncle Sam's army is over."

He looked her directly in her eyes, his own slightly watering in the memory.

"Flory, I loved every precious minute of it! As an aged wise sage of a friend once said, These are all memories in the book of life. He was so right."

David then turned once again to Flory took her hand and gently pulled her towards him and kissed her quite passionately on her voluptuous reddened lips. This kiss took Flory completely by surprise, not that she really minded, after all it was nice and to her David was more a man than many of the much older men she had been with in the past. No, what troubled her was what people who were around maybe watching, what would they think? She was after all twice his age.

She made a small gasp and pulled away from him, though not in a very convincing way. Flory had gone bright crimson in colour, which made David smile inwardly.

She grabbed at his arm and decided there and then that if he was going to get too fresh, it must happen back at her flat and not here in the open for all of humanity and neighbours to see. So they walked around Kelsey Park enjoying one another's company, Flory with her arm through David's. They talked about some of the events that happened in Vietnam, also about the forthcoming house and college. Flory was well and truly enamored by this young man and his tales that didn't seem to be so much nonsense.

After the sun was setting hard and casting long shadows, a park official warned them that if they didn't leave now, they may well have to spend the night there as he was going to close. It was only then that Flory and David realised just how dark it was becoming, so they left being the last to do so.

"So Flory, what shall we eat? What do you fancy?"

As he said that last sentence, he noticed that she went slightly red once more.

He knew he had made a double meaning from the sentence; he also knew that the response was what he hoped for. She was indeed receptive to his amorous advances, albeit that they were done in a very roundabout way.

They went out the park with Flory's arm well and truly pushed through David's. Flory now felt like she was a young girl again, not a forty odd year-old divorcee.

Flory had lived all her life in Beckenham, she had been born in Stone Park Maternity Hospital between the wars and had grown up in a very middle-class environment having lived in Manor Road, a quite exclusive area of Beckenham. Her father had worked up until his death in 1959, as a station manager for Imperial Airways out at Croydon airfield.

The pay had been good, so the lifestyle had improved as the years passed. Flory went to a private school on the outskirts of Hayes. She prospered well and got her certificates of passing her final exams almost a year before she should. On leaving school, Flory got a job at Heathrow working for British Overseas Airline Company where she very quickly climbed the career ladder to become a chief secretary to the then second-in-command. She was extremely highly thought of, that was until she met Harold Hooper one of the leading pilots for the company. Though he was supposedly happily married with four children, both Flory and Harold entered into a very open and torrid affair. After what seemed like years, but instead was just eight months, Flory fell pregnant. Harold was over the moon with joy and promised to leave his wife Gloria and move in with Flory, but on the way home from a very taxing flight from Cyprus, Harold drove into an oncoming bus and was killed instantly. This left Flory with a sad and serious problem, she would soon have to leave her job as the pregnancy progressed, her parents had more or less disowned her as a disgrace to the family name of McDownley, especially as her father was a very upright elder of the Scottish Presbyterian Kirk. The shame was just too much for her parents to bare.

Eventually her bulge became a very large embarrassment to BOAC, thus she was asked to resign. With no job and now only a small room to live in off Village Way, Flory was mortified by the lack of help and interest in her plight. After eight months she started with serious constrictions, she was rushed to Stone Park Maternity Hospital, but the baby was still born.

Still her parents rejected her and as her mother and father died, even the house and money were left to the Scottish Church. She had been completely abandoned by her family and that disgrace lived with her always. Flory met another man called Hedley Graham, they quickly married but it didn't last, and they divorced after just one year. Flory had made up her mind after that disaster never to fall in love again. She felt more than a little reticent about caring for anyone after her experiences. When she recovered from that debacle, she got a job in the Labour Exchange and that is where she stayed.

"Well, my dear lady friend, again I ask where would you like to eat?"

Flory stopped dead and managed to yank David to a halt as well.

"Eat, yes you are taking me out to dinner, I remember now. Let me think, what do I want to eat. Well, if you are feeling wealthy, we could go to the Grand Sasso, they do fine Italian come French style food, but it is very expensive."

And the putting her left-hand index finger up onto her chin she feigned concentration.

"Let me think, we could go to the new Chinese restaurant that has opened halfway down the High Street, or if you really want to push the boat out, why not try fish and chips, cheap, good and healthy, well cheap anyway."

They both laughed, and then in a quieter voice she added,

"Get fish and chips and we can eat them at my flat, if you would like?"
They ate their fish supper extremely quickly and retired just as fast to Flory's bedroom.

She had over the years managed to buy a small one-bedroom flat in Village Way very close to the railway station. The entire flat consisted of a hallway to leave coats and shoes, this came with a toilet off it, then a dining room come kitchen come lounge, then off of that came her bedroom which had a closet sized bathroom, with a small bath with shower and a sink and toilet. Cosy wouldn't have described the space, cramped was more to the point. But having said that Flory had everything in place and every place had something within it. It was very true to say she did own a lot of nick-knacks. The bedroom was incredibly tidy, it virtually sparkled, but with a full-size bed in it there was left just about one foot anywhere else to spread oneself.

"David, it has been a very long time for me. Please be gentle!"

David was climbing out of his pants when Flory had said these words.

"Flory, are you sure you want to do this? I don't want to push you into something that you will regret. But I have to say that I want you very much. You are beautiful and extremely sensual, to me you just ooze sex appeal and sensuality, and I love it."

He stared directly into her eyes.

"Standing there with the streetlight coming through the window, making you cast shadows around the room, why you are looking so very virginal in your panties and bra, I just incredibly lust after you and if that's wrong, I am sorry, but there it is!"

And then grinning, not that Flory could see that smile, he carried on with,

"I know, I know, there is an age gap between us. But you are young, and I might just be a little too old, so I think we owe it to ourselves to make mad passionate love together and then we can see where this is going to go after exhaustion takes over."

Almost laughing, he finally stated with a flurry of conviction,

"Flory, you are gorgeous and wasted on anyone other than me, so please get onto the bed and let us start the proceedings."

David waited for some sort of answer but none as such came back, so he walked around the bed to where Flory was standing, took her hands in his and kissed her very gently on her hands, arms and then lips. He could feel her trembling from the top of her head to the bottom of her toes as he tenderly kissed her. Young David then put his hand behind her back and undid her brassiere and laid it on the bed, her breasts were large and rounded and yet for a woman of just over forty years of age they stood out well, though of course there was some southern movement. Cartier leant forward and kissed very gently the right breasts nipple, to which Flory very nearly fainted, he then cupped the left one and caressed it very carefully at the same time he sucked on the right one. Flory was already exploding, or at least she was about to.

"Oh David, I had forgotten how nice a man's touch can be. Let us climb into the bed."

"Ah, before we do that, I want to remove your panties, it is my job and I will not slack where work is concerned, I am always and will always be the diligent one."

He sat on the bed and took her knickers with both hands and very carefully removed them. He was amazed to see how much pubic hair she had, so he parted it all as best he could then slid down from the bed to the floor so that he could get his mouth and tongue into that special area. As David worked his magic Flory trembled more and more, her breathing became so heavy and laboured that David was more than a little concerned that she was about to have a heart attack. Flory didn't have a heart attack instead went into a near state of ecstasy. She had now sunk onto the bed with her legs akimbo and David between them licking frantically on her clitoris, she rocked gently backwards and forwards to the rhythm of his tongue seemingly having orgasm after orgasm. All that could be heard was a very long drawn out,

"Oooooooo!"

And then after some time had passed a small but deliberate moan was heard and then as if in a dreadful panic, Flory cried out,

"David, stop, stop. I am not sure I can take any more. It's wonderful but you must be patient and slower. Come and lay beside me."

David lay there gently caressing her right breast as he thought of Megan, wondering how the baby was and whether he should take the trouble in contacting her. And then he remembered that he was going to telephone Louisa and see if she could get time off and fly over and be with him. It was really time to see with Louise if their relationship was actually going to be permanent, or not?

All the time they lay there Flory was trying hard to recover. She had never experienced anything quite so intense in her life. 'Calm yourself woman, breath gently, let the feelings roll over you and then when really relaxed again, get him to finish the job. This young buck seems to have powers, plus more than a few stories beyond his young age.'

Just as David was starting to nod into the land of erotic dreams, Flory gently touched his penis which had long since shrunk back to a somewhat more normal size, immediately it sprang back to life regaining that vital spark, David came out of his state of illusionary slumber and extremely quickly expanded into life. He just as quickly sank down between her legs again and started to get her onto a higher plain once more and then he drifted upwards and on doing so allowed his member to find its own way into her vagina. David was extremely tired so his rhythm was slow and circumspect, this couldn't have been better for Flory, she wanted slow and deliberate. He thrust in as deep as he could and as he did so Flory would ever so slightly arch her back as the feelings intensified themselves and not before too much longer, they both came in a feeling of flashing fireworks and light displays. Both had enjoyed the experience; both were now replete and satisfied. But one small snag played badly on David Cartier's mind, all the time he was having sex with Flory he was thinking about Megan and Louisa. Not for the first time this indeed worried him, to the extent of leaning towards Flory, watching her gentle face moving in rhythm with her breathing and then her mouth dropped open slightly and a very small and delicate snoring sound emerged, this startled David as he really wasn't expecting this and then he noticed that she was dribbling from the side of her mouth as she snored. David was not enamored at all by this show of passion, or now lack of it? It was time to gently withdraw and dress and leave, allowing Flory the obvious sleep she needs.

The next day when rising from his camp bed on Steven Preston's dining room, he had already made up his mind to four different things.

Firstly, he wasn't going to see Flory again, she was too old and as it wouldn't be going anywhere it seemed appropriate not to screw up her life any more than it already was. Secondly, he was going to telephone Louisa and see whether he could talk her into coming over, thirdly, he would try and contact Megan and then play that telephone call by ear as to what to do next. His thoughts quickly excused that ridiculous pun, maybe he would take a trip to Wales and see her and the baby? Fourthly, he wasn't going to try for a temporary job with the baker's, Ackerman's Bakeries, he would try and get some playing work instead, after all he was a musician and now had plenty of experience under his belt.

He looked at the clock and was horrified to see that it was only nine thirty-four in the morning, he should still be sleeping. But there were now things to do, so he got up and did his ablutions, stole some of Steve's cereal and milk and started to think out his plan of action for the day.

Firstly, he wrote out a carefully worded letter to Flory. This he would explain that it wasn't her or the age gap, just a pressure of work on his viola that he realised that they shouldn't see one another again. Sorry, but there it was!

Secondly, he went to the local post office and asked to make an overseas call to Germany.

He got through to Louisa very quickly and started talking to each other in a very loving way once more. She was ecstatic on hearing his voice and jumped at the chance to fly over and stay for some days with him. She suggested that it be on the twenty-first of July, which just happened to be his twentieth birthday, she would stay for just three days and then return to Berlin. He hung up the receiver and was in a state of shock, what had he done, did he really want her to come over? He wasn't at all sure whether this was indeed what he wanted and now it had all been agreed.

He went to directory enquiries to find out Megan's number, this was quickly found. He dialed the number, and an elderly man answered.

"Can I please speak to Megan! Tell her it is David back from overseas."

There was a long cold silence, then a very deep sing-song voice said,

"David, you say! I am not at all sure she will want to speak with you, but I will ask."

David heard him call out to Megan and then quite obviously a hand was put over the receiver so that David couldn't hear what was being said, just a muffled murmuring sound. A long pause came before a very demure but ever-so pronounced voice said,

"Hello David, how are you?"

"I am fine Megan, got back the other day!"
He lied.
"So, I was wondering, did we have a boy or a girl?"
"We have a son. He weighed nine pounds three ounces and is beautiful to see, but with very Welsh lungs on him. His high-pitched screaming keeps me from sleeping most nights."
"A son you say! That's fine, just fine. Was it a hard birth?"
"Well now! It could have been easier if I had had a man to help me, but then he was away in foreign parts. Just kidding, don't panic."
Her voice had so quickly become very broad Welsh with its lilting way, that David could hardly recognise it as being his Megan.
"Megan, how do you feel about me coming down across to Neath and seeing you and the baby?"
There was a long pause, so David added,
"I will get a hotel and stay just two days and two nights. I must be back in South London for the nineteenth, I am working in a pub playing with a jazz band after that date."
It was a huge lie, but he would see if he could get work with a group to make some money.
"When are you thinking about then?"
She said, as if confused at the actual time and date of coming.
"I could come today; in fact, I could be on my way within the next thirty minutes. How do you feel about that?"
"Yes, that would be acceptable, get into Neath's station hotel. If you leave within the next hour, you will be there when I call at say, six-thirty tonight."
And then she went into a whisper,
"Don't call here and I shall not let on that you are coming. My father just might come and give you a

huge piece of his mind and neither of us would like that, that I can promise you."

David left for Neath just after forty minutes were up and got there just after five o'clock that very afternoon. He went into the hotel lobby and enquired at the reception desk as to obtaining a room for the next two nights. He had the choice of any, there could only have been five or six taken up on. David picked the room furthest away from anyone, right up on the fifth floor. The room was spacious and though extremely old fashioned, it had a certain old-world charm about it.

The curtains were a darkish brown and had seen far better days than nineteen sixty-four, the carpet was very threadbare but had once shown the grandeur of a Persian past. The wallpaper was a striped pattern that had some colour still showing, though whether that was the original colour or just the way it had all faded was hard to tell. There was a washstand and basin with a bar of new soap and the towels had once come from the Imperial Hotel in Brussels. How they ended up in Neath was anyone's guess. It all seemed unreal to David even though he really hadn't known what to expect when he arrived. It was warm but not hot, but somehow it oozed a certain charm and that made him feel comfortable there.

He placed his small satchel on the rack, he hadn't brought much with him, what for he wasn't going to be going anywhere special that night or the next. In fact, he started to wonder why he was there at all, even though in the pit of his somewhat debauched mind he had an inkling.

Knock, knock, the door was rapped which made David somewhat jump. He looked at his watch, it was dead on six o'clock. He looked in the mirror and examined himself, his hair looked good, though maybe getting just a tad too long. He walked over to the door and there standing there was Megan, but she was alone, no son!

"Wow Megan, you look good enough to eat! Where is that fat and flab which seems to go with childbirth?"

It was true Megan looked better than he had ever seen her before. She had cut her hair in a short style with beautiful streaks of shades of her own colour running through it. Her face was soft and gentle looking, with her skin almost shining and yet if it was made up it was very well placed for it looked completely natural. She wore a light blue dress that flared out showing at least light blue two petticoats underneath and a top made from white pure lace that displayed her bigger than remembered breasts to the full.

"You are so beautiful, wow, I cannot get over it, you are just, wow!"

"Well David are you going to make me stand here all night, can I come in please?"

"Er, sorry Megan, of course come on in. But where is our son?"

"He sleeps now, but he will be awake again roughly twelve o'clock until two in the morning. I Might be able to grab a couple of hours before he wakes again and demands more food. I love the little bugger, but he makes me work hard for any love he reciprocates back to me."

She entered the room and surveyed it as if she was a decorator. She looked to see what David had brought for their son, but she could see that nothing was forthcoming.

"Megan, what have you called him?"

"I thought I would call him Stuart David Cartier; how do you feel about that?"

"Well, I am flattered that he has me as a middle name, it's more than I deserve. Please sit down. Oh dear, there is only the bed to sit on."

"David come and sit next to me and tell me all the news."

David did sit next to her, and he explained about the tour and all the playing that he had done, he did leave out his sexual exploits, he knew those would only upset her.

"God, Megan you smell so wonderful, what is that stuff you have on?"

"It's called Midnight Passion, by Imprardi. I am glad you like it, I hoped you would."

David knew exactly what was coming next and he could already feel his loins expanding to meet the possible request.

"I thought about you a lot while I was away!"

"I have been thinking about you too. I won't lie, I have missed you. I don't expect you to give everything up and come and live with me, but it would be nice if we could still see one another from time to time. You showed me things that I never want to be shown by any other man."

Megan went red just like he remembered and then carried on,

"You don't have to worry about me, I shall never hold anything over you. All you have to do comes and see Stuart from time to time, maybe bring him some toys as he grows older, things that you and he can both play with together. As for money, that is not important, I know you don't have any so we will forget all about that. It just so happens that a great aunt of mine, auntie Lucy, died a couple of months ago and left me a sizable amount of money, nearly three hundred thousand pounds and that is after all the taxes have been paid. So, you can see I am in quite a good position after all. She was my father aunt, but she couldn't abide his religion and what she thought of as pompous ways, so when she heard I was pregnant she was delighted and left me everything, she had been a suffragette and was extremely liberated in her thinking."

Again, she went red.

"I am living at home at this moment as I need the physical support that only parents can give with young Stuart, but as soon as all the taxes and death duties are paid, I shall move into her house in Cardiff, it's very close to the castle in the centre. It is a fine old Victorian six-bedroom house, so you can even come to visit me there, that is if you want to?"

David was dumbstruck, yet somehow delighted with Megan's good fortune, or was it that he now realised that he had been given a get out of jail free card?

"I will of course come and visit you and I will try and do the right thing by Stuart, but can I see him tomorrow? Maybe we can all have a walk somewhere?"

"Why of course we can, Stuart can meet his daddy, and you can meet your baby son."

"That's settled then, now can we make love, your perfume is driving me wild with excitement?"

Megan didn't go red, she just gave a small laugh and then said,

"I have done something just for you?"

"Oh, what's that then?"

"Lift up my petticoats and see for yourself."

David's hand trembled with anticipation as he carefully went to lift her skirt and petticoats. Underneath was nothing, no knickers and no pubic hair get in his way. Her mound was beautiful to observe, so he just watched and was enjoying this very special moment.

"Can we both take off our clothing?"

"Why of course, I have been left mesmerised by the beauty of your pussy, I just love it without a mass of hair covering it all up. I just want to eat it and I am going to make you ejaculate with just my tongue, I remembered that you liked that being done to you."

Megan was out of clothes before David and immediately lay back on the bed with her legs akimbo awaiting both their pleasures. Megan's breast was quite a bit bigger than he remembered and her nipples showed that she was indeed feeding young Stuart herself, she was already lactating slightly.

It was a nice surprise to young Cartier to see that there were absolutely no stretch marks on her stomach, he was pleased for her and it pleased him to see that her age had gone down, not up with childbirth, to him she was a small teenage girl, and he was going to deflower her once again.

David slid between her legs rubbing himself against her, he allowed himself to slide down completely and with his legs on the floor he could kiss and lick that all important vital area. This he did with a will, and before many seconds had passed Megan was in full ecstasy mode, she moaned and groaned as if she was in pain but they both knew better than that, she was ecstatic with pleasure. Megan rolled her head from side to side; her eyes were wide open but she saw nothing.

David having reached his goal of creating an orgasm for Megan, he moved up a notch and got his penis in a position to enter her.

"Are you sure you want me to do this Megan?"

"Get it in, get it in, stop wasting time you silly boy. And don't withdraw it will be okay."

David started to pump away, very slow at first and then quickening the pace somewhat. He moved his position a little so that he was rubbing against her wall, this heightened his feelings. He soon became close to orgasm, when he realised what Megan had said,

"Leave it in!"

That simple phrase made him hold back just a tad. 'I am not going to leave it in when I come, she wants another baby!' He knew he couldn't hold out too much longer so as that moment occurred, David withdraw and managed to leave a deposit on her tummy. Megan came too immediately.

"Why didn't you leave it in as I said?"

"Because my dear Megan, neither of us are ready for child number two. If you want another child, we sit down as two adult people and discuss it, this way is trickery."

David looked sternly at her for a moment and then his feelings melted into one of caring father whose wife now wanted their second child. But then reality hit home again. 'I haven't even met Stuart yet and she already wants another sprog. No chance!' They lay in bed together and David already realised that coming to Neath was probably not such a great idea. He always knew it would end up in bed, his weak will and her determination were a bad combination. He knew he would have to make an excuse to leave, possibly tomorrow afternoon after he had met Stuart. They didn't make love again that night and Megan went home to her child just after eight o'clock.

The next morning was an overcast day, which didn't surprise David or anyone else, that part of Wales was known for its inclement weather. They had arranged to meet on the seafront next to the small arcade that stuck out like a sore thumb, but it was an obvious place to meet. So, there was baby Stuart and Megan walking along pushing the pram like a real proud mother should.

"Meet your son. Stuart this is your father."

The baby was sound asleep, quite content within his small world of sleeping, eating and being cuddled twenty-four seven. He most certainly wasn't interested in a viola player from London. Stuart was Welsh and if his relations have their way, he will grow up being extremely proud of his heritage.

"Megan, I cannot stay long as I have to get back to London, I have been asked to go on a small tour with the Festival Ballet and as I haven't had a legacy from a dead great aunt, I have to take the work."

"Oh, I thought you might stay for another day or two. Let's walk along the promenade then."

David immediately noticed how Megan had taken to motherhood, there she was walking beside the seaside with her beautiful young infant and her man tailing awkwardly beside her, she loved it all, but David was cringing badly.

"Do you want us to go back to your hotel and make love again?"

"Oh God, Megan you sure know how to kick a man while he's down. You know I want your body, but what I don't want is another child, not yet maybe never. If you want sex, then fine we can go back and screw till I must leave, it's up to you." There was a hint of a threat almost permeating from David's last sentence and Megan was fully aware of it. She stopped pushing the pram and looked hard at David.

"If you wish to leave now, I won't stop you. But if you wish to stay here with me and your son, then please speak a little more conciliatorily, your words sounded almost like a threat."

Tears were welling up in her eyes, but she carried on speaking,

"I have been more than considerate to you. I pose absolutely no threat what-so-ever to you, but I get the feeling that somehow you are afraid of me and what I might do. I am not the same person that spat and clawed at you all those months ago, I am a woman who cares for her son, and maybe her son's father, but like I said, that is entirely up to you."

Megan withdrew a largish handkerchief and blew her nose so vigorously that it made a smile return to David's countenance which broke the mood.

"Look!"

She said,

"I do have extremely strong feelings for you, but I am not looking for a husband. Yes, I agree, I do want another baby at some time, but like you said we should talk it out first. Then if you agree we will go for it together, but if you don't then I have two options, don't I?"

Now she was staring him down! Megan was gaining a foothold in this conversation.

"First option is that Stuart is an only child, or second option is that I find a man that I like, and he should be that willing donor."

Game set and match. Megan had learned well, she knew how to get around David, she knew exactly the right buttons to push, now she was doing just that!

"After all you are not the only fish in the sea, and I am not that ugly that I couldn't attract another man if I wanted too."

David was now very confused, he had over the years come to see himself as something special, maybe, just maybe, God's gift to women and sex, it seemed that maybe he was somewhat a little mistaken.

"Look Megan, let's start again. I didn't mean to come across authoritarian towards you, of course you are your own woman. Oops, I nearly said man."

David could hardly disguise his smirk from his silly mistake.

"And you can do as you please. But I really don't like the idea of another man screwing you with the intention of producing a brother or sister for Stuart. We will talk of this, but not today. If you want to have some fiddlydee, then let's go back to the hotel."

But he then added with a very wry smile on his countenance,

"I think I could muster up the energy for a little more horizontal sexual exercise."

And then in a more serious voice he ended with,

"Though Megan I do have to leave early so don't get offended will you, it's not you, just work and money."

They went back to his room and made love one more time, but David was very careful to withdraw before he actually came.

Young Cartier was back in South London by ten fifteen that night. He had to waken poor Steven up to get in because he had forgotten his keys. They didn't talk, David was confused and very tired.

Strange as it may seem, the next morning there was a call from the office of the Festival Ballet, asking him if he was free to join the tour which was in Swansea. He would be away for another three weeks. It seemed that one of their viola players had gone sick with appendicitis, David was starting to wonder if through other people's illnesses and misfortunes, was this going to be the only way he would obtain work?

It was perfect for David; he could play everything with his eyes shut and the music was somewhat mundane and very easy to play. They were performing Swan Lake, Giselle, and Sleeping Beauty, nothing taxing for the viola, except for Giselle, which had a big viola solo in it, but then he wouldn't need concern himself with that problem, he would be sitting on the back desk.

The nicest aspect was that he was now on his twentieth birthday and Louisa would be flying in, he was given permission to go to Heathrow to meet her and she would spend a couple of days with him while on the tour.

When she did come, they were playing in Darlington, an interesting railway town with a wonderful Edwardian theatre. Louisa was so happy to see her David, she had too wondered whether the romance had gone cold as she didn't hear from him quite so regularly, but there he was waiting by the customs station at terminal one with a huge bunch of flowers. She now knew once again that his love was still intact and that their lives together was looking more and more promising. In fact, she was now ready to come to live England, just so long as he married her.

David was completely overwhelmed as he watched this beautiful woman approach him. Could any man be this lucky? She was looking so chic in her mini skirt and high heeled shoes. Her hair was now much longer than he remembered but she had put it into two pigtails, and they suited her so much. Many eyes were following her, and one could believe that some men were told off by their wives for staring too hard. They kissed passionately and tears were streaming from Louisa's eyes, she was in a state of bliss. They caught the bus into town and then went to catch the train to Darlington.

Louisa would have preferred to have stayed in London, but she understood the situation, her David was trying hard to save money for their future home.

The train to Darlington was an aged post train and would arrive there at five in the morning which was a problem as what would they do while waiting for things and hotels to actually open? The good aspect of the train was that it was sparsely charged with human cargo and as the train went further north, the fewer people remained on it. David and Louisa had managed to get a compartment carriage which meant they could pull down the blinds and the chances of anyone else coming into their cubbyhole was somewhat remote. David once again felt love surging through his veins, all thoughts of Flory or Megan had disappeared out into the ether, it was all Louisa, his beautiful oriental lady. Good looks, and a great deal of class and charm that was Cartier's Louisa.

"I have missed you so much Louisa. But my time has not been wasted, I have been earning money and am in the throes of buying a house in Beckenham, an Edwardian semi-detached in a road called Clockhouse Road. It was built in 1908 it is now separately sectioned into two different flats, a bloody-minded old man lives in the top flat and is playing a silly holding out game, otherwise I could now be in, but truth be known I shall not be taking residence before November this year. I shall be starting college in September, so things are going to be tough and extremely busy. I thought, if you agree we could get married next July time, which will give me lots of time to get organised, plus I will be twenty-one years of age and therefore will not have to ask my mother and father for consent. So darling Louisa, will you marry me?"

The words shocked David, he just let it come out. But was he really ready to ask such a question? The answer came much quicker than the question.

"Of course I will marry you, I have been waiting for just such a question. Next July, mm, probably better if it was August or even September, then after we are married, I will try and get a decent job here in England. What is this house like, tell me more about it."

"Well don't get too excited, this property is in a fine location, but it needs a lot of restoration, nothing structural just cosmetic. Plus, it will need a new kitchen downstairs and a decent bathroom upstairs. Of course, almost every room will need decorating, but all of this we can do over a long period of time, as and when money starts to roll in."

David had his eyes shut and was daydreaming as to how they would bring the place to life.

"There is quite a long garden with a small allotment right at the back next to a railway line. But don't worry about the train noises, it is a small branch line to Hayes in Kent, nothing special and anyway, the trains are far enough away from the house as not to be heard. Also, the line is electric not coal or diesel."

Louisa contentedly nestled up to her man and in ten seconds they were both sound asleep. The train reached Darlington to a sunny warm day, no one was around, the streets were quiet except for some early birds. David knew what hotel most of the orchestra were staying in and so decided that they should make their way there just in case there was a night porter. There was and he let them in and David retrieved his room and they both went back to sleep for a few more hours. When they next awoke it was ten o'clock and the maid had mistakenly entered thinking the room had been empty. They got up bathed in an antiquated bath where the water came out either steaming and dangerous, or icy cold and even more dangerous.

Louisa got into the bath and David sat beside it admiring her form and beauty.

"Let me wash your back?"

"That would be nice, then I shall wash you."

Cartier lathered her rear and scrubbed in a gentle way, of course Louisa was not dirty but the action of David touching her sent quivers of pleasure down to her toes. David then stripped and got into the same tub. A lot of water splashed and went over onto the floor only to end up dripping into the bath below, on the next floor down. He very carefully caressed her legs, allowing his hand to gradually go up and in between, he touched her pubic hair and ever so gently pressed his finger along her valley. Louisa was almost having her first orgasm.

Knock, knock. Someone was trying to stir them both. David immediately climbed out, wrapped a towel around himself and went to see who was there. It was a fellow member of the viola section, one Amos Russell, a fine musician who had befriended David.

"Front desk said you had returned. So, when are we going to meet the next Mrs. Cartier then?"

"Give us fifteen minutes to wash and get dressed and I will meet you in the dining room. Maybe two coffees and a couple of rolls would be nice. Give us that time and I will gladly introduce Louisa to you."

Down in the dining hall were several members of the orchestra and all had taken a shine to this young talent on the viola, so all of them were curious as to what this young woman would be looking like and what sort of personality she would have. They didn't have to wait long, a few minutes later in strolled David with Louisa on his arm. The four men who were there immediately became jealous of the young pretender, likewise the five ladies also went down the same road, except they were sad that their chances weren't looking good now for bagging David, whom they all wanted to mother one way or another. As David hadn't leant all their names he just said,

"Good morning, all. I would like you to meet my fiancée Louisa Young, she flew in from Berlin yesterday, we got back here roughly five-thirty this morning having caught the post train from London. I really cannot say that I recommend it to anyone, the post train that is."

There was absolutely nothing to do until seven o'clock that night when a magical performance of Swan Lake was to take place in the theatre. David suggested that he should take Louisa to look around the town, it was Friday so the local town market would be there to see. Louisa would be staying with David until the Monday and then in the evening she would catch the flight back to Berlin. But today was a day for just mooching around, both were tired, and both wanted to get some more sleep, so wondering around taking it easy seemed a sensible thing to be doing.

The market was selling mainly vegetables and farm produce and though it was obviously cheaper than the local shops it wasn't all that interesting to either of them. They walked down the High Street in an easterly direction and came to the local town museum. Like all British museums it was free to enter. It was crammed full of stuff found in and around the town. Dinosaur bones by the bucket load, some even quite interesting.

There was masses of knowledgeable information concerning the first steam railway that was established in Darlington and known as the Stockton and Darlington Railway. It was first brought to life in 1825 with the running of the first train which happened to be called, Locomotion.

This small but highly important railway was the start of an epoch-making journey that so quickly spread so completely around the world. They read and read all the history that this insignificant little town, what it brought to the world, changing the lives of people forever. They read that when Locomotion reached Stockton, there was a crowd of over forty thousand people there to greet the new-fangled device, all ecstatic, all realising that their lives had now been given a certain freedom which they hadn't had before. That new freedom was a chance to travel, before the trains came the only way someone could travel was either to go on horseback, which meant you had to own a horse, or walk.

Most of the population of Britain never got outside their own little confines, as going somewhere was costly and time consuming.

There were many things of interest including scenes from World War One, at least small sections of film about the Darlington pals that fought and died at the battle of the Somme on the first of July 1916.

Louisa now felt that she had seen and heard more than enough from Darlington, it was time to get some lunch and then maybe try and grab a couple of hours more sleep before tackling Tchaikovsky's ballet Swan Lake.

They quickly found a small café, which could just about manage a couple of plates of Shepherd's Pie. They then ambled their way back to the hotel and went to David's room. They both got undressed and lovingly sank between the sheets and found their own way of lying and sleeping.

They were woken at six o'clock as the corridor became very noisy with the tramping of feet going to and fro. David thought another bath was the order of the day, if for no other reason than to properly wake himself up. He was about to get out and dry himself when Louisa came into the bathroom, she was completely naked and looked divine in David's eyes.

He immediately got an erection and thought it might be an appalling waste, to waste the opportunity of having sex over the bath. Louisa was extremely receptive to his advances and quickly assumed the position of almost lying over the bath. David entered her to both their delights and all it took for David to ejaculate was maybe two minutes, which sadly wasn't quite enough time for Louisa. David didn't try and withdraw but allowed his semen to enter her vagina, his thoughts at the time were, 'If she gets pregnant all well and good, she is going to a make a wonderful wife and I suspect a fabulous mother to boot.'

That night the ballet went very well, it was a wonderful company that had been formed in 1953, after the Festival of Britain and was very quickly competing with any dance company throughout the world. As it spent its life touring it had a huge turnover of dancers and musicians as the life more or less permanently on the road was very tough. Louisa sat in a complimentary seat in a box that possibly had the best view in the entire theatre. She adored what she was watching; to say she loved every romantic magical moment of the production, was a huge understatement.

The next day was the twenty-first of July 1964, David Cartier's twentieth birthday.

Louisa woke first, she got out of their bed and went to her suitcase, in it she had bought a small piece of mans jewelry it was a gold chain that one could hang a watch upon. She laid it beside his pillow and then went and washed herself thoroughly, she wanted to smell right when he awoke. He was still asleep when she came back to the bed. Louisa approached his side of the bed and now only wearing a very short see-through night top. She looked stunning, which is more than can be said for David who was now snoring gently and dribbling from his open mouth onto his pillow. Louisa sighed deeply, hoping this might stir her man somewhat, then she sighed even deeper, this time it had the desired effect. David' right eye opened just a tad, but enough to realise that he should be awake. He opened the other eye, so what was so wonderful as to be awake, sleep seemed a much better idea.

But then he noticed that there was a small parcel not more than four inches away from his eyes and nose. He tried to focus in on the obstacle that was spoiling his view of the world. It was then that he heard another sigh, and this time realised that it must be Louisa creating all this fracas. He gently raised himself to look around, and then a voice said in a sweet loving way,

"Happy birthday darling. Aren't you going to open your present?"

Now Louisa had his full attention. He now took in all that was around him and spying the present once again pretended that it wasn't there.

"Come on open it up, I spent weeks wondering what to buy you."

"What are you talking about, present, what present?"

Louisa clambered across him and snatched at the wrapped little box.

"Well of course if you don't want it I shall just have to take it back and get something for myself."

"Oh, that present."

David kissed her gently on her cheek and took back the little box and then opened it up.

"It is beautiful, I shall have to buy a watch to suit it though. I have never owned such a beautiful object before. Let me have a shower and get dressed and then we can grab some breakfast. Come in the shower with me, we can Christian it."

That breakfast was a huge surprise for David as most of the string players in the orchestra had gathered there to not just welcome him in officially to the orchestra, but someone somehow had got wind of young Cartier having a birthday and they were there to greet him and Louisa. Everyone was extremely curious about this young oriental beauty. And as they both entered into the dining room a chorus of,

"Happy birthday to you..."

Rang out loud and clear! David had already become a welcome and important member, all be it temporary, of the orchestra and the viola section had immediately recognised his worth.

Introductions were made and everyone made the young Louisa feel welcome.

It was then suggested that they all were to spend a day in Richmond, a beautiful medieval town with many interesting touristy features to suit everyone. Louisa loved the countryside with all the rolling hills and dales. She adored Richmond, especially enjoyed her first cream tea in one of the many tea shops. She had never experienced clotted cream before and along with her Earl Grey tea, she understood why the British saw themselves as the superior race within this small spinning globe.

The weather was clement with a wonderfully sunny day roughly seventy degrees, with a small light north-easterly breeze just to make sure that it bordered on perfect. Having done the tourist tour of Richmond, it was soon time to think about returning to Darlington for the next performance which was going to be

Giselle. Everyone on that crusade to Richmond had caught the sun and one or two were indeed suffering from a combination of too much sun, plus too much sunny wind creating yet more trouble for their delicate skins. The real problem occurred when the first clarinet player, a very fine musician called Thomas Whitestone had been burnt on his lips, so much so that he couldn't play that night it was just too painful for him. Tomski as he was affectionately known, was a very fine player, in fact good enough to be in any of the London orchestras, but somehow by a combination of fear of doing the audition for a fine orchestra and the simple expedient that he was also far too lazy about actually following up leads, also probably the simple truth was that having landed the job in the ballet orchestra, why change? Tom had no real ambition and though he enjoyed what he did, his real love was magic and to that end he really was bordering on being a genius. The tricks that he could do always fooled all the people all the time. But that evening, for once Tom sat in the audience with Louisa and watched a performance instead of playing in it.

Soon it was time for Louisa to leave for Berlin again, back to the toil of hotel work. David took her back to Heathrow and watched with tears in his eyes as she went through immigration and out of his life for what was going to be some time yet. David now knew that Louisa was most definitely the girl for him. He loved her and loved the fact that she blended well with musician in general and her taste in music was most definitely on the up. As far as David was concerned, he realised quickly that she had loved her introduction into the fine arts, thus passing one vital test in young Cartier's eyes. He now had made a very conscious decision not to allow other women into his life, he was truly going to be faithful to his Louisa.

Two weeks later in Newcastle David's tour came to an end. He had become a very important member of the viola section and had been given the task of playing the big viola solo in Giselle on his last evening's performance. The solo went extremely well, though the conductor had no idea that someone else was up for playing it but got a very pleasant shock on hearing the sounds that were being developed.

Not that anyone gave so much as a hoot for his well being, as a conductor they all thought he would have been better at being a conductor on the 12A route to Crystal Palace, not overseeing an orchestra. After that solo had concluded David got a larger than normal banging of bows on music stands and scraping of feet, which were done to indicate approval.

He arrived back at Steven Preston's flat to discover that he had now been booked for yet another tour, this time with the Welsh Opera, that is to say a section of it. This jaunt really intrigued David, it was the thought of this small touring band, and this turned out to be a tour with a small section of the opera to many of the Scottish islands, something that many companies do to attract arts council rewards, plus to keep singers/dancers and musicians working when they might be resting, as known in the trade.

There were going to be just thirteen musicians and six singers, no props or scenery, just the local landscape to back up whatever opera that was to be performed. But the really exciting aspect was that the tour ended just one week before college was to start.

David quickly telephoned his Louisa and told her the news. He then got in touch with the estate agent to make sure that things were still ticking over and when could they arrange his solicitor for him, he was going to leave on tour the following Monday and this was already Wednesday, could things be moved along before Friday this week?

David then went to his bank and paid in the cheque that had been handed to him by the Festival Ballet Company.

He was getting his act together well and really thought that by the time he the exchange of contracts was supposed to take place he would have plenty of money to get furniture and pay for extras that he would surely be needing.

For a young man he was doing very well, everything was sort of tickety-boo so far, he was in fact earning the money he needed to get the things he thought he needed. The next three years had seemed to be taken care of and for such a young man to own his own house seemed some sort of miracle. On the way back to the flat David did some shopping for food and plenty of it. This was because he was determined to cook a meal for both of them in way of saying thank you to Steven for doing the work of an agent for him.

Strange thing was, how did the companies got to know about him, he guessed through the musicians union, which all musicians in Britain had to join, the music profession was a completely closed shop, if you wanted to work the only option was, JOIN THE M, U!.

Steven came back to the flat, happy to see his friend. David told him all the news and then explained that he was going to make them both a meal for that evening. The meal was not very good as the lamb chops which he had put into a casserole dried out and became tough to eat, but the four bottle of wine later and the case of Irish beer, plus the half bottle of Bells went down a treat.

David told him all the stories of the tour, but ended with the story of the last night in Newcastle when after the concert the entire orchestra, that being thirteen happy contented musicians went out to a Chinese meal, a youngish bassoon player called Katherine Childs sat next to David and after many courses had been consumed, a finger bowl was passed to her, she turned to David and asked what it was for, he immediately said,

"It is a consume soup, just drink it."

Katherine promptly did just that, except for a girl opposite who exclaimed in a startled throaty voice,

"You're drinking a finger bowl that has been used by almost everyone!"

Katherine immediately threw up her dinner all over the table and then turned to David in tears and said,

"David, how could you? I thought you liked me?"

What with the smell and the vomit gradually spreading across the table, everyone was very put off from continuing their repast. David felt like a complete heal and got many scowls from many of his colleagues from around that long table.

It was time for him to leave, which he did after apologising and then going around the entire room shaking everyone's hand whether they were orchestra or just Joe public.

Steven fell about laughing and just literately fell of the seat onto the floor in a dead drunken faint, he was total out of it. Steven Preston one of the greatest flute players this country had produced in many years was dead drunk to the world and come to that, so was David Cartier his best friend.

The next day David telephone Louisa, just to make sure that she was back safely within the fold of the hotel. She had enjoyed herself immensely with David and could hardly contain herself at the thought of them soon being married and living together in England.

Words of love were spoken, and David made a quick excuse to say a loving goodbye as the calls to Germany were costing serious money, money that was better spent on the forthcoming mortgage and furniture for their new home.

Four days later David had caught the train to Charing Cross where he was to meet his fellow musicians for the start of their tour to the Scottish islands.

What a huge disappointment greeted David as he discovered that the coach was actually a very old post war rambler and had most certainly seen better days. It was a petrol driven coach made in 1948, it sadly had been thrashed into the ground over to last sixteen years. It stunk of fumes, blew acrid black smoke from its exhaust pipes which somehow managed to find its way into the seating area and generally stifle the people sitting within the area it chose to pollute. It was most definitely underpowered for the sort of journey that was going to undertake. The seats were worn through to the springs and the suspension was a real bone shaker. But to David this was going to be a real treat as he was once again going to see parts of Britain that he had never seen before.

Once everyone appeared on board the coach started on its long trek. They weren't expected for their first concert until the next evening and the plan was that they would stay overnight just north of Carlisle, a small town called Rockcliff, which was off the main A7 route and nestled beside the Solway Firth.

All thirteen of the musicians turned up on time, the only person they had to wait for was the conductor, a young man who had been given this chance to conduct an opera company and anyway of course he came extremely cheap. His name was Bergman Soloman, a Danish scholar who had come highly recommended by the famous conductor Sir Adrian Bolt. No one knew anything about him but everyone had high hopes, but as the Leader of the small ensemble said,

"Live in hope, but like pretty well all conductors you die in despair!"

The clown that led this band of hopefuls was someone called Brian Thomas, a very fine violinist who never made the real big-time because he really couldn't keep his mouth discretely shut. He was indeed good enough to lead any orchestra but instead was happy to be on the periphery of the best players.

The journey was to be via Liverpool, there the bus would pick up the six singers, plus the road manager and porter. With everyone, there was to be twenty-two people which did give some room to all that was already uncomfortable on the coach.

The coach left Charing cross at approximately ten thirty in the morning, it reached Liverpool at six fifteen that evening. It was going to take a hell of a lot longer before they reached Rockcliff Hotel. They didn't make it to the hotel until twelve-sixteen that night. By the time they reached the place everyone was in a bad tired, half drugged state from the fumes, or drunk from alleviating the stress by drinking from various bottle of whiskey which were being passed around. The coach itself was passed caring for as they pulled into the hotels driveway the exhaust pipe fell off and the engine died. There was some frantic telephoning, and a newish coach was promised for breakfast the next morning.

One can never quite understand why coach companies think they can palm off lousy coaches on anything to do with the arts.

People fell into their beds as quickly as they were shown them. Exhausted, hungry and extremely bored, not a good start to any tour.

The next morning as the band and singers were the only guests, breakfast was served as people rose. Absolutely no pressure was put on anyone. The new coach arrived at ten-thirty sharp, it was almost new, it smelt nice, had comfortable seats and didn't have a petrol engine so there were no fumes blowing back into the seating area, this time everyone was happy.

At eleven thirty everyone was ready to leave, they had to get to the island of Bute in the river Clyde, they would be giving their first performance the following day, but this evening was earmarked for a rehearsal.

Now things were looking up for them all.

The singers all grabbed the front seats, just in case there were going to be fumes. David sat next to Cynthia Stonebridge, the flautist. Cynthia was a largish woman very much the spinster sort. David wondered just how often she had to shave her rather greasy looking face. But she was a pleasant enough person who was keen to know all about David and his sister Nevillia, who she admired almost to the degree of adoration, her feelings of esteem came through, everything she said about Nevillia by using the word tremendous all the time, she is tremendous this, or tremendous that, it was completely sycophantic.

They both talked for several hours until they got their first stop at a café come garage, when they had eaten and returned to the coach, David put his head against the window and was sound asleep in seconds.

When David had finally woken the coach which had already stopped twice before now stopped waiting for the ferry Skelmorlie which would take them to Rothesay on the isle of Bute.

There was no time to go to the hotel that they were all staying at, they now needed to rehearse for the next two night's concert. The first night would be a medley of Mozart's operas and the following night would be Verdi, this was so the local people could get a serious contrast in music styles.

The journey by the ferry only took thirty minutes, which was just about time enough for David and the other musicians to wonder around the deck and get some fresh cold sea air on the faces.

Most of the people took the opportunity to smoke as the coach had a no smoking policy, which to everyone surprise was a very unusual thing to be introduced on transport indeed. So, there they were lined up on the starboard side of the ship puffing away on their Players or Woodbines, believing that they were now halfway to heaven, but not realising and taking into account that after another thousand or two cigarettes, they would be.

David was always so glad that he hadn't taken to the weed. He had tried the odd cigar, even a puff or two on a dodgy Acapulco Gold Marijuana cigarette in Vietnam, but as all that happened was a complete feeling of nausea, he was ecstatic at not liking anything that took smoke into his lungs. Strangely enough none of his girlfriends had smoked either.

Once landed at Rothesay the journey was literally five minutes to the theatre that was going to be theirs for the next three days. The establishment was an aging Odeon cinema which had taken its screen down for this special event. There were posters hanging everywhere which was nice to see and everyone wondered how many customers they would get at each performance?

The staging area was small not being meant for concerts performers, but the musicians got themselves seated and even made room for the singers to come on to the stage. Sadly, the acoustics were almost completely dead, which meant they would have to play as loud as possible to be heard, plus it meant that intonation would have to be very carefully watched as it would be easy to play out of tune without easily being aware of it. The next problem was the lighting, sadly it was nearly impossible to read the music with such dim lights. The engineer of the cinema spent the entire rehearsal time grubbing around for extra lighting.

Even so the musicians and singers knew their stuff well enough to get through without any major problems. After two hours, everyone had had enough, fatigue and complete boredom was taking its toll, so it was unanimously decided that a jaunt back to the hotel was in order, obviously by now along with some food.

The hotel, which was named the Pride of Bute, was a rambling old early Victorian mansion which served the local community as a hostelry and pub, plus it served the best fish and chips on the island. It wasn't long before all the musicians were sitting eating and then taking the odd whisky or two, supposedly for personal medical reasons only, at least that was the drunken joking argument.

The next day they had an early morning rehearsal which lasted from ten until one in the afternoon. The concert was going to be seven-thirty that night. Everyone was buoyant about the show knowing that it should be a great success, as they were going to repeat all the concerts throughout the entire tour, it was unanimously decided that only sound checks would take place at each new venue, there would be no more rehearsals, this annoyed Bergman the conductor, as he was the one that needed to get to know the works in hand.

This free time meant, that they were free to go and explore these ancient islands as they were to come across them.

That night David with the others arrived at the Odeon at seven o'clock, he would spend some time making sure that the intonation was good and then go over some of the more difficult passages in the works.

Seven-thirty came, but an audience didn't, at quarter to eight people started to drift in. By quarter past eight the conductor decided that enough was as good as a feast and brought the orchestra on to start the overture to Don Giovanni. There were no more than twenty-five paying customers sitting in the auditorium and everyone was incredibly disappointed by the turn out.

They all went through the motions, but to a man or woman they were very upset by the few people that had decided to come. The singers did their bit, and the orchestra played well enough for them, but the clapping lasted ten seconds and the audience was out and through the exit before one could say anything.

So much for the Mozart evening.

The next day David rose at the crack of dawn with his new found friend Callum McGregor who played the bassoon, Callum was going to hire a car, and he was going to explore the island and David and Jane Davis, second violin was going to come with them.

Once again, the weather was somewhat inclement but with a promise of maybe some sunny spells. They went south along the A844 road until they reached Kingarth, there they stopped for coffee and some cakes. The town itself was nothing to write home about, a small Kirk, two pubs and a small café come grocery store. But there was an interesting war memorial in the shape of a Celtic Cross that they decided to look at, it had the names of twenty-two men who had died on the Somme in 1916, all in the one battle.

'Twenty-two men dying in one battle, how many men actually went there? How many men could this little town have had to sign for the King's shilling in the first place?   They must have been part of Kitcheners army, part of a Pals Brigade. What a terrible waste!' David could see them in his mind's eye walking across no-man's-land into a hail of lead from the German machine gunners. And he knew that they were actually ordered to walk, and woe betides anyone who ducked into shell holes. They could have been immediately shot by their own officers. All three of the musicians felt the agony of those men caught in the mayhem of that First World War battle.

It spurred them on to finding somewhere else to visit. They drove on another mile and found a small road to a village called Kilchatten, this really was a tiny little hamlet with no more than twenty houses down one road. Sure, enough at the bottom of the road was yet another Kirk, so they stopped to view it. It was extremely plain inside, yet it was obvious that it was in constant use. As they looked around the inside of the building there was yet another memorial to the fallen of the 1914-18 war. On this plaque were the names of thirteen men all of which died on the Somme.   Thirteen must have decimated this tiny community, a hamlet that would have relied entirely on farming and fishing as they were quite close to the sea.   Young Cartier was astonished and deeply saddened by the complete waste of life, he thought that the loss must have been awful, what those few people went through beggar's belief.

They decided to drive as far along this road as they could, even though it had turned into a dirt track. After what seemed an eternity, but in fact was less than ten minutes of bumping along they came to another hamlet called Garrochty. Once again there was just a few houses and a Kirk and of course, yet another memorial to the fallen, but this time it was just two men, one of which was a Lieutenant Cummings, the son of the local Laird. Both men had died on sixth of July 1916, at the battle of the Somme.

This time though, the inscription on the memorial stated how and where they both met their Waterloo. They were opposite the huge explosion of the mine that the allies had dug under the German trenches. But these two men, plus other men from different parts of Scotland were caught in a huge shell hole when the debris that went up from the mine, came back down again. Fifteen men were buried alive by the miscalculations of the miners. Feeling thoroughly depressed from reading the account of the men's death, they decided to walk down to the sea, which was called Garroch Head. The first thing that came to them was just how fertile the soil seemed, vegetables were growing in abundance and looking like bumper crops. After fifteen minutes they reached the head and stared out into the sea. As they looked Jane pointed towards Arran.

To their extreme delight, there in the sea they could clearly see a pod of Humpback Whales. And joy of joy for the onlookers, they were breaching and crashing around looking as if they were thoroughly enjoying themselves. And then as suddenly as they appeared they were gone and could after some minutes be seen heading outwards to the ocean. Though they tried to count them all three came up with different numbers. David thought there were four, Callum said five and

Jane said six. But all three agreed that it was an incredible sight to behold, but more to the point, it had elated their spirits once more and stopped them all thinking of war and death.

On the journey back to Rothesay they came across a field that had a sign pointing to some standing stones, so as a last excursion they went to investigate. They had to climb over a barbed wire fence, thrash their way through overgrown weeds and sapling trees and eventually after one hundred yards they came to their first ancient sight. There were six huge monoliths standing ten to twenty feet high in what once had been a circle, plus in the middle was another large monolith that had either fallen over or been pushed horizontally in the distant past, but it all was so very impressive to behold. There was a very mystical element about the place that didn't go unnoticed by any of the three. The shame was that the entire area was so overgrown and inaccessible, this place could and should be a huge tourist attraction. Older people than the three musicians, would have found the going hard to impossible there.

"Callum, you know these stones are supposed to be no older than eighteen hundred years, laid down by the people that fought the Romans. But I once talked to a very serious scientist who estimated that the stones around Britain were at least five thousand years old having found the remains of bones that could be carbon dated underneath each stone."

Callum said nothing but looked at Jane, who was now giving him a knowing look.

"David, be a pal, take the car keys and wait for us. We won't be long."

David was shaken and surprised by the request, but he understood that the two of them, though both married to other people, they were obviously having an affair. David made his way back, got into the car and promptly went off to sleep.

Much to the surprise of the musicians that night concert was full to overflowing. They had squeezed into that cinema, now concert hall, nearly one thousand people, so once again the concert started late as the people tried to settle down. But the people made it an interesting event and subsequently the orchestra played well, and the singers responded well to the efforts of the orchestra.

The next morning, they were off to Arran, which meant taking the same ferry back, driving down to Ardrossan and catching yet another ferry there to Strathwhillan on Arran. This time the coach got them to their hotel in plenty of time to have a fine meal and take some leisure time around the golf course. They were staying at Brodick Castle Country Club, a very up-to-date country club that had a fine restaurant and hotel. The owner had paid a lot of money to get the opera company there, he wanted to entertain all Brodick and Strathwhillam's people to the two free concerts. It was a selfless act of kindness.

To this end he had acquired the biggest marquee anyone had ever seen. Everything within the bounds of the country club was free for the musicians and singers, so that day a lot of drinking and eating went on. There was a sound test that evening and as expected the sound was hopeless being completely dead within that huge tent, but no one gave a hoot, this was going to be fun.

That night as the musicians walked onto the makeshift stage the rest of the marquee was crammed full of people all enthusiastically clapping and whooping with great expectations. The conductor came on to the stage and promptly fell off his rostrum, the crowd thought this was all part of the show and cheered and laughed at Bergman Solomon, the young man completely shaken by his experience thought that the audience were rude laughing at his unfortunate situation, but what could he do, he stood brushed himself down and then proceeded to act just like Charlie Chaplin. He waddled from one side of the stage to the other half tripping on every step he took. And while the audience were ecstatic with mirth, he then gingerly climbed on to the rostrum once again, lifted his baton and proceeded to bring the orchestra in with the Mozart overture to Don Giovanni.

Somehow the man had got away with the shenanigans and the audience just loved every second of the performance, though one would wonder how much of the music they heard. After the overture on came the singers and none of them knew if they should act like clowns or just do their normal straight singing. The spell was broken when the tenor went to shake hands with Solomon, and he missed his hand and he too went sprawling much to the delight and amusement of all there. By now all the musicians were almost crying with what was happening. So now to be outdone the bass player feigned a swoon and fell carefully backwards managing to lay his instrument as he went. From then on mayhem ruled the evening. With clowning going on all the time. But somehow the music got played and the singers performed with a certain grace and elegance, even though they now all clowned around.

The evening was a great success and only ended when Bergman Solomon put his hands in the air and thanked the audience for being so patient, even this made them laugh, partly because no one knew that the entire evening had been an accident, they all thought it was a well rehearsed choreographed show of excellence. After the people had left and the musicians were enjoying a well-earned drink, the conductor came in and said,

"Whatever happens, there must be no repeat performance of tonight's nonsense. Obviously, it was just one of those things that happen, but what if it hadn't turned out well, what then?"

Then the leader turned to Solomon and in a more severe voice answered,

"Please get the perspective right! It was you that took the tumble, had you risen showing that it was just an accident, the audience wouldn't have carried on laughing and you would have got your normal concert."

He sniggered but carried on regardless,

"I don't know what the local papers will make of tonight, but one thing is for sure, the people who were there went away having had a wonderful evening. So don't start laying blame at our door."

There was a small cheer from the other musicians and then he finished in an almost threatening tone with,

"Bergman, I suggest you go to bed and forget tonight. Sometimes strange things happen."

The next evening the concert went extraordinary well with no slips of any sort, but somehow the audience was more subdued, one would suspect that they were expecting a French Feydeau Farce as opposed to a serious classical concert.

The next day was completely free, and the coach driver was ordered to take everyone around the island and show them all the highlights.

The next island was going to be Islay and that involved two ferry rides, of which the second which was from Kennacraig to Port Ellen. It took three and a half hours across quite rough seas.

They were all packed and ready to board the coach at ten that morning, the last man to get on was the conductor, who was then annoyed as the front seats had been taken, so he moved towards the rear mumbling some unpleasant oaths under his breath. David on watching this came to a rapid conclusion. 'A petulant spoilt, no nothing conductor! Bloody typical!' David was already developing a hard-bitten attitude to conductors, not altogether healthy.

They drove up the A841, all the way to the Lochranza car ferry. This small ferry service was an open platform which strained under the weight of all the cars and coaches that boarded her. It pulled away from the quayside and immediately hit roughish seas. It was at the discretion of the skipper as to whether the vessel would leave the harbour area, if the weather was too inclement. The fact that the ferry was soon awash with spray and some of the waves were even crashing over the deck making the crew rope down the lighter cars to the deck. One aging Singer open top pre-war sports car was almost swept overboard as the further out they got the more the waves became higher and wilder. Everyone had taken to the small cabin that was situated overhead which was also were the vessel was steered from. There were some brave souls that were playing dare with the spray, but all were soaking wet before the ferry had gone more than half a mile. Though to some on board, the whole experience was one of great fun, there could have been a dangerous element to the trip, it would have been fatal had any one person slipped and got themselves washed overboard, or a car had come loose and got damaged by knocking into another vehicle. As it was the poor Singer was practically filled with corrosive sea water and had to be bump started when the sea water had at last been removed.

Once off this ferry they drove across the huge spit of land to the town of Kennacraig, though one would hardly call it a town. There was a ferry terminal but not much else. A mole stretching a hundred yard out into the sea was all there was to see of anything. There was a hut where one bought tickets and there was a café, which sold the most basic needs for survival, tea, instant coffee and mangy looking sandwiches, which made British rail sandwiches look like some specialist food from Harrods.

They had to wait an hour before the ferry showed itself to them, and by that time there were quite a few vehicles including another coach and two largish lorry's carrying succor to the locals of the island. There were also ten cars of various age and size and bringing up the rear was a very ancient pre-war tractor. All these had somehow to get on the ferry. The small wide ship docked and down came the gangplank and to the surprise of everyone on the coach, off came a cavalcade of cars and lorries, so it was perfectly obvious that the small contingent that had gathered were going to be a doddle as far as loading them on was concerned.

The vessel was expected to leave immediately it was loaded, but to the surprise of all the passengers, all the vehicles were pushed onto the starboard side of the ship, leaving a long empty space on the port side. But nothing moved, the skipper and crew just left the ferry and went to the café, drinking copious amounts of tea and coffee, there they waited.

After nearly one hour and thirteen minutes of frustration for the paying passengers had passed, along the road came a huge low loader lorry carrying an enormous electrical generator, which must have weight twenty to thirty tons let alone the weight of the lorry that was toting it. By now the tide had dropped about a foot, and it became clear to see that this was what they had waited for, now the gangplank was level and the huge load creaked and groaned as it slowly eased it way aboard. It really was heavy enough to tilt the vessel slightly, but not enough to seriously fret about. The captain and his crew now came back on board laughing and chattering as if this was just another normal day. The heavy gangplank was raised, and the ferry got under way and not too soon, as most of the passengers were extremely fed up with the hanging about and from the lack of any information concerning the hold up.

Now the longest of the ferry journeys so far was to begin. It was now two o'clock in the afternoon and finally for the first time since coming to Scotland the sun broke through the distant rain clouds and a huge spectacular rainbow spread itself before them showing the way to the port on the isle of Islay.

Three and a half hours later the ship docked at Port Ellen, and everyone disgorged themselves and so very happy to do so, it had been a long tedious trek over beautiful countryside and very choppy blue-green seas, that all the time displayed small white horses, warning everyone that this area of sea was indeed dangerous and ever changeable.

Once off that vessel the coach only had a mile's journey to the hotel which was situated around the bay of Kilhaughton overlooking the sea. It was a beautiful rambling Victorian establishment that had kept its charm and warmth. The entire hotel had been set aside for the musicians and singers and though food was free at mealtimes, whisky from the local distillery cost four shilling and six pence a shot, but the upside was that it was an honesty bar which meant you could drink anytime you wished with no restrictions on timing at all.

Single malt Islay whisky was a wonderful elixir that cleansed the soul and heightened the spirit, everyone loved it and partook in the imbibitions of this God given nectar.

The room that David had was a double and he was asked to share with the oboe player, one Stuart Gegarian, an Armenian musician who had escaped in the early nineteen fifties and found his way to London. He had married a wealthy older woman who though he was very fond of her, he could never satisfy her needs as he was a homosexual and just loved young boys. She knew he was gay when they married and though they did achieve a daughter it was with most stressing difficulty that consummation was performed by Stuart. As the years had gone on, his wife Cynthia had grown older and wiser, the daughter kept her busy and to a degree contented in life, but Cynthia now accepted that her younger husband found his sexual satisfaction in much younger men than himself.

The strangest aspect of Stuart Gegarian was not that he hated communism, but had for some inexplicable reason become a great admirer of Adolf Hitler, so much so that when he obtained British citizenship he had joined the brown shirt party of Sir Oswald Mosley, in fact he had become his personal bodyguard of that fascist leader when they toured around the British Isles trying hard to still drum up support for their neo Nazi ideals. Even stranger was the fact that he didn't hide his beliefs but shouted them out to anyone that wanted to know about him and the so-called party. Yet even stranger, still everyone just loved him, despite his appalling politics, he was a complete pussy cat, adored by all.

They were going to be staying at the Hotel Slaggentor for three nights. The next day there would be a small rehearsal at the Port Ellen town hall, where they were going to perform to a specially invited audience of the local dignitaries. But after that one and only performance, they had free time as they were not going to be leaving the isle of Islay until the Tuesday and they had arrived on the Saturday. Sunday rehearsal, then free from lunch time, Monday free all day but evening concert, Tuesday free in the morning but leaving early afternoon to coincide with the hopeful ferry and tide times. There was plenty of time to explore and enjoy oneself, or just relax and thus partake in what was on offer at the hotel.

Once everyone had stowed away their belongings it was decided by the majority to take a walk along the beach. It wasn't a clean area with golden sands, but it was sort of sandy, but a very gritty sand that scratched your feet if you walked barefoot. And though there wasn't human detritus lying there, there was a great deal of wooden flotsam. Many roots of trees and branches that had obviously swept inland and just lay on the seashore for many years. Occasionally there were the remains of fires that had been lit to get rid of some of the trees and any other burnable rubbish. They were all happy and thrilled by the prospect of some good breezy weather as opposed to the cold rain that had been forecast. They walked for about a mile when suddenly, the smell became somewhat overpowering. Then turning past a small chalky cliff, they came across a sight that they all wished they hadn't. There on the shoreline was a large pod of porpoises, and they were all dead and starting to stink. Sea birds, crows and rooks, were pecking at the meat they could get at with the claws and beaks. There were at least twenty lying there with skin and guts hanging off. Thomas Typhon was the first to throw up and this prompted several others to follow suit. What with the aroma of dead animals and vomit, it was more than mind and body could take by most of them. David felt no pangs of problematic stomach complaints, in fact it just made him feel hungry. They then made their way back to the hotel where most of them immediately went to their rooms to try and sleep off that nightmarish image.

The next morning everyone was up reasonably early, they ate their breakfast and then found their way to the coach. The town hall was a typical Victorian building, but it surprised everyone by its large size. Where did such a small island get the sort of money to indulge in such extravagance? The entrance was vast, in fact the whole edifice was supported by two huge Greek Corinthian columns. The lobby was totally lined with fine Victorian paintings, many of which were obviously worth quite a lot of money. There were several typical Scottish scenes, many showing Lochs and rivers, all showing stags and highland cattle.

But interestingly there were two fine quite small paintings of the Great War. One was a scene of a Zeppelin going over London with a searchlight catching it in the near darkness, the other was a more obscure scene of a battlefield somewhere around Flanders. Those two paintings had all visitors stopping and viewing them. Then they entered the chambers which were extraordinarily large, quite capable of seating a thousand people, which was almost the entire population of Islay. It had now been cleared of all the councilors seating and was now set up ready for the musicians and singers.

"How many councilors do you think they have here on the island?"

That question came from Bergman Solomon speaking to no one in particular and at the same time looking around at the incredible décor that the inside of the hall had to offer to the viewer, but then he answered himself in a very sarcastic way.

"Hundred's? No, half a dozen, of that I am sure of!"

The rehearsal was over in less than one hour and the rest of the day was going to be spent sightseeing with the local Laird, one John Campbell of the Campbell clan, a tribe dating back many hundreds of years. He had bribed the coach driver to allow him to escort the entire ensemble around the island.

"Ladies and gentlemen, I would like to take this opportunity of first thanking you all for coming here to entertain us and then to offer you this golden chance to see one of the best islands for history and beauty, it had over the centuries become known as the queen of the islands, with our drivers help I will show you why."

He took a deep breath and carried on talking,

"I am going to start our little tour by showing you Port Charlotte, sleepy but an incredibly picturesque little fishing ports, much nicer than anywhere else to be seen."

He tapped the driver on his shoulder and requested him to drive.

"Driver take the left and follow the road."

They drove in the bright windy sunshine for roughly twelve miles before they turned on a left-hand bend, they then saw this sparkling little village port loom into the foreground.

"This bay that we have driven around is called Loch Indaal, it is a very deep-water bay which is great for sea bass, mackerel and lobsters, Plus also lots of varieties of shell fish, all of which we eat here on Islay. There cannot be more than two hundred people living within the reaches of Port Charlotte, but it is a friendly sociable place which will make any money bearing tourists welcome. In fact so welcoming, we are going to stop and have some fish and chips for a lunch. No arguments they are on me."

Before anyone could say a word, he continued,

"Oh, by the way, this port is called Charlotte after an ancestor of mine, Lady Charlotte who was the daughter of the islands owner, my great, great and many more greats, grandfather."

He smiled at the thought of his own joke, or to be more honest, nearly a joke.

"We have a painting of them both somewhere on the island."

There was a titter from some of the listening people, but most were fascinated by the beautiful countryside that manifests itself to them all.

Campbell was most eager to show them the small intimate church that stood in the middle of the village right opposite the actual port area. And of course there was the proverbial Celtic Cross, giving the names of the local fallen of two World Wars. David asked John Campbell how many people lived in the area during the Great War, especially if so many had died in battles?

"Yes, it makes one wonder how many were left when the war had finished with its slaughter. Crazy as it seems, more than three quarters of the men that enlisted for the war's duration, died, mostly at the Somme battle in 1916."

He looked sad as he thought about the wasted lives.

"Such appalling slaughter, such a waste of manhood. When the survivors returned, there weren't enough left to man the boats or plough the fields, so it quickly emptied the entire area of people. It was like the great clearances of the early twentieth century, people just up sticks and left either for the cities like Glasgow or Edinburgh, or they went south to England or across the sea to America. It wasn't until after the second war that people started to return and work the land once more."

They then went just around the next bent and came across a largish fish and chip restaurant. This establishment surprised everyone, but in a nice way. The food was good, plentiful and very welcome and, though the only drinks were water, tea or coffee, it all went down extremely well.

"I now want to take you to see a very beautiful part of our scenic landscape. This is a small mountain which anyone could climb called Dun Nosebridge and when you see it you immediately understand why it was given that name."

They all clambered back onto the coach and drove for yet another two miles around the coast and there for everyone to see was this special area called Dun Nosebridge. It had the appearance of a man lying prone on his back and his head and especially his nose was in profile for all to see. This was as far as they were going to drive in a westerly direction. John Campbell spoke quietly to the driver, and he then turned the coach around to retrace some of the steps already taken.

"I have asked the driver to now take us to Mull of Oa. This is a peninsular of land as far south as the island goes, apart from the great beauty of the area, there are two special things I want to show you all. But you will have to be patient as I am keeping quiet until we get there. Have a sleep for twenty minutes, err, I know I will be!"

Actually, the drive took nearly one hour even though it was only thirty miles away. But the nearer they got to their objective the worst the roads became. Eventually the coach was almost scratching itself on either side against bracken and shrubbery. The last two miles there was no road just a cart track, but that was okay as they were now in complete open country.

"Stop driver, there's a good fellow."

John then pointed to a large standing stone that overlooked the beach.

"That big monolith is said to be the grave of one Godred Croven, the King of the Isle in the dark ages. But the stone does have some supposed magical powers. As it is windy today the magic might just work, please follow me and we will put the legend to the test."

As the people got closer to the stone there came a three toned whistle directly from it, somehow as the wind coming from a south westerly direction, hit a point on the stone and that created the whistling sound. Everyone except John Campbell was totally taken aback by the eerie sound that came from it. The sound couldn't be heard unless one was within twenty feet of the monolith, it wasn't that loud, but in many ways because of the volume of the whistle it sounded more like it was coming from deep within the ground as opposed to the actual stone. The legend was that Godred Croven was calling to passersby to help lift him from his tomb. The stone itself was roughly seven feet high and was quite obviously hewn as opposed to being natural.

"I cannot tell you much about Croven, but the chronicles state that he was an unjust king, who wielded his power everywhere just for his own ends. He was supposed to have died from pestilence around 970, give or take a hundred years or more. But another tale tells of how he took advantage of the first night rights, thus raped a young girl on her wedding night once too often, this incurred the fury of the locals who came in the night and caught him red-handed, castrated him there and then and then hung draw and quartered him. The legend goes on to say that each quarter was taken to the furthest reaches of the island and buried there. There is another grave mark north of this island, but it is too far and too difficult to get to, something you do yourselves when you have the time."

A small appreciative ripple of applause came from the entire band, they then boarded the coach once more.

"Now the last place I am taking you to is literally a mile down this track, whether we can get the coach down there will be in the lap of the gods."

The driver struggled with the track but after getting most of the way there he gave up and said that they would all have to walk the last few hundred yards, which they all did.

They came to the cliff edge and there before them was a large monument which had been constructed by American money between the wars, it was there to commemorate the sinking of two troop ships in the Great War.

Now the Laird John Campbell was in his stride.

"Here you see this monument to the fallen, but it wasn't the British fallen it was Americans, all part of General Pershing's AA (All American) army."

He was already rippling with the energy of excitement of relating the story.

"If you look out to sea in the direction of the arrow pointing on the monument, roughly four miles out lies the wreck of SS Tuscania, this was a cargo vessel converted to troop ship. She was loaded to the gunnels with a human cargo, who had come all the way over to fight the allies cause in Flanders against the Kaiser's army. They reached this point on the fifth of February 1918. It was early in the morning and most of the men were asleep. It was a very bright sunny morning with everything glowing reddish from the rising sun."

At this point in the story, one could tell that the relating person, the one and only John Campbell was actually there, reliving the entire experience.

"The ship must have stood out along the horizon like a sore thumb and there lurking just below the surface was one of the Kaiser's submarines, one U-77. The submarine used only one torpedo and struck the Tuscania amidships causing her to sink within a three-minute period. Only one hundred and sixty odd souls managed to be rescued, over one thousand drowned. So, there is a war grave carrying the youth of the United States. No one is allowed to dive on the wreck, though it is in a very deep part of the ocean anyway. A very great sad loss. The islanders rallied for the rescued soldiers and crew and many of those men come back here from time to time to give thanks for the lives."

He looked out to sea as if searching for the victims to float ashore.

"I have met many of the veterans from the States, all so very grateful to the locals for being looked after until another ship came to take them to the mainland."

His eyes had once more watered up.

"Yes, quite wonderful people and what a terrible experience to go through."

"Are any of them here on the island now?"

David asked in a hopeful way.

"Not that I am aware of. Most would be in the eighties and nineties now, so it's not easy to travel here as you well know. There was a chap from

Milwaukee that came to live here between the wars, married a local girl and then stupidly signed up for round two, he was killed in North Africa in nineteen-forty, I think his name was Lee Leonard, or something like that."

And then before anyone could interrupt again, he carried on,

"And then what do you think? On sixth of October 1918, there was a collision just out there between HMS Otranto and HMS Kashmir in extraordinary rough seas, the two ships were part of a convoy carrying troops from New York again to Flanders. The Otranto lost her ability to steer and drifted onto the rocks just down there. But only four hundred and thirty-one lives were lost, everyone else was saved, thanks mainly to a quick distress call which alerted a destroyer, HMS Mounsey. The destroyer managed to pick up survivors from their lifeboats. On very low tides you can still see the rusting remains of the wreck."

John paused for effect and that did the trick, he had their interest and apart from the wind that still blew quite fiercely you could have heard a pin drop.

"Right then! Back to the hotel."

He had had them fascinated and, just as quickly he had broken the spell. There was a spontaneous round of applause, not for the hotel, but indeed for the trip around the island. Everyone had enjoyed this tour with John Campbell's rather eccentric approach to public speaking, immensely. It is strange how a good day out can lift the very souls of lonely, depressed peoples, not that anyone in particular was either lonely or depressed, but had they been, then this tour would have been just the tonic for them.

Everyone got back on the coach and was laughing and chattering together, theirs were at least lifted spirits from a tedious rehearsal and an even more tedious conductor. And on the way back to the hotel, John gave out yet one more piece of useful information,

"If any of you are into trying very fine Malt Whisky, you will be happy to know that we have two really fine distilleries here on Islay."
He waited for some sort of reaction,

"One is the world-famous Laphroaig and the other Islay, both are absolute world beaters. If you don't get a chance to visit the distilleries, then buy a bottle of two in the hotel."

It only took twenty minutes to get back to the hotel and as the coach pulled up into the car parking space the conductor decided to say a few words,

"On behalf of my musicians and singers, we would like to thank you for showing us all what you have shown us today. And if you have yet another half hour to spend, I would like to invite everyone on board for a drink of these whiskies at the bar."

There was a spontaneous cheer and a thunderous clap that made the coach actually shake.

The concert the next day was a moderate success, the singers performed well as did the musicians, but there were less than one hundred and fifty people attending in the audience. It was the same on the Verdi night, but nobody minded as the orchestra and singers did their combined bits well.

The next day they were to leave and go north onto the next island which was going to be the Isle of Skye.

They left early, after a quick breakfast and a letter of thanks was read to all of them, also a bottle of Islay Whisky was handed to each and every one of them.

To all the musicians and singers, it had been the best island so far. They got the ferry back to Kennacraig from Port Ellen and this time the sea was like a millpond with the sun blazing down on them. And everyone smiled when they received the weather report for the rest of Britain, south of Glasgow the weather was cold and rainy with gale force winds, but north was sunny and still, with a nice high-pressure zone standing quite still offering good weather for at least the next four days.

They reached Skye very late that night having driven through the most beautiful countryside, viewing lochs, lakes, mere's, forests and mountains all the way. They stopped off at Fort William for and early evening meal and made it to the last ferry across to Skye from Mallaig to Armadale. The moon shone just for them, their coach was the only vehicle but there must have been one hundred bicycles and five-hundred-foot passengers, all happy and singing and dancing upon the car deck. Once on the island they still had another forty odd miles to drive before reaching the hotel. They arrived in Portree at one-thirty in the morning only to find that the hotel was closed and they had to telephone through to the night porter to let them in.

Though it hasn't been spoken about it ought to be said that David had written to Louisa almost every day. On this tour of duty, he had been totally loyal and true, hadn't so much as looked at any of the available women that were on this trip. That was up until they reached the Isle of Skye. When the porter was allotting the rooms to everyone, there was just one double room left over and two people to share it. One was David Cartier and other was June Summerfield, a second violin who though nicely young and pretty, was somewhat overlooked as she had a very retiring nature.

But the porter somehow assumed that David and June were together as a couple, but as David had gone to the gentlemen's toilet to perform an act of nature, June had been given her key and gone up to the room, David then came out of the toilet and a second key to the room was handed to him.

Now the entire musical ensemble and singers were well on their way to getting a night's sleep. The hotel was completely full no more space at the inn, at this point David went to the room opened the door and to his and June's horror found themselves having to share, with David looking on at a half naked June.

"June I am so sorry, but maybe you have got the wrong room. You can see I have the key to this room."

"David, will you please turn your back to me while I get some clothes on. I have the same key, or how else would I have gotten into the room?"

David had as ordered turned away but was still enjoying the sight of June struggling to get back into some clothing, whilst watching her within a life-size mirror. He hadn't thought about any women at all and like most of the male musicians, he hadn't given June the time of day, as she tended not to want to talk being somewhat shy. But now watching her curves and breasts in the mirror, David understood his ardor was indeed rising rapidly for the first time since getting on the coach at Charing Cross in London.

"I will go back down and demand another room."

David quickly turned and left the room, but as he did so he said,

"June, I have a feeling that the hotel is completely full, if so we will have to somehow divide the bed into two compartments, his and hers. But I will do my best."

He left the room and retraced his steps to the reception area. Luckily for him the night porter was still entering names into the register.

"Excuse me, but you have put me into a double room with a woman."

"Aren't you a couple then?"

"Would I be here now if we were?"

"Well somehow, I got the feeling that you were. There are absolutely no more spare rooms, either you share tonight or you can sleep on the sofa in the lounge, the trouble is that the cleaners will be arriving in a couple of hours so you won't get much sleep."

"Oh shit! I will ask if we can share, I would sooner sleep with her than share a special moment with bloody cleaners."

David then turned and made his way once more to the room with June in. He no longer felt like a gentleman, in fact his mind had wandered to a much more carnal state as all that his thoughts went to where that image of June in the mirror, showing bare breasts and very flimsy knickers.

He entered the room to find that June was already in bed and the lights were out.

"June, I am sorry but there is absolutely no more room at the inn. We must share, just put a pillow down the middle and I will try and keep to my side of the bed."

"Oh, stop fussing and come to bed. I somehow knew you would be back; we will just have to make the best of it."

David went into the bathroom and washed and changed out of his clothing and just left his boxer shorts on, they were nearly clean and probably didn't smell too bad. In the darkness he clawed his way to the right-hand side of the bed, pulled back the sheets and was about to crawl in. Much to his amazement and joy, June was there almost on his side with absolutely no clothes on.

"Well, you said we will have to make the best of it, you had better be the best."

"What you mean? You want me to make love to you?"

David was somewhat dumbstruck by this obvious blatant attempt of seduction, but never-the-less climbed into the bed as quickly as possible. He hadn't written to Louisa that day, nor would he be doing so until the tour was over.

They spent four days on the Isle of Skye, most of the time David and June hired vehicles and toured the island sightseeing. June was the driver and very competent she was too. They saw everything there was worth seeing and when no one else was around they would christen the area with their own brand of quickies to mark the various spots.

A lot of their time was spent looking for standing stones and walking over hills and dales yet finding none. But the exercise did them both a power of good. The air was breezy but incredibly clean to the taste, plus the walking made their collective legs stronger and healthier. To both David and June, this was a wonderful interlude, quite unexpected, but never-the-less delightful in its casualness.

The concerts were held in an old cinema that had seen better days, it was drafty and cold and not at all conducive to performing at ones best.

To be perfectly honest most of the musicians were very disappointed by firstly the lack of audiences, second the conditions that they were expected to play in, thirdly the real lack of interest that was shown to such a worthwhile troupe of musicians and singers and, as the weather had somewhat worsened by becoming overcast cold and windy, it didn't go down well with anybody.

No civil dignitaries had come to show themselves, which had now become something they expected. No one presented any sort of acknowledgement as to them even being there in the first place, they had just come, rehearsed, did the concerts and left. So much for the Inner Hebrides.

The next island was going to be much further north and much harder to reach. If the weather was too inclement the ferries would not run and that would put their schedule right out. As it was, they would now have to travel to the southeast to Aberdeen and there they would catch the ferry to Lerwick of the Shetland Islands.

The journey from Portree back down to Aberdeen was roughly one hundred and fifty miles, but a journey that would take them across some of the most beautiful scenic landscape in the entire British Isles. They saw the mountains and lakes, lochs and rolling hills. Everywhere was shown at is optimum, the lousy windy rainy weather that abounds in the far north of Britain also goes to make everything look lush and rich in green colours. It was the natural weather, anything else just wouldn't have been right.

The Highlands just like the Yorkshire Moors, being witnessed in bleak harsh weather, that is when you see the countryside at it real and possibly its best. Crossing through the Highlands, showed an exciting landscape that shone beautifully in the now clear bright sunlight that abounded. Everyone on the coach enjoyed the journey, especially when they stopped for toilet, lunch and general muscle stretching comfort stops.

It was evening when they approached Aberdeen, though some of the architecture was of interest, most people felt a little depressed at the grayness of the city, everything was built from grey granite. In the twilight of the evening that drab colour only brought on drab feelings of sadness and even slight depression.

They were to be staying that one night at the newly built Holliday Inn, a very American influenced construction but once again drab and grey and extremely cold looking, though once inside the opposite was true. It was now taken for granted that June and David were an item, so a room together was the order of the day. June had completely come out of her shell and was so enjoying the company of this younger man, but not much younger as she was only twenty-four and had just left the Royal Academy of Music that year. This was her first professional tour since leaving college. June was a first-class violinist who could sight-read just about anything, but she was somewhat shy about putting herself about.

Her auditions for various posts hadn't gone well, but not because she couldn't do the job, no her problem was a musical world problem, one to do with just plain nervousness.

To get on this tour all she had to do was to play to the leader of the ensemble. Surprisingly, that was easy, she played part of the Bruch first violin concerto, then sight-read some typical opera parts which she sailed through, but she was playing to someone she knew and only that person not a board of musicians and officialdom. But the tour had been good for her just as it was for David, touring means getting along with your fellow musicians. As you are all the time in close proximity, so one needs to be affable in nature, or things will and do get out of hand quickly.

On a tour such as this opera stint the music is easy, one is repeating the performance night after night, so plenty of time to master the difficult passages. Sight-reading becomes harder when one is in a major symphony orchestra, one that does a three-hour rehearsal in the morning and supposed to give the ultimate performance in the evening.

June really had grown fond of David, so much so that she clung to him everywhere. At first this was exciting to David, June was young, pretty and extremely sexy, but even when he went to the toilet, when coming out, there would be June ready and waiting for her new man, there never seemed to a minute when he would find himself alone.

The trouble was that David now wanted to practice more, yet June was always there more or less stopping him by just staring, plus giving advice that wasn't asked for. It quickly became a burden that David was not going to tolerate for much longer. The night in the Holliday Inn was typical, one could possibly say probably the straw that broke the camel's back.   David wanted to sleep as they would have to rise at five the next morning, but June had now developed a lust for sex. Thinking that David was just playing a game she persisted in tantalising him. David grimaced, he was bored with June as he found her shallow and somewhat cheap, her mind dwelt on clothes and fashion, she wasn't even interested in the arts, so how she became a violinist was to David a minor miracle, yet somehow, she was really quite good.   'Where was the culture of this new generation?' A funny thought for a young man who was at least four or five years younger than June.

"Look June, forget the joking, I am shattered and really do need to sleep. Sleep, not making passionate sex. Just plain old sleep!"

"Anyone would think you don't love me anymore?" She looked at him in a quizzing manner.

"You do love me, don't you?"

David didn't answer but jumped into bed turned over and was almost immediately asleep. The next morning June was still sulking and creating a bad atmosphere. She was extremely unhappy as to why her David rejected her passionate advances, she just didn't understand that he might find the entire aspect of sex every night tedious and boring, as for the need for sleep, this was almost too much.

"David before we go down to breakfast, I wish to state something important and then you can make your comment should you wish."

She took a deep breath and looked quizzingly into his eyes.

"David, I think we should part company, I see no point in keeping this relationship going as I can see and feel that you have completely lost interest. May I suggest that from now on we remain friends but have separate bedrooms?"

David didn't blink an eye and came back with,

"Yes you are right, we should go our separate ways. Thank you for your friendship, but it is a wise person who knows when enough is indeed enough."

June's jaw dropped open as this wasn't what she expected, she was hoping he was going to beg and plead his case, instead he wanted to leave her. She immediately started to well up and sank back onto the bed and felt the tears start streaming down her now flushed cheeks.

"David, don't you love me? I love you; you must know that?"

"Well, I am sorry June, but the truth is I don't love you. I know nothing about you or you about me. How can you possibly talk about love?"

As he spoke, he was wincing in an obvious way that didn't go unnoticed to June.

"Please try and remember who seduced who in this relationship? If you can recall, you more or less dragged me into your bed even though sex was the last thing on my mind. We have been good for one another, but good doesn't necessarily mean love. Sure, I like you and I like you a lot, but you have never enquired as to whether I might have a girlfriend or not, you have just assumed that sleeping with me means we are an item."

David tutted extremely loudly before carrying on with his oration,

"Sorry June, we are not an item! In fact, you should know I am engaged to be married and that is happening very soon. Sorry but you suggesting our end has helped me with my thoughts concerning fidelity, so I am going to be true to my oath from now on, so separate rooms are a must."

There came a slow moan from June, gradually this turned into a long low wailing sound that quickly turned into a scream. Soon, the person sleeping in the next room came out to see what all the ruckus was about, the man was a complete stranger and he looked at David and then at June, she was now purple in her face with rage and was just sitting on her bottom looking through everyone and everything, her only thought was of losing the man she had decided she was going to marry. It was because she had come to that decision concerning her feelings of love, June hadn't taken any precautions concerning love making and what is worse she had also told David that she was in fact on the pill though she actually wasn't. Somehow in her rather contorted mind the next and obvious step was to have a child, yet she somehow decided that it might be better not to tell the father to be.

David looked at the man and just shrugged, he didn't know how to calm her down. Soon many people came to investigate the sound of a dying person, that also meant many musicians and singers. Then finally the conductor stood and looked at this wretched person wailing on the ground.

"What the hell have you done to her? Why is she screaming so much? Have you hit her?"

David looked at the baton waving fool with complete contempt.

"Why do you assume that it is something that I have done. Isn't it more likely that she has done this to herself."

"What on earth do you mean to herself, June is quite obviously very distressed and that means someone has upset her badly, as you are the only one sharing a room with her, one must assume that you have something to do with the distressed state she now finds herself in! So, I ask you once again, what the hell have you done to her?"

David completely lost his cool with Solomon and gave him both barrels all at once.

"Listen you stupid interfering idiot, the only thing I have done to June is to agree that we should indeed split up."

At that she gave off an even bigger noisier burst of wailing, this time it brought even more people to their room. At this noise, which was bringing people from all parts of the hotel, David made a decision and one that was going to affect everyone.

"Right, that's it, I quit, I am stopping here and then I shall catch the next train back to London. Thank you for your friendship, but this is enough bullshit for me, I am out of here. I need a holiday!"

And then he added,

"Bloody conductors, bloody women and bloody stupid idiotic fools that call themselves musicians. I'll show you all."

He went downstairs, had some breakfast and waited until everyone had gathered at the coach before packing his clothes and making his way to the train station.

'What have I done; will this be a huge black mark against me?'

David reached his friends home that day and there he found a small amount of solace from Steven Preston, who though he thought he was stupid to have left the tour, as things would have probably sorted themselves out, he never-the-less understood the position that he had taken and explained that it wasn't serious enough to give him a lasting black mark against future work, though it might be a good idea to write to the management explaining your position in the affair. And this David did, then a week later came a very complimentary reply plus his cheque for the tour, the completed tour.

Anyway, he had now three years ahead of him while at the Royal College of Music to allow things to cool down.

The next stage of David Cartier's life was now about to start.

You can follow the further adventures od David Cartier in 'Yet More Bullshit'.